"It's been a very trying day,"

Alexandra's gaze wandered to the closed library doors, "for *both* of us. If you would be so kind, my lord, I'd like to be excused. I'd like to retire."

He stood. "No, don't go away." He then appeared to want to bite the words back. Small forlorn words they were, but they seemed to have popped from his mouth like his own devil.

"It's so late," she whispered, amazed by the intensity on his face. Newell looked down at her as if he wanted to grab her and keep her from leaving. As if her presence, her very being, were something he drew comfort from.

"You said you had questions."

"I'm beginning to understand now. I promise to be good to Sam. He'll never have cause to fear me." She stole a glance at him. He seemed preoccupied, as if trying to figure how to keep her from wanting to leave.

She stepped back. He followed. It was almost a waltz.

"May I be excused, my lord?" she asked, fear making her a little breathless.

His gaze rested upon the gilt doorknob that she now clutched like a crucifix. An inexplicable anger seemed to grip him. He looked to the ceiling as if gathering the strength to control himself. There was a heart-stopping moment when she almost suspected he might grab her, hold her in the library against her will. But in the end, he wore the veneer of a gentleman well. He didn't try to stop her. He merely looked at her, then gave a curt nod, acquiescing to her desire.

BOOK YOUR PLACE ON OUR WEBSITE AND MAKE THE READING CONNECTION!

We've created a customized website just for our very special readers, where you can get the inside scoop on everything that's going on with Zebra, Pinnacle and Kensington books.

When you come online, you'll have the exciting opportunity to:

- View covers of upcoming books

- Read sample chapters

- Learn about our future publishing schedule (listed by publication month *and author*)

- Find out when your favorite authors will be visiting a city near you

- Search for and order backlist books from our online catalog

- Check out author bios and background information

- Send e-mail to your favorite authors

- Meet the Kensington staff online

- Join us in weekly chats with authors, readers and other guests

- Get writing guidelines

- AND MUCH MORE!

Visit our website at
http://www.zebrabooks.com

GENTLE
FROM THE
NIGHT

Meagan McKinney

Zebra Books
Kensington Publishing Corp.

http://www.zebrabooks.com

ZEBRA BOOKS are published by

Kensington Publishing Corp.
850 Third Avenue
New York, NY 10022

First Kensington Hardcover Printing: February, 1997
First Zebra Printing: December, 1997
10 9 8 7 6 5 4 3

Printed in the United States of America

For Pamela Gray Ahearn.
My dear friend, this one is solely
dedicated to you.
May we all live to tell.
God bless.
                                    —M.M.

Do not go gentle into that good night. . . .
Rage, rage against the dying of the light.

—DYLAN THOMAS

Chapter One

Hath not a Jew eyes? Hath not a Jew hands, organs, dimensions, senses, affections, passions? Fed with the same food, hurt with the same weapons, subject to the same diseases, healed by the same means, warmed and cooled by the same winter and summer, as a Christian is?

—*The Merchant of Venice*

In the years to follow, she would recall that it was his name that first drew her to him. John Damien Newell. Just a signature at the bottom of a letter; three words penned in a neat, arrogant script, with no forewarning of what was to come.

The name had left her curious. Alexandra wanted to see the face of this man, this John Damien Newell. The man who needed her, and yet didn't know it. Perhaps it was simply the great need that beckoned. But in the quiet hours, she found herself repeating the name and trying to imagine a face that as yet had no definition in her mind.

John Damien Newell.

The name spoke to her. One day she might believe it had somehow awakened a part of her, a part she had thought was to remain forever silent, forever empty. But that was not what she told herself on that gray, drizzling London morning, when she struggled with her reply.

In the library, pen in hand, Alexandra was convinced that it was only youthful foolishness that made her answer Newell's letter; foolishness and hurt, the kind that ran deep and gave one the wild desire to steam forward like an out-of-control locomotive. The kind that made one answer a letter that should have been ignored.

She set out to answer the letter right after Mary had served her coffee in her father's old library. The flames from the coal hearth backlit the vellum of her reply as she held it up and examined her signature. She stared at the inky scrawl and wondered what it revealed about her. *Lies,* she thought, guilt darkening her hazel eyes. She hastily blew upon the wet ink. Her hands shaking, she read her letter again, convinced she was being reckless and unwise, still not yet knowing she was placing her life in a stranger's hands.

19 April 1858

My Lord Newell,

I am sorry to inform you that your request to summon my father, Dr. Horace Benjamin, to Cairncross Castle is impossible. Dr. Benjamin died this past December from influenza. His notebooks have been donated to the Royal College of Surgeons so that they may continue his work. I hope this is of some help in curing your brother's affliction.

If you can find no recourse through the College, I would be willing to offer my services. I've not the formal education of my father, yet I was his assistant in all his later works and can say with veracity that there was no theory, no experiment, we did not discuss.

I await your reply. Until then, I am,
                              Your most humble servant,
                              Alex Benjamin

Alexandra stared at the letter, guilt making her hand itch to pick up the glass pen and finish her name. She was lying to the man. Indeed, if he offered to fetch her, she would have to write him and decline the work for fear of his righteous anger over the deception. But there was no other course but to fool him. If she signed her response Alexandra, she might as well not even reply. He would never consider bringing a mere woman, let alone one who possessed no physician's degree, to Yorkshire to help his brother. True, it was more than likely once she arrived at his home that he would show her the door, but she at least had to try. She couldn't bear London any longer. Leaving London was imperative. This baron, this John Damien Newell was her only road out.

Suddenly melancholy, she looked at the room she knew so well. Once there had been heavily patterned green and black Axminster carpet warming the floor, silk taffeta drapery shimmering in shades of pea green and purple hanging at the windows, and the room sentineled with bookcases, each filled with tomes on every subject from polychrome-painted Roman antiquities to French parlor etiquette. Now Alexandra numbly gazed at the bare room. The carpets were gone, revealing the raw, unfinished floorboards that had been covered from the first day she and her father had moved into their new townhouse. The room once had smelled of claret and beeswax, now it merely smelled of old lumber. The windows were now as bare as the floors, the drapery gone, sold to a rag merchant out of Whitechapel. As she stared, she could see every drop of London rain that wept against the naked panes. It had been a fine home. Alexandra had been only ten years of age when her mother had died and her father had informed her they were to move to London so that he might better pursue his experiments. A motherless child could not be impressed with the Egyptian tomb-shaped doorways and the curving shape of the structure, but fifteen years later, Belmont Crescent had proved a reasonably fashionable and comfortable place to live, even for *their* kind.

Alexandra felt the old hurt creep into her heart like an inconsequential vine that, once twisted around a brick, could make it crumble. She was what she was and her father was what he was. He had been a good and kind man, ever the one to toss a penny to a beggar, even if three times his purse had been snatched in the effort. The college had respected her father. His studies had come out of the fact that he had married a deaf woman, a beautiful, neglected woman whose family had treated her cruelly because she could not hear and, thus, could not speak. His greatest wish as a husband and a physician had been to hear his name on his wife's lips, so he had taught her to speak, and began a lifetime of study that had taught others to speak as well; others who, like her mother, had been thrown from society and branded a cretin simply because they could not express with words the outrage at their ill-treatment.

But Alexandra knew well enough that all the good deeds in the world would not erase the spot on Horace Benjamin's irredeemable soul. He had been a Jew. A Christ-killer unwilling to be herded into the folds of Anglican salvation. She, Horace Benjamin's daughter, could cry all she wanted that her mother had at the very least been an Irish Catholic from Wexford, but it didn't matter. She was judged solely by her father's blood and defiance. The prejudice laureled around her shoulders as it had around his, and she had paid the cost.

Yet anger was a fine thing, she had come to realize. It was always timely, arriving just at the moment of helplessness and surrender. Alexandra knew that she herself was not a Jew for her mother had not been a Jew. But if all the world wanted to believe her one, then by God, she would claim it, and claim it proudly, and they could all be damned. Especially *him*.

Her gaze slid to the library's bare window seat where she had spent many hours perched on the satin pillows, ostensibly to read a book, all the while looking out the lace curtains to see if he had come to call. Even now she could remember the sweet pleasure when Mary would find her at the window seat and whisper that Brian was "a-waitin'" in the drawing room to see her father. For years her heart had leapt in excitement just by the mention of his name. Being her father's assistant, she worked side by side with his students, and she supposed she had been susceptible to falling in love with one of them. In retrospect, she could see now that the tragedy could have been neatly sidestepped if he had not said he'd loved her too, but she didn't know that then. She didn't know how politely cruel he was, and how cruel love was, and how it crept up behind one with kind words.

"Miss?"

Alexandra raised her gaze. Mary's lace-capped head peeked through the door. Perhaps it was merely age and not the agonies of the past months, but Alexandra saw for the first time that the servant's red curls were finally showing their gray.

"They're a-comin' fer the desk, miss. What'll I tell them?"

Alexandra stared at the letter that lay unsealed on her father's old beloved desk. She stood and melted a wax seal, then poured the scarlet puddle onto meeting folds of the letter and stamped it with her father's signet ring. The wax cooled, leaving a perfect impression of the letter B surrounded by the Star of David.

"Would you post this for me?" Alexandra handed her the letter. She nodded toward the foyer and the waiting scavengers beyond. "You may tell them to come in."

Alexandra Benjamin had been an unusual child, studious, quiet, and prone to reverie. She herself had preferred to think she'd turned out the way she had because she had been motherless at ten and had spent the rest of her childhood a lone female lost in the company of men; indeed, it was not uncommon for her father's house to serve as a dormitory for the many various male colleagues who took to bivouacking in the library when the hours spent in the laboratory grew late. Yet those who knew Alexandra, like the cook and Mary, did not blame the overwhelming male company for her shyness. For years, they had whispered amongst themselves and shaken their heads in pity whenever little Alexandra's plight was mentioned. If they had been asked, they would have explained that Alexandra's inward turn had been caused by a father whose drive to help the helpless had left him blind to the little soul that worshipped at his knee. Horace Benjamin had one overriding passion in his life since his wife Hope had died, and it was his work. In the Benjamin household, it was not uncommon for days, even weeks, to go by without little Alexandra seeing her father, even though she and her father occupied the same building. Tearfully, Mary once claimed to cook that it had broken her heart to see the child run into her father's laboratory, her eyes shining in delight so anxious was she to show off her new blue satin sash. "He didn't hear her. He didn't see her," the housekeeper wept, sharing a late night tipple with cook. "He might as well ha' been just like one of his patients, for he was deaf and dumb to her presence. Oh, and the little child. The light just died in her eyes. I couldn't bear it. She slipped out of his laboratory, the sash falling off behind her, her brow furrowed, her thin little shoulders held high, as if she were fightin' off tears. And you know," Mary blew her nose into a hankie and leaned a little closer to cook, "the poor little thing never did retrieve her lovely sash. You see, it proved no use to her whatever."

But to Alexandra, the idea that perhaps her father had neglected her wasn't even possible. Her father provided her with everything a little girl could want—toys, pretty dresses, ribbons. Everything, except companionship. Yet, even as a child, Alexandra had found she was self-sufficient to a fault. Without any playmates, she had learned happily to play by herself; without a mother to guide her, she had taught herself the gentlewomanly arts of needlepoint and watercolors.

Then came the day of discovery. Her father had been bent over his notebooks scribbling his latest technique, and Alexandra happened to enter with a pot of tea. As usual, his thoughts were elsewhere, littered by hypotheses, clouded by theorem. Normally she would not have bothered him, but this day he was working with a deaf five-year-old child, a little boy whom she noticed had slipped from his mama's grasp, walked right into their parlor and had begun to pound on the piano keys in earnest.

Without even thinking about it, Alexandra mentioned before leaving that she believed the child had responded to the various vibrations of the piano. She then placed the tea tray by her father's elbow and to her surprise watched her father's head jerk upright.

Horace Benjamin stared at his daughter, then fourteen, as if he'd never quite noticed her before. Intrigued by the possibilities, he dragged Alexandra into the parlor with the child and began experimenting. It was the first time Alexandra ever really felt a connection with her father, and she never let it go. From that day forward, she had found her place in her father's life. Science was essentially closed to her, given her sex; there was no hope of a formal education because even the well-respected Dr. Benjamin couldn't break the barriers his colleagues had placed before women. Nonetheless, she became his assistant.

Alexandra found that if she could talk to her father about his work, then all the lonely hours in the schoolroom seemed to melt away beneath the warmth of his attention. The work, while at times monotonous, was interesting, and her father never treated her like a woman. She had always been a special kind of colleague to him. He gave her everything her mind could absorb. Regardless of her sex, regardless of her youth.

But youth itself was a harsh teacher. And Alexandra was unusual in that she knew precisely the time when her youth had ended. It perished December 24, 1857, moments after midnight. Her father had been buried that very day; she was adrift with grief, yet still there was Brian; blond, handsome, witty Brian towered in her mind like a shining beacon of salvation. Finally, amidst sorrow, her dream might come true. With her father's death, there was no reason not to let work temporarily take second place to more earthly needs such as the need for love. And surely Brian understood this too, she had told herself that terrible, solemn night when she waited for him to respond to her note.

Indeed, he showed up. He appeared at her door right before midnight, his brow clear, his eyes lit with a dark wistful expression. He confirmed it was true, just as she had written in the letter. For several years, between long glances in the laboratory and whispered encounters in the hall, they had both developed the belief that they possessed a destiny. In her letter, she had confessed every burning wish, how she ached to be by his side morning and night, how she longed for his children and a home and hearth as her parents had had in the few blissful years they'd been together. She'd let the ink bleed for her, but her wounds could heal and it was time to speak. Their own silence must be banished.

With tears streaming down her face, she had penned of her long-unrequited love for him and her hopes for the future. Marriage and children weren't completely out of their reach, she had explained, not even for two such workhorses such as themselves. Her father's death had shown that they must take what life had to offer. The time had come for them to enjoy the freedom of being open with their affections, to seize the permission to at last give words to their loving thoughts.

The time had come, she had begged, for them to unite in marriage.

Afterward, she realized that two paths had been laid before her that night. She could have cried and begged and pleaded with him to understand that what he thought of her wasn't technically true. She didn't have to wear the taint he put upon her because in the literal sense it wasn't really hers to wear. Her mother hadn't possessed it and so neither did she. In the eyes of God and the Church, it was nothing but a relic of her father's, a man who was now in the grave.

But Brian had laid *two* paths before her that night. Defiantly, silently, she took the latter. She realized that once tainted by another's misguided prejudice, there was no compunction to wash it off. It wasn't true what Brian believed her to be, but to correct him meant a worse injustice than the one he was inflicting upon her. It meant dishonoring and distancing herself from a man she admired and loved as no other. She would not do it.

So her youth passed, and she began to understand how easily one lonely woman could be duped. Brian had never taken her to the opera because, as he told her, his mother couldn't abide him escorting someone other than herself; he never bought her gifts because, in his words, a *true* gentleman would never presume upon a lady's charity to assume his trinket worthy of her adornment. So Alexandra had had no evenings at the opera, no tokens of affection. She'd stupidly tried to the bitter end to understand, and only afterward had she realized that another woman had been accompanying him to the opera, and that same woman had worn his small gold trinkets bought from Bronwyn and Schloss.

In her letter on that fateful Christmas eve, she had begged from Brian revelation and the truth, and in his midnight visit, he had given her those things. He had whispered of love in the same breath that he murdered her dreams. He cast every moment of the night into permanent memory. Even now she could recall every emotion; in the beginning there had been the sweet, unspeakable relief of seeing his face at the door, then came the ache of the bound-up desire in her heart and the sweetness of her hope. He had kissed her just as the clock chimed twelve times. Memory was merciless. He pressed his fine, handsome lips to her needy ones and he moaned how he had longed to do such a thing for years. Breathlessly, she whispered back, giving voice to her deepest dream: that finally there were no more obstacles to prevent her from accepting his formal proposal of marriage.

He pulled back from his kiss. Her gaze, alive with expectancy, met his.

Then he patiently explained why the answer was no.

Chapter
Two

Approach the chamber, look upon his bed,
His is the passing of no peaceful ghost ...
                                   —Robert Ruthven

The ride to Cairncross became long and muddy with spring. Alexandra sat with Mary at the depot at Stirrings-in-Field, waiting interminably before the next train north was due to arrive. As she shifted her bottom for the twentieth time, her stiff, horsehair petticoats no match for the far harder board of the bench, she couldn't help entertaining the possibility of sending Mary to the village pub to request a room. But she forced herself to refrain. When all debts had been paid and the town house sold, she'd been left a small inheritance, one that could afford luxuries now, but wouldn't see her through the rest of her days without extreme penny pinching. Perhaps if Horace Benjamin had been a less generous man there would have been more left for his daughter, but Alexandra couldn't begrudge him the past. He had wanted a certain address and lifestyle for his family, and he had gotten it, even if it meant being less than judicious with a physician's income. Some would have called him a fool for pursuing medicine when he might have been a banker, as many of their kind in London had been—those Jews who flaunted their wealth as if hoping it might offer a panacea for their social ostracism—but Alexandra knew Horace Benjamin could never have even entertained such ideas. His thoughts had always been more lofty. He had wanted to help people and helped them he had. Her own mother had been one of the many souls who owed their lives to him. Alexandra could not, would not, find fault with him, even though her home was gone, and with it, all the happiness she had believed she once possessed. Horace Benjamin was who he was, she comforted herself even now, and not without a little defiance.

She and Mary sat primly on the short wooden platform at Stirrings-in-Field, the minutes passing at a tortoise pace. Alexandra sighed and closed her eyes and wished that she could instead loosen her corset and rest on a feather mattress until the 9:36 to York steamed into the depot. Around the two lone women, a fog cloaked the landscape, giving the new front of the depot an aged, menacing patina.

"Miss? Are you sure you want to do this?" Mary asked, her black-gloved hands holding her purse in a nervous death grip. "You've lived so long in London. What if you don't like York? What if you don't like Lord Newell and Cairncross?"

"I should hope we can stay long enough to find out," Alexandra answered, the spirit of a rueful smile crossing her lips. She had thought it prudent not to mention to Mary that Lord Newell expected a man. Now she wondered how she would break the news to her.

"I cannot help but feel we've made a mistake. It's me being superstitious, of course, but I've a bad feeling about this place we're a-going to."

Alexandra thought a moment on Mary's words. She had never quite sorted out her own feelings about this trip. That was the odd thing about escape. One never thought about where one was going; one only focused on the means to get out.

"We'll be all right. Lord Newell might be quite charming."

Her voice sounded strong and assured. Confident. It even con-
soled her own suddenly jittery nerves.

Mary peered around the foggy depot and at the lantern swing-
ing in the distance which foreshadowed the arrival of the train.
Mumbling, she said, "I just don't think this trip is proper for
a young lady such as yourself . . ."

A young lady such as yourself. Such as yourself.

Alexandra squeezed her eyes shut. She never wanted to hear
those words again. Those were his words. *His* words.

A man like me can't marry a young lady such as yourself.

Slowly she opened her eyes again and stared at the misty
yellow light that was moving toward them down the tracks.
Against her will, her mind drifted back to finer days when her
father was alive, and the world had made sense.

Her youth wasn't completely spent working on models of
the muscles of the mouth and tongue, or assisting a patient
with lipreading. She spent many a free hour curled up in the
library window seat with her novels, and there she lived another
life.

Her favorite naturally had been Sir Walter Scott's *Ivanhoe.*
It had been much beloved for two reasons. She had once heard
the story that Sir Walter Scott had derived his inspiration for
Rebecca from a trip made to New York. There, in an unassum-
ing brownstone, perhaps one that faced a lovely tree-lined
square, he had met a beautiful, dark-haired Jewess and, some
said, fell in love with her. Secretly, though Alexandra loved
taking up the gauntlet of her father's work, her soul was not
inspired by medicinal powders, glass beakers, and long, tire-
some hours enunciating phonics. She had wanted a father and
science was how she kept him, but deep inside, her passion lay
elsewhere. The Waverley novels incited that passion; *Ivanhoe*
inflamed it.

Her romantically inclined imagination placed herself in the
role of Rebecca. She was not as dark as Rebecca; instead her
hair, while blessed with thickness, was a tedious medium brown
with corkscrew curls she was forced to brush a hundred times
a day to tame. Her eyes weren't dark and sultry either; rather

they were hazel and, some said, overly large for her fragile face. Her father always used to tease her about the expression in her eyes; he'd said she always looked slightly devastated. Thinking back on the night Brian had come to give his sympathies, and how quietly she had sat on the settee listening to his reasons, she was strangely glad her father was gone, so that he could have not seen the expression in her eyes then.

In her reveries, Brian had always been Ivanhoe. She'd daydreamed that it was he who fought gallantly for her salvation and he who went to the grave with his thoughts captured by a beautiful Jewess.

As it turned out, fiction had strangely twisted into the truth. Brian *had* been Ivanhoe. For Ivanhoe had married Lady Rowena.

"This is the right thing to do. I feel it," Alexandra found herself saying even though Mary was up off the bench and distractedly instructing a boy to gather their bags.

"I feel it," she whispered later on the train as she looked out the window of fog and watched the depot become lost in the steam.

John Damien Newell leaned his head back in the iron chair and stared at the lightning that flashed silently across the Thames. Even on the rooftop, the night was warm for London in May. Already there were thunderstorms. It had been a violent, unsettled spring.

Two pale feminine hands slithered down his naked shoulders and raked at the burnished gold hair covering his bare chest. Abbey had come up behind him from the garret window and now stood at his back, her hands as always, eager and lascivious. But he didn't notice; he was waiting for thunder. He was always waiting for thunder. There was none.

"Must you return so soon?" she whispered, burying a kiss in his neck.

His gaze blithely held the velvet blackness above the rooftop flat where he so often found himself. The sky boiled with thunderheads and the sludge of coal dust from hundreds of thousands of hearths. He was entranced by the beautiful void of darkness above, the one he yearned to lose himself in.

"Don't go," she whispered, her nails raking down his belly, her fingers tugging at the waist of his trousers.

"I'll be back," he said hoarsely. "I always come back."

"Yes, yes, but never soon enough." Her words were petulant. With a sigh, she left him and sauntered over to the other iron chair that had been dragged out to the rooftop from the attic windows. Behind her, she trailed the ends of the sheet that was coyly wrapped around her bottom.

"Why do you have to go this time?" Abbey took the chair and held Newell's glance. The sheet slid, no accident for she had once been an artist's model and was well-educated in erotic draping.

She seemed unable to hide the self-satisfied smile that tipped the corner of her rouged lips. "Don't go. I'd think you'd find York dull after . . . after this . . ." she whispered.

"York is dull." His gaze flickered across her taut alabaster breasts, then he looked up to the London sky overhead. The storm churned like black soup, creating shadows like the ones that were always there within himself. "Still, I must go."

"But can't you send a servant?"

"No." The tone of his voice was the quiet thunder missing in the night. He looked away when she visibly shivered.

Lightning, a breathless white fire, shot across the sky in the pattern of a spider's web. Below them, the wharf was dark and silent, eerie in its desolation. Execution Dock it was named two centuries past, when pirates were hanged, tarred and preserved as a deterrent to others. Now Wapping was only another London port built upon the mud of the Thames, a place where even an artist's model could find a cheap attic flat amongst the taverns and storehouses. For years, he too had called Wapping, home.

"Perhaps I should come with you. I've never been to York." Abbey rose from her chair, an enticing smile tipping one side of her mouth. The sheet remained behind.

He felt his breath catch. His loins reacted to the tableau of her nakedness like an animal's, absent of emotion, devoid of thought. As always, the physical response was there, willing, always willing, except the completion of the act now struck him as futile, melancholy, ultimately defeatist.

"I think I'd like to be mistress of your new castle, after all," she whispered, straddling him between her pale soft thighs.

His hands rested on her hips and stayed her. "You've told me time and again how much you like your independence. Yet you offer to give that up and come with me to York."

"You're gone too much these days. Ever since you inherited that castle and that title, you haven't been the same. I thought it would be good for us. Now I hate York. I hate it," she repeated like a spoilt child.

"I see. You must be lonely without me."

"Yes," she hissed fractiously.

"But what about Charles? And James? And Thack?"

She stared down at him, surprise slackening her features. "But—but—how did you know about them?"

A dark smile crossed his lips. "They'll miss you if I take you away. And I couldn't have that."

"I've only dallied because of you!"

He laughed. He couldn't know what a beautiful, cruel sound his laughter was.

"If you weren't in York so much I wouldn't need them." She pouted. Leaning over, she pressed her chest against his and again slid her hands into the waist of his unbuttoned trousers. "Take me with you to York. I'll be your mistress. Just take me with you."

He stared at her. Her loveliness was indisputable. She had glistening black curls and bewitching green eyes. As a creature, she'd been much in demand by painters seeking to find a subject worthy of their masterpieces; as a woman she was just as coveted, for she was as willing to pose as she was to perform. She was perfection in every way, except that her soul was shallow and filled with vice, and, if the truth be known, she was not much company. Wit simply eluded her.

He stared at her and the old desolation weighed down upon him. This new girl, Abbey, was just like all the others; another small depravity in a string of excesses. The Newell poison was pushing the extremes. Satisfaction and feeling, from joy to torment, was always just around the corner, just another dark experience away. Always just out of reach.

"Cairncross Castle is not the place for you. You'd be bored out of your mind with nothing but moorland and the occasional storm that blows in from the North Sea. It's not the place to put up a coy mistress," he said with a slap to her behind and a sarcastic bite to his words. "Already a physician has arrived at Cairncross to help with my brother. I'm leaving tonight."

"I'll go with you." She stared at him, defiant.

He stared back.

His expression clearly frightened her. He wondered what his face looked like with anger glazing his features. From the beginning of their liaison she'd said she'd been captured by his handsome English schoolboy face. Now he wondered if the face had grown cold. If the humanity—what little he possessed of it—had bled from his eyes.

She went to him and placed her hand tenderly on his face. "Please," she whispered. "Don't turn away. Don't be cruel to me, not this time."

"You want to go to Cairncross but how long will you be faithful?"

"Forever," she whispered, as if she really meant it.

"Still, there's one requirement to being at Cairncross Castle that a baggage like yourself will never master."

"Whatever it is, I'll do it." She snapped her fingers. "If it's the servants you're worried about, I'll treat them like the curs they are. I won't let them get the better of me."

"I've no doubt about that." A shadow crossed his eyes. "You're just the one to be amused to by a beating." His gaze dipped to the red marks still swelling on her thighs and bosom, and he remembered, and the remembrance gave him pause. "You like it too well yourself," he whispered, his insides torn apart as if a battle were being fought inside him, as if he haunted himself.

He pushed her off his lap. To his annoyance, she followed him from the rooftop through the flat's bedroom window, and she watched, her expression filled with forlorn appreciation, while he buttoned up his trousers.

Crossing the room, he snatched up his shirt. He dwarfed her lithe, tall form even as she stood on the threshold of the flat's attic dormers and as he well knew, his height, his heavy musculature, his blondness never failed to arouse her. She'd once called him part Viking, part schoolboy, and, when he slipped the curled arms of his gold-rimmed spectacles around each ear—part schoolmaster, from whom, she'd whispered, she was eager for discipline. Disgusted with her and with himself, he'd given her that and more. Now he wondered if she might have developed a fondness for him after all. Despite their experiments in dark ecstasy, the pain that swept her face seemed to give proof she would miss him. Her expression was so genuine it gave him pause.

"No woman can come with me to Cairncross," he said, his words bare and harsh and truthful. He buttoned his shirt and stepped into his shiny black boots. With a violent tug, his heel met the bottom of his boot. The finality left his spirit in an even deeper state of destitution.

"You've inherited your father's lands and his title. Why do you insist upon enjoying them alone?"

Enjoying them. He wanted to laugh out loud. As if there was anything in his life that he really enjoyed.

He pulled on his other boot. The truth was a hard, brittle biscuit to swallow. Without a heart to break and a soul to feel, he knew he would never find real intimacy with a woman. And yet, he knew too, that if he ever did come across the one who could chase away the stark ugliness of his existence, he wouldn't be able to keep her. These other women, creatures like Abbey who ran with the darkness, who folded themselves in dangerous shadow, he could hold every one of them in his fist. It was easy when they took might as a metaphor for love.

But his longing, and thus, his torture, was for the opposite kind. The kind of women who loved their children and honored their husbands, the kind whose silver laughter he heard tinkling like angel bells down the long length of a crowded dinner table. He had never personally known women like that. They didn't pose nude for painters, they didn't throng the docks at Wapping, coming out like cockroaches when dusk settled in on the city. He'd known few good women in his life and the deepest truth was that he almost feared them. He'd no experience with them and only recently had his life crossed paths with theirs. He might be a baron now, a peer with all the might and money of his father, but they, *they* were goddesses he encountered in mundane incidence on the street, passing him in their carriages, waltzing with him at a ball. Now after years of poverty and struggle, he ran in the exalted circles that had so captivated his parents, even to the exclusion of their sons' needs, but still he had nothing in common with the kind gentlewomen and noble peeresses that surrounded him.

And should he ever fall in love with one, he almost winced from the agony of it. His fine, moral, *good* woman would be the death of him. She would only serve to remind him that his body was separated from his soul by many abysses.

"Please take me," Abbey pleaded softly, her voice taking him from his terrible thoughts.

"No." He grimly knotted his black silk cravat.

"What do you require that I'm so lacking in?"

She waited as if yearning for the painful words that would flail her more than even he had. He knew she wanted to hear that it was social position that kept him from taking her, but that was not part of it, and it was an excuse that was weak, in his mind, to the point of inconsequence. Still, she appeared to want to hear him say it. It was another form of the abuse she craved.

He walked to the flat's peeling-varnish door. Twisting the knob, he was anxious to leave. Behind him, he knew she waited. Darkly he gave her the answer she so foolishly sought. "Be thankful I'm not giving in to your desire to see Cairncross,

Abbey. Truly there isn't a woman alive I would put through that ordeal." He watched the lightning crackle across the sky through the bedroom window, his expression static, hardened. He departed, but before he closed the door behind him and abandoned her for what he knew would be forever, he voiced the truth that had pressed on his mind all along.

"You see, the mistress of Cairncross cannot be afraid of ghosts."

Chapter Three

The depot at York was like nothing Alexandra had imagined. Perhaps because of the gloom of Stirrings-in-Field, she imagined the city to be covered in a shroud of fog, its inhabitants pasty-faced, even ghoulish, the famous York Walls surrounded by empty, endless moorland. Certainly the morning's blue skies above aided to a feeling of optimism. She and Mary disembarked from the train, but neither woman was ready for the rush of crowds at the station, the flurry of ladies bedecked in cut-velvet traveling suits, and the smartly dressed top-hatted men who laughed and cheerily greeted their friends arriving fresh from London.

"Now what'll we do?" Mary asked, clearly dazed by the boisterous, colorful crowd. The old maidservant clutched her worn carpetbag like a talisman against the surging throng. Her familiar red curls—probably the remnant of a Scottish ancestor—escaped in corkscrew fashion around her forehead, making her appear just a little bit mad.

Filled with an unexpected affection for the woman, Alexandra suddenly took Mary's arm in her own. Mary had always looked after her, even long ago when Alexandra had been a child. Now she had dragged the maidservant far away from London, the only town they'd ever known, and it was time for Alexandra to look after her. The responsibility weighed heavy upon her.

Alexandra searched the crush of travelers on the platform and searched the sea of unfamiliar faces again, her optimism and confidence sinking like a ship. In dismay, she murmured, "How foolish of me to think this a small provincial town. I just assumed the driver would be waiting and that . . . we could *find* him."

"Did the letter give a clue as to who was to meet us?"

Alexandra shook her head. "The last correspondence was from me, informing his lordship when we were to arrive." She looked around the milling, hugging, laughing crowd. There wasn't a soul who seemed to have not yet hooked up with their party.

"My bottom's plumb worn out from all the sittin'," Mary sighed as she heaved her stocky form down upon a bench.

"Don't fret. We can always hire a coach to take us to Cairncross." Alexandra watched the crowd thin. Porters and servants grabbed the handles of trunks and carpetbags. Slowly, one by one, the passengers and their respective parties dribbled off the platform.

"This isn't right. We can't go galavantin' across the countryside not knowin' a body or soul. 'Tis below your station. Besides that, I think it must be dangerous." Mary shook her bonneted head and let her gaze wander up and down the now-empty platform.

Alexandra clutched her beaded purse and took a deep breath. She was going to handle this. She strode to the front of the platform where she could see around the depot. There wagons and carriages lined up to meet the passengers. The last one pulled from the slate curb and began ambling toward the minster. The depot was completely deserted. The only sign of life was a painted "open" sign over the ticketmaster's window. With spreading unease, Alexandra watched as a hand appeared on the other side of the glass and turned the sign. Now it read: "Closed for Dinner. Return at two o'clock."

"Wonderful," Alexandra whispered under her breath, afraid to look at Mary's I-told-you-so expression.

Helplessly, she searched either end of the platform one last time. The depot was situated beneath one of the town's famous Roman walls. Besides the tower of thick gray rock that made up the wall, there was nothing around them but trees and the occasional rusting water cistern.

"We'll just have to acquire a hack. Lord Newell will surely reimburse us for the charges. After all—" Alexandra stopped. Mary sat on the bench transfixed by something above them.

"Mary?" Alexandra whispered. Mary was pale. Her frozen expression sent a foreboding shiver of ice down her spine.

Alexandra followed the old woman's gaze to a point atop the wall.

"Do you see her?" Mary choked.

"See what? Who?"

"She's a-starin' right at you, miss. Right at you."

Alexandra looked at the ridge of the wall. It was more than fifty feet above them. She saw nothing. "I don't see anything."

"She's gone." The words were a whisper of relief and terror.

Alexandra turned to Mary. The maidservant was now standing, as if whoever had been upon the wall had beckoned her forth.

"How could you see anyone up there? It's so far away."

"Oh, miss. She was terrible. Terrible. I never want to see such a figure again. Never again."

A tendril of cold seemed to wrap around her heart as Alexandra noted Mary's ash white face. She took the maidservant's hand and found it like ice. "I think the journey must have taken its toll on you," she said gently. "Perhaps it was selfish of me to take you with me—"

"But who else would you have? And you need someone. I know that now." The woman seemed on the edge of hysterics.

"Come, sit here and rest. I fear you look as if you might faint." Alexandra helped her down onto the bench. "Rest here.

Perhaps we could find an inn and take refreshment. That might make you feel better.''

Mary just shook her head as if a tragedy had already occurred. Her head rocked back and forth in the slow manner of a matron at the funeral of a youth. So mournful of the waste.

"What was it that you saw? A woman?'' Alexandra patted her shoulder to comfort her. "Was she so ugly then? Perhaps whomever it was was staring because she was supposed to notify the driver from Cairncross to pick us up. No doubt he's dallied at the pub and that's why he's not here.''

"No. No.''

Alexandra bit her lower lip, perplexed. She'd never seen Mary in such a fit. Nice, sensible Mary. It was unusual for her to have fits.

All at once Mary grabbed her arm. "We've got to leave here. Find the ticketmaster and tell him we want to return to London immediately.''

"How could a woman who's merely standing on the wall put you in this state? What's this all about?''

"She was ordinary, ordinary. Except for her hair. She had great gobs of it, quite red. And it was all unpinned. Brazen-like. Blowin' back in the wind.''

Alexandra looked up at the wall, a small furrow lining her brow. "But it's not windy today, Mary. I haven't felt a breeze since we disembarked the train.''

"Exactly.'' The word was barely a whisper.

Alexandra took off her glove and held her hand high. The air at the depot was graveyard quiet. Several tourists paraded along the wall now, maps and books in gloved hand while they strolled the perimeter and studied its history. The ladies' skirts did not flag in the breeze. "I suppose it's entirely possible a wind touched upon the wall moments before. Why, that must be what happened. Oh, you goose. All you've seen is a tourist—''

"She was evil. And she was staring at you, miss.''

Alexandra locked gazes with her. A funny, skittering feeling took hold of her stomach, but she willed it away. They had

enough worries given no driver had come for them and Cairncross was all the way on the coast and the master was expecting
a man. She couldn't succumb to hysteria now. Nor could she
allow Mary to. "But how do you know this?" she asked. "Was
this woman wearing a witch's costume? Carrying a pitchfork?"

"Nay. She was in simple garb. Dressed all in black. A
horrible sight she was. A horrible sight . . ."

Alexandra stared at her, helplessly searching for words of
comfort. Mary had always been much older than herself, old
enough, in fact, to be her mother. It was always she who was
comforted by her, not the other way around. Until that very
moment Alexandra had never considered Mary aged, but now
it struck her with all the force of a blow how old Mary really
looked. The dear face beneath the shabby chip bonnet was that
of a geriatric. The beloved, comforting visage was now masked
with lines and worry. And as she stared at Alexandra, she wore
the face of a mother who feared for her child.

Alexandra took the servant's shaking hand and stilled it in
her own. "There's nothing to be frightened of, I swear it. Think
about it, Mary, a woman in black is not so strange. You yourself
are wearing black, and so am I, for that matter."

"She wore a dress much as your'n, miss. But 'twas old-
fashioned. Without any cream lace."

"Then I must get the name of her dressmaker," Alexandra
quipped lightly, anxious to remove Mary from whatever spell
had passed over her. "You know I hate the cream lace on my
gowns. It's practical and serviceable and I hate it. White looks
so much better, but now I must refrain from spending the money
it takes to replace it when it soils or tears—"

"Please let's return to London. I—I have a terrible feeling, of
a sudden." The heavily wrinkled folds of Mary's eyes revealed
irises the color of periwinkles. Alexandra always thought Mary
had such comforting eyes. Now their expression terrified her.

"I can't return." She pressed the woman's hand, her face
an apology. "If you're so frightened of whatever this thing
was you saw on the wall, then I'll help you return to London.
But I can't. I . . . won't." Alexandra drew herself up. Even

scary, flame-haired trollops on the York Wall wouldn't force her home.

"I'll be comin' with you then." Mary dug through her ancient reticule and found her handkerchief. She patted the perspiration on her upper lip and forehead and staunchly looked up at the wall.

"See? There are only tourists up there," Alexandra said, rubbing the hand that was still clutching her own.

"No. What I saw, I saw. She wasn't a tourist. She was . . . evil. I haven't children, Alexandra and you're as close to a child as I'll ever have and I can't bear the idea of you being looked at by—by *her*."

Alexandra opened her mouth to reason with Mary, but she stopped herself. She knew her maid too well. A stray black cat had shown up at their kitchen door one day and Mary had nearly burned Alexandra at the stake to find the girl pouring it a dish of cream. Mary had hated the cat and nothing would convince her it wasn't the devil's own spawn, and the servant didn't change her mind in all the nine years the cat frequented the kitchen begging cream and fish. If nearly a decade of little-girl pleas couldn't convince Mary to allow the cat to live in the town house, a few words now were not going to convince the woman she had not seen something evil atop the wall. Alexandra could see it in the set of her jaw.

With a great, weary sigh, Alexandra looked around the platform once more. Nothing broke the empty stillness, not footsteps, not carriage wheels, not even a breeze.

"We'll not speak of this anymore," Mary whispered, her expression losing some of the terror.

Alexandra nodded her head. "Of course. We'll forget this ever happened."

"Are you with Dr. Benjamin?"

The voice nearly sent both women clutching for the hartshorn. Alexandra spun around and stared at a neatly dressed older man who stood behind them. He wore corduroy breeches and a brushed black coat over a plaid vest. He was obviously a driver for a country manor house.

"We've—we've been waiting for you," Alexandra stammered, wishing she could instead ask how he had escaped their notice and managed to come up behind them.

"Are you in Dr. Benjamin's party?" He removed his satin top hat to reveal a head as bare as a billiard ball.

"We are the Benjamin party, but there's no doctor. I'm afraid you're mistaken," Alexandra said as crisply as she could to cover her nervousness. It was time to face the piper and reveal Alex Benjamin as a woman.

"But I was sent from Cairncross to pick up Dr. Benjamin." The driver frowned in confusion.

"I'm Alexandra Benjamin and this is my maid, Mary. We've come from London as sent for by Lord Newell."

"But Lord Newell said in his letter 'twas to be a Dr. Benjamin."

"I never professed to be a doctor. And indeed I'm the one he sent for. There is no other," Alexandra corrected coolly.

The driver stared at her and continued to frown. He looked up and down her black silk gown and finally rested his gaze on her bonnet-framed face. It was obvious that she was not as he had expected.

"Our bags are there." Alexandra pointed to a cluster of carpetbags and leather satchels. Imperiously, she asked, "Where is the carriage?"

" 'Tis over yon." He nodded toward the front of the depot. "I'll take you to the castle if you like, but you may as well know, his lordship's expecting a Dr. Benjamin."

"Then my appearance shall correct that error." Alexandra bristled at having to discuss her situation with the coachman. It didn't help matters either to see the terror on Mary's face melt into the old disapproval.

So we'll be booted out anyway, she thought to herself as she gathered her skirts. *At least we tried. At least we came this far.*

The carriage driver reluctantly loaded them into a green lacquered landau, his expression a strange blend of worry and warning. They wheeled into the city through Micklegate Bar. All the while, Mary pointedly refused to look at the wall again, though they ran parallel to it for nigh a quarter mile. But if the woman—or apparition—atop the wall was not on Mary's mind, she had returned with a fury to Alexandra's. Fighting an unwanted foreboding, Alexandra gazed upon the ancient city of York.

". . . and that there be Micklegate-bar. 'Tis an old gate. The arch was built in Roman times . . ."

Alexandra heard the driver's voice but didn't listen as he droned on about the turrets and embattlements of the gate, one of the four main entrances to the city. Vaguely she heard him mention that York was once the British capital of the Roman Empire and later that of the Viking conquerors. It had been a stronghold of the kingdom of Northumbria, and York Minster was one of the largest and oldest cathedrals in England, whose foundation was begun more than twelve hundred years before. The details of architecture bypassed her, however, along with the stories of kings and ecclesiastics who'd shed blood like rain to keep York within their grasp. At any other time she'd have found such history fascinating, but now her thoughts were centered around her reception at Cairncross, and she was anxious to get there and be done with it.

"Isn't there something a little odd about this fellow's tour?" Mary whispered to her as the driver negotiated the crowded street of Micklegate.

"I've noticed he never gave us his name," Alexandra quipped.

"But listen to him, miss, it's downright gruesome the tales he's telling."

Alexandra turned her attention to the loquacious driver. At the moment he was dribbling out words about York Minster and there seemed nothing unusual in his talk. Her gaze drifted to the cathedral; she'd read enough about it to not be surprised to see that its magnitude equaled its magnificence, but she was astonished to discover that the massive edifice had been enclosed in an area that would have cramped a moorland church.

In the background, shouts of hawkers, squeals of rusty carriage wheels, and the waterfall of slop pouring into open sewers obfuscated the driver's speech, but she found the man's endless, unintelligible talk almost soothed her. At least he hadn't the power to tell her to leave.

"See what I mean, miss?" Mary nudged her.

Alexandra sharpened her attention.

"Over yon, 'tis the front of the minster." The driver slowed the carriage to a slug's pace in order to join the stream of vehicles in the crowded thoroughfare around the cathedral. The slow gait gave them ample time to study their surroundings, and also to pay attention to the driver's presentation. While he spoke, the man constantly turned to look back at Alexandra. As much as she didn't want to acknowledge him, she found herself hypnotized by his warning-filled glance.

"Look closely at the pavement, Miss Benjamin. 'Tis built right over the ancient graves of bishops." He leaned back to give her a better view, his mouth curved in a wretched twist of pleasantry. "Now and again a ruby or sapphire ring used to pop up from the soil—you know how 'tis, miss, when them coffins give way to the soil and there ain't nothing left in the dirt but bones and jewels—so to keep away the thieves, they paved over all them bishops, and they cut the paving stones you see right now from their old marble grave markers." His teeth, crooked and weathered as tombstones themselves, bared in a smile. "Now what do you think them bishops think o' that?"

Alexandra didn't know how to reply. She stared at him, for the moment, mute.

"Left you speechless, did it?" He tipped his hat and held Alexandra's stare. "Nigh forty year before there was an old public house what sat next to the minster. They tore it down and found it covered the entrance to the old Saxon prison. 'Twas a rude piece of sculpture they found. A screaming man in the last agonies of death, his body mangled in torture, his soul seized by demons. Sits in the minster library now it does."

The man stared at Alexandra. "Be happy to take you ladies by it, if'n you like."

Alexandra slowly released her breath—unaware that she'd even been holding it—and leaned back against the seat. "That won't be necessary, Mr . . . ?"

"Jaymes, miss. Roger Jaymes. I been with the master near all his life. A good servant I am. Always will be." His expression turned dark. He seemed suddenly troubled. He glanced at her as if there was something he wanted to tell her, but then, as if he thought better of it, the stony Yorkshireman expression returned and he looked away.

"Why don't you take us to Cairncross, Jaymes," she commanded gently.

He turned around.

They drove through the narrow medieval streets while he continued to narrate its past. Even once outside the city walls, he still played the tour guide.

"See them old stone crosses?" he pointed out. "Them was erected during the terrible distemper. The King's Evil, they called it. Nigh every one in the city died. So the peasants put up them crosses as a way to meet with the city folk and barter their goods without entering the deadly walls of our fair York. They weren't a stupid race of people. They were simple creatures, country folk, they were, but they didn't blunder into places where they didn't belong. That be true." He gave Alexandra another foreboding glance before he returned his attention to his driving.

In the silence, Alexandra leaned toward Mary and whispered, "Renounce me as a critic, but I daresay his tour exhibits a lack of charm."

"He's nothin' but a curmudgeon," Mary whispered behind her gloved hand.

"He's certainly not happy we're here. I believe he's deliberately trying to frighten us with his macabre tour—" Alexandra's voice lowered to a hush, "—to frighten me."

"We shouldn't be here, miss." Mary wagged a finger at

her, hiding it behind her reticule. "You mark my words. Nothin' good will come of this."

Alexandra gave her a disparaging look, one that belied the worry gnawing at her stomach. Ever since the talk of the woman on the wall, a strange sense of dread seemed to cloak her and she could not shed it. Now as they wheeled along the road that cut north through the haunted scrubbed moors, she wondered again about her reception at Cairncross. She would either be taken in by the master and told to go to work, or she would be sent back to London.

"The castle is two hours and then some," the driver called back to them above the moorland wind. " 'Tis right on the chalky cliffs north of Whitby. A beauty, it is, Cairncross Castle . . . a terrible beauty."

Mary stared at her. Alexandra could feel her gaze driving into her like a spike.

"Then it's good we're on our way. I'm anxious to get there." She hoped her words sounded confident and unruffled. No despicable carriage driver was going to scare her away. She was not going to return to London.

The driver drove on. They reached the crossroads to Scarborough and Whitby with Cairncross beyond. Alexandra expected the driver to take the north road without hesitation, but he suddenly stopped the open landau and looked back at her as if he had something he wanted to tell her.

"You should have been a man," he said, his voice barely discernible in the moorland wind. He looked at Alexandra, his lined mouth tightened, but not with disapproval. Disapproval she could understand and cope with. Mary had disapproval. But the driver's emotions seemed beyond even that. His mouth was turned down in despair.

"You should have been a man, Alexandra Benjamin," he repeated slowly as if waiting for her to change her mind and tell him to take her back to York.

"Why?" she said, compelled almost against her will.

"The master's expecting a man." He shook his head. The mouth grew more despairing. "For your own sake, Alexandra

Benjamin, you should have been a man. You—you don't know how cruel the master is.''

Mary clutched Alexandra's hand, her old woman's eyes popping out of her head.

Bless her, Alexandra thought. Bless Mary for her homey ways and her melodrama. The maid gave some mortal normalcy to a situation that was fast sinking into the surreal.

"Drive on," Alexandra told him, anxious for him to turn away so that she would not have to see his wretched expression.

He touched Newell's fancy matched bays with the whip, his actions more reproachful than if he had spoken.

The moors, in their unnatural silence, passed slowly. There was little in the lifeless monotony of the landscape to cheer the lonely traveler. The worn colors of heather and bracken looked like rotting drapery too long exposed to the elements, and the unchanging expanse of emptiness left a solitary ache in the heart. As if each breath of wind carried a cry marking the demise of another doomed soul.

Alexandra felt Mary's fear like a palpable creature sitting between them, one difficult to rout, yet infinitely human, and therefore, in theory, able to be chased away by reason. She wished she were merely afraid like Mary because the emotion that gripped her now went beyond fear. She felt the inevitable. The man of the letter beckoned as much as her past sent her running away. The only thing that was not inevitable was Lord Newell's reaction to her. He would be displeased, that much she knew, but the rest of the future was still an enigma. For right now only two questions remained: whether she would be taken in or thrown out.

And, of course, which would be worse.

Chapter
Four

Alas, how many hours and years have past,
Since human forms have round this table sate,
Or lamp, or taper, on its surface gleam'd!
Methinks, I hear the sound of time long pass'd
Still murmuring o'er us, in the lofty void
Of these dark arches, like the ling'ring voices
Of those who long within their graves have slept.
                              —Orra, A Tragedy

Cairncross Castle *was* a terrible beauty. Its gray mossy battle-ments perched on chalk white cliffs like a gargoyle crouched by the sea. The castle was enormous, the sprawl caused by a millennium of military architecture and bloodshed. End to end it took near a quarter of a mile of coastline. It was a breathtaking homage to greed and the human need for protection.

The modern age had yet to dawn upon Cairncross's fearful visage, yet peace had long settled upon the coast. Romans, Vikings, they were no more. Still, the castle seemed tensed for battle. The windows still stared out to the roiling sea as if waiting for the next marauder.

But the marauder had crept upon Cairncross unnoticed. She had arrived the back way, by land. And all it had taken was a train ride from London. Alexandra smiled at the thought and gathered her courage.

"Quite impressive," she announced, nudging Mary who sat next to her as silent as a freshly dug grave.

"I can't change your mind, so I'll just keep my lips together." Mary clutched her reticule and sourly watched the driver dismount.

A mousey, black-garbed woman appeared at the doors that opened to the castle from the bailey. Her brilliantly white starched collar and the gray in her hair seemed to pronounce her the housekeeper. She stared at their party with large, confused eyes as if their presence had proved a terrible shock.

"Is Dr. Benjamin arriving later, Jaymes?" she asked while lifting her skirts and nearly running down the marble stairs from the front doors, her face a mask of worry. She looked at Alexandra and said, "He didn't say there would be others. I thought it was assumed the doctor would be traveling alone."

"There's been a mistake." Alexandra held out her hand for Jaymes to help her from the landau. "I am Alexandra Benjamin. I'm the one for whom Lord Newell sent. This is my maid, Mary Taggart."

The housekeeper stared at both women as if she were stunned into disbelief. "Oh dear," she murmured, the shock on her face melting into a faint despair. "Oh dear." She turned to Jaymes, worry lines woven along her forehead.

"She's insistent his lordship sent for her," Jaymes muttered, helping Alexandra to the ground.

"But we thought—*his lordship*—thought you were to be a man." The housekeeper resumed staring at Alexandra.

Alexandra straightened her cream lace cuffs, a nervous habit she was beginning to pick up. "Lord Newell called for my father. My father is dead and I offered my services. So here I am."

The housekeeper's eyes darted to Jaymes and Alexandra swore she saw the carriage driver give an almost imperceptible shrug.

"Would you be so kind as to show me to my room so that I may freshen up before I meet with Lord Newell?" Alexandra hated the supercilious tone she was forced to take but she didn't know what other recourse to take.

The housekeeper worried at her lips with her teeth. She gave another surreptitious glance to Jaymes. "Lord Newell won't be here until tomorrow. He's come up from his house in London to meet Dr. Benjamin." Anxiety masked her face. "Follow me. I'll take you to your rooms."

The housekeeper nodded and Alexandra, arm in arm with Mary, followed her through the front entrance. Still, Alexandra was unable to hide her gasp of awe as she took her first steps inside the castle.

"What is this room?" she asked reverently, her gaze darting around as she tried to absorb the scope of the enormous chamber in which she stood.

"This is the Great Hall. His lordship sometimes has dinner here for five hundred guests." The housekeeper brusquely walked through the enormous cavern ignoring her awestruck behavior.

Alexandra tried to keep up but everywhere she looked there was distraction. The room's four walls were entirely lined with armor and as she stumbled along she found a most gruesome display of maces and the rusting chest plates they had gouged. Ancient triangular wooden shields marked one section of the wall, then flowed into a field of small Spanish fist shields. Finally the dais wall was tapestried with the gaily emblazoned steel shields of mere centuries past. Sentineling the banquet table stood pedestaled displays of armor, each knight holding a raised broadsword inside a locking—or as she had come to learn of them through Sir Walter Scott's novels—a "forbidden gauntlet."

It was easy to think of romantic tourneys, of knights jousting

with their paramours' brilliant silk scarves tucked near to their
hearts. But the unique collection of broadswords that daggered
the opposite wall like deadly teeth testified not of men being
accoladed to the magical state of knighthood; instead they spoke
of war and death and defeat. Each bronze sword pommel wore
the arms of the knight who had gone on Crusade, and each
steel blade was blasphemed with an Arabic inscription, no
doubt bequeathing this most precious object of the fallen knight
to the sultan. Alexandra was particularly disturbed by the last
sword on display. A small gold plaque proclaimed it the Cairncross sword. It was nicked and battered by the armored bodies
it had cut down. Engraved on its pommel was the motto of the
ancient Barony of Cairncross: *Sunt hic etiam sui praemia laudi.*
"Here too virtue has its reward." There was a certain incredulity to the motto that disturbed her. Yet it rang true. It was all
in keeping with the gloomy castle, the crumbling battlements,
the well-used armor.

She followed the as-yet-unintroduced housekeeper through
the shadowy torchlit passages of the castle while Mary, her
face drained of blood after the view from the Great Hall, brought
up the wake. Alexandra tried to keep her thoughts from wandering to Lord Newell but it was impossible. She didn't know
how he was going to react to the surprise of her womanhood,
but she was determined to play her role to the finale. There
was nothing her father could do for Newell's brother that she
could not do with equal skill and intelligence. Audiology was
in its infancy; there just weren't a large number of practitioners
upon whom he could call. The Right Honorable Lord Newell
had to accept her services, or toss his deaf brother to the ama-
teurs. Her abilities were strong and she must remember this
when she met Lord Newell. And she must keep her head high.
It would probably behoove her to keep his family motto in
mind also, should he disparage her weaker sex. All in all, the
Cairncross motto, haunting as it was, was eminently truthful.

Here too virtue has its reward.

* * *

"You may have this room for the night, miss." These were the housekeeper's first words since they left the hall. The woman flung open a door in one of the castle's newer wings and stood by while Alexandra stepped inside, Mary at her heels.

A peat fire blazed pleasantly in the hearth, and tea was set on a table between two leather club chairs. There was a puffy, buoyant appearance to the mattress that made Alexandra think it was freshly aired. The room smelled of beeswax and oil soap. The place had clearly just been prepared, no doubt, in anticipation of the illustrious Dr. Benjamin's arrival.

"I'll send supper up at eight." The woman paused as if her throat were caught with fear. "You understand that his lordship is expected to arrive at the castle any moment—"

"Oh really?" Alexandra spun on her heels and stared at her. "I hadn't realized Lord Newell's arrival could be so imminent."

"There's an evening train up from London. He could be on that one, or tomorrow's nine-fifteen, the train you arrived on." During this exchange, the housekeeper seemed to gather her courage and take a long hard look at Alexandra's face. The woman's entire expression seemed to say, "What has possessed you to come here?"

"The wardrobe's over yon," she finally instructed Mary as if shaking herself back into the role of servant. She walked around an awkwardly placed iron-strap traveling trunk while her expression once more fell back into appropriate disconcern. "There are extra bedlinens in the bureau, and under the bed you'll find a trundle. I believe that's all you'll be needing."

Alexandra opened her mouth to say something about the master having all these hundreds of rooms and not a one to spare for Mary, but she closed it again, already knowing what the response would be. She would be told that she and Mary probably weren't going to stay more than a night so there was no point in messing an extra room, even in the servants' quarters.

The housekeeper pointed to a door opposite the carved oak four-post bed. "That door goes to the old schoolroom. Don't bother yourself with a tour of it for it's kept locked at all times. Poor old Sam gets rattled when he finds himself inside it, so now we keep him out. I hope you understand." She looked expectantly at Alexandra.

Alexandra didn't know who poor old Sam was or why the old schoolroom rattled his nerves, but she felt it best to nod. The questions and answers would come later if she stayed.

"I'll be by at ten with cordials and your bedwarmer. Sleep well this night." With that, the housekeeper closed the door behind her.

"But wait!" Alexandra could only stare at Mary while they both listened to the click of heels on the passage's floorboards. "She didn't even give us her name," she said, dumbfounded.

"I can't imagine what's going on around here, but I know one thing: that woman, she doesn't want us here, and that's for certain." Mary clucked and threw open the luggage like a mad hen.

"She doesn't. Even a fool could see that." Alexandra pensively stared at the closed door. "I rather think she and Jaymes are wary about their master's wrath. I think they believe my 'unfortunate' sex will somehow be blamed on them."

She went to the windows that looked out to the moorlands, hoping the view would take her mind from her troubles. Mists from the channel had begun to drape the countryside like cobwebs, but beyond the coastline, the huge emptiness of the moors lay naked, too far away for the comfort of the sea.

She wished Lord Newell had been at the castle when she arrived. She could have been done with it by now.

Her gaze wandered down to the trunk at her feet. It was a curious old piece; the black leather straps were cracking and even the padlock was rusted shut with age. The name Pole was embossed in tarnished gilt along the front of the lid.

"I wonder why they keep this here—?"

"What's that noise?" Mary interrupted, her voice a sudden

whisper, her hands locked on the door to the massive mahogany wardrobe where she was just hanging dresses on the pegs.

The hair prickled on Alexandra's nape. In the dimming light from the window she thought she saw a shadow pass beneath the door that led to the castle's old schoolroom.

"I think there's someone in there," Mary whispered. "But Mrs. No Name said it wasn't in use."

Alexandra felt her heart beat an unnatural staccato against her ribs. "Perhaps she has gone in there to check on things, or such." She looked at Mary. "It's none of our business what goes on in this castle outside this room. They have every right—"

A great thud sounded from the schoolroom beyond. Alexandra swallowed her words.

"Lord a-mighty, what could that be?" Mary gripped her arm with such force Alexandra was sure she would have no feeling in it the rest of the night.

"Perhaps someone knocked over a chair." Alexandra extricated herself from Mary's terrified grip. "Let me see if I can check on it. Perhaps someone has fallen ... or such." She reached for the door to knock but when her knuckles met with the wood, the door swung open wide releasing a long, painful screech.

She nearly jumped at Mary's gasp.

"I thought she said it was kept locked?" the maid whispered behind her.

Alexandra shook her head, unable to explain it. She took an old Argand lamp from the mantel and lit it in the fire. With light in hand, she stepped into the abandoned schoolroom.

"Stay here," she snapped when she found the servant right behind her. Peering into the shuttered dimness, she whispered, "I don't want you screaming if you see a chambermaid. That's not the way to win a welcome. I'll be right back."

Alexandra held the Argand lamp high and studied the beautiful schoolroom. The wainscotting was hoary with dust but even so she could see it was carved of once-gleaming walnut. There were two slanted desks with little lordly chairs to match and a larger desk at the front, one with a delicate pierced skirting of mahogany. A woman's desk.

"Why, there's no one in here," she whispered to herself, shivering with a sudden chill. She could understand the reason that they'd abandoned the blasted room. It was downright drafty.

"We didn't imagine that noise."

Alexandra looked behind her and found Mary at her elbow. The dear, as usual, was pale with fright yet determined to be at her side.

"Look. The dust hasn't been touched by feet." Mary pointed to a second door that obviously connected to the corridor. The dust on the floor going toward it was as unmarred as virgin snowfall.

Alexandra thought of the darkness she believed had passed on the other side of the door to her room. The schoolroom was dim, but there was still enough late-afternoon light leaking through the closed shutters to create shadow. She was convinced something or someone had moved on the other side of her door.

A sudden, irrational thought made her veins turn to ice. If whoever was in the schoolroom was not in front of them, then perhaps. . . . In a rush of primeval fear, she whipped around to look behind her.

No one stood there. The door from her bedroom was only half ajar and it was impossible to hide behind it. The room was empty save for a cold wind or two.

Mary was nearly choking from shock. "You nigh took a decade off me with that maneuver."

"It's just that . . . well, I thought I saw a shadow before we came in here. I just can't understand what could have caused it since the room is empty and clearly has been for years."

Frustrated, Alexandra stared at the path of scattered dust in their wake. If there were another's footprints there they were gone now. With their two silk gowns serving as dustmops, the path was swept clean of any footprints, even their own.

"Looky, miss. There is the answer to this mystery." Mary pointed to a book that lay on the floor.

Alexandra looked down. The book had obviously fallen from the shelf above for it was one of a matched set.

"I see I must resign the shadow to my imagination." Alexandra stepped over to it. With all the shift and decay in the abandoned room, it was surprising more of the books hadn't fallen.

" 'Tis a beautiful book. Even from here I can spy the rich leather. Everything in the room's beautiful. Almost too fine for children . . ." Mary chattered like a wren.

"Let's not speak a word of this, shall we? I have a feeling they don't want us in here. It won't go over well." Thinking of the mysterious Lord Newell's reaction to their trespass, Alexandra absentmindedly picked up the book.

"Why 'tis the Waverley novels. A whole set of them. By the great Scotsman himself," Mary exclaimed, running her finger along the matched volumes.

Alexandra looked down at the novel in her hands. She felt an unnatural cold run through her that seemed to lay a frost even to her bones. The novel she held was *Ivanhoe*.

"You don't look a-rights, miss. Whatever is it?" Mary whispered.

"I'm—I'm fine." She hastily placed the novel in the empty slot where it belonged with its mates. The bookshelf was covered with tomes—atlases, novels, books about science, history and mathematics lined the entire wall. It was mere chance that *Ivanhoe* had been the one to tumble from the crowd.

"You don't look a-rights, miss."

"No, really, I'm fine." Alexandra ran her knuckles down the gilt-lettered spine. Her thoughts pressed down on her. Brian and *Ivanhoe*. They were inextricably intertwined. She wanted nothing more to do with either of them.

She tightened her mouth. Without offering any more explanation, she turned to Mary and said, "Come along. Let's leave this place. It's cold in here."

Mary followed her out and resumed unpacking. Alexandra went twice to the schoolroom door just to make sure it was firmly closed.

Chapter Five

Were she ten times a witch,
provided she were but the least bit of a Christian . . .
— *Friar Tuck*
IVANHOE

A loud knock suddenly sounded. Alexandra bolted upright in the bed. The knocking continued relentlessly and she groped for her old velvet dressing gown. Unable to find it in the dark, unfamiliar room, she threw her shawl around her shoulders and stumbled to the bedroom door.

"Who is it?" she called.

"His lordship's arrived, miss. He demands to see you right away."

Alexandra opened the door. Earlier it had seemed absurd to have had cordials and slip into bed when she still had not met her nemesis, but there had been no word of Newell's arrival. All evening she and Mary had had nothing better to do than work on their needlepoint canvases and stare at each other.

Now, looking at the housekeeper's grim face, the time had come to meet him.

"But—but it's so late," she stammered. "His lordship can't think I'd be dressed to meet with him now." She clutched the shawl around her slim shoulders. Her hair had already begun to escape its plaiting. Two particularly annoying curls kept falling over her eyes.

"Miss, he's called for you. 'Tis best you come now." The housekeeper still wore a nervous, birdlike demeanor, except that now, Alexandra was distinctly aware that terror lit her eyes.

"He'll have to wait until I'm properly dressed—"

"No, miss. Come now. He said he wants to see you now."

She just looked at the housekeeper, a stupefied expression on her face. She couldn't believe it. Newell was a tyrant to do this at this hour.

"Very well," she answered slowly. She turned and stepped to the bed. Mary was still in her trundle, the covers frozen in hand. Alexandra could almost read her mind. To her old maidservant, she probably looked like a child with her unruly curls braided down her back and her bare toes barely covered by the hem of her pristine white nightrail. But Alexandra was no longer a child. And while Newell may prove more of a dragon than she could fight, she was going to defend her position until he booted her out Cairncross's front door.

"I'll come with you, miss," the maidservant whispered.

Alexandra flicked a glance at her. Mary was straightening her frilly night cap and reaching for her faded maroon-colored robe with an old purple wine stain down the front.

"No. There's no point in you suffering this humiliation too." Alexandra grabbed her velvet dressing gown, slung an arm through the sleeve and trailed after Lord Newell's cowed housekeeper into the darkness of the passage.

She half expected to be taken to the baronial hall where Newell might view her from the dais and direct Jaymes with the instructions, "Off with her head!" Instead she was taken to the other side of the castle, to a handsome pair of walnut doors that appeared to lead to a man's study.

"He's in there," the housekeeper whispered behind her.

Alexandra felt as if she were some kind of lion tamer being told where the escapee was hiding. She waited a second, expecting the housekeeper to at least open the door for her, but the timid woman made no such effort. The absurdity of not even knowing the housekeeper's name struck her; the situation was ridiculous, yet it was not amusing because waiting to enter the maw of Newell's study made her heart pound with an unnatural fury.

No man could be this much of a terror she told herself. Trying to forget the housekeeper's wild-eyed face, she placed her hand on the door handle and opened the door.

In the back of her mind, she supposed she half pictured Newell as some kind of ogre poised by the fire salivating from a feast of fresh servants. The handsome, bespectacled blond gentleman who perfunctorily rose upon her entrance couldn't have been less like her imaginings.

You don't know how cruel the master is. Jaymes's words seemed to taunt her.

"My lord," she whispered in the shadows by the door, momentarily shocked by how much Newell looked like Brian; the blond hair, the balanced and precise Anglo-Saxon features, the broad-shouldered, masculine figure. She was so struck by the awful comparison that she became unconscious of her own appearance; that she stood before a peer barefoot in only her nightrail and dressing gown. She didn't know what she had expected John Damien Newell to look like, but she hadn't counted on this.

"Sit down, Miss Benjamin." He nodded to the armchair across from the hearth.

While his own luxurious chair was upholstered in the finest purple damask, the one he offered her was made of near-petrified wood, torturously designed in medieval times from turned spools and spindles. She sat and found it as stiff and uncomfortable as it looked. Vaguely, she wondered if the chair was normally kept in Cairncross's dungeon.

Newell resumed his seat and she took in more of his appearance. His charcoal frock coat elegantly fit his enormous frame as only the finest tailor could make it. Even so, she could see the muscles in his arms bunch against the fabric, straining it, testing it, a small clue that this man was not quite the civilized, sedentary peer one would expect of a baron. And when he reached up to the mantel to where he kept a glass of brandy, she could almost imagine those same muscular arms raised with the Cairncross broadsword, eager to slam it down upon an enemy's skull.

She touched her forehead and let her fingers run along her scalp. It was then she remembered that her hair was in a plait and that she was dressed in her night clothes. A betraying, panicky flush crept up her neck.

"Miss Benjamin." Newell finally gave her his attention. Despite his imperious, bored expression, she could tell he found her appearance an aggravation. "I did not send for a governess. I sent for a doctor. Why have you come here?"

She met his cold stare. One not unexpected given the circumstances. Neither was the anger that lit his cerulean blue eyes. The seconds ticked by as she rallied her thoughts, groping for the best explanation of her lie. He watched in a decidedly lordly fashion, as if, not being a peer herself, she were just a kind of creature brought into his richly appointed study to amuse him.

Still unable to find the best approach to begin her explanation, she merely returned the stare, noting that he appeared almost as tired as she felt. He possessed lines of fatigue that creased either side of his well-formed mouth. With silence damning her, she gazed at him while he removed his spectacles and rubbed his bloodshot eyes. He seemed to wait like a bowstring ready to be let loose upon her lame words.

"You have nothing to say for yourself." It was not a question. It was a sentencing.

She stared into his eyes, imploring for what, she didn't know. She wanted compassion, understanding, respect. She wanted to appeal to the human side of him and tell him she was just as qualified as any man he might bring to Cairncross. The only difference between her and her father's assistants was that in society they were afforded the dignities of a formal degree and the esteem of other men. She was not.

Their gazes locked. She realized that this time she saw him without the cover of his spectacles. He was a handsome man. More handsome even than Brian, but now experience told her to give such handsomeness pause. As did such an expression.

Anger, betrayal, ridicule; she had anticipated that. But not this. His eyes disturbed her. There was a wastedness she had never seen in eyes before. It was as if they had never seen anything but the dark side of life. They held a dangerous beckoning. A lost beauty. She found she couldn't quite bear to look upon them.

"The explanation." He settled the gold-rimmed spectacles back on the bridge of his nose, and an arrogant, finely crafted nose it was. The vanquished mortal she thought she'd seen in him was now shielded.

"You—you would not have sent for me if you had known I was a woman." Her voice was weaker than she would have liked, but she was shaken more by the indefinable emotion she'd seen in his eyes than by the confrontation. Nervously, as if it were a gesture of protection, she pulled the lapels of her dressing gown together, almost clutching them.

He stood. She was already dismissed. He'd obviously found her words trite and unimpressive. He meant her to go without further explanation.

"Wait." She clenched her hands and stared down at the gaudy gold and purple carpet as if for strength. Slowly she rose to her feet, and even more slowly she tilted her head upward and met his foreboding stare. "Forgive me, Lord Newell. It was an inexcusable ruse, but as one can already see by your reaction, I had no choice. If I'd signed the letter Alexandra, you would have tossed it in the paper bin, and I would not be here now trying to help—"

"I asked for a physician, not a governess."

"I am not a governess. The rest of my letter was true. I studied my father's work for years. There are few more qualified than I—''

"You're no doctor.''

"I never claimed to be. You must understand, there are few who specialize in this area. No qualified man would be willing to come all the way up here to help your deaf brother—''

"Sam is not deaf.''

The quietness of his words in the midst of the argument had the effect of a boulder falling from the ceiling. She could only stare at him until the words once more came to her lips.

"I—I don't understand.'' Her mind clicked with previously ignored facts. She recalled the housekeeper saying that poor old Sam avoided the schoolroom. She had thought she'd been referring to an elderly befuddled servant; now she understood she'd been speaking of the lord's brother. "My father specialized in helping the deaf,'' she nearly sputtered. "Why would you summon him if your brother can hear?''

Newell resumed his seat, leaving her to stand awkwardly in the middle of the room. He pinned her to the thick carpet by his stare. "Dr. Horace Benjamin specialized in audiology. He helped deaf people speak. If he could do that, I thought he could help Sam.''

"Your brother never learned to speak?''

Newell slid his gaze to the fire. The flames reflected in his spectacles with an almost satanic glee. "My brother is . . . slow. He was born that way. It took many years but he eventually learned to speak. He lost the ability, however, and now I'm here to take care of him again. I want to bring his speech back.''

"He *lost* the ability? But how did he lose it? I've never heard of such a thing. Was it a blow to the head? A fever—?''

"Fear.'' Newell's gaze slid back to hers, strangely taking her breath.

"Fear?'' she repeated numbly.

"He was frightened so badly he never spoke again.''

The baby-hairs stood up on her neck and she felt the gooseflesh rise on her arms. Eventually her breath came back to her but only in short, thick puffs. If the afternoon hadn't been full of haunts, she might have been able to control her reaction better, but this particular story disturbed her because it was not speculation or the ruminations of old men. It was fact. Something—a person, an incident—had frightened the speech from this man's brother and now all she could think of was that novel lying on the floor of the abandoned schoolroom.

Ivanhoe.

"You look pale, Miss Benjamin."

She reached behind her for the medieval chair. Slowly she sank into it. "What frightened him?" Her voice was low and trembling. After looking into this man's eyes, she was not sure she wanted to know.

His gaze raked over her, studying her as if weighing the possibility of answering or not. Finally he said, "I was gone from Cairncross by then and not privy to the incident. That's why I wish to hear him speak again. I want to know exactly what was done to him. Right now all I have is a recounting of the day by my old servants. I had hoped with the right physician, Sam would be given back the ability to tell me what really happened."

She looked blankly around this lord's elaborate study while her mind raced with images of horror. She'd been given enough veiled warnings and malevolent forebodings to be impressed by them. She couldn't help wondering if now wasn't the time to bow out and for the first time in her life be grateful she was a woman so she would not have to hang on a man's kind of honor and keep her commitment.

Her gaze trained on Newell's face once more. The one so like Brian's. She was grateful for the spectacles. They kept a distance between her and those eyes. Those terrible eyes.

But if she left now and returned to London, Brian's kind of thinking would have won. Her forlorn acceptance of the circumstances would only serve to strengthen the prejudice she could see Newell felt for her. Yes, she was a woman and no physician, but she was the best this man could ever get to help his brother, despite her sex. She couldn't leave without a fight as she had let Brian leave that night long ago, his thinking intact. To let this particular man believe he was correct in his thinking would be ruinous to her pride. She had to stay at Cairncross. She had to prove to someone that her kind, whatever that was, was good enough.

Besides, she had nothing to fear. Newell's story of his brother proved nothing. There was wickedness and evil in the world outside of this castle, so what did it matter that here at Cairncross evil cast a more obvious shadow? If anything, she could almost take succor in it. Sometimes the worst sort of evil was performed in quiet formal parlors, with all the manners of a courtier.

"Lord Newell, I believe I can help Samuel and unless you plan to take him to London, I'm the only one who can. I think you must let me try." She gave him her most level-minded, serious stare. She could see he was pondering it; she could see he hated the idea.

"You're not a physician. It doesn't matter who your father was, you're a woman and of limited use."

His words were like a punch in the gut. It was the expected attitude, but it was still grossly unjust.

She stared at him. "I can help."

His expression hardened, and she realized the battle was lost. He was more like Brian than in mere appearance. There would be no fighting him. She was on his ground, not hers; looking down at her nightrail, she wasn't even dressed for the battle. And one certainly couldn't argue with a peer when one was further handicapped by being a woman.

Releasing a dark sigh, she rose and walked to the study doors. Disappointment tugged at relief. At least Mary would rejoice.

"Why did you want this job, Miss Benjamin?"

She let her hand slip off the carved brass doorknob. The curiosity in his voice seemed to lend her a second chance. She faced him but she was still wary. Backing against the walnut doors, she said, "I thought to come here because I wanted a chance to leave London. My father recently died, as you know from my letter.''

His gaze flickered over her appearance. She couldn't tell what he was thinking. His expression was a hard opaque mask of hidden emotions. ''The way you signed your answer to my letter, I know very little about you.''

''What do you need to know about me?'' She looked at him, at a loss whether to hope or despair.

''If I give you this job I don't want an irate husband coming here to drag you away just when Sam's making progress.''

''I haven't any husband.'' At his knowing look, she stammered, ''I—I had expectations once but it's over and done with now.'' She wondered why she had volunteered that last piece of information. She could have kicked herself when he asked his next question.

''You were engaged?'' He lifted one dark gold eyebrow.

''Something like that.''

''And yet . . . no longer?''

She didn't want to speak of Brian, especially to this stranger who damned her by his resemblance to him. Besides, she had only realized afterward the true picture of her ''expectations.'' Science had been everything to Brian and so it had been everything to her. Years had passed in a limbo of quiet yearning because she had always thought marriage and babies were able to wait. But now she fully understood that she'd mistaken a passion for science as a passion for her. Only later had she realized how it had all ironically managed to pass her by: Brian, marriage, babies, and now, if she didn't get this job, even her beloved science.

She gave him a look of reproof and hoped he could see he was out of his boundaries. ''We had an 'understanding,' 'tis all.''

He stared at her. He liked her discomfort. There was a smugness to his gaze, a slight quirk to his lips, but whether it was flirtation or malice, she didn't know.

''How long of an 'understanding' did you have, Miss Benjamin?''

She prayed she kept the hurt from her eyes. She didn't want to answer but to not answer would make it seem more important than she wished it to be.

"Five years." Had her voice trembled? Could he see the wounds were still fresh?

At her answer, his eyes widened imperceptibly. Then, without warning, he laughed, a big, white-toothed snarl of a laugh whose sound felt like a hot iron on her sores.

She shot him a furious, insulted glance but it didn't quell him at all.

"You mean to tell me this man had a chaste little 'understanding' with a young woman such as yourself for five interminable years?" His face was a sardonic mask of disbelief.

"Yes." She wanted to reach for the doorknob and slam out of the room. This was no business of his, but she couldn't bring herself to leave, not while she stood on the precipice of his employment.

"The bastard must have been Irish to have had an understanding with a woman for that long."

She made no comment. It was probable that the Honorable Brian Denys Tewesbury, the second son of a viscount, was part Irish, but she was half Irish, and though it would no doubt shock Newell right out of his arrogant assumptions, she felt no compunction to explain that the *Irish* in either Brian or herself had never been the problem.

Newell stood and stepped toward her, brandy glass in hand. In a slow whisper, he said, "You needn't tell me the rest, Miss Benjamin. I take it, like most 'understandings' between men and women, he got married, but you didn't, am I correct?"

"Yes," she hissed, hating to admit that he was right about Brian when she had been so wrong. She willed away the tears she knew had sprung into her eyes. Staring at him, she relished the fact that this handsome peer looked so much like Brian. She wanted to remember Brian, not because of the tenderness she had once felt for him, but because of the lessons he had taught her.

A silence ensued between them. Her answer seemed to temporarily satisfy his curiosity and he appeared content just to watch her. She thought she might be dismissed with the issue of her employment still unsettled, but he never told her to leave. Instead he seemed to enjoy studying her, his gaze wandering down her small figure as if it were property, his eyes fixed on her face as if he were trying to read the intelligence there. Any other woman might have taken his rakish attention as flattery, but she knew it meant something else. Something more. He was assessing her.

She could see by the brief light in his eyes that he noted her lack of stature. She was a petite woman and next to his giant form she did seem insignificant, but she would not allow him to treat her as insignificant and this defiance that must have lit her eyes was a thing that seemed to intrigue him. He probably couldn't reconcile her strong opinions with her inconsequential appearance. No doubt she made a childish picture, standing with her back to the door, her dusty bare feet hidden beneath the even dustier hem of her nightrail, but she could not let him treat her as a child. She was a grown woman, worthy of respect, and he would respect her or she would leave.

Their gazes met. He seemed to be able to read her determination. The cruel amusement died in his eyes. Slowly, his expression turned grim.

"When they told me a woman came in the doctor's place, I thought to find a silly girl running away from her father or such. I have to admit I looked forward to chasing you away."

"And now?" she whispered.

"Now a part of me wishes you could help Sam."

"I think I might be able to. My father is dead, my lord. If anyone can do it, I can do it."

"You're determined, I see." His eyes flickered down across her small figure, her chaste nightclothes. His gaze returned to her face and by his expression, she couldn't tell whether her implacability pleased him or infuriated him. "I'll give you a warning, Miss Benjamin." His eyes filled with a strange loathing and despair. His expression hardened with frustration, as if he couldn't quite reach for the words to explain it to her. "You should leave here."

"I've already been told to leave."

"Then why don't you take such good advice and go?"

She looked at him steadily, frightened, yet still willing to hold her ground. "I want to help your brother."

"You want to help yourself. That's why anyone does anything. And your reasons for coming here are more influenced by your 'understanding' that went awry, than the need to help Sam."

She was stunned how well he could read her. But he couldn't read all of her. Not her innermost heart. At least not yet. " 'Tis true I was glad for the opportunity to leave London, but I still want a chance to help your brother. My father is dead and I fear his work will go to the grave with him if I don't carry on, and that is why I came here, my lord."

He stared at her for a long assessing moment. As if he were on the verge of believing her.

She suddenly felt encouraged. "If I do not heed the warnings, my lord, have I the option of employment?"

"You'd be a fool to stay."

"I've already heard that, my lord."

His gaze locked with hers. He seemed ready to point to the door and order her out, but something in her face caught his eyes. She didn't know what it was that stopped him, perhaps it was simply her determination or her need that gave him pause. A muscle tightened in his jaw and he ran his knuckles over it as if in an effort to hide it. He glanced at her one more time, then he said, "If you're foolish enough to stay, Miss Benjamin, I'll employ you . . . for as long as you remain here."

Her heart drummed. She hadn't missed his implicit threat, but somehow she didn't care anymore about warnings and foreboding. Despite his unkindness, she'd stood up to him and convinced him. The job she had desperately wanted, needed, was hers. She could stay.

"You must know," he said in a hard, raspy voice, "that if you stay I'll hire you only in the capacity of a governess.

You're no doctor and I won't have you pretending to be one. Sam is near my age, but he's still a child. He needs looking after. I'll employ you to do it. If you can manage your father's techniques and get him to speak again, I'll pay you as I would a man. Otherwise, you'll get fifty pounds a year, and it's a generous man who gives you that.''

"Aye," she whispered, not caring about the money.

"Gather yourself up now. I'll take you to him tonight so that you may be acquainted."

"Tonight? Now?" she almost gasped.

He peered down at her, the shadow of arrogance on his lips. "Are you already complaining?"

"No, but—"

"I don't spend my time at Cairncross. My agent runs things." He folded his arms across his chest in the manner of a king. "I'll be returning to London tomorrow. I won't waste a day in my schedule for the convenience of a governess."

She glanced at him and bristled. She already didn't like the image of governess he'd forced upon her.

Suddenly, he laughed. "Miss Benjamin, has anyone ever told you you have the most remarkable eyes? They hold . . . a certain expression. A mystery. I must admit it challenges me to solve it."

She opened her mouth, to defend, to reproach. It was no place of his to comment on her eyes.

But before the words could leave her lips, he took her hand in his and dragged her out of the study.

Chapter
Six

Alexandra knew she would never forget the night that Newell pulled her through Cairncross's dark hallways, her small hand tucked firmly, helplessly, within his large one. Once outside the library, he'd grabbed a candelabrum and now held it before him as a staff, the light creating demon-shadows along the damp walls. Even later, she knew she would be able to vividly recall the comfort his warm hard hand gave her amidst the gloom of Cairncross's maze of passages.

There wasn't a soul to disturb the unearthly quiet of the stone passages. The servants had all retired. It was just she and Newell. The Right Honorable Lord Newell, a great big giant of a man who towered over her like the steel knights in his hall. He was a man built for a destrier, not a carriage. He was a man made for the wild, haunted moorlands of York, not the dirty, elegant streets of London.

They walked through the halls for miles it seemed, and more than once, she whispered to him, "My Lord Newell—" but never finished. She couldn't quite bear the thought of him pulling his hand away. Without his warm, alive clasp of his hand over hers, she would be left to face the darknesses of Cairncross alone.

"He's in here," he said when they at last reached a passage lined with carved oak doors from the Restoration period. She was beginning to realize that Cairncross's sprawl was mappable if one only knew the architecture of English history.

"He may be asleep, my lord," she whispered anxiously.

Newell looked down at her as if weighing her comment. His lips hinted at a terrible smile. "He would rather meet you as you are, Miss Benjamin. Now you look like a girl. Tomorrow you will look like a woman and then, I fear, he could react differently."

She could feel her blood slowly turn cold. "You speak in enigmas, my lord," she murmured, half desperate to know what he meant, the other half not sure she really wanted to know.

"Yes," he said, gently pushing open the door where blackness lay within.

She ducked beneath Newell's outstretched arm and stepped into the bedroom. It was a grand room, from what she could tell by the thin light still alive in the hearth. A bedstead, carved with acorns and crowns, draped in a wool damask, seemed made for a prince.

"He's over there. By the hearth." Newell cupped her chin and turned her head. She spied the "prince" himself sitting in an armchair, his profile almost exactly like his brother's while she had seen Newell staring into the fire. He had Newell's blond hair and giant build. Short of a slight difference in the bridge of his nose, he could have passed for Newell himself.

"Speak to him. Tell him who you are."

She glanced at Newell. Everything about this meeting was unorthodox. He was testing her. He wanted her off-balance. It explained the midnight visit to this place, it explained everything except his motivation for wanting such things.

"My lord, he doesn't appear to see us . . ." She waited for Newell's response, all the while wishing he would see the folly in the situation and allow them to leave.

"Go and talk to him. It might go better for you tomorrow if you do. He just might remember you." Newell stepped back into the doorway. He folded his arms across his massive chest and achieved a lordly expression of expectation.

Resigned, she turned back to the young man in the armchair. Samuel wore a brocaded dressing gown in the same tarnished-gold shade as his hair. He appeared freshly bathed, and she remembered the crisp edge of the turned-down sheets on his bedstead. A servant had probably prepared his master for bed. He lived the life of a child and in the back of her mind, she somehow expected him to be a child. She was dismayed to find that he was not only a grown man, but a handsome and extraordinarily large one, just like his brother.

Slowly she stepped toward him, feeling the fool because she was still barefoot and in her wrapper. Her appearance held no authority and when she stood in front of the seated giant, her petite form dwarfed by that of her pupil, she acutely longed for some.

"Samuel," she said in a low, gentle voice.

The man looked up at her, a man who looked so much like Newell one could mistake the two except for the dull expression in this one's eyes.

" 'Tis late, I know . . ." she whispered, unable to shake her dismay. Samuel was so much like Newell.

"Samuel, I'm Miss Benjamin. Lord Newell has hired me to teach you and look after you." She held out a trembling hand wondering if he would take it.

Samuel Newell stared at her outstretched hand like a dog stares at a bone. His head cocked slightly and the glazed, benign expression in his eyes vanished long enough for her to know he seemed to want to take it. But the look disappeared as quickly as it had appeared. Soon he shrank away, his dull gaze returned to the fire.

"Take her hand, Sam. Be a gentleman," Newell prompted.

She looked behind her at Lord Newell. There was a cruel iron expression on his face that held no patience, no gentleness. She had the feeling that if he could, he would have stepped up to Sam and beaten him into speaking and behaving the way Newell wanted him too. But something kept him from doing it, and she wondered if it was his love for his brother. Perhaps it was just the fact that as cruelty-bent as Newell was purported to be, he still possessed a small modicum of human compassion. A diminishing amount of goodness. In her heart, she believed both hypotheses.

Samuel slowly looked behind her where his brother stood in the shadows. He seemed to find assurance in his presence, for all at once he reached out and laid his hand in hers.

"There. I'm not so bad, am I?" she whispered. She begged for his gaze to meet hers but he resolutely refused to look at her. There was a dog she'd found starving on the streets once, and she had tried to befriend it. She had sat on a park bench with a bowl of stew and softly, gently, coaxed it to come out from underneath the bushes. Closer and closer, she edged herself toward the creature, ever conscious of its fear. It would not meet her gaze; it would not look at her. Some children came running down the park lane and their noise and laughter caused the cur to put its tail between its legs and run off. In the morning the stew was licked clean from the bowl, but she never saw the poor thing again. And she could never quite shake the sadness of the fact that it had been too terrified to even look at her.

"Samuel, you and I are going to be great friends, did you know that?" She knelt down before him, reminded of all the deaf children she had cajoled into trusting her and her teaching methods. She had learned that gentleness and a smile could go a long way. She wondered if such things would work on a giant too.

"Miss Benjamin is here to help us, Sam." Newell's chilly voice broke into the silence. "I want you to listen to her and do what she says. Do you understand me, old boy?"

Samuel turned his head toward his brother again. Newell never left the shadows, but it was obviously enough reassurance. By Sam's expression, the message had gotten through.

Alexandra looked down at the big hand in hers. Samuel's

hand was strong and fine, like his brother's. But while Newell
had held hers with strength, assurance, Sam's was limp. Afraid.

"Do you like music, Sam? It's a blessing you can hear.
We'll be playing lots of music and letting you listen to the
sounds . . ." She leaned back, saddened that he still would not
look at her. He was as terrified of her as the dog had been in
the park.

She stood and stiffly returned to Newell. There was a long
pause while she tried to formulate her words. She brushed the
wisps of dark hair out of her eyes and straightened the lapels
of her robe all the while trying to formulate the best approach.

"My Lord Newell, if you'll pardon my presumption . . . I
dare say that Sam isn't in need of an audiologist. He needs
someone to overcome his terror. Whatever frightened him still
holds him within its grip and must be dealt with. I understand
there is an entire school of physicians in Vienna who aim to
specialize in such disorders—"

"I know what he needs," Newell said fiercely. "I'm the
best to judge, not you."

"His fear must be overcome. Only then will he trust enough
to speak."

"Then you will overcome his fears."

"I'm not equipped to do that."

"I think you are." Newell watched her from the shadows,
the changing, reflecting plane of his spectacles the only hint
that he moved at all. "Because you are what he fears most."

She stared at him, shocked.

Without further comment, he left the bedroom.

Alexandra found her way back to her bedroom by sheer dint
of will. Anger and confusion guided her through the daunting
maze of the castle as well as any beacon. She was too preoccupied with Lord Newell's mysteries to be frightened about
becoming lost.

John Damien Newell vexed her. He seemed unwilling to be
anything but needlessly obscure, and then he had the temerity

to demand treatment for his brother without even the slightest
explanation of what it was that had caused the affliction in the
first place.

To add fuel to the fire, Newell had never even returned to
his brother's bedchamber. He'd abandoned the poor man to a
stranger, and she knew just by instinct, it was because he
couldn't shake the speech right out from Sam. He was an
impatient, hard man, and these very characteristics made him
an angry man. So he'd decided to blame her.

She almost wept for the expression on Sam's face when
Newell left. If he could have, she swore he would have crawled
right into his bureau drawers if that would keep her away from
him. Sam had been terrified of being alone with her. Even his
commanding, bullying brother gave him more comfort than a
minute alone with her.

She left Sam immediately after Newell, her heart twisting
at the picture of the man sitting by the fire, frightened out of
his mind of a woman who was less than half his size. There
had been no helping him. Now she had the enigma of Newell's
words still rattling within her mind like an echo. She couldn't
decipher the accusation, but she had known, looking at the
forlorn figure of his brother, that she would have to understand
it before she could help anyone at Cairncross. She had departed
the bedroom, reassuring Sam that they would soon be friends,
but when he refused to meet her eyes, she had left feeling
despondent.

Once back in her own bedroom, she'd brushed off Mary's
interrogation with a few obligatory phrases describing Lord
Newell and their discussion of her post, then she went directly
to bed. She was bone tired from the journey. By all accounts
she should have slept like the dead, but she instead lay awake,
staring at the shadowy damask canopy of the bed, not comforted
by Mary's pleasant snores coming from the trundle.

What had he meant by *you* are the one he fears? His vagueness
frustrated her. She knew very little about the situation at Cairncross, but she knew one thing about Newell: he wanted very
much to keep her off balance. She wondered if it were a game

to him or a necessity. Whichever it was, she understood that this was how he controlled people.

She might never solve the mysteries of Cairncross, but whatever Newell had meant, she knew intuitively that he hadn't said it as a personal statement. He'd said it in order to comment on a generality.

She tossed and turned, unable to discover the truth with so little information. The morning would bring further news but it would all be bad. Newell might well have decided to dismiss her after the botched meeting with his brother. And if he let her stay, she had no idea how to go about her task without more background on her pupil. It would be difficult stuff to dig up given that it wasn't her place to request a meeting with Lord Newell, and even less so to ask him prying questions. Should she be allowed to stay on, she had doubts whether she would see Lord Newell again. He would leave the mess of his brother to her care and tally-ho back to London, and she almost couldn't blame him. Frequent escapes from the depression seemed almost a necessity at mighty Cairncross Castle.

Dawn crept into the room like a spider through the cracks in the heavy velvet draperies. The hearth was dead, full of cold white ashes, and an unshakable chill seemed to clutch the still air. Despairing of ever getting any sleep, Alexandra sat up in the bed and untied the hopeless mass of her hair from the plait. In minutes she expected a servant to arrive to put a brick of peat in the fireplace and to deliver morning coffee. She wanted to be dressed and ready by then. Lord Newell was probably leaving for the city first thing and there was greater chance of seeing him again if she went downstairs.

"Are you awake?" a whisper came from below.

She looked over the edge of the mattress. Mary smiled at her and raised herself to a sitting position all the while rearranging the frilled cap that had come askew in the night.

A knock pounded on the door. Before Alexandra could say "Good morning," a servant had entered with the prerequisite brick and pot of strong coffee, then promptly left.

"Will you be startin' the work on the young lad today?"

Mary asked as she wolfed down a strawberry-laden pasty from
the silver tray.

"I can't quite say as yet when I'm to start and in what
capacity. Lord Newell's plans were quite nebulous last night."
She sloshed warm water into the bowl from the ewer and bathed
her face, hoping Mary couldn't see how evasive she was being.
She didn't like keeping things from Mary, but she almost felt
as if this was necessary. As if she were protecting Mary. Plaiting
and twisting her hair, she pinned a neat chignon to the back
of her neck and netted it beneath a crocheted lavender-colored
snood.

Mary watched her from the armchair while Alexandra threw
petticoats over her head and nervously tied them.

"Are you meetin' Lord Newell again this morn? Is that the
reason you're so pale and quiet?"

Alexandra paused and looked up at Mary. Without answering, she grabbed her gown and carefully drew it over her coif.

"Why are you afraid to talk about Lord Newell, love?"

"It's not that I'm afraid." Alexandra furrowed her brow as
she hooked the front of her bodice. "I'm just perplexed by
him, that's all. He's a strange man and difficult to read. To tell
the truth, I'm not sure about the position here. I think I'll know
more today."

"Then why are you rushin' about like a chicken ready to be
beheaded?"

She opened her mouth, ready to deny all, but then when she
looked into the glass, she realized she'd been in such a rush
to dress, she'd hooked her bodice crookedly. "Don't let my
silliness bother you, Mary," she finally confessed, impatiently
ripping open the numerous tiny iron hooks to start the process
again. "I suppose I'm a bit anxious to get started this morning
because I'm hoping I'll see the master before he leaves. There
are just so many things I want to be made clearer before he
leaves and since—"

"So that's the reason for your poor color. He's handsome,
then?" There was a tone of doomed disapproval in Mary's
voice.

Alexandra froze. She was stunned by Mary's interpretation. All thoughts of completing her dress were forgotten. "That's not it at all," she blurted out.

"Then what is it?" Mary prompted, bobbing her cap.

"Well . . . h-he is handsome actually," she stammered, "but don't go thinking I'm smitten on him. He's my employer. When he tentatively offered me a job last night he spurned my knowledge of father's work and told me he could only use me as a governess. It wouldn't do for the likes of one with the station of a governess to aspire to his, now would it?"

"You're not a governess. You're educated, and young, and most assuredly not in the poorhouse. Your father didn't leave you a rich woman, but he left you a decent enough sum at his death in spite of the fact that you had to give up Belmont Crescent."

"You forget, however, that I didn't come here to find a husband. Besides, he's not how you picture him, Mary."

Mary looked up from her large white cup of coffee and sagely nodded her head. "You know how I picture him, miss. Remember, I heard what the wretched driver said yesterday about Lord Newell."

Alexandra frowned and became pensive. "I agree that there's a coldness and distance about him that I can't quite explain even by his lofty station. He's mannerly, yes, but rigid about it, certainly not friendly. But is he cruel? I don't know yet. I can see a part of him that can be cruel but there's a part of him that seems . . . well . . . lost, adrift. Oh, I know it sounds absurd; it is absurd, only . . . only I don't know."

Mary stared at her, her face lined with that all-too-familiar concerned expression.

Alexandra forced herself to brighten. She felt as if she were compelled to chase away goblins. "He's not going to be around much, I daresay, so enough of this speculation. I only thought to see him now because it may be my last chance to discuss his brother with him. The lad we thought we were coming to help is no lad. My pupil is much older and larger than I thought he would be. I don't find it fitting to be his governess, but he does need someone. He's slow, more like a child than a man.''

''Is that so?''

Alexandra nodded and finished her hooks. When she was fully dressed, she told Mary she would be back after a stroll on the ground—and after a discussion with the departing Lord Newell, should she be granted one. She grabbed her shawl from a nearby chair, then sought the chilly morning gardens.

There wasn't a sign of the master in the great hall, nor a hint of the housekeeper. A young lad carried a whisk and a pan and set about sweeping the many hearths while the butler, or at least a man dressed in a black frock coat whom she assumed was the butler, gathered the stray silver candelabrum that had missed being polished the night before. To her left, a maidservant feather-dusted a piece of the armor and as Alexandra walked by, she noticed the unfortunate piece was a large brass and silver breastplate with a hole through it the size of a cannonball.

''Good morning, miss,'' the young maid said tentatively as she noticed she was being watched. From her difficult perch on the ladder, she attempted a respectful curtsy.

Alexandra nodded pleasantly but her gaze was riveted to the breastplate. ''St. Albans?'' she asked softly, wanting to know more about it.

''Waterloo, miss.'' The maid gave it a reverent pause, then continued her dusting on pieces just as gruesome.

''Can I help you?''

Alexandra nearly jumped at the voice that seemed to have come from nowhere. She spun on her heels and found the nameless housekeeper standing behind her, wearing the same grim black gown and nervous, wary expression as yesterday, but today the woman had pinned her gray-streaked bun into a netting that was as fine and translucent as cobwebs. She looked elegantly severe.

''I thought a walk in the garden would do me good after the long journey yesterday. I hope there's no objection to my taking the air?'' Alexandra said.

The woman stood perfectly still, her hands in a white-knuckle clasp.

"If Lord Newell should like to see me before he departs, I'll be at his disposal."

Again the woman said nothing, merely watched her with anxious eyes of indeterminate color.

"Well, all right then ... I'm off ..." Alexandra gathered her shawl more tightly around her shoulders.

But then the woman blurted out, "He's now not going to London, Miss Benjamin."

Alexandra paused. She looked at the housekeeper and said, "You know my name, but as yet, I don't believe you've ever given me yours." She watched her with an imperious gaze and waited.

"Mrs. Penrith," the woman offered, not quite as cowed by Alexandra's show of spirit as Alexandra might have wished.

"Well, *Mrs. Penrith,* I suppose if Lord Newell decided it's best to stay with his brother a while, then that's all there is to it."

"Did you know there was another governess here once?"

Alexandra paused. She had the notion that Mrs. Penrith was challenging her somehow, and she didn't like the feeling at all. "I fear it isn't an extraordinary occurrence to have a governess for a child. And Sam is really a child, isn't he? The fact that there was a governess here before me is mundane at best."

"There was nothing mundane about *her,* miss. Oh, no. Nothing commonplace at all."

Alexandra found herself losing patience. She wasn't pleased having to wear the label of governess in the first place, and here the housekeeper was trying to make her feel inferior to her predecessor. "If she was so extraordinary, why did she leave? Clearly Sam still needs her."

"She didn't leave, miss." The fear that always seemed present in her voice now came to the surface. "She *disappeared.*"

"Disappeared?"

"Yes. She disappeared. That's something altogether different from leaving."

"Did she just up and leave the castle in the middle of the night?"

"No. One day she was here and the next, nary a trace could be found of her. All her worldly goods are still in your room, miss, packed away in the large leather trunk by the window."

Alexandra could taste fear in her mouth. She didn't know why, but the old rusty black-strapped trunk had remained in the corner of her mind, tickling her with its importance. Perhaps it was only natural that she should have wondered about it; now she never wanted to think of it again. The idea of a missing woman's possessions locked up in a trunk in her room, waiting for an owner who was long since gone, left Alexandra with a strange, inarticulate terror.

Mrs. Penrith came close and almost whispered in her ear, "Will you have tea in my room and allow me to tell you some stories of the castle, and those who've lived here, and those who live here still?"

It was all Alexandra could do to keep the shriek out of her voice. Finally, in a low, even tone, she said, "If you think to tell me tales to scare me off, let me inform you right now that—"

The housekeeper unclasped her hands and placed them on Alexandra's arm in supplication. "I'm not trying to frighten you. I just think you should know what goes on here at Cairncross." She stole a furtive look at the man in the black frock coat who stood clear across the baronial hall. With hushed words, she said, "You must have tea with me in my rooms. There's a lot you don't know about the master and his poor brother."

Alexandra wanted to disapprove. She wanted to hold herself above servant's gossip and tell Mrs. Penrith that recounting old fables was not the way to introduce her into the household. But her curiosity wouldn't be quelled. She was desperate to know more about the situation she was in, especially if she was going to help the lord's brother. Besides, the housekeeper had such a sincere, frightened look in her eyes that she found it difficult to admonish her. Also, the housekeeper was clearly taking a risk in telling her these things, and Alexandra knew it every time Mrs. Penrith glanced nervously at the butler.

"I should like to hear more about Sam . . ." Alexandra watched the housekeeper; after the cold, disjointed welcome the day before, she was unable to keep suspicion out of her mind. "It'd be a pleasure to take tea in your rooms."

The housekeeper looked unspeakably relieved. She turned to the girl on the ladder and asked her to fetch a tea from the kitchen. The butler, or whoever the man was in the black frock coat, watched them from alongside an enormous medieval kas, his arms filled with stray silver.

"Mr. Featherstone, if you please, I'll be in my parlor with Miss Benjamin should my services be needed," Mrs. Penrith said in a subservient manner.

"Very well," he croaked, his rigid, jowl-draped face turned toward Alexandra. She couldn't shake the feeling that he wanted her gone, too.

Mrs. Penrith led her belowstairs to a neat little parlor especially designated for the castle's housekeeper. When Alexandra was seated and tea was finally poured, she dared to begin her subtle interrogation.

"So is Mr. Featherstone his lordship's butler?" she asked, setting her cup onto a wafer-thin china saucer.

"Indeed." The housekeeper nervously primped and straightened the antimacassars. She was a good housekeeper because even in her own rooms she could not stop attending to details. "He, of course, sees to all the pertinent goings-on in the household. I, naturally, am left the lesser duties."

"And am I a 'lesser' duty?" Alexandra took a sip of the hot brew.

"I don't quite understand." The housekeeper looked puzzled.

"He's failed to introduce himself, nor has he yet to take any part in seeing to my welfare. I presume, him being a butler, that those are his duties. So I can only conclude he's ignored me because he deems me beneath his concern."

"He doesn't want you here, miss. Make no mistake about it. Mr. Featherstone's had a run-in with her himself many a year back. It's upsetting to everyone to see another young woman here after so much time having passed."

"Are you referring to the old governess?"

"Yes." Mrs. Penrith's mouth squeezed into a rosette of lines.

"How long ago did she disappear?"

" 'Tis been twenty long years."

"She's been gone for *twenty* years?" Alexandra couldn't hide her shock. For some reason she wanted to believe that the woman whose belongings were abovestairs in her room was going to show her face once more and retrieve them. It wasn't easy to believe it would happen with twenty years under the bridge since the woman was last seen.

"Sam and Lord Newell were hardly more than boys when Miss Pole vanished. Sam was a child—no more than ten. Lord Newell was thirteen. Certainly no more than fourteen."

"She was *his* governess too? A normal boy of fourteen? Why, he was much too old."

"It was wicked." Mrs. Penrith poured herself more tea and slowly stirred several hard brown rocks of sugar into it. "Lord Newell should have been sent away to school, or at the very least been given a schoolmaster to come to Cairncross. His mind was quick and he was extraordinary apt at any subject, but I fear his parents, Lord and Lady Newell, neglected their children. They spent all their time on the Continent and couldn't be bothered with the details of John Damien's education. Besides, Ursula Pole wanted to educate him. Being cousin to Lord Newell's father, the old baron, she was a governess who possessed infinite power. The parents remained *in absentia;* she remained with John Damien. Though the boy loathed her, she grew to become obsessed with him. Sam, by the grace of God, she left alone, probably because the lad was slow, but her feelings for John Damien . . ." the housekeeper shook her head, "well, 'twas a wretched arrangement that went on *too long* . . . if you understand my meaning?"

Alexandra met her gaze. Slowly revelation opened up to her like the granite door of a crypt.

"You look horrified, Miss Benjamin, as you should."

"But you can't mean what I think you mean? Lord Newell was young, yes, and perhaps easily swayed by a woman of poisoned morals, but from our brief meeting, he seems like a person who cannot be easily led. Even as a boy, it's hard to believe—"

"Even as a boy he could not be easily led. The lad refused her, is the way the story goes. But some say Ursula Pole was in love with him," the housekeeper lowered her voice to the barest whisper, "and some say she's in love with him still."

Alexandra stared at her, frowning. "So you're saying she's been heard from after all?"

Mrs. Penrith looked her right in the eyes. "Not in an earthly sense."

"You can't mean what I think you mean." Alexandra wanted to scoff at her, but she found she was gripping the arms of the chair as if she somehow needed to hold herself aright. The conversation made her feel as if she were inside a bouncing carriage and not sitting in an armchair in the staid little parlor of a housekeeper.

"Perhaps 'tis only servants' gossip, but that's the story as I know it." The housekeeper finally picked up her teacup and sipped from it, her hand trembling slightly. Giving her away.

These were lurid tales, no doubt embellished so as to shock. It worked; Alexandra was almost speechless, still, she found her tongue. "So what do they think became of Miss Pole? If you say she's not been here in an earthly sense, then you must mean—"

Mrs. Penrith nearly slammed her china cup down onto the saucer. "She's gone. Do you understand me? She's gone and we in the household who once knew her thank God every day that the woman left."

Taken aback by the woman's vehemence and contradictions, Alexandra sat numbly and sipped her tea, each clink of porcelain against porcelain magnified amidst the tension in the room.

Mrs. Penrith seemed to gather herself once more. Quietly, she asked, "Do you know what evil is, Miss Benjamin? I'm not talking about naughty children or even poor wretches driven to thievery and murder. I'm talking about evil. The complete absence of guilt or moral conscience. There are those amongst us like that. They look just like you and me, but they're not like us. Not a bit."

"I think I know what evil is," Alexandra answered, her mouth gone dry, her teacup forgotten on the lace-draped tea table.

"*She* was evil." Mrs. Penrith's voice lowered to a hoarse whisper. "She could never forgive the boy of his rejection of her. She wanted his attention even if it were acquired in the most hateful way. Years ago, John Damien had a favorite hound as a boy and one day the poor old thing just up and died—very mysteriously. She gave John Damien all the false consolation she could muster for the boy's grief. Then one day, she appeared in the schoolroom with a most unusual pair of gloves. Green leather, they were, with orange trim, but they weren't made out of cowhide, or lambskin, you understand. They were made out of a unique leather. They were, as I said, a most unusual pair of gloves. Do you know what that woman did?" Mrs. Penrith leaned closer. Her face was masked with a nauseous expression, as if she were forced to swallow her bile. "That creature, Miss Pole, told John Damien that she'd had his old hound's body taken to the tannery and herself made up that pair of gloves. She told the boy that, and if you think about it, Miss Benjamin, you'll see that the cruelty of the story was that it didn't matter whether it was true or not. The only thing that did matter is that she wore those every day, and it was to make John Damien never forget what she told him." Mrs. Penrith's voice lowered to a wretched whisper. "She did unspeakable things. Unspeakable things."

Alexandra stared at the woman. She was sickened by the story and her heart twisted in empathetic torment for young Lord Newell. But then a worse revelation came to her. "Mrs. Penrith," she began, "Lord Newell told me last night that Sam was frightened out of his speech. Do you think it was something that she—?''

''She did it. Of course she did it. I don't know what, or how, but I know 'twas her, I'd stake my life on it.''

Alexandra felt her stomach give a tiny lurch. The nightmare at Cairncross was only getting worse. This latest horror made her doubt her sanity at staying. No position seemed worth becoming embroiled in such circumstances. She was beginning to wonder about her capacity to help these people. Lord Newell and his brother's problem went far deeper than the loss of an ability to speak. She hated to think about it, but if what Mrs. Penrith had told her was true, then Sam and Lord Newell might both be beyond help.

The housekeeper outstretched her hand to implore her. ''You understand now, miss, why we all think it best that you leave? There's nothing here for you. Things can only get worse.''

Alexandra grew quiet, pensive, as her mind and heart were weighted down with the magnitude of the problem. It was probably all beyond her abilities, and yet she couldn't get the forlorn picture of Sam out of her mind as he'd sat before the fire last night, eyeing her with a terrified gaze. There was no one else to help him but her. No man would come to Cairncross and waste his time with a frightened idiot man, particularly not for the unenviable task of returning his speech. And she wondered if another would feel the grip around her heart as she had at the story of young John Damien and his hound and those hellish gloves.

''Someone needs to help Sam. *Someone.*'' Her soft words were filled with an unwarranted amount of determination.

''Sam should have been put in an asylum.'' Tears sprang to the housekeeper's eyes. It was such a genuine display of grief and despair, Alexandra felt her own eyes blur. ''He's such a handsome one. Looks so much like Lord Newell. What a pity it is . . . so much wasted. But there's nothing we can do for the soul here. Why, old Sam hates this castle. If it weren't for his brother's regular visits to Cairncross he would know no happiness at all. You must understand, the poor lad knows no sense of time. In his small thinking, 'twas only yesterday that *she* walked these halls. He still won't go into the schoolroom. To him, she's in there waiting. Just waiting . . .''

"Lord Newell should send him to London. I know of a hundred doctors who would treat him with kindness—"

"His lordship tried taking him to London once, but Sam's never known any home than Cairncross. Just the trip to York unnerved him so, John Damien was forced to bring him back. In Sam's case, perhaps 'tis better to have the devil you know than the devil you don't know."

"Is that why Lord Newell never sold this castle?" Alexandra said.

"That's the tragedy. The castle is entailed. John Damien would have nothing if he tried to rid himself of Cairncross, but more than that—he fought so hard to come back here, to regain what was his. He won't let anything out of his control now. Even with the best land agent, Lord Newell still oversees everything. The castle holds bad memories for him; nonetheless, he stays here regularly. I think to watch over Sam and to keep him company."

"Why did he have to fight to come back to Cairncross?"

It seemed a natural question, one that begged for an answer, but it robbed Mrs. Penrith of her obviously uncharacteristic openness. The spider's web of lines returned to her puckered mouth and she said, "If you stay, miss, that story is for Lord Newell to tell you, not me. I—I—" The housekeeper paused as if she were chastising herself for her loose tongue. "I've just told you these things because I think it in your best interest to leave. Cairncross is not the place for a young lady. I implore you to use your common sense and allow Jaymes to take you and your maid to the train station today."

Alexandra stared; she was on the precipice of being convinced to leave.

"The master can be a rabid wolf when he wants to be, miss. There's no point in your going up against him," Mrs. Penrith added.

"He was nothing but a gentleman last night—mannerly and soft-spoken—"

"He wants someone to make Sam speak. Perhaps he thinks you're the one to do it after all."

"Perhaps I am."

"Now don't go thinking you can help. What good would it do anyone to hear the boy speak? What's he going to tell? Nothing but horrible things. There's no point in it at all, miss."

"But perhaps returning Sam's speech isn't for Sam. Perhaps it's for Lord Newell. Have you ever thought of that possibility?" Quietly she added, "As you've just told me, he, too, bears scars of his childhood."

"He does." Mrs. Penrith suddenly looked decades older than she had before. "I know he wants Sam to talk again, to be the brother—such as he was—that John Damien used to know. I've known his lordship all his life, miss, and my sympathies go with him. Yes, they say he's cruel and uncaring. The only kindness he's ever shown is to his brother. We all find him fearsome," she caught Alexandra's gaze, "but he loves his brother, and that's saying a lot for a man who never knew any kind of love himself. Many a lord would abandon a simpleton such as Sam. John Damien didn't."

"Then that is the reason to stay." Alexandra looked wide-eyed at the housekeeper. "Someone must help them both."

Mrs. Penrith stood. Her expression looked ready to explode. "But you're not the one to do it. Don't you see? Not a young woman like yourself. You'll only get them upset again."

"Lord Newell was not upset by my presence. He admirably hid his irritation at finding me a woman—"

"He's a master at hiding his true feelings and true thoughts. She made him like that and now he's brilliant at it."

Alexandra stood also. She dropped her linen napkin to her chair. "But that is exactly why I should stay. They need to get over Ursula Pole. She's long gone. Why, she probably *is* dead."

Mrs. Penrith looked as if she wanted to put her hands over her ears and block out her words. "I beg you to be gone, miss.

Now is your chance to leave. Leave before you get much more entrenched.''

"I may leave anytime I wish. And whether I stay or go, it will be my own decision.''

"Lord Newell's not like Sam, Miss Benjamin.'' The house-keeper's voice turned shrill and urgent. "Sam is a hulk of a man like his brother, but he's slow and gentle; why, I've never even seen him trample a flower in the garden. But his brother—his brother is something else altogether.''

"Some would say that the gentleman I spoke with last night was nothing less than a saint, given the trying circumstance my deception put him into.'' She grew impatient to leave.

"Miss, you've got to see—''

"I'll do my best to consider what we've spoken about this morning. I think I'd like to go to the gardens and ponder it awhile. If you'll excuse me?''

"Take the train this afternoon, miss. It leaves at 4:11. I beg of you, be sensible.''

"Is it sensible to abandon those in need?'' Alexandra made to leave.

She was already out of the apartment when the housekeeper cried out in one last impassioned plea, "John Damien was a normal boy, you see, miss? The cruelties done to him aren't easily forgotten in a mind as sharp as his. He had a terrible time as a child . . . and *some say he's not right in the head because of it.*''

Alexandra stopped dead. The words hit her like a blow to the temple. She turned back to the housekeeper to ask for an elaboration, but Mrs. Penrith's door was closed, as if the woman couldn't bear to face the consequences of her revelation.

Alone, Alexandra gazed at the closed door. Mrs. Penrith's words tumbled through her mind like boulders crashing down a cliffside.

But she was her father's daughter; eventually reason took over. She clenched her jaw and steeled herself from the fear. Lord Newell must be given his chance. It was her decision to stay or to leave and she wouldn't make it in haste. She had her own reasons for making this job work, so she would take her time; she would weigh every possibility, every consequence.

And she would make the decision herself.

Chapter Seven

To buy his favour I extend this friendship:
If he will take it, so; if not, adieu;
And, for my love, I pray you wrong me not.
　　　　　　　　—THE MERCHANT OF VENICE

The Cairncross garden was the antithesis of the castle. If the castle had been hewn by a warmonger, the garden had been cultivated by a romantic. Forty rosebushes bloomed in heavy-petaled extravagance against the garden's brick walls. It was a bower of perfume and color, from pink to lemon to scarlet. The crumbling gray stuccoed walls blocked the relentless wind, and the inhospitable soil had been worked with humus and peat. Wrought from the blank despair of the moor, the walled garden was a place where even the most fragile jasmine vine could climb and flourish.

Alexandra entered the enormous quadrangle through a pair of wooden gates. The green paint was bleached and peeling, and both doors were off one hinge, forcing them permanently open. In the far distant corner, she spied a moldering statue of

St. Francis hid between sheafs of blooming lavender. Next to it an ancient, gnarled lime tree bowered over a carved marble bench, one that begged a visitor to sit and experience the sensations of an English garden run wild.

She sauntered to the corner, taking her time to bend and experience each heady fragrance of rose, narcissus, and mint. Her thoughts seemed to want to drift away on the perfumed air, but again and again they returned horrifically to Mrs. Penrith's tale. Finding a seat on the mossy bench, she soothed herself with the pattern of shadows from the twisted limbs of the lime tree. Her horsehair crinoline kept away the marble chill of the bench, but the sun beat warmly, and she wondered if she might regret not having spent money on one of the new caged crinolines that were taking fashion by its throat.

She leaned her head against the ivy-carpeted corner of the wall and inhaled the sweet bathwater scent of lavender mixed with roses. The stillness of the garden was almost palpable, broken only by a lone brave butterfly that flitted across the thorny bushes. The silence was so great, it seemed to possess a power of its own, willing her thoughts onto subjects she wished could be left alone.

She thought of Newell.

She was here to help his brother, and yet it seemed from the moment she saw John Damien Newell, he was the one who commanded her attention. She wondered about him, what he felt, who he was, how to help him.

The notion was absurd. She was here to aid Sam. Besides, what did a rich peer need that she could ever give? Nothing. But still, she couldn't shake the notion that the only way to help Sam was to help his brother.

She tilted her head up and watched a breeze waft overhead, just barely trembling the upper branches of the lime tree. Clouds scrubbed the blue sky overhead and she knew without even peeking over the wall that the empty moorland beyond would be dotted by their swift-moving shadows.

What a glorious place this garden was. She mused about the soul who had created it. Newell was not the type to garden.

Besides, his lordship had made it clear that he didn't tarry long at the castle. So someone else from Cairncross had wrought such loveliness from the inhospitable moorland soil.

"So you've found it."

She started at the voice. She spun her head around and discovered Newell standing not four paces from the bench, arms crossed over his chest. His figure was elegantly attired in morning dress: a charcoal frock coat and gray-checked trousers. A cravat was precisely tied into a barrel knot. The color of deep blood.

"My lord." She glanced up at him, confusion sweeping across her face as she met his gaze. She tried to stand but he waved her back down.

"I see you've discovered the garden. Sooner than I would have thought." He walked over to the wall and leaned against it, unmindful of his expensive clothing. She watched him, again amazed at how large he was. Even in the bright light of morn, he loomed at least a head taller than she and weighed double the stone. If Brian had stood next to him, he would have been dwarfed.

"I've always enjoyed a garden. We had a small one behind the town house." She rattled on, dismayed at her sudden loquaciousness. "Of course, it was not as glorious as this one. Still, it gave me much pleasure." She felt strange pinned beneath that inscrutable, bespectacled stare. The urge to protect herself was strong. A primal instinct warned her to increase the distance between them.

If Newell had been an old man, she might not have minded the intrusive gaze, but he was not an old man, he was young, clearly very robust, and inexplicably very fixated upon her.

"Sam and I used to play in this garden. We were children then. Young lads perhaps no more than ten and five. We would hide in here and laugh and run. The roses were planted by our grandmother."

Alexandra forced herself to meet his gaze. It took more bravado than she could account for. "So your grandmother cared for you and Sam. I'd been led to believe you and your brother had lived virtually alone at the castle.''

He studied her. His face grew taut as if he were fighting the desire to ask her how she obtained such information, but he clearly knew without asking. It was the servants who disseminated information and it had been that way in English great houses for centuries. ''We did not live here alone,'' he said. ''Our grandmother lived with us, as she does now. It was she who planted this garden. Lady Bess's rooms are in the north tower.'' He pointed to the turret that looked far out to sea. ''She lives up there with her servants, usually in quite a temper. Her bones ache and every chill draft causes her torture. Yet she remains on this earth, though past ninety.''

''So she's been here all those years?'' Alexandra couldn't quite mask her incredulity. She couldn't understand how anyone could have lived with those two boys and not see the agony Ursula Pole was inflicting on them.

''Lady Bess, is . . . how should I put this? . . . she is an ineffective person.'' He looked at her as if to see if she understood.

She did. His grandmother was oblivious to the goings-on about the castle, which was why she had never interfered on behalf of her grandsons.

''Still, we tolerate her quite well here. She loves her flowers.'' He paused. Out of the blue, he said, ''This is a good place.''

Alexandra found herself mesmerized by him. His words, the deep timbre of his voice, seemed to cloud her thinking as sure as the sky was clouded above. She had questions—about Sam—about him—that she urgently wanted answered. But now, with her gaze captured by his, her mind seemed only concerned with inhaling the suddenly intense fragrance of the blooms. And with watching him.

It was almost a need, this watching him, this scrutinizing of his face, his expression, his form. Even she knew her stare was like none she had ever given before. It was brazen and thorough. An almost desperate seeking. But it went beyond the mere

dress of female watching male. It was a sudden, needful, helpless search. It sought the essential, sublime goodness that she
irrationally wanted to find in him.

But hadn't yet.

"Yes, this is a good place." Her whisper was lame, the
words gray and mundane as washwater, yet the truth in them
left a bittersweet taste on her tongue. The garden was a good
place, and goodness was only judged and identified by the evil
that surrounded it. It suddenly came to her that the aura of the
garden was unlike that of the castle. The castle was darkness; the
garden was light. In fact, she could see now that the Cairncross
garden wasn't really a garden at all. It had roses and lime trees
and moldering old benches from the last century, but looking
beyond those things, she could see that the garden was also
the physical metaphor for all that was right in the world. All
that was good.

"It's a lovely garden for two boys, I should think," she said
softly.

He looked at her, his gaze hard. "Because she never came
in here. This was our place, Sam and I."

Alexandra wondered if her face had lost color. Somehow,
she knew in her very soul who he meant. "You mean Lady
Bess, your grandmother?" She had felt compelled to ask the
question, yet her denial of the obvious was a fraud.

The expression in his eyes was kept shuttered behind cloud-
swept spectacles. He didn't appear bothered at all by the fact
that she knew. Against her will she began to tremble.

Ursula Pole, she thought. *He means Ursula Pole. Just say
the name out loud. She can't hurt you anymore, John Damien.
She's gone. Remember? She's gone.*

He never answered her; she surrendered the pretense. They
both knew who it was he referred to. With their gazes, they
had just had a silent dialogue.

"The servants say she was very unkind," she whispered,
her shoulders slumping with the weight of her imagination, the
breeze overhead carrying her words far.

He reached out and lifted her chin so that she looked fully

up at him. The reflection in his spectacles was gone. "Not unkind . . . a demon," he answered, his handsome face ravaged by his belief.

She leaned back, gripped by a sudden instinct to flee. The horror of his words sent ice through her heart.

"She's gone now," she heard herself saying, as if in a dream.

"Is she?" One dark gold eyebrow lifted in a taunt.

"The memory may linger but she herself is gone. Sam must learn never to be afraid again." You must learn never to be afraid again, she thought, but could not quite bear to say it.

"Yet fear is what teaches us manners, Miss Benjamin. It's what keeps us in our place." The expression on his face was steeped in dark sarcasm. "Otherwise we would just be savages, wouldn't we?"

"I was never taught by fear," she said staunchly.

"No?"

"No."

"And yet, what about him? What was his name? What did you call him? You phrased it . . . ah, yes, your 'prospect.' What lessons did he teach you, Miss Benjamin?"

She could feel the blood drain from her cheeks. "He had no effect on me whatsoever. We parted. That was it."

A cruel smile lit his mouth. "Five years of your youth spent waiting for a man and he taught you nothing? But I think he taught you a lot, Miss Benjamin. I think if you were married right now, you would not have come here in your father's place. Indeed, I think your young man was a fine tutor. He taught you most eloquently the fear of being alone."

She stared up at him, the frozen ball of her heart melting just enough for tears to spring to her eyes. The look he gave her told her he knew exactly what he was doing. In just a few minutes of their acquaintance, he'd gauged her weak spot and rammed a sword right through it. It was suddenly clear that every warning she'd been given about this man was true. He was indeed cruel. He enjoyed tormenting people. But he would never reap the satisfaction of tormenting her. She wasn't going to cry. She'd cried her last for Brian. Nothing was going to make her weep again.

"Did *she* teach you such manners?" she asked acidly, brushing away his hand from her jaw; viciously forcing back the tears.

"She never taught me anything, Miss Benjamin." He took her arm in that savage Norman grip and pulled her up to him. He was so still and so close she could hardly breathe from the terror constricting her chest. "And do you know why?"

The answer was almost too simple, but looking at him she believed it. John Damien Newell could face the fires of all hell and he would do nothing but embrace them. "Because you have no fear."

In all probability, it was this flaw in his character even more than his real cruelties that made people fear him. People always reacted more by instinct than actuality, because instinct was usually right.

"We'll speak no more of Miss Pole." He stared down at her. His placid tone only heightened the implied violence in his touch. "Sam is the one who needs your help." He glanced at the grip he had on her arm. Slowly, as if warring within himself to let her go or to take her even more ferociously, he released his hold.

She slid down onto the bench. With a shaky hand, she ran her palm over her temples to push back the curls that had escaped the pins. *Leave this place, leave this place,* she thought in a futile attempt to collect herself.

She looked up at him and shook her head, her hands still shaking. "I'm beginning to heed the warnings about you, my lord," she said angrily. "You must know that I cannot battle for your brother and battle you at the same time."

Newell removed his spectacles. He leaned once more against the crumbling, ivy-covered wall and turned his face toward the sun. The hollows of his cheeks seemed to match the pale etchings of weariness around his eyes. Some would call such crinkling of the skin at the corners of the eyes laughter lines, but she somehow knew he had not acquired them by laughing. This man, this brooding, melancholy, emotionally distant lord hardly ever laughed. It was a foreign thing to him, as foreign as that blasphemous Arabic writing was on the old Cairncross sword in the hall.

Her attraction to him, or perhaps just the realization of it, came upon her savagely. With just a glance at his face, his eyes serenely closed and the anger gone from his finely-formed lips, he beguiled her beyond anything she'd ever felt before. His handsomeness was so like Brian's. He was just another English schoolboy set out to crush her with his dispassionate cruelty. And yet, like a moth to a candle, she felt herself drawn to him. Even though she knew better than most how utterly fatal the flame could be.

"I spent last night trying to decide what to do about you," he said, not opening his eyes. "I felt my decision to let you stay might have been hasty. But in the end, I concluded that you must stay. If he can trust you, he'll overcome his fear and speak. A woman took his speech away. A woman can bring it back."

"I can't promise miracles." Her defensiveness even startled herself, but it was a reaction to her sudden attraction to him. Inside, her venomous anger toward Brian roiled and demanded release. She had never wanted to feel this way again. In fact, she'd believed she never could feel this way again, and now the emotions were upon her, as strong and violent as this man's character.

"I'm not a man who believes in miracles, Miss Benjamin."

His expression was so void of hope she felt a lump in her throat. He moved her. She didn't want to react emotionally toward him, but by his very hopelessness, she found herself drawn to him. Before, her succor had always been that a heart could only break once; there would never be another Brian. But now in one swift moment, her theory had proven wrong. Next to this powerful haunted man, Brian was weak and pale, only a sniveling memory.

"Last night I was naive." She glanced at Newell, almost hating him for the forbidden, unavoidable attraction she now felt for him. "I wasn't clear on the scope of the problems. Now I know more things and the difficulty—"

"You will stay."

The words weren't an invitation, they were fact. By the set of his chin, she could see the iron-willed determination that backed up his decision.

Then he stared at her, his unnerving gaze unfettered by spectacles. The color of his eyes was one shade deeper than the sky overhead. Blue and just as barren.

"Common sense and instinct tell me to leave. Even you yourself warned me away from Cairncross. 'Tis perhaps good advice," she said.

"It's very good advice," was all he said, as if his words alone defied her to stay.

She looked away, despising his manipulations. "Sam may be beyond my help. He may be beyond anyone's help." She added softly, "And yet, he does compel me . . ." Without really wanting to, she returned Newell's stare. Her confession made her feel vulnerable and exposed. As if picking the path toward good was no match for selfishness and evil.

"I would suspect you of a lack of feeling if he did not," he said.

She half-expected him to release a wretched smile. He'd caught her. To accuse him of a lack of feeling would have made him laugh, but to throw the same noose on her would only serve to force her to acknowledge her more altruistic side. One he didn't seem to possess.

"I might bring him around, yes," she said to him, "but have you thought of the possibility that I might also destroy whatever chance you have to get him to speak again? It's in his mind, his not being able to speak. I'm no expert on the mind."

Newell didn't answer. Instead he leaned toward an old rose-bush and plucked a dead, gone-to-seed blossom. "What does this represent, Miss Benjamin?"

She found herself unable to answer.

He glanced at her, then back at the brown, dried-out blossom.

Without warning, he pressed it into her hand. It crumbled like burnt paper.

"It's death, Miss Benjamin. Death," he whispered as if they were alone in an attic and moorland wind didn't blow overhead. "You can kill a rose just by crushing it in your palm. Once it's plucked you cannot return it to the stem for no matter how you tend to it, it dies.

"But a rose is also life," he said, staring at her as if into her very soul. "A rose in full bloom is the metaphorical pinnacle of life. And life is strong. The cycle continues. In the spring and summer, this bush will be full of new blossoms, and the dead ones will be gone and forgotten. That is the sublime brilliance of life. Life is good, life is beautiful, but most of all, life is resilient. It does not possess the static nature of evil."

She watched him in silence, her gaze unwavering.

Abruptly, as if he'd said more than he'd wanted to, he left his place at the wall and sauntered to the garden's dear lopsided doors. To her chagrin, his speech was over, and she had just been dismissed without even the most uncivilized word of farewell.

"My lord?"

He stopped.

She felt a new power rush through her veins.

He turned to look at her, his expression impatient.

"My lord, I would have you treat me at least as well as you would my father. I require a greeting upon your arrival, and a farewell when you leave."

"I'll see you at three in the schoolroom. We'll begin with Sam there." He looked at her, her requests ignored. "I think you're our last hope."

She gazed at him, this time trapped by the desolation she saw in his eyes. The agony there compelled her as no other, and she knew that it was going to be very hard to stay distant toward this man. But she must. She could already see that it wouldn't be the lord's cruelties that would hurt her. No, indeed. It would be the tantalizing, forever out-of-reach lure of his better nature. She'd fallen into that abyss once before, and found her hands full of nothing. As wretched an experience as Brian was, it had at least been an education. She was stronger now. She'd never do anything stupid again.

"I'll meet you in the schoolroom at three," she said, walking past him without a backward glance.

Chapter Eight

Newell stood in his bedchamber window gazing out to the walled garden below. The relentless wind shook the panes of glass, but down in the walled garden, the large square of vegetation was almost completely still, spared of the violence scrubbing the moorland around it.

She was like that garden. Placid, pretty, promising life in a place where no such life should grow. The very idea made his mouth grow dry with fear. He didn't want to be attracted to her. He wished desperately he'd found her plain. She was no ravishing beauty, but there was a gentleness about her, an innate femininity and strength; he found himself being drawn to her like a dog to poisoned meat.

He shut his eyes to will the image of her away and instead pictured her again as she had been in the garden. There she was, unremarkable, really; in many ways a mouse of a woman; the daughter of a Jew. But he couldn't stop himself from seeing her in his mind. It was her eyes. They sought so much. Too much. And they seemed to promise everything. Her eyes gave him the same feeling he felt when he was in the garden. An escape from the darkness. She chased away the depression that clung to him and to Cairncross like an inky shadow. Even now he could feel himself in her presence and the darkness within him seemed to recede, if only for a moment. It was all in her eyes. They sought what he feared no longer existed.

His eyes flew open. His mouth grew drier. He wanted nothing to do with her. It was one thing to have a sexual need for a trollop in Wapping, it was another to find oneself wanting a woman of goodness and gentleness and intelligence. It would mean he would have to be worthy. He would have to assess himself and he wouldn't do that. Nor would he allow any woman to get so close to him that he needed her. The very thought, if he were truthful, terrified him. He would never need a woman. He would never let down his guard with a woman again.

It had been odd that he'd let her stay. Even now he wondered why he hadn't sent her back to London. He'd never had any intention of letting some young woman come to Cairncross.

But things seemed to change when she was near.

He changed.

He paced the chamber, absentmindedly running his hands around the thick, carved post of his tester bed, wishing it were instead someone's neck. He didn't like this feeling she gave him. It was too foreign, too out of control. It left him on edge.

He didn't like to think about it, but there seemed no getting around the fact that he was irrationally attracted to her. If she'd been a woman like Abbey, a beauty with nothing on her mind but carnal gratification, he might understand the attraction. If Alexandra Benjamin had even been a peeress, he might find himself challenged by the seduction. But she was nobody, just a woman one step above the working-class.

His mind wandered back to the moment he left the garden. He was astounded at her demand for a proper farewell. Alexandra Benjamin was merely a woman, but she was one of strength and conviction. With a noble set to her mind.

If he let her stay here, she would affect him. She might make him want to deviate from the path he'd set for himself. Long ago he'd chosen darkness over light, cruelty over understanding.

He wouldn't change now. A woman had pushed him onto this path. No woman was now going to make him turn from it.

The thought gave him pause. He wondered why he was even thinking of Alexandra Benjamin. He needed to will her from his thoughts, but she represented a challenge he ached to meet. That he wanted to toy with her was undeniable, but such a thing might prove dangerous. He couldn't allow it. The goodness in her wouldn't metamorphose him. His philosophy had taken years to develop. Years of anguish and agony. Years of hurt and the wild instinctive need for protection.

She wasn't going to change him.

A knock sounded at the door. He strode to it. Mrs. Penrith was there, her face drawn and lined.

"My lord," she began, "Nancy, one of the scullery girls, has come down ill and cannot clean the schoolroom. I don't believe I can have it ready in the time you specified."

He peered down at the tiny, black-gowned housekeeper, a terrible anticipation suddenly thrumming in his veins. "Then you must let her go, Mrs. Penrith."

"But, my lord, she's in the family way and she spent all night scrubbing the stone stairs in the great hall as you requested. The stones are shiny clean now; she did an excellent job though her hands were rough and bleeding from the lye. You must understand—"

"She's not ill, she just doesn't want to go into the schoolroom."

"The servants have always talked of ghosts."

His mouth tipped in a dark smile. "The servants are worse idiots than Sam. Tell the chit she's to be let go."

"But she needs the work, my lord. Think of the babe."

"She's to be let go, and if the schoolroom is not clean by three o'clock, you may pack your bags as well."

Mrs. Penrith gasped. "But I've no relations; I've nowhere to go. I've been with the family for twenty-five years, my lord."

"You presume a security you do not possess. Good day, Mrs. Penrith."

He closed the door. The schoolroom, he had no doubt, would be spotless by three o'clock.

The satisfaction was dark and sweet. He smirked as he again thought of the new governess and the expression in her eyes that made him feel wild with rage. It questioned the goodness in him and he'd cleansed himself of that vulnerability long ago. He couldn't change, even if he did long to taunt her, to shock her. To test the very righteousness in her that she held up to him like a shield.

If she were going to stay, and he continued to find himself taken with her, then the easiest thing to do would be to change her. In his mind, he pictured her again in the garden, so full of life and resilience and challenge. He almost anticipated the clash.

Good versus evil. It was an age-old battle he intended to win.

In the course of twenty-four hours at Cairncross, Alexandra had had two conversations with Lord Newell, and both times the subject of fear had arisen like a piece of statuary between them, hiding each other from view, demanding it be noticed and commented upon.

Alexandra thought of this as she paced her bedroom, waiting and watching the clock while it chimed the second hour. Mary was gone and so were Mary's trunks. Mary had either been diabolically spirited away, or, as she really suspected, the maid had been given a room of her own down with the other servants now that her mistress was going to be remaining a while.

Nervously anticipating the meeting at three, she went to the bureau mirror to check her hair for what seemed the hundredth time. "A woman who can control her hair can control anything," she proverbially assured herself, while smoothing back the hair on her temple with her boar-bristle brush. Finished, she laid the brush down on the lace lambrequin, and suddenly noticed a small corner of a piece of paper that had been stuck beneath it.

She removed the brass candlestick that was on top of the bureau, then pushed aside the lace. A piece of yellowed paper slipped to the floor. She picked it up and noticed that one side of it was ragged as if it had been torn from a sewn binding.

Slowly, she began to read the thin, scratchy, faded handwriting:

15 December 1837

He refused to look at me today. He sat slouched in his chair in the corner of schoolroom, and he wouldn't even meet my gaze. But I don't worry. Last night I entered his bedchamber and found him slumbering; the young lord, so handsome and smooth-skinned. I touched his face. I wanted to kiss him, but then he awoke. He sat up in bed as if he'd just seen a ghost and I began to laugh. It was so funny, you understand. Here, he thought I meant him harm, and yet, all I wanted was a caress in return. I know he knows how. I see him watching the scullery maids, that gleaming look in his eyes just as if he were a man full-grown. If he will look at them, then why not me? I laughed and laughed, and he cursed me as I stood over his bedstead. I took the candle and left, but he knows I'll be back.

He refused to look at me today. But I don't worry.

Alexandra lowered the paper and a strange, sickening emotion settled in her belly. She didn't know why or how, but it was obvious this was a page from a diary, Ursula Pole's diary. The boy was Newell.

So the next question was how had the page gotten beneath the lace lambrequin on her bureau. It hadn't been there for twenty years. Someone who had the diary had placed it there, as if expecting someone to find it. Her.

But who would do such a thing? Mrs. Penrith? Featherstone? The next thought struck her like a wave of nausea. Could it have been Lord Newell himself?

She put the page on the bureau. She didn't want to read

Ursula Pole's diary. Just from the one page, she'd found it like living life through the eyes of a monster.

She glanced down at the paper, then carefully folded it and placed it in her bodice. Someone had put it in her room. It would be very telling to know who, and she was determined to find out.

A rattling noise went along the passage outside and drove her attention from the diary. It stopped in front of her door, and she had a moment or two of irrational terror, as if her mind had lapsed, and she could indeed believe in ghosts.

"Is that you in there, miss? Could you get the door?"

Alexandra released a sigh in a gush and flung open the door. Mary stood there, a silver tea tray in one hand laden with currant scones and pink-iced petit fours; in the other hand, she carried a tray of newly-cleaned oil lamps, their loose glass covers making a terrible racket with her every movement.

Relieved, Alexandra took the lamp tray and placed it on the bureau.

"They're short of help belowstairs today. I offered to bring all this up, but it almost got away from me." Mary whisked into the room in a flurry of lavender water and serviceable black taffeta. She began to set up tea by the fire, and again Alexandra found herself grateful for Mary's homey ways. They were so *normal*.

Alexandra sat in one of the oxblood leather club chairs and motioned for Mary to take the other. Being at times more a relative than a servant, the maid sat herself down and began buttering a scone while Alexandra poured out.

"You do look peaked, love. I can't imagine what the ogre said to you. You should hear the talk about him belowstairs." Mary concentrated on buttering the scone as if her nonchalance might get Alexandra to talk.

"I'll concede that he's an odd man. A very odd man." Alexandra handed her a steaming cup of oolong and squelched the urge to pinch her cheeks in hopes of bringing life back to them. The diary page was just so unexpected. She still felt the oozing sickliness in her belly. But she wasn't going to tell

Mary about it. She had enough concerns on her hands to have to deal with another's hysteria.

"From what I've heard today, he's every bit as cruel as they said." Mary stopped chewing long enough to look at her.

Alexandra didn't quite meet her gaze. She forced her attention on the sugar bowl so that Mary wouldn't see the worry shadowing her eyes. "So far, in my presence, he's acted just as I would expect from an English baron, no better no worse."

When five lumps of sugar had gone into her cup, Alexandra finally noticed what she was doing and ceased. She took a sip, then grimaced; she hated anything too sweet, especially her tea. "I imagine most servants don't like their masters. Lord Newell is probably callous at times. He's distant and a bit cold, but, no doubt, he's got much on his mind, and so I don't wonder that he comes off as cruel. They probably can't articulate how to describe him so they've latched onto this word 'cruel' when they don't mean 'cruel' at all, they mean . . ." She stopped and stared into her teacup.

"What do they mean?"

Evil, Alexandra thought, remembering the diary page and Mrs. Penrith's warning. *The servants mean to say that they think John Damien Newell is evil.* The bile rose in her throat. Certainly John Damien had been through enough to turn a young boy astray. It was probable that those in the household were noticing it.

"What is it, miss?" Mary prompted, unable to completely cover the anxiety in her voice.

"I just had a thought, but it was nothing. Absurd really. My instincts have gone awry. There's just something about him. As I said, he's an odd man. Big, quiet, abrupt, distant." She took another sip of her sickeningly sweet tea to hide her worry. "Well, with all that, 'tis no wonder he makes a bad impression."

She didn't even notice the way Mary stared at her. She was too engrossed in her thoughts and in stirring a cup of tea that she was never going to finish.

Why had she thought of the word evil? She herself didn't

believe Newell was evil. Evil was the complete absence of good and there was good in the man, she knew it. He cared about his brother. She could see it in his face when he spoke of Sam; he even said as much in the garden. An evil man wouldn't have done such a thing. He found refuge in the garden as she did. An evil man might admire the walled garden for its innocence and beauty, but he would never take solace in its inherent goodness as Newell had.

So why did she think the servants believed Newell to be evil? Was it just that evil always seemed to accompany sadness and tragedy, two things that Cairncross had seen a lot of? She would have to give the servants more credit than that. They might be uneducated, but Jaymes and Mrs. Penrith and the elderly, sour-faced butler, Mr. Featherstone, weren't fools. They sensed the dichotomy at Cairncross, the polarization that she had only begun to notice. Her first clue had been in the garden. Now sitting in her room, she couldn't understand the aura of evil that seemed to possess the place. She had only noticed it in the garden; she only took note of it when it was absent.

That was why Newell was misjudged. He himself wasn't evil, but there were those in the house who had been. Ursula Pole, for one. Alexandra knew very little about the woman, but it was not difficult to put a fix on her. The woman must have been mad. The diary page proved that. In 1837, Newell had been perhaps thirteen. Ursula's feelings were unnatural for a boy of that age. They were wrong and sinful and damaging. Newell had escaped her in the end. His banishment—whatever the cause of it had been—had probably been a blessing. But he'd had to leave Sam behind. And Ursula had done one last thing to Sam before she'd disappeared, and now Alexandra braced herself to confront the horror of it, the *evil* of it. Lord Newell had called Ursula Pole a demon. It sent a cold, sliding fear down her spine.

But the woman was gone. She was so long gone, she'd never bothered to return to claim her belongings even as she'd left desecration in her wake. Even a vile, abusive governess couldn't be as evil as the history of Cairncross—all the battles fought, all the men who died to protect its boundaries. Besides, first and foremost, Alexandra considered herself a scientist. She couldn't allow that the tearing asunder of Cairncross was caused by the residue of memory. The people and their terrible deeds were over and done with. The past was gone, overridden by the present.

Slowly her gaze drifted over to the locked trunk beneath the window. The past had indeed departed, but if the memory of Ursula Pole was ethereal and fading, her belongings were not. The page slipped beneath her corset cover was no fantasy. The trunk was no lingering residue of memory. These things were as tangible as the woman herself had been. Call it wild irrational instinct, but Alexandra hated the trunk, in fact, she despised it, and at first opportunity she was going to get a servant to take it away.

"You're a thousand miles away, love. As far as London itself."

Alexandra focused her gaze on Mary. Mary whom she'd forgotten was even in the room, let alone directly in front of her.

"Has he done this to you?" Mary asked.

"He hasn't done anything to me. He's not evil. I know he isn't." The confession wasn't quite what she'd meant to say, but the words had erupted anyway.

"I never asked you if he was evil. What made you think it?" Mary's face was the face of last night: wary, lined, aging by the minute.

"There's something about him that isn't quite right. Lord Newell isn't really evil, it's just that I think . . ." Alexandra groped for the words to express her theory. "It's just that I fear he has grown to embrace too closely that side of our nature. Does that make sense?"

"I'm not sure." Mary put down her scone, her appetite clearly gone.

Alexandra's face grew pensive. "He's already asked me about Brian, and I told him. I told him more than I've told hardly anyone. I can't say as to how Lord Newell thought that would be my Achilles heel, but he knew it, and he took a strange kind of amusement in asking me about him.''

Alexandra watched the mélange of emotion flit across Mary's dear features. The maid had had very little information about what had gone between Brian Denys Tewesbury and Alexandra, but it had always been enough to simply say he'd broken Alexandra's heart. From that and that alone, the woman had been as protective of Alexandra as a lioness toward her cub. The secrecy and silence about Brian was their pact. A pact now violated from the outside.

"The wretch," Mary cursed.

"But, still, I say he's not. Not completely." Alexandra frowned, the idea in her head difficult to put into words. "As much as he enjoyed asking me about Brian and digging up that hurt, he knew he enjoyed it." Her brow furrowed deeper. "He might hurt people, Mary, but he knows he's hurting them, and I tell you that's why he's not like Brian. Brian rationalized his prejudices as being the right and proper thing to do, regardless of the cruelty of it. He felt no guilt at all over his abandonment of me, but Lord Newell would have felt the guilt. He might have been just as cruel, perhaps even more so, but he would know he was being cruel. He would feel the guilt. That's why he's different. That's why he can be—'' *Saved,* she thought, astounding even herself at the deduction. It seemed to have come from nowhere, but she believed it. She believed it utterly.

"But if Lord Newell is hurting anyone and enjoying it, then I say he's a wretch." Mary stood and began to put the cold cups of tea onto the tray.

"Yes, I suppose in some manner he is a wretch. I'm not sure I like him. I only know that he's not like Brian. He's not beyond the point of no return." Alexandra rose and quietly stood in front of the looking glass, smoothing again her rebellious curls. Her hell-spawned attraction to Lord Newell once again reared its head in her thoughts and taunted her with its obtuse meaning. She didn't really like the man. She knew this now. Still, she was powerfully drawn to him.

So she must force herself to remain sensible. She would keep her distance from Newell. She lectured herself on this while the clock on the mantel rang thrice. With each chime, her nerves pulled taut to the snapping point.

There was nothing to fear as long as she kept her head. She must always, *always*, remember to keep Newell emotionally and physically at arm's length. If she failed, then she might be lost, but if she succeeded, instinct told her she could take comfort in the fact that then she would never have to come face to face with the thing that was so very wrong at Cairncross.

Chapter Nine

A servant had entered the schoolroom and cleaned it. The carpet of gray dust had been removed from the floor, a cheery little peat fire burned in the stove, and the window shutters had been flung wide allowing some of the thin moorland sunshine to flood the room.

It was almost a pleasant place, Alexandra thought, being the first to arrive. Still, there was something chilling about the room. Its emptiness, its silence was alienating. The woman was still a part of the room. It was no wonder people avoided it. Sitting in an empty schoolroom made one feel like one was in permanent detention.

She set about rearranging the furniture. The small chair and desk, while perfect for a little lord, were hardly going to hold a grown man. In fact, Alexandra couldn't shake her amazement that the old furniture was still in place. The boys, even at nine and thirteen, would have dwarfed it. But obviously no one had cared. Perhaps that was the effect striven for. If the boys—or at least John Damien—were humiliated by it, that might have been how Ursula Pole took her control of them.

Alexandra shivered and stepped over to the teacher's desk.

The chair had been upended, no doubt left by the careless servants who had swept the floor. She straightened the chair and scooted it beneath the beautiful mahogany ladies' desk. A *bonheur du jour* she had heard these little escritoires called. They were all the rage in the last century, but now were relegated to attics and old schoolrooms, left derelict for governesses to use. A trite inadequate desk for a trite, inadequate education.

Alexandra fetched an old blackened Windsor chair from her room. It was ridiculous to think she could do anything with Sam and these petite little furnishings. The schoolroom might be the place to start with her treatment, but she would speak to Lord Newell first thing about setting up elsewhere. The music room, if there was one, was usually the best place for her patients. Even the most profoundly deaf could discern the vibrations from a piano or horn. That was the beginning in helping them understand that speech was only so many variable vibrations and sounds.

"Prompt. I admire that."

Alexandra turned around and found Newell standing—or rather filling—the schoolroom doorway. He seemed to be always sneaking up on her, as if his footsteps weren't quite mortal. But perhaps it was only that she was so terminally preoccupied at Cairncross. It was probable that even an elephant could have tiptoed past her notice.

"Where is Sam?" she inquired, pushing the two little desks against the bookcase that held the Waverley novels.

"He's coming. Featherstone should be up with him soon." Newell entered the schoolroom. His gaze darted around as if he almost expected her to have company.

Inexplicably nervous, she reached for her black satchel and extracted her teaching aids. There was her "timpani" section, a xylophone and chimes, also several three-dimensional drawings of the mouth and tongue creating certain sounds. As she put the pictures up against the various bookshelves, she couldn't stop herself from realizing the hopelessness of the situation. She was used to working with children, not adults. Children were the ones generally who could be helped because they were still open to speech; the stage of such learning had not yet been passed. But Samuel Newell was thirty years old. And he'd already learned to talk. There was no teaching one who already knew the subject.

"Before I begin, I must confess that I'm a bit out of my element." She fingered her satchel, then nervously clasped it on Ursula Pole's writing desk. "You must understand that I've never taught someone to speak who already could. Those who lose their hearing once they master speech don't need to bother with my father's teachings." She glanced at Newell, then took a step back. It amazed her how much presence he had. She felt suffocated next to him in the tiny schoolroom.

He quirked his lips. "You may teach him geography, if you wish, as long as you teach him."

"But the point is—"

"The point is for him to get used to you." He looked around the room and added, "to this."

"You think when he overcomes his fear, he will speak."

"I do."

"And if he should not? His slowness won't help us. He may never speak as he did."

Newell stepped closer to her, his eyes sparkling behind the clear crystals of his spectacles. "He will never be anything else unless we show him—you show him—that she is gone."

"Ursula Pole."

It was not a question but he answered it anyway. "Yes," he rasped.

"But she is gone. I was told she disappeared."

Newell glanced at her. She could see his restraint. It was in the manner in which he controlled the muscles in his jaw, the stiff, unyielding posture of his back. He appeared as if he wanted to pin her against the wall and demand all that she'd been told about Cairncross and Ursula Pole and himself. But he performed no such violence. Instead, he said calmly, "Yes, she disappeared. Sam must be told that time and again. He must know that she left."

"Does he think she never left?"

"Possibly."

"He knows no time but his own," she whispered, her heart aching for poor old slow Sam. To him, twenty years was but yesterday. The workings of his poor tortured mind must be a snakepit. One she longed to free him of. Her gaze met with Newell's.

Featherstone led Sam into the room much as one might escort an old, frail, delusional woman. Sam clung to his arm, a wild light in his beautiful blue eyes that only turned calm whenever he looked at his brother.

Alexandra stiffly walked over to the small ladies' desk and sat down in the same chair as Ursula Pole had sat in.

"Come sit down, Sam. We thought it best to start in the schoolroom. It's a place you're familiar with now, aren't you?" Alexandra waved to the Windsor chair. Sam pulled upright and refused it, backing away.

Slowly Alexandra rose to her feet. She didn't understand the point in beginning in this terrifying place. It would have been better to be in the drawing room, or even beneath the willow by the pond. She met Sam's frightened eyes and said haltingly to his brother, "Lord Newell, don't you think another room would be better to—"

"No," Newell whispered at her elbow, his gaze as intent upon his brother as any.

"Sit down, won't you, Sam?" She again motioned to the Windsor chair. Sam shook his head and turned toward Featherstone. With just a nod, Newell motioned for the butler to depart. The old man did, all the while glaring at Alexandra.

He thinks I'm going to hurt Sam, she thought to herself, finally understanding the butler's look of anathema toward her. The old man must have been in the service of these two men for decades. Just like Mrs. Penrith, he didn't quite approve of the Newell men, but his cold, Yorkshireman loyalties had been cast with them long ago.

"Sit down in the chair, Sam. Miss Benjamin is here to help us. She's not going to hurt you." Newell took his brother's arm and led him to the Windsor chair. Sam sat in it, reluctantly, and watched in terror while his brother walked toward the door.

Newell turned. "Begin, Miss Benjamin," he commanded.

She looked from his face hardened with studied inexpression to Sam's, so handsome and innocent and full of fear. She could hardly bear it. The contrast was so stark.

"I always begin with sound. Music is so beautiful, so . . . good." She picked up a felt-covered hammer and let it fall upon the chimes. "Can you hear that, Sam? Can you tell the different sounds?" She looked up at Sam and could have cried out from horror. She followed his terrified gaze to her hand that held the hammer. A sudden, awful thought occurred to her and she dropped it like a fire iron. It clattered thunderously to the wooden floor.

"*Sam,*" Newell rasped as Sam lept from his chair. Alexandra shrank back but Sam didn't lunge for her, rather it was the door that he wanted.

"Stay here, Sam! You must stay here and face this thing!" Newell tried to push him back, but Sam would have no more of his brother's reassurances. He lunged and lunged again for the open doorway and the blessed passage beyond.

"Let him go. I beg of you, don't force him to do this terrible thing." Alexandra could hardly believe it was she who spoke these words. She ran up to the two brothers locked in what seemed to be a life-and-death battle, and she tugged on their meaty arms, begging for a separation. Finally she caught Newell's gaze, unaware that she had tears streaming down her cheeks, unaware that the blood had left her face, giving further impact to her supplication. He released Sam, and they both watched him clutch at the plaster walls of the passage while he stumbled away, gasping and groaning for breath.

"It shouldn't be this way. This is not going to help," she choked, her sobs heaving within her chest.

Newell didn't look at her. She could see he considered his brother's fear a failure. But whose? His or hers? Or Newell's himself? She would never know.

"I don't see how you can accomplish anything." He turned an accusatory eye upon her.

She stammered, groping for an exclamation. "I—I—didn't mean to drop the hammer. It's—it's—just that I thought perhaps she might have hit him—he looked at me so fearfully and—and I couldn't bear to see it."

"You'll see more than that."

She stared at him, despising the implications. "Did she use to hit him?" she asked in a small, hopeless voice.

"She did not. Is that the worst pain you can imagine, Miss Benjamin? A cut across the cheek from a whip?"

"Nay," she whispered, suddenly chilled to the bone.

"Which is worse? To feel the lash yourself, or to see your most beloved cut beneath it instead?"

"It would be worse to see it than to feel it."

"Exactly." He looked down at her, his expression hard and wrathful. Knowing. There was so much he knew that she didn't, she didn't even know how to ask the right questions.

"Tell me about her. If I'm to help him, I must know. Tell me," she repeated, grasping at the basic need to know one's nemesis.

"I'll tell you tonight. At dinner. I eat precisely at eight." He stared at her for a good long while, as if he were battling some kind of decision.

Then he turned and strode down the long passage, leaving her alone in the schoolroom.

After many hours in her room reliving the few minutes spent in the schoolroom, Alexandra found she had no one to blame but herself. It had been a foolish thing to do. She was the one who had possessed the overactive imagination; she was the one who had pictured Ursula Pole beating Sam, and, with hammer in hand, Alexandra had been the one who mistakenly thought that Sam believed she would beat him also. If she hadn't dropped the hammer, if she hadn't played into a fear she couldn't yet begin to understand, the afternoon might have

gone more according to plan. They would have begun a friendship, she and Sam, one that they could build toward getting
Sam to speak again.

Now they had only moved backward. Sam, in his small,
simple world, would associate her with the former Miss Pole,
and so she would have to break that association and break it
immediately. Tonight she was somehow going to have to prove
to Lord Newell that it was of utmost importance that she be
allowed to perform in the manner she thought best. No more
throwing the lambs to the wolves. Sam for all his age and
size was nothing more than a frightened child. He needed
comforting, not confrontation. Lord Newell would have to see
that, and he would have to accept it or watch her leave by the
next train south.

"I don't remember you being this quiet back in London,
miss." Mary shook out her lavender silk twill gown for the
evening's repast with the master.

Alexandra didn't know how to respond to the silent accusation in the maid's voice. She hadn't asked Mary about her new
room belowstairs, nor about the other servants Mary would be
forced to seek out for company now that her mistress was above
stairs. There was a lot Alexandra wanted to tell her, but the
words didn't seem to come. She was reluctant to explain a
feeling when there was no evidence to back it up. There was
Ursula Pole's trunk, for example. Alexandra was repulsed by
it. Revulsion had replaced curiosity ever since Mrs. Penrith
had told her about the woman. Now she spied the trunk beneath
the window and whereas before she saw little more than a
worn, locked trunk full of mysterious possessions, she now
saw something dark and unaccountably repugnant. To her, the
trunk had become bad. Even evil. Mary with her hard-cast
loyalties would believe her if she told her how she felt, but
Alexandra also knew she would alarm her and she didn't want
to spend the rest of her time at Cairncross battling her maid's
desire to flee. Too, she also believed that once she put her
feelings and suspicions into words, she would no longer be
able to give them credence. Being a well-educated woman, she

would be forced to announce such things as ridiculous. Ghosts and goblins and suspicions of evil were not something she could take seriously. Her father had not raised her to be so simple-minded.

And yet . . .

And yet, there was another reason not to put words to her growing unease. If she spoke her fears aloud, she would be forced to mock them, and she had the unsettling notion that to do such a thing would be to invite trouble. Even a scientific mind knew not to scoff at the unknown. Such actions made fools. And victims.

"My thoughts are on Sam. I'm not sure how to go about teaching Lord Newell's poor brother, 'tis all." Poor Sam. *Poor* Sam. Alexandra now knew why no one could speak the name Sam without preceding it with the adjective. Sam's appearance didn't dovetail with his simple mind. His physical self seemed only there to mock the child that lived within.

"Something isn't right here at Cairncross," Mary said gravely. "The other servants speak of things—"

Alexandra stared at her.

The maidservant drew herself up. "It's not gossip I'm speaking of. It's a feeling. A sense of darkness. I can't quite put my finger on it."

"The castle is old. Going on a thousand years, I daresay. It's all alone on these moors and our welcome was less than convivial. Anyone would have a dark feeling about it."

"But you've got it too. Look at you. You're so pale, miss. Pale and quiet. You know something's not right about this place. What is it?"

Alexandra lowered her gaze to her bodice. She thought to bring out the diary page and unburden herself, but she knew it would only aggravate things. Besides, it was soon to be eight and she still had not changed gowns. "I agree with you that there seems to be a bad feeling here, but perhaps the gloom is because of Sam. We can't let our wicked imaginations run wild just on a feeling, now can we?"

"Feeling is all we've got." Mary tightened her lips and

helped her step out of the black silk gown and into the lavender. "It's the only real thing we know, now isn't it?"

Alexandra stared at her own pale face in the mirror above the bureau. Her heart pounded against the page folded inside her corset cover. "Yes," was all she whispered.

Twenty minutes later, with her hair braided and twisted beneath a black snood, she said goodnight to Mary and left for the baronial hall. Lord Newell hadn't told her where he usually dined and she now meant to seek out Featherstone in order to find out where the lord's eating room was.

Walking alone through the wing, she couldn't shake the notion that the castle seemed darker than normal, the shadows twice as long as the night before. She found the stairs and took them four flights down to the floor she believed held the great hall, but the maze of passages soon bedeviled her, and she quickly found herself in a dead end. Perplexed, she turned around and faced the opposite, as-yet-unexplored, end of the passage.

A slow, narcotic horror seeped into her veins.

There stood a woman. The figure hovered in the darkness at the other end of the shadow-draped passage, a frozen black-swathed form that seemed almost needy for the gloom around her. The woman didn't speak, she didn't move, there wasn't a breath of rustling silk, yet her stance, her veiled featureless face, seemed intent upon Alexandra, drawn to Alexandra. Alexandra could almost feel her watch her.

At first, she believed—or perhaps wanted to believe—the woman was Mrs. Penrith. The black-clad woman was petite and wore a gown much like the housekeeper's, but when Alexandra called her name, she didn't respond. The figure—the *creature*—remained silent.

Her face was in half-shadow, blurred by the black translucent netting of the veil, but Alexandra could almost make out a visage, one that stared in her direction, still as death, with no identifiable emotion in the sunken valleys of her eyes. As if it were an afterthought, a heavy black woolen cloak was thrown haphazardly over her shoulders, the kind one donned in winter. to keep out the frigid winds.

"Who are you?" Alexandra called, anxious to close the great distance between herself and the woman. Yet, terrified to. "Can you tell me where the master takes his dinner of an evening?"

There were probably fifty servants in the castle. Certainly Alexandra had yet to lay eyes upon them all, but she felt this woman wasn't one of the help. The obscured, static expression, the shadowy stare, could never be mistaken for a servant's demeanor. There was a stillness, a malevolence about her, that was unnatural. Though Alexandra was a hundred feet away, herself cloaked in the darkness of the passage, she could not quell the tremor of apprehension that took hold of her. There was something terrible about this woman. It went beyond the quiet of her form, beyond the staring, veiled obscured face. This woman looked as if she should not be here. And that she was here, intent upon Alexandra, frightened her to the core.

"I ask that you identify yourself," she said, stepping closer to the shadows wherein the figure dwelled.

The answer was silence. Cold, ever-present silence.

"Lord Newell shall know about this. I daresay, he won't like his servants skulking about the castle, rudely hiding in the shadows . . ." Alexandra stared at the creature, praying for any small movement from the static form—a release of breath, a shudder, a sigh, anything that would proclaim this figure mortal.

"Why are you hiding in the corner there? Is someone looking for you? Mrs. Penrith will be most unhappy to hear of this." She moved forward, the baby-fine hairs rising on her nape like the hackles of a dog. In the fog of her memory, she recalled the figure of a woman on the York wall that had scared Mary. If this were the figure, Alexandra could finally understand the fear. Even as she stepped closer and closer, the figure didn't move, didn't flinch, not once.

"Are you trying to frighten me?" she whispered. "Is that why you won't answer? Is it me especially that you want to scare?"

The woman said nothing. She just looked at Alexandra from the soulless black hollows where her eyes should be.

''I said speak to me! Do you hear! Speak!'' Rage giving an edge to her fear, Alexandra rushed to the black-clad figure. Her hands reached out to claw off the veil, to confront the gaze of this wicked thing, but she only took hold of the scratchy black wool of the cloak. The dead weight of the woman's body seemed missing and instead the figure seemed wrought out of air. Her lunge caused the woman to tip like a wooden clown Alexandra had seen once in a toy shop, first to one side, then to the other, almost comically. The woman tumbled to the ground, cloak, gown, and all.

Alexandra screamed.

Chapter Ten

It took a lifetime in the darkness for Alexandra to reach the gas lamp affixed to the far wall. She scrambled back from the disassembled figure and ran, tripping and gasping, toward the light fixture at the other end of the long hall.

There must be light, there must be more light, she prayed as she bumped into tables and trunks, then stumbled and fell to her knees as a hail of spools of thread rained down upon her back. She tripped once more on a stack of cloth bolts and she cried out loud when a pair of footlong dressmaker shears fell like a spear from the table above and landed within a hair's breadth of her nose.

Her entire body shook with terror while she fought to stay on her feet and continue her quest. The path was littered with shadowy obstacles but she maneuvered around each one, determined to get to the gas lamp. She was going to see that creature once and for all.

With gasps of gratitude and relief, she came to the lamp. Her fingers stretched to reach the key, just inches too high on the wall for her, but she wasn't discouraged. Fear and anger drove her like a madwoman. The gaslight would be turned up to its fullest, and she would return to the end of the hallway to find her nemesis even if it took every ounce of bravery and strength she possessed.

She reached again and again, still not quite able to take hold of the key. Then, to her shock, a pair of strong hands reached from outside the weak sphere of light and twisted the key.

She spun around and came face to face with Newell. He was dressed in fine evening clothes. He wore an elegant black frock coat and his shirt sported a freshly starched collar. He looked at her not as she would suppose he would. His eyes were not mocking, his mouth held no hint of derision. She knew she looked like a lunatic, clawing along the passage wall for the gaslight as if it would save her miserable life. In the back of her mind, she even wondered if he'd heard her scream, but she didn't ask him. She didn't give him any greeting at all. She took her comfort in the bright glow of the flaring gas lamp, then walked to the other end of the hall where the woman had once stood.

"I see you've gotten lost and frightened yourself," Newell commented as he stepped behind her.

Alexandra just stared at the black pile of clothing and the drab linen-covered dress form that was now knocked to the ground beneath it, its head a smooth molded composition of the human face.

"This is a servant's wing." He turned her head to the staircase. "You came down five flights from your room when you should have gone only four."

She nodded, unable to find her voice. In the gaslight she could suddenly see the plainness of the passage's walls and woodwork. The fine walnut wainscoting of the upper floors was missing; so too, was the rich Turkey carpet that covered the hallways in the newer wings. In one corner of the hall, a dressmaker's dummy and endless bolts of black worsted were stacked. A bay of windows covered this end of the passage and in the day it would be flooded with light. Judging by the scattered chairs and tables, the rainbow of spools, and the flash of steel shears, it was obviously the place where the seamstress and her army of girls sewed the servants' clothing.

"There's nothing here, you see?" he said lightly.

She looked down at the dressmaker's dummy, sickened by the sight of the naked featureless head and the deep hollows of its face where two eyes should have been, eyes that she'd believed were staring at her beneath a veil. She picked up a worker's black-crocheted shawl realizing that it had been left ignominiously draped over the dummy's head. There had been no veil at all. Everything could be explained as the work of her childish and overactive imagination.

"Come. Now that I've found you, let's have our supper, shall we?" He held out his arm.

She looked up at him, frustrated that she couldn't meet his gaze beneath the spectacles. "She seemed so real." She didn't know why she had just whispered the words, but somehow, she needed to say them. She wanted desperately to relieve her fears, and the only way to do that now seemed to be to finally speak them.

"It was nothing more than a dress-form hidden in a darkened passage." Was there finally amusement in his voice?

She took a step backward, her instincts driving her away from him. A terrible suspicion sprouted in her thoughts. In the back of her mind, she recalled Mrs. Penrith's chilling words: *. . . and some say he's not right in the head because of it.* "She was real. I know what I saw and what I saw was a dressmaker's dummy set up in order to frighten me. Someone did this and so therefore, it was very real. Not an accident."

"How could anyone know you would make a mistake and come down here?" There should have been patience in his voice, the tried, exasperated tone of a father speaking to an irrationally frightened child. But there was none. Instead, he seemed almost bored by her fear, as if he had expected it and now thought less of her that she had succumbed to it.

"Did you dress it like this? Are you trying to frighten me?" Her gaze was level and accusing. She was now more bewildered than scared. The thing she had seen was real, real at least in the sense that it had been manufactured to terrify, and it had terrified. And his reaction—the vague amusement in his voice, the bored tilt to his head—was not right. His reaction left her almost as chilled as when she had first laid eyes on the figure in the corner. Earlier today someone had placed a page of Ursula Pole's diary beneath the lambrequin in her bedroom. Now she couldn't stop herself from wondering if ghosts were walking the halls of Cairncross, or if these events were just the product of a sick amusement on the part of this man who stood before her.

"I don't spend my time trying to frighten little women." He looked down at her, his obfuscated eyes still giving away his lack of confidence in her and her small stature. "Besides, I could not have known you would come down here to see it."

"Yes," she agreed in a whisper, turning back to the crumpled figure on the floor. "It's almost as if someone knew I would come down here . . . or . . ."

He lifted one gold eyebrow questioningly. "Or . . . ?"

"Or that someone was following me." She looked down at the other end of the long passage. It was now the one cloaked in darkness. "I went down to that end of the hall first. Someone might have had time to set her up while I wandered down there." She lifted her head and gave him another accusing stare.

"I might have had time, is that what you're saying?"

"Perhaps you want to test me for Samuel. Perhaps you want to know if I'm easily frightened."

"I only want to know what you can do to help Sam."

"She was made to look like that." Her defense seemed as weak as a child's.

He lifted the corner of his mouth almost as if in a smile. "Let's have our supper, shall we? And I'll tell you ghost stories about Ursula. Will that calm your nerves?"

"I thought Miss Pole merely disappeared. I didn't know she was dead."

"They've never found her body, but most of the town thinks they have the killer." He took her by the arm and laid her reluctant hand firmly on his forearm. The expression on his face was deep with pleasure. "Did you know, Miss Benjamin, that they think I killed Ursula?"

Alexandra sat numbly across from Newell at a large walnut dining table. She stared at him, giving long furtive glances that retrieved very little information. For the most part her appetite was gone, trifled away, minute by minute, as they pretended to have a civilized meal.

His lordship took his meals in an eating room off the cavernous baronial hall. The walls were upholstered in the latest fashion of maroon cut-velvet. An enormous chandelier hung overhead, its countless arms were topped by etched globes each held up by a snarling gilt-bronze gryphon.

Somehow, Newell didn't fit with the room. It had recently been decorated, all with the most modern gas fixtures and coal grates. The darkness suited him, but the puce satin drapery with the enormous fringes and cording was almost too perfectly executed. The room was tasteful, modern, and calculated—to the point of sterility.

It had probably been redecorated when he'd come back to the castle. Lord Newell had probably had many of Cairncross's rooms modernized. It was interesting to her that he enjoyed comforts, especially since he never seemed prone to handing them out. On the contrary, except where Sam was concerned, Newell seemed bent on discomforting those around him, as his last statement in the servants' hall had proved.

Alexandra looked down at her small little hen stuffed with orange peel and dripping with burgundy sauce. She had rarely tasted such delicious fare; Newell must pay his cook a fortune. Still, none of it was enough to take her mind from the figure in the hall and her burning questions of the past.

"You're disappointingly quiet, Miss Benjamin. I would have thought you'd have more to say after all we've been through tonight.'' He took a large forkful of pheasant and put it in his mouth with the neat, expedient motion of a carnivore.

''I don't know what to say. I don't know what to think.'' She looked at him, her gaze unwavering.

''You think you want to leave.''

Their gazes locked. She felt a strange tingle run down her spine.

''But you haven't left yet,'' he observed, ''and do you want to know why, Miss Benjamin?''

''Why?'' she whispered, the tingle becoming more like cold fingers.

''Because as much you're afraid, you're also curious. You've inherited that fine curiosity of yours from your father. The fine Dr. Horace Benjamin, the physician, the man I thought might come here and cure Samuel.''

''Curiosity is not always a good thing.''

He laughed. ''It wasn't good for the cat—if that's what you're implying.''

''Partly.'' Her mouth felt dry. She had difficulty speaking. ''I keep telling myself that this is your business, not mine. But if I stay, I must make it my business.''

''And you find that daunting.''

''Yes.'' She looked at him. ''Wouldn't you?''

He sat back in his chair and stared at her as if contemplating her question. As usual, his cravat was perfectly knotted, and of a shade of gray that was studiously in the best taste. He had a striking appearance anyway, but his austere, somber dress only served to further highlight his boyish features. He always made her feel shabby with his elegant, dark clothing. Her half-mourning lavender gown made her seem like a wren beneath the gaze of a peregrine.

Her eyes fixed on his spectacles, the two shields behind which he hid. If the eyes truly were the mirror of the soul, there was no telling about his soul for the reflection of it was distorted and eventually lost in those two circles of glass.

''I want you to stay,'' he said slowly, cautiously, as if choosing his words. ''Your curiosity is what makes you a scientist.''

"But I'm afraid you need to feel this situation and my feelings tell me that to stay may not be productive, nor prudent."

Her answer seemed to impress him. He looked upon her with a new respect. "What are your feelings?"

"I'm indignant. Someone set up the dressmaker's mannequin to frighten me. It was done on purpose and in ghastly taste, and I think it's imperative to know who did it."

"Perhaps it was just a servant's prank," he offered lightly. "They never like newcomers, you know. It ruffles their feathers."

"Again, you must feel this and my instincts tell me this was no servant's prank. There was a message there." She stared at him, waiting.

"Which was?" He raised one dark gold eyebrow and she had the distinct notion he was mocking her.

"Which was," she repeated, *"personal.* The message was to me and to me alone. But perhaps you'd be a better interpreter than I." The accusation was as much in her words as her voice.

He laughed, a deep-chested snarling sound, the kind of noise she'd expect from the mouths of the gilt-bronze griffins above. "Come now, Miss Benjamin, you must believe I had nothing to do with this." He leaned across the table and caught up her hand. "It was a prank at worst, all in your imagination, at best."

"If it was a prank, I'll not abide such things. I was singled out personally to frighten and I want to know who it was. Someone followed me to perform that gruesome trick or else how could anyone know I would get lost and miscount the floors? How could they know it?"

"Unless they know things that we could never know," he said eerily, in a tone much too accepting of such a theory.

She sat, not speaking, her gaze slowly wandering to his hand that had captured her own. It grasped hers in a brutal, viselike grip. The emotion it represented was truth—the truth of fear and malevolence—even though his words, his voice, lied.

"Please," she gasped, realizing he was almost crushing her.

He let go. There was a flash in his eyes, or what she could see of them, that almost seemed like that of a wounded animal.

She stood, rattled by the exchange.

He stood also, violence suggested by the quickness of his actions.

She stared at him. He suddenly seemed to realize how he appeared. He sat down again, implying this time, a more non-threatening facade.

"This isn't how I thought to spend this evening," he said. "I had hoped to discuss Sam. To let you get to know him better."

"I want to get to know him. I have questions—"

"Then ask them."

She felt herself almost swallow a sob of fear. "I want to know about the other governess. I want to know about Ursula Pole. About her years here."

"She's dead. What else is there to know?" The glimmer of a smile touched his mouth. "You think too much of the past and not enough of the future."

"The future comes from the past. If we don't know our past, we cannot know our future."

He stared at her for a long painful moment, then he stood, mannerly this time. The perfect gentleman. "Let's have a sherry in my library, shall we? We'll talk about all this. Come clean, as it were." He finally smiled. His face was relieved and handsome. Abominably attractive.

He took her arm in his and led her from the room as if she were an invalid taking her first steps from bed. She could only stare at him, paralyzed by her wrestling emotions. "I want to know about Ursula," she whispered, an effort even to do that.

"Ah, you want to know about Ursula," he repeated as if he were talking to a child. "Then, come, Miss Benjamin, let's have a sherry. If I find I've had enough wine, I may tell you the grisly story of Ursula Pole." He looked down at her, clearly amused at how she stared at him like he was a madman just escaped from St. Elizabeth's. "And if I find you pleasant enough company, Miss Benjamin, I just might let you ask me if I *did* kill her.''

The library held a warmth even as the night wind whipped at the forest of shrubbery on the other side of the bay of windows. Alexandra sipped her sherry and mused about her situation, all the while staring at the lapis-tipped flames of the hearth. No peat fires in this part of the house. It was modern coal all around.

''Such a faraway look.''

She glanced up and found Newell staring at her, his face taut with expectation and yet, distrust.

''Come, tell me what you're thinking.''

She was instinctively afraid to breach Cairncross's forbidden thresholds, yet desperate to understand the maze of shadows she'd found herself in. The diary page burned, in its nearness to her breast. ''I'm thinking about Miss Pole. And about you.''

''What do you want to know?''

''I think I must know everything in order to assist Samuel.'' Her throat choked with something akin to dread.

He studied her for a long moment, whirling his brandy round and round in his glass, mesmerizing her, making her feel she was on a carousel which she could not get off.

''As you may have already gleaned from the servants, Ursula Pole was hired here in the absurd capacity of governess.'' He began slowly, almost with caution. His voice was harsh, halted, as if it tore at him to speak of her. ''By all rights, two young men, even one who is slow, should have had a schoolmaster, but—'' he met Alexandra's gaze, ''she was father's cousin, destitute and at our door, and our father was in Paris. He couldn't be bothered with the situation, so he merely left it up to her.

''She was here four years, then she disappeared. I was four-teen at the time.'' He ran his thumb and forefinger up beneath his spectacles and rubbed the bridge of his nose. A gesture of weariness. "I hardly need tell you this, but we didn't like her, Sam and I." He paused. "Sam was afraid of her."

"But not you," she whispered, needlessly. What she had read in Ursula's diary told her exactly how Newell felt about his old governess; still, she wanted to hear it from him. She wanted so terribly to understand.

Their gazes locked: her own, wide and honest with emotion; his, thunderous and cloaked behind the treachery of those spectacles.

"I was not afraid of her, I despised her," he said, his voice carefully cleaned of all emotion. "The two are altogether different."

She suddenly felt a surge of pity for the boy he had been. As a child, he'd been sexually hounded by the woman, and given no recourse to protect himself. It was no wonder Newell had grown into such a dark figure of a man.

"Why were you forced to leave the castle?" The question came out before she could stop it.

The brandy in his snifter swayed up and back. He laughed again. Another dark, mirthless sound that echoed through her heart. "Are you asking if they set out to lynch me for murdering her? I had reasons, you know. Not everyone would have blamed me for it. However, I'm sorry to disappoint you, Miss Benjamin, I was gone from Cairncross before our dear Miss Pole even disappeared."

"You were gone?" she asked in amazement, her beliefs and the small truths she had constructed from them suddenly thrown into turmoil. "This doesn't make sense. Why are there rumors that you killed her? You yourself have implied—"

"An implication is not a confession. I've no control over the servants' tongues."

"Perhaps, even if you were gone, it is believable you could have returned—"

"But I didn't. My destiny here was over and done with by then. Father had me disowned the night before and I was in an oxcart headed for London the day she was never heard from again."

Alexandra took a sip from her glass hardly aware of what she was drinking. A numb bewilderment laureled around her. Nothing seemed to be as she thought it was. That was, if Newell was telling her the truth.

"Why?" she asked.

His eyes were unreadable, an opaque, shielded void. "What happened back then to me has nothing to do with Sam, but I'll tell you this much, believe if you will: I was banished from Cairncross because I was accused of behaving improperly with Miss Pole."

She glanced away, wanting to hide the empathy in her eyes. After reading the page in the diary, she could see such a scandal was bound to occur. It was a tragedy that the axe had fallen upon young Newell and not upon his wicked governess.

"You may check these facts with anyone, Miss Benjamin. Featherstone remembers the day well, as do Jaymes and Mrs. Penrith. I was gone from here."

She was silent while she thought about the diary and the past.

"Do you think I murdered her, Alexandra?"

She raised her eyes and found his gaze nearly drilling into her. If the naked bluntness of the question shocked her, she was even more troubled by his use of her first name. "I wasn't here way back then. I never met her. I've only my instincts to guide me in this matter." Of course, he didn't murder this woman, and the reason left her as unsettled almost as if he had. As little as she knew of him, she was convinced she knew him well enough to know he would have admitted it if he had taken Ursula Pole's life. It was a twenty-year-old murder. There would be no price to pay, and even if the law did come to his door, Newell's wealth and position would protect him. Without witnesses and evidence, there would be no case put against him.

"What do your instincts tell you, Alexandra?"

"That you didn't do it," she whispered.

"Interesting."

She felt the sharpness of his smile even before she saw it.

There was no humor in it. Nothing happy. But it was the smile of someone who had just won.

Her stomach tightened into a ball of anxiety. It was more than lack of reprisals that drove Newell now. She knew enough about his personality to understand that he would be all too happy to volunteer the truth if the truth were ugly. He'd revel in such effective torture. To keep her here at the castle while gruesomely detailing the previous governess's death would only be joy to him. The Right Honorable John Damien, Lord Newell, was a dark enough character to appreciate the irony in it.

He would have admitted it. If it were true. She could only conclude now, with heart and soul, that it was not true. He'd never touched Ursula Pole.

He looked at her and though it was a captivating look—filled with masculine appreciation—especially for a labeled Jewess who'd been bedazzled by such looks before, his expression still had a steely edge to it, one that gave fair warning. "Miss Benjamin, you look almost disappointed."

She had no way to explain to him her genuine disappointment in discovering yet another diabolical side to his character. Never in life had she encountered such a man as he, one who seemed so willing and able to accept the evil men do.

"Disappointment is hardly appropriate in this instance, is it not?" She studied him. "I'm most certainly relieved. I don't want to share quarters with a murderer, not even this large castle. It's heartening to see it is not within your character to do such an atrocity."

"Yet."

Her eyes met his. "I suppose the potential for murder is within us all, but I would not make light of this, my lord." She paused, keeping her gaze cool, level, chastising.

He stared back as if her admonishment, her normal grasp of virtue, intrigued him. As if it were something new and foreign. "What do you think about when you grow so quiet, Alexandra?" he asked softly.

"I think of many things, my lord, such as why you called me Alexandra."

His face seemed to grow taut, much like how warm pliant flesh might look at the very point it turned to marble. Pygmalion in reverse. "Did I call you that? It was an accident."

He glanced at her quiet, small form as she sat opposite him. It was a raking gaze, as if it sought things she hid. She was sure of it when he searched her face. He was searching to see if she believed him.

She did not believe him.

"You sit there so demurely, Miss Benjamin, with your honest face and your memorable eyes. You desire to help Sam, my own flesh and blood. If I'm becoming too familiar with you, it's because I want to become familiar with you." He watched and waited. His lips thinned into an enigmatic line. "And too . . . I think you might want to become familiar with me as well—"

"Indeed, no." She stood as if the action would deflect the words he'd just spoken. As if the very idea of his notion was absurd. She knew she couldn't let him see how his words horrified her. He must never know how precariously he had skirted the truth.

Her head rose in a haughty position of superiority even though her insides churned like butter. She groped for something quelling to say, a short quip that would put him in his place and make him realize how he'd offended her. She was an employee at the castle, not a friend nor peer. She could not let him treat her with such familiarity. They couldn't continue in this vein because he just might begin to see how great her attraction was to him, and how completely Brian had destroyed her. After their first conversation they'd had in this same library, she knew it would be suicide to ever let him see those wounds again.

"I'd like to retire for the night, your lordship, but before you dismiss me, I must remind you that I came here to work with your brother. Perhaps it would be more convenient for you to return to London and allow me to befriend your brother without assistance.''

He stared at her and rubbed his jaw where an evening shadow of dark gold beard was just now appearing. ''Thank you for the suggestion, Miss Benjamin, but let me make one of my own: it's not the place of a servant to reprimand the master.''

''I'm not a servant, I'm the governess.''

She closed her mouth, taken aback by what she had said. She didn't like being called a governess; it was unsettling to hear herself draw claim to it. Yet the words had just popped from her lips like some kind of demon.

''It's been a very trying day,'' her gaze wandered to the closed library doors, ''for *both* of us. If you would be so kind, my lord, I'd like to be excused. I'd like to retire.''

He stood. ''No, don't go away.'' He then appeared to want to bite the words back. Small forlorn words they were, but they seemed to have popped from his mouth like his own devil.

''It's so late,'' she whispered, amazed by the intensity on his face. He looked down at her as if he wanted to grab her and keep her from leaving. As if her presence, her very being, were something he drew comfort from.

''You said you had questions.''

''I'm beginning to understand now. I promise to be good to Sam. He'll never have cause to fear me.'' She stole a glance at him. He seemed preoccupied, as if trying to figure how to keep her from wanting to leave.

She stepped back. He followed. It was almost a waltz.

''May I be excused, my lord?'' she asked, fear making her a little breathless.

His gaze rested upon the gilt doorknob that she now clutched like a crucifix. An inexplicable anger seemed to grip him. He looked to the ceiling as if gathering the strength to control himself. There was a heart-stopping moment when she almost suspected he might grab her, hold her in the library against her will. But in the end, he wore the veneer of a gentleman well. He didn't try to stop her. He merely looked at her, then gave a curt nod, acquiescing to her desire.

She nearly dashed out the door. There was a wide passage-way, carpeted in ruby wool, that led to the main staircase, and she almost tripped in her rush to get there. She half-expected Newell to follow her, to chase her down the hallways and when he caught her, do with her what he would. She didn't want to be afraid of him, in fact she knew she didn't even really have cause to be afraid of him, but it was ungodly how he unnerved her. He was unpredictable, and big, a fair giant of a man. And now he'd tried to be familiar with her. While he had never even made a move to touch her, while his eyes never seemed to hold any licentiousness, there was something in his voice, a gentleness, an inquisitiveness, that was too intimate.

She must stay clear of him, she told herself while climbing the stairs. She couldn't let him get close to her. He was her employer and nothing more. And no matter how strange and compelling his problems might be, they didn't concern her.

"Sleep well, Miss Benjamin."

She whipped around and found Newell standing in the shadows at the bottom of the enormous oak staircase. Her hand grew slick on the railing, her palm suddenly sweating.

"Good night, my lord," she whispered, unable to make eye contact with him through the shadowy reflection of his spectacles.

She turned around to continue her climb, but he stopped her with one word.

"Alexandra." The name twisted her heart.

She turned back to look at him as he stood so woodenly in the shadows below. "Yes?" she whispered.

His voice was thick with some kind of grim, unnamed emotion. "Help Sam."

She closed her eyes, unable to bear the surge of emotion. Slowly, she nodded and gathered herself once more. She forced herself to turn and continue her climb up the stairs. And she discovered much to her shock that her eyes were filled with tears.

Chapter Eleven

Truth is a thing that ever I will keep
Unto thylke day in which I creep into
My sepulchre—

—Cartwright

"Wake up, miss! Wake up! There's been a terrible accident! The master's hurt! You must come at once!"

Alexandra thrashed from the tangle of bedclothes and stumbled in the dark toward the door. She had been half-asleep when the pounding came upon the door and with it the cries of Mrs. Penrith.

"My God, what is it?" Alexandra gasped when she saw the bloodless face of the housekeeper nearly hidden behind the large oil lamp she carried.

"Miss, he's hurt. We've sent for the surgeon, but he's asked to see you."

"What happened?" Alexandra asked as she reached for her black shawl draped on a nearby chair.

"It was in the passage, miss. Right at the foot of the stairs.

The parlormaid thought he was speaking to you. She said she heard voices and then a crash. The old iron chandelier snapped right over him. He's got a slice along his arm the length of a sword. Aye, and so much blood I've never seen. 'Tis lucky he wasn't killed altogether."

"How awful . . ." Alexandra followed the woman down the hall, hardly registering the ice-cold stone floors upon her bare feet. All she could think of was the melancholy figure of him as he stood at the foot of the stairs, and the unbidden tears that had stained her face as she left. Even now, there was a deep ache inside her that felt strangely like regret. She'd lain awake for a long time thinking of him. Hating the fact that she had hardly been able to bear leaving him when he had looked almost vulnerable.

"I think the surgeon will be able to put him arights. But he's quite agitated. Called for you, miss. That's right. He called for you and told us to give the parlormaid a good dose of laudanum to cease her crying."

"Is she that fond of his lordship?" Alexandra felt an odd twist inside her heart. It was cheeky to ask such a question, in fact it was downright cutting, but the parlormaid's reaction seemed a bit strong. Ostensibly, it could only be explained by the girl having an unnatural fondness for her master. And as much as Alexandra wanted to deny it, it was something she could understand, for she herself was beginning to feel unnaturally fond of the master also.

"She's a loyal one, that Sally, but not that loyal. No, miss, the foolish girl's not crying about the master. She swears the crashing chandelier was the work of Satan. She says she saw a darkly draped figure at the end of the passage just before his lordship was hurt. Oh dear, it's a wonder we can even keep servants at Cairncross with what goes on around here."

Alexandra felt her heart stop in her chest. A stream of terror filled her veins. "So have the servants seen this figure before?"

"She's been here for years, but the sightings come and go."

Alexandra ran a hand down the back of her neck as if to smooth the rising hackles. She wanted no more talk of draped figures again in her lifetime. "What does his lordship think of this?" she asked quietly.

"His lordship is nigh delirious from all the laudanum, miss. He's in terrible pain; still, he rallied enough to tell us it's all stuff and nonsense. He denies talking to anyone and mumbled something about everyone and their mum seeing black figures in the castle's passage today."

"He's correct in that regard." Alexandra picked up the dragging hem of her nightrail in order to keep up with the housekeeper.

"And he called out for you, miss. For you and only you. Laudanum, pain and all, he still bade us fetch you." The housekeeper turned back and gave her a scrutinizing glance. " 'Tis a strange thing that's happened down there in the hall. Whatever it was, I really think the poor parlormaid was worse for it all. Even with all the tincture of opium, she's still ranting and raving about this figure she's seen."

"How is Lord Newell?" She desperately wanted to change the subject. The parlormaid and her visions were beginning to unnerve her.

"The master's holding his own." Mrs. Penrith gave a nervous little smile. "As bad-tempered as he can be, he's not the type to succumb to a wound."

Featherstone was in the passage when they arrived, holding vigil over the carved double doors that led to Newell's bedchamber. Mrs. Penrith set down the oil lamp on an ancient Chinese war chest and motioned for her to go in.

Featherstone gave Alexandra such a look of utter dislike, it caused her to catch her breath.

As she passed him, he whispered in a voice well beyond the housekeeper's hearing, "She wants to take him with her now and all because of you."

Alexandra looked up at the old butler, unsure of how to defend herself, even unsure of his cryptic remarks. His distinguished, wrinkled face held no malice, only anger and distress.

She passed him without a word and entered Newell's bedchamber.

"God dammit! God dammit, can't you do that more quickly!"

She heard Newell's curse emanating from the room beyond the antechamber. She saw, in gaslit silhouette, his supine figure upon a bed, the surgeon bent over him with needle and thread.

"My lord," she said at the entrance to his bedroom. Newell jerked his head to see who it was and even the surgeon looked up, but only briefly before continuing with his sutures on Newell's thickly muscled upper arm.

"Ah, Miss Benjamin, come in, come in. I've been waiting for you." Newell's tongue was thick with laudanum. Each word seemed to cost him. His eyes, now a brilliant azure blue in a field of bloodshot, blazed with pain and the drug they had given him. The laudanum dose had probably been strong, but not strong enough to bring this man peace.

He nodded to a crewel-work armchair, a vestige from the last century. "Sit down. Give an audience to this butchery." He shot the surgeon a black look. The man's hands began to shake.

She sank into the cushion, unable to take her gaze off of him and the blood. There was an astounding stain of crimson on the sheet and a wretched amount awash on the surgeon's hands. Gently, she said, "I see your temper is in fine form, my lord, even if your arm is not. Undoubtedly, it must mean you'll live."

"If I survive this needlework." He turned to the young doctor. "God dammit, man, aren't you through yet?"

"There, my lord. I'm finished." The man clipped the violet threads that had been previously soaked in gentian. He dabbed the snake-like wound and began wrapping it in bands of bleached gauze. Newell watched on, his glazed expression the portrait of impatience.

When the wound was wrapped, and bloodied sheets discarded, the young surgeon picked up his black satchel and said, "I'll give Mrs. Penrith direction on your care and I'll check on you in the morning." The doctor nodded and Featherstone conveniently appeared to escort him downstairs.

Left alone with Newell, Alexandra felt a small tingle of foreboding. There was nothing to fear, certainly. In his present state, his lordship looked unable to battle a kitten. Still, she watched him cautiously, unsettled by his proximity, and even more unsettled by the warmth she felt at sitting at his bedside.

"Are you in much pain?" she asked softly.

"I've had worse. Tomorrow it'll swell and then I'll really be a bear."

"Remind me to wait a day before I bring you flowers." She smiled slightly.

His eyes met hers and then he smiled too. It was nothing more than a small lift to one corner of his mouth, but she found it an all-consuming captivating moment. Especially since she knew this man gave out smiles about as often as the Borgias gave out alms.

"I'm glad you were still up so that Mrs. Penrith could summon you," he said, easing his head back against the pillow.

"I was certainly not up. She roused me from a dead sleep and well you know it."

He smiled again, then released a chuckle from deep in his chest.

She laughed also. Never in her life had she met a man who possessed this one's gall. When not being a tyrant, at least Newell proved he could be amusing.

"Pour a cup of tea. The maid left a tray on the table near the mahogany bureau. There's a silver flask in the top drawer. Bring that as well."

"Am I now nursemaid as well as governess?" Without waiting for a reply, she went to a black tole table set near his immense bureau and poured a cup of tea. The flask was where he said it would be, in the top drawer, nestled among starched shirts. The drawer smelled of vetiver and soap. She found herself almost longing to touch the pristine shirts, to see if the batiste was as fine as it looked. To feel a further intimacy with this man she knew she must have nothing to do with him.

She quietly closed the drawer and went back to the bed. It finally dawned on her that his room was nothing like she had

imagined. It didn't resemble the downstairs chambers at all.
Newell's bedroom was more like a court than a bedchamber,
she decided first, glancing at the Dark Ages tapestries of indigo,
scarlet and gold that covered all the walls, each portraying one
of the four seasons. The bedstead, a huge tester carved with
oak leaves and acorns, rested in lordly fashion upon a stone
dais. The room had not been modernized as she had supposed.
Ivory-colored tallow candles the thickness of a man's wrist
burned on the walls. Bog-cut peat burned in the grate. If the
parlor stank of new carpet and polish, Newell's chamber
smelled of very old red wine. It was velvet and cobwebs.

"My lord," she said, holding out the cup of tea and the
flask.

He took the flask and waved back the cup of tea. "For you,"
he said and took a deep dram from the flask.

A silence ensued while she sipped her tea and wondered
why exactly he had summoned her. It was not at all proper for
her to be at his side, unchaperoned in his bedchamber, but it
didn't quite feel as wrong as she supposed. Perhaps it was only
because he posed no threat with his fresh wound; still she felt
comfortable by his side, more so now than she had in the
library.

"What do you make of my accident, Miss Benjamin? I
suppose you've heard the gossip." He took another long gulp
from the flask and eased back into the pillows, his handsome
face etched with pain.

"I heard about the parlormaid," she answered softly.

"A flighty creature, that one. Never could abide her, whatever her name is." He kept his eyes closed. The spectacles
were laid upon his bedside table. Off of his face, they were
now only an innocuous contraption of gold wire and glass.

She took a sip of her tea and almost longed for the false
bravado available from his flask. It was the last thing she wanted
to bring up, but she was compelled to speak. Lightly, she began,
"It seems the girl apparently saw a figure much like the one
I saw in the servants' passage."

"So she did."

"Was there a figure?"

He opened his weary eyes and looked at her. She was taken aback by the forsaken soul she saw there. "What would you say, Miss Benjamin, if I told you that there was indeed a figure with me in the hall this night. And that it was this figure and not an accident, that broke the chandelier chain. What would you make of that?"

In a hushed voice, she answered, "I—I would wonder why you've tried to keep it a secret."

"Your thought process, as always, is quite logical. Quite logical. Scientific even." He looked away and a muscle tensed in his jaw. "You don't linger on ghosts and demons, because you're an intelligent woman, Miss Benjamin, and such things are unproven. Instead, you hone in on the facts. And the fact is, I've led all to believe what happened to me was an accident, when it was most definitely not an accident." His words slurred from the laudanum. "Not an accident at all."

"Who did this?" She pressed closer to him, concerned by his mental and physical state.

He bent his head as if he were unspeakably weary. "Not who, but what."

"What then," she whispered, another lump of inexplicable tears in her throat.

"Evil, Miss Benjamin. It was Evil." He raised his head and looked straight at her, his eyes were like beautiful blue stones, brilliant and hard from the pain that wracked him.

Alexandra sat back in her chair, chastened by his answer.

His face, so handsome and taut with implied cruelties, menaced in the gaslight's half-shadow. "You look at me as if you don't believe me, Miss Benjamin."

"You're in pain. You've been given laudanum for that pain."

"Yes. The logical conclusion. I would have expected no less."

Her gaze flickered along the length of his body. A sheet barely covered his hips and she could see the top of his trousers along its edge. He was bare-chested, his broad torso gridded with hard muscles, matted with sweat-glistened tawny hair, a feast for feminine eyes. He was beautiful. Godlike. Thor in all his magnificent fury lying naked from the chest up in his lordship's bedstead.

And enveloping him was this evil he spoke of. A notion that could be as easily harbored in beauty as ugliness.

She licked her dry lips, unnerved that, even drugged as he was, his gaze riveted to her every motion as her tongue flitted over her mouth. "The thing set up in the hall to frighten me was no evil phantom. It was a manufactured thing, as real as the person who dressed it."

"But that is where your logic fails you. Evil doesn't just exist in shadows and in our minds. It is *real,* Miss Benjamin. It exists in many forms and in *any* form. A child, for instance." His eyes grew dark; his mouth hard. "Once that child sees what a banquet evil has spread out before him, he may want to pull up a chair."

"Are you that child?"

He stared at her; their eyes held.

"I could be . . ." he replied, slowly.

A lump caught in her throat. She couldn't believe they were having this conversation, and she couldn't believe she was believing it. "Do you want to do evil things?" She held her breath. He had her mesmerized, trapped in the foreboding terror of his answer.

"There is power in evil. Such power has been used against me." Despite the laudanum, his voice turned hush and diamond-hard. "Never shall it be so again."

She stood, her heart beating furiously in her breast. "It has been used against me also, my lord, but I don't relish being a part of it. I spurn it and I spurn those who would nurture it."

His fingers reached out and touched hers. His caress was warm, gentle, yet his presence was strong, much too strong, overpowering and overwhelming, like the clasp of his hand had been. "You curse yourself with answers like that," he whispered. "Don't you know—it's why I find—I'm drawn to you." His confession was given haltingly, as if by inquisition.

"If we speak in metaphors, my lord, who was this figure of

evil the palormaid saw then? What did it represent?'' Her hand, her lips, trembled with fear.

His hand took hers and pulled her toward him. His face was as solemn as marble. ''I fear the figure seen was that of Miss Pole.''

She stilled. The room grew so quiet, the silence turned into a roar. She knew he must hear the staccato of her heartbeat. ''It couldn't have been. She's never been heard from since the day she left here and some even think she's dead.''

''Exactly.''

''Are you telling me what the parlormaid saw was a ghost?''

''Such things have been called ghosts.''

''This can't be.'' She gave him a wild-eyed stare. Her voice, she realized, was but barely a squeak.

''A good Jew would not believe in ghosts.'' He glanced at her. ''And a good Christian should not believe in them either. Yet they do.''

''The issue is not whether we are good Jews or good Christians. I may believe in them or not. It's that I *don't* believe in them,'' she gasped, not collected enough to understand that he was slowly pulling on her arm, drawing her near him with every second.

''It's your choice. Ever your choice.''

She shook her head. ''Ursula Pole, I was told, disappeared. You yourself cannot even say if she's dead or not. If you believe it was her standing with you in the hall, couldn't it be that she's come back? Could she have disappeared only to find her way back to the castle of late?''

''Are you implying that she may be wandering these hundred rooms of Cairncross undetected?''

''It is a possibility. After all, she was—'' Alexandra clamped her jaws shut. Her thoughts astounded her.

He stared at her, his gaze holding her like a spider's web. ''Yes. Yes.''

''But you don't know what I was about to say,'' she confessed in a small, fearful tone.

''You were about to say that she's here because she was

obsessed with me.'' He raised himself and took her chin in hand. ''Wasn't that what you were about to say?''

''Yes,'' she gasped, unnerved by his abilities to almost read her mind.

''Again your reasoning powers are excellent, Miss Benjamin. You took all the facts and deduced them down to their logical conclusion.''

''You must search the castle. She must be here somewhere. There are so many wings and passages. I know some of the castle is abandoned. A search will turn her up and then you may be rid of her. Finally, forever.''

''Have you asked yourself why she wanted to hurt me?''

She looked down at him, forced to do so by the grip on her chin. His face was very close, impossibly fine, with the veneer of pain on his expression that tortuously compelled her feminine nature. ''I don't know why she would want to hurt you. Perhaps her madness is evil.''

''No,'' he whispered, so close his breath heated her cheek. ''Her madness is not evil, *she* is evil. But she's an obvious evil and so not much to be afraid of. She's but one small drop in a wretched vat of evil that stains our entire beloved earth. She only wants me destroyed now because of you.''

Alexandra shook her head, too stunned and fearful to speak.

He raked his hand down the veil of her dark hair. ''She wants me dead because then I'll be with her . . .''

''But if she's dead and haunting these halls, she's with you every moment,'' she choked out, battling his logic.

''Yes, but now she has you here.'' His breath quickened like the sound of a rasp. His eyes were heavy-lidded, distrustful and yet hungry. A wolf's on the empty moor. ''And she knows that I want—I want—*this*—''

He pulled her down to him and he stared at her, waiting for something—revulsion, hatred, anger. When none of these crossed her face, when none of these saved her, he slowly raised his head until he covered her mouth with his own.

The shock of his lips was like a charge that ran through her entire body, soldering her figure to his lap. She drew back, a violent instinct, but his hand clamped on her nape. He held her head to him and his kiss grew more fierce. Lips that looked hard and merciless, were. She had never liked the shape of her mouth; she'd always felt her lips were too full to make a really pretty mouth, but he seemed to relish how they mirrored his. Where she was soft, he was implacable, where she was vulnerable, he greedily robbed.

His tongue ran like fiery velvet along her front teeth and a sob caught in her throat. Her mind screamed for her to run, to break away, to not even let this man touch her. But as much as he'd once reminded her of Brian, she knew he was not Brian. This kiss was not Brian's. She had always imagined when her wounded heart had healed that if another man tried to kiss her as Brian had, his kiss would be received without passion, without anticipation, participation, nor hope. She would allow it, but only perhaps, and then she had resolved to judge the kiss as mercilessly as Brian had judged her. In her vengeful schemes she had always pictured herself coolly assessing the action. The man's kiss would be evaluated, ridiculed and probably dismissed.

Oh, but she had never counted on this.

This was something else altogether; she knew it as sure as she knew her heart thumped in her chest, as sure as she knew her father could recite the Torah.

And she most definitely knew it when this man, this Right Honorable Lord Newell, blinded her better judgment so completely that when he bade her open her mouth to him, she did it. With a terrified, exquisitely grateful heart, she trembled and let him have it all. Every last taste of her that he could take. Because she wanted him to; because he was blessedly inescapable.

"Oh, God," she cried softly when he broke from her mouth.

Their eyes were only inches apart. She was so close she could smell him, the coppery scent of blood, his blood, the dark, smoldering essence that clung to his skin and now tasted in her mouth. His scent hinted of male biology and yet something else that could never be extracted, distilled and analyzed because it was his and his alone. The elixir of his soul. Her very lips now burned of it.

She turned to flee.

"No," he said, grasping her arm.

"You shouldn't have done this. Not with me," she choked out, her gaze cast to the floor in mortification.

"Why not with you?" he asked, his voice terrible and unforgiving. He took her chin and tilted her head up so she would meet his gaze. His eyes were azure in a field of blazing red. The pain she saw there left her breathless. "What makes you think you're immune to this?"

"I am *above* it," she cried out angrily.

"Yes, yes, I see." He leaned back against the pillows, his face pale and drawn from his wound. Still he did not release her arm. "You with your goodness and your manners and your wide, hurtfilled, spinsterish eyes." He pulled her to him and she was nearly forced to kneel on his mattress. ". . . and you with your soft, pink mouth that could earn a whore's fortune where I've been."

She moaned and felt her cheeks heat with embarrassment. Against her will, her hand went to her lips as if to hide them.

"Don't you see? You *are* above it," he whispered to her, drawing her ever near. "You don't know how you tempt me, prim little Miss Benjamin? I've never had your kind. The very righteousness of your being calls to me and how dearly . . ." he paused and reemphasized the word, ". . . how *dearly* I would like to make that righteousness mine to mold as I wish."

Like an animal that smells danger, she pulled back, suddenly terrified. There was a menace to him she had only glimpsed before. His words, his manner, his inexplicable wanting, left her chilled to the core of her soul. "You've been damaged by her," she whispered harshly. "You and your brother. This isn't you speaking, it's *her*."

"Great minds, perhaps." There was glee in his voice. "But the past is gone and I'm a man of my own destiny now. I speak *my* mind."

Her lips quivered but her voice was strong, her words concise.

"I won't tempt you, for I won't stay long enough. I came here to help Sam, not for," her gaze flickered downward to where he gripped her arm, "this."

"You could have slapped my face and run, but you didn't," he taunted.

She couldn't look at him. She wanted to scream that she had only been attracted to him because he reminded her of Brian, the man she had loved, the man who had broken her heart. But she couldn't because it was a lie. Newell no longer reminded her of Brian and she most assuredly didn't love Brian anymore. There was only one reason why she hadn't protested the kiss and that was because she had wanted it. Newell's handsomeness and deviltry intrigued her. But never again, she reassured herself while she ever so slowly tugged on her arm for him to release it.

"This has all been a mistake," she said evenly, praying she hid her worried gaze. "You've been given drugs . . . remember your wounded arm, my lord. You clearly don't know what you're doing, and I've been party to it only because it surprised me." She quit tugging on her arm and became deathly still. In a soft, angry voice, she said, "So, I bid you release my arm and we shall forget this ever happened."

He stared at her. The stoic line of his mouth turned into stone.

"Please release me," she said. "You mustn't forget your arm, my lord."

The corner of his mouth turned up into a smirk. "Yes, of course, my wound."

"It must hurt terribly. 'Tis no wonder your thinking is not clear."

"Yes." He looked down at his bandaged bicep. Thickly, with a strange note of amusement in his voice, he said, "It's killing me."

A cold wind seemed to pass right before her. She couldn't enjoy the irony in his words. She thought of Ursula Pole and his insane reasons for his accident, and she longed to run away. On winged feet.

"I should get the physician for you." Her gaze left the hand clamped on her arm and moved to his other shoulder. There was a bright line of scarlet banding the top of the pristine linen bandages.

"No. I'll sleep."

"But—you must be in—some pain—" Tears misted her eyes and maddened her. One minute, he frightened her to death, the next, he made her ache with a wild inexplicable sadness.

"I only need sleep."

To Alexandra, Newell seemed to pull away physically as well as in spirit. His mood now seemed almost self-chastising, almost like the way he had appeared in the library after he'd angered and dropped his polished manners.

"Go, Miss Benjamin. I'll spare you such a night again." He shut his eyes and leaned back once more against the mound of pillows. "The laudanum has caused me a weak moment. We'll never speak of such things again."

"Yes, my lord, but what about Ursula Pole? Could you be right? Was it really her figure down in the hall? I feel it warranted to summon the servants for a search—"

The eyes flew open. The grip left her arm. She stepped back as if from a snarling dog.

"What I spoke of here, I will never speak again. I will deny I ever told you such things. This night, this conversation, never happened, do you understand?"

"Yes," she answered, "but, my lord, why—?"

Their gazes locked. She felt her feet go leaden; she felt her arms ache to cover her face as if to ward off nameless, and therefore ever more frightening, fears. Within his eyes, she seemed to glimpse a ravaged, vanishing soul, one whose tenuous hold seemed not destined to remain long. And as much as it terrified her, it moved her. Her heart wrenched inside her.

"You don't believe in ghosts, do you, Alexandra?"

She trembled, but managed a swift shake of her head.

"Then that is why." He closed his eyes and leaned back against the pillows. He spoke no more.

Chapter Twelve

> But I have griefs of other kind,
> Troubles and sorrows more severe;
> Give me to ease my tortured mind,
> Lend to my woes a patient ear;
> And let me, if I may not find
> A friend to help, find one to hear.
> —CRABBE'S HALL OF JUSTICE

"How does a honey bee sound when he's hovering over a flower? Buzzzzzzz . . ." Alexandra scratched at her xylophone.

She looked up at Samuel who still sat stiffly on the garden bench, not watching her exactly, more feeling her presence and giving indication of it with every stiff muscle of his body. It had been ten days since Newell's accident. To divert Sam from his brother's condition, she'd taken him to the garden and slowly introduced her therapy. Afterward, she always made it a point to take him to see Newell. It was the reward for trusting her. Though Newell was in a fever and not much company,

Sam seemed to take comfort in the visit. Their relationship moved quickly.

"Can you make that sound, Sam? Buzzzzz . . . ?" Her face held anticipation.

Sam didn't move. He merely looked at her with the same hooded blue eyes of his brother, then let his attention drift like the puffy clouds in the sky overhead.

She heaved a sigh and cast her weary gaze down to the black watch tartan of the blanket on which she sat. It had been her idea to bring Sam out to the garden. It was imperative they become friends, because only then would he trust her enough for her to begin her work. But now it seemed a pointless endeavor. She was stiff and tired, not only from perching herself amongst the garden grasses in her crinoline, but because she had slept so little in the past nights.

The hours she'd spent tossing within her bedstead, thinking of Newell, left her exhausted. Worse was the imagining of all the spectres that floated within her mind just on the perimeter of her reason.

There were no ghosts. She was positive about that. The very idea was absurd. Even as she walked back to her room that night after leaving the baron's bedchamber, she experienced no fear of phantoms. They existed only in the minds of children and the mentally unstable. No, her only worries and fear centered around Newell. It was feeling and only that, but something made her think he was fighting some sort of invisible battle. Good and evil seemed to war within his heart, taking grip on his soul.

And he was losing. And he had begun to accept his impending surrender.

Their conversation had haunted her like the imaginary shade of Ursula Pole. With distance and the light of morn, she had been positive her disturbed feelings would have settled, but they hadn't. She still wondered why she had let him kiss her. Was it the draw of his physical beauty? Or, worse, was she compelled by the darkness he held inside of him?

She didn't want to know. That was why, at first light of day, she had breakfasted and made her plans to begin with Sam. She was going to throw herself so completely into her work that she was never going to think of Newell again. She would teach Sam to trust and to speak once more, then she would pack her carpetbags and be off to London to begin a new life. And if she did a good enough job with Sam, Lord Newell might even recommend her. She might even be able to make a career of her father's work despite not possessing her father's credentials.

"Sam, come with me," she said, taking the man's hand. She felt him draw back, but she held on tight as if the giant were a toddler and she was trying to cross an avenue clogged with fast-moving carriages. "Let's take a walk along the garden wall and I'm going to tell you a story."

She led him to the mossy stone wall, beginning at the decrepit gate. "Now there once was a boy named John Damien who used to take his brother here to play. His brother's name was Sam." She smiled at him, hiding her despair that he didn't smile back. Running her hand along the crumbling limestone, she said, "They played all kinds of games in this garden, safe within these high stone walls. Sometimes they got into mischief . . ." She bent down and scooped up a handful of green hazelnuts, the first of the season fallen from the old gnarly tree. "But mischief is usually the best kind of play, isn't that so? Even I felt that as a little girl." Her gaze lit upon him, hoping against hope he was interested. To her cautious delight, he was.

"So there were times, just for fun, when John Damien would throw these old hazelnuts just to see what he could hit . . ." She wanted to prod some long lost memories, but she wasn't sure if she was going in the right direction. She knew very little about boys, even less about their mischief and play.

"So they threw these in the direction of the house—" She tossed several with all her might but because of the tightness of her bodice and sleeve she could barely manage to heave the hazelnuts over the stone wall, let alone manage to make them ricochet off the leaded windows of the castle.

All at once, Sam pulled her away. She feared she might have frightened him somehow, but she was quickly convinced this wasn't the case when he led her, hand in hand, to the south garden wall.

He pointed upward. The wall was covered with wisteria vines, so thick even pruning shears would be useless against the tangle.

"What's up there? I can't see it?" she said to him, confused, but deeply heartened that they were finally having some kind of discourse between them, even a silent one.

Sam pointed to the wall. The middle of the wisteria seemed especially thick. From the ground, she could just barely spy a small granite paw perched on the top of the wall.

"Why, there's something behind there. You're right, Sam." She looked around the overgrown garden for a ladder. In the back of her mind, she recalled seeing one abandoned by the last gardener to tend these few acres, but where it lay, she couldn't quite remember.

Sam left her side and disappeared behind a scrub of once-sculpted yews. She couldn't as yet get the connection between her throwing hazelnuts and the stone creature that was hidden behind the wisteria, but she was convinced there was one for Sam, and she would have to wait until he could make it clear.

Sam returned with the small gardener's ladder, dwarfing it with his warrior's height. She took the ladder and set it against the limestone, and hoped he would have the forethought to catch her should she fall. She climbed the ladder and began to pull at the thick, twisted wisteria.

She uncovered two granite paws, one completely green by the moss that grew upon it. It was a dog, it had to be a dog, she mused as she pulled wisteria until her hands were cut and blistered.

A heavy chain carved from the granite soon appeared and it dangled from the creature's neck. She pulled the last bit of heavy vine from the animal's face and almost giggled from the shock of what stared at her. It was a hideous lifesize gargoyle, chained in stone to the top of the garden wall.

A hazelnut sailed past her and bounced off the gargoyle's

salivating mouth. It nicked the top of its canine teeth, then tumbled to the ground.

She twisted on the ladder to see who had thrown the hazelnut. It was Sam. In childish glee he was retrieving nuts from beneath the hazel tree and running toward the gargoyle with the intention of pelting it.

She ducked and admired the man's aim. The gargoyle was hit right between the eyes. Upon closer inspection, she saw that there were hundreds of nicks and scars on the granite where it had been bombarded through the years.

She scurried off the ladder and joined in the fray. She gathered handfuls of hazelnuts and acorns in her skirt and let Sam do his worst. Sam was a good marksman and more than once she laughed as the grotesque animal was bullseyed.

"You used to do this with John Damien, didn't you?" she asked, still laughing from the latest hit of the evil creature's face.

Sam didn't respond. He only pelted the gargoyle more.

She gathered more hazels and acorns. Sam seemed to find enormous release in grapeshoting it.

Then all at once the sound came out.

"Bzzzzz . . ."

Alexandra grew still. She dared not to hope. Her gaze fixed on Sam.

"Bzzzz . . ." he said, pointing to the gargoyle.

Her heart beat frantically with joy. She had finally made him make a sound. He was trying to speak. At last, she had broken through the ice that he'd hid behind.

"Bzzzzeb," he said again.

She wanted to throw her arms around him and hug him, then skip along the garden paths and laugh as if she hadn't a care in the world. He was trying to speak. Her therapy was working. The old Sam was trying to come back.

Quietly, she watched him struggle with the sounds. At first she thought he had finally taken some interest in their earlier lesson and was now imitating the honey bee sound she had made, but as he grew more and more adamant in pointing to the gargoyle she was convinced he was actually trying to tell her something. She listened and a tiny, almost invisible frown marred her forehead.

"Bzzzbb . . ." Sam said in his slow, dense manner.

"Bezzzeb . . ." she repeated, trying desperately to understand what he was saying.

"Beelzzzb . . ." he tried again, pointing desperately to the evil creature salivating stone.

"Beelzebub," she repeated softly, ominously, her eyes widening at Sam's look of relief.

"Beelzebub." She stared at the gargoyle, now hating it.

"Bzzzebub," Sam repeated, throwing another acorn at its snarling face.

"Is that what you and your brother named it? Beelzebub. The name of the Devil?"

Sam nodded and pelted it again. But now he glanced at her distrustfully, as if he were afraid of her again, as if he thought she was angry.

She took two whole handsful of hazelnuts and threw them at the gargoyle as if to prove she was on Sam's side. He watched her solemnly as if judging whether she was good or bad, like that dog had watched her once in the park in London. She suddenly smiled and took his acorns and threw them at the gargoyle too. With her demons exorcised, she suddenly laughed and found that he was smiling at her. At least almost smiling. It was the haunted smile of his brother. A half-smile, that only turned up one corner of the mouth, showing only the half of the man that trusted.

"Beelzebub!" she cried out, hoping he would follow her.

"Beelzebub," he repeated, more schooled this time, watching her like a child watches Punch and Judy.

"You've both managed to keep him out of the garden this way, haven't you?" she said to him.

Sam nodded. And she laughed, now knowing why this place was so wonderful. Because in the silly imaginings of children, the Devil rested on the top of the wall and he couldn't come in. He wasn't invited. The image of the gargoyle perched precariously on the wall of righteousness was so strong, she almost swore that if she tipped the piece of granite into the garden, it would disintegrate before it crumbled to the earth. It couldn't exist in the garden. It was doomed to perish in such a place as this.

She took Sam's hand and squeezed it. The fearful, slow-minded giant seemed to have suddenly diminished. Where before she had seen a towering man who overwhelmed her, now she saw only the young boy he'd once been, simple perhaps, but smart enough to know when the devil came knocking, one didn't answer the door.

"Beelzebub," she whispered, repulsed by the name and yet almost loving it because his fear of it had made him speak.

"Beelzebub," he repeated slowly, the fright gone from his eyes when he looked at her.

She walked in light; he, in darkness. She was born of the permanence of the Old Testament, he was born of the violence of the new. He either had to leave her alone, or risk destroying her.

Damien stood at the garden gate and felt the ecstasy of hearing his brother speak his first words in twenty years. Though she didn't turn and see him, Damien saw her. He gazed at Alexandra for long, still moments, and he knew she was an angel of mercy who'd come to save his brother.

And come to damn him.

He could feel the tautness in his jaw as he clenched his teeth while thinking of her. She was more than any woman he'd ever encountered. More goodness, more intellect, more spirit. The ache to possess one such as her came as a slice to his gut. The want was sharp and pitiless. The challenge to destroy what was so unlike himself was exquisite.

But his decision was right. He must leave. Leave at once. Or he might see the tables reversed. He might grow to need her.

The thought left him with the familiar terror. He didn't trust women. His mother had abandoned her sons practically right out of the birthing bed. And then came Ursula, the one who'd taught him the most about women. There was no getting over his physical desire for them, but the baser they were, the better he liked them. It was a comfortable, one-dimensional need he'd developed for them. The desire had a beginning and a completion, and his kind of women didn't dig deep. They didn't ask for love when all he knew was hate. They didn't ask for light amongst the shadows. They didn't hold out their hands and ask to be the sole guardian of his vulnerabilities.

But he knew this woman would require that. Alexandra Benjamin had already challenged him to find his heart and his soul. And even now though he shouted silently that there was none to find, the expression he pictured in her eyes denied it.

So he had to go away. The night in his bedchamber when she'd come to him haunted him as much as a ghost. To his shock, he'd found he'd come to like her, respect her. But worst of all, he was attracted to her. And he knew no gentleness toward women where there was attraction. In bed, he'd developed a preference for reciprocal need and reciprocal violence. He'd always done his best to stay away from women like Alexandra, gentlewomen who were easily undone by brutality. But it really wasn't for their own good that he'd stayed away, it was more for his own. No woman was going to make him lay open his heart. Because he didn't know what frightened him more: the fact that he might confirm as he suspected that his heart was black and empty; or that there still might be in it a tiny live ember of the boy he used to be, the one who loved and wanted love in return. It sickened him to think of vulnerability that might still be there, buried deep inside him, just waiting for a woman to come and give it the agony of a final execution.

No, he told himself as he looked at his brother, who was doing his best to smile at Alexandra. He was going to leave that woman alone, and to do that, he was going to depart Cairncross.

Because if he stayed, he might grow too fond of Alexandra

Benjamin. And in order to protect himself, he might be forced to take her with him on his walk through shadows.

A noise made Alexandra turn her head. Far behind them at the gate, Newell stood watching them. He appeared like a ghost of his formerly brawny self. His face was drawn and pale. His arm was limp by his side, and all the finery of his black greatcoat couldn't hide the fact that it seemed to cause him silent agony. But even from a distance she could see the light in his face. The openness. Just by his expression, she knew he'd heard Sam speak.

"My lord," she called to him, hesitant to go running to him and share in his joy, especially after their disastrous encounter almost a fortnight before.

Newell nodded and stared at her for a long moment.

Then he disappeared, ducking behind the gate.

In a flash of understanding, she suddenly realized he had on traveling clothes, and she found herself running to him after all.

She crossed the garden in all speed, the urge to see him growing stronger with every step. His promise that he would never again tell her of ghosts and the darkness surrounding the castle disturbed her now more than ever. He was keeping that promise, for he was returning to London. She knew it.

She picked up her skirts and fled toward the bailey and the waiting coach. She barely cleared the barbican before the coach door was closed by Featherstone. The carriage rolled by, its anonymous ruby velvet window shades looking down upon her figure as if she were merely a street waif and its occupant a king.

"Miss, his lordship has returned to London. He left you instructions. Shall I bring them to you in the garden?" Featherstone peered down at her in the usual manner, but some of the malevolence was gone from his lined face. It seemed he trusted her a bit more now that she'd been at the castle a while.

She suddenly wondered what Ursula Pole had done to him to make him such a suspicious old man.

"Yes. Bring it to me in the garden. I left Sam there." She took one last look at the departing carriage. The glossy black Newell landau was cutting through one of the distant cairns, a trail of Yorkshire dust the only memory. She wondered when she would see John Damien Newell again. And a strange ache lay heavy within her heart at the thought that it might be never.

23 June 58

My dearest Miss Benjamin,

It should be of no surprise to you that I chose to return to London. I cannot help you with Sam, indeed I find I may be a hindrance. I know you can help him. He will speak again if one is patient and kind. You are both.

I leave Sam to you and to this place. It is unfortunate to keep him here, perhaps, and yet the castle is the only home his simple mind can comprehend. He is trapped in childhood. Therefore, I cannot wrench him from his home for fear of what it may do to him.

We may never see each other again, Miss Benjamin. Truly, I believe I would prefer it. But I want you to remember, whenever you should think of me: Here too virtue has its reward.

Yours in faith,
Damien

She felt a wetness on her cheeks and realized that tears were streaming down her face. The garden that had once seemed so overgrown and happy, now appeared to be only empty and unkempt. The ground grew cold beneath the blanket where she had returned to read Newell's letter.

He had left. He didn't want to see her again. It felt as if he had taken her heart and twisted it until it was wrung dry of its life's blood. She had let him kiss her, she had wanted him to kiss her, now he had left her. He'd chosen to do without her as Brian had.

A hand came to rest on her shoulder. She looked up and found Sam touching her, his face a mask of awe in the presence of her tears.

She patted his hand and thought how much he looked like his brother. In his finely-tailored forest green corduroy trousers and black checked jacket he could almost pass as Newell's twin.

But he was anything but Newell's double. Especially as he leaned down to her and fingered the tears on her cheeks as if they were as rare as diamonds.

"Did she never cry?" The question was pointless. Alexandra didn't expect an answer, because she already suspected Ursula Pole was too heartless to shed tears.

"Your brother has returned to London." She retrieved her hankie from her sleeve and patted her face and nose. "He thinks it best that we work without interruption, and I agree." She blew her nose and hated the way it sounded. No doubt, Newell thought her nose too large to be ladylike. Her curly brown hair was probably something he was deriding even now, its color and the incompetent manner in which she attempted to control it.

Her insides throbbed and then turned to ice. No, she wouldn't punish herself as she had done when Brian had first rejected her. She was good enough, for anyone, she told herself silently, because she was the daughter of a man who had helped the deaf speak. She was the daughter of a man who had loved his wife. She was the daughter of a man who knew compassion and honor. She was staying at this Godforsaken place to help the man who stood beside her now. Oh, yes, she was good enough and the world be damned.

"How silly I am," she said lightly, scooping up the blanket and rising. "Now let's get back to where we were. I must tell you, Samuel, if you continue along in this manner, we'll have you talking before December. Then you and . . ." She paused. "You and his lordship will celebrate a most joyous Christmas."

"Dam'en," the man uttered, looking forlornly at the abandoned gate.

"He'll be back. Don't you worry. He loves you, Sam." She took the giant's hand and said quietly, "I'll do my work and when I'm finished, he'll be back."

"I love . . ." Sam said, tears coming to his blue eyes.

"Yes. Love . . ." she whispered, unable to finish.

Alexandra took the numerous steps to her room as if there were a guillotine waiting for her at the top. She'd had tea with Sam in the drawing room and while it had been amicable, there had been a pall over them. Newell had returned to London. All the household was buzzing about his quick exit from Cairncross, particularly in light of his accident just ten days before. It was too early for him to travel, Mrs. Penrith moaned, while she instructed the parlormaid to bring in the tea tray.

Samuel already missed him. She could see it in his glum, innocent face. It was an altogether unhappy situation; Newell could not stand to be at Cairncross and his brother could not comprehend any other home but the castle. He should stay beside his brother, she thought, watching Sam's melancholy face, remembering how he had searched and searched the bailey for signs of the Newell landau. It broke her heart to see Sam search for his brother who wasn't there, but she knew until John Damien had made his peace with the past, he would never choose to stay at Cairncross long.

Her mind instructed her that it was for the best. With his talk of ghosts and evil, John Damien Newell had proved he was not the kind of man a woman took for a beau. Their social positions made it virtually impossible for a union. This time she was not so naive to believe affection and a midnight kiss could lead to anything desirable.

Yet her thoughts remained captive to him even now that he'd departed. She hated to admit it, but she mourned his absence as much as Sam did. The night when she'd gone to his bedchamber—and even before that, in the library—she sensed he'd needed her, but she hadn't understood why. Now she had the strange suspicion that he had left Cairncross to spare her. Her conflict now was that she'd discovered she might not want sparing. She wanted his presence, even if that meant discovering demons.

Depressed and melancholy, she arrived at her landing. The door to her room was open and she thought the chambermaid might be in there, but when she got to the threshold, the room was empty. The hearth was cold; Mary had not been up to see that it was stoked.

From where she stood, she looked around the room at how the fading summer light painted it. The room seemed to glow in an ethereal mist. Instinctively, she turned toward the schoolroom. The glow spilled from there. The door had been left open again and now long lines of light were thrown in from the schoolroom's louvered shutters.

It wasn't Sam who had been in there, she was sure of that at least.

Tossing her shawl on the bed, she made her way to the schoolroom door. It wasn't like her to be afraid, but she was different now. The woman who'd first arrived at Cairncross only days before hadn't seen that monstrous contraption dressed up in the dark hallway belowstairs. Hadn't glimpsed the evil in it. Even now all the explanation of dressmaker's forms and artlessly draped shawl fell on deaf ears.

A tiny sliver of cold trailed down her spine as she stepped into the schoolroom. The place had been newly cleaned again, by, no doubt, some unfortunate scullery maid who hadn't the position to protest. The room seemed almost pleasant with the late sun streaming in and the walnut and mahogany gleaming with a fresh application of beeswax.

Still, it was not a pleasant room. And there was no way to explain it. Perhaps it had been the carpenters who first cursed this place. Alexandra always felt that the floor in the schoolroom was not quite even with the rest of the floors in the castle. The floorboards seemed to slant in odd levels that were not quite visible to the eye. Whenever she walked into the room, she had a terrible vertigo. The floor seemed to fall away and come up to meet her at surprising angles. It left her feeling unbalanced. It left her vulnerable. She longed to leave the room now, and looking around, she reassured herself twice that nothing was wrong, that everything was in its place except that some uninformed servant had left the door ajar.

But then she saw what had made her pause and peruse the room twice. She saw what was wrong and why staring at the room tickled and disturbed the edge of her thoughts. She stared at the bookcase opposite her, inexplicably frightened by what she saw.

Ivanhoe was gone.

Chapter
Thirteen

By St. Dunstan, this is no Jewess, but an angel from heaven . . .
          —On Rebecca, from IVANHOE

Alexandra still did not believe in ghosts. Even with the disappearance of *Ivanhoe,* she refused to believe in the supernatural. There was earthly evidence to account for any occurrence, even what was going on around Cairncross. The only thing she could not reconcile with herself was the book. *Ivanhoe.* It meant so much to her, it stood for everything that had molded her into the person she'd become. Rebecca's ache was her ache, but no one could possibly know that. Not even Mary or her father had known what *Ivanhoe* had meant, had come to mean, to her.

Coincidence did not happen in science. But coincidence, she told herself time and time again whenever she felt that small, icy panic invade her soul, had happened here.

Alexandra's work with Sam progressed from their first breakthrough in the garden and she looked forward to their lessons almost as much as he seemed to now. Sam grew to trust her with every meeting and once, when Alexandra had just awakened, she heard shuffling outside her bedchamber door. When she opened it, she found a bouquet of limp nasturtiums tied together with a length of hemp. She saw Sam at tea and she showed him the flowers, then she kissed him on the cheek. Sam simply stared at her as if he'd never seen such a creature as she in all his life. Indeed, he probably had not.

There was one incident—if Newell were to return, Alexandra knew she'd be obliged to tell him about it. The occurrence happened one night when a storm raged across the moorland like a scrubbrush in the hands of an overly enthusiastic scullery maid. Alexandra had trouble sleeping, her thoughts still clung to Newell. She decided to go downstairs and find a volume in the library. Naturally, there were books in the schoolroom she could have chosen from—all the Waverley novels were there, except *Ivanhoe,* of course—however, she could never bring herself to enter the schoolroom since she had discovered the novel missing, and that particular night, when she was restless, her mind encased with thoughts of a bleak future, she was assuredly not going to venture into the old schoolroom.

She descended the main staircase, chamberstick in hand, for the gas was turned low and the servants abed. Belowstairs she could still hear the murmurs of the undermaids as they finished polishing the brass. A servant appeared at the landing below and began to climb the stair. At first Alexandra thought nothing of her. There seemed to be thousands of women in the castle from scullery maids and undermaids to parlormaids and assistant housekeepers. This one appeared no different in her black serge dress. But something intangible, instinctive, even primeval, made Alexandra stop on the stair tread and look at the woman.

She passed Alexandra without incident. Only in hindsight did Alexandra recall that the woman wore no kind of cap indicating her position in the household, nor did she bother to answer Alexandra's greeting, a serious infraction considering the governess was even higher in position than the housekeeper. But at the time, Alexandra didn't notice these things. She was instead struck by the woman's face. The servant was sublimely beautiful, her face sculpted as if from marble, and yet it possessed a complete stillness that Alexandra had never seen before. Even her eyes held no brilliance. Instead they were as flat as chalk, and without focus; they seemed sightless, or worse, all-seeing. They turned to Alexandra only once, and Alexandra knew she would never forget it. As they passed on the stair, the woman ignored her greeting, and Alexandra felt those vacant, omniscient, horrible eyes upon her. She found herself leaning back against the banister, suddenly unsure, as a doe is unsure when it hears a twig snap in the glade. Her feet seemed to freeze to the treads; she discovered that she was suddenly too afraid to follow the woman and ask who she was. Alexandra could only look up at her as she climbed the stairs and disappeared into the shadows above.

And that was when she noticed the woman's hair was red.

She never told Mary about her. The next day, she blithely inquired through Featherstone if there were any female servants with red hair. As it turned out, there were two, and Alexandra knew both of them. Neither of them was the woman on the stair.

"You've been here almost two months now." Mrs. Penrith left the statement hanging in the air like a net. She poured from a silver teapot and handed the china cup to Alexandra. In the weeks the master was gone, the two women had forged a tentative friendship, which Alexandra was grateful for in the loneliness of Cairncross.

"Sometimes it feels like I've known this place only a few days, other times . . ." Alexandra didn't finish. The answer involved her continued thoughts of Newell and she saw no point in revealing them to herself or the housekeeper.

"I thought it would go worse than it has." Mrs. Penrith smiled. The servant was definitely thawing toward the new governess. "You've been very good for Sam. I think our boy has developed a certain fondness for you."

"It's wonderful to watch him come to life, to find out some

of his feelings. I expect he'll be speaking quite well before Christmas. I shall hate to leave him."

"Oh, but you won't be leaving us, miss. So soon?"

"I'm not really here as governess, you know. Lord Newell hired me to regain Samuel's speech. When he's done that, my job here'll be done." Alexandra took a sip of her tea and stared pensively at the changing oak outside Mrs. Penrith's window. Already the leaves were yellowing. Time was passing.

"Does his lordship really believe such a quick departure is prudent?" Mrs. Penrith asked, still wearing the surprise on her face.

"I don't believe I'll be seeing Lord Newell again to consult him. I imagine I'll be gone before he returns." Once she spoke the words, she felt a hollowness settle inside her. Already, she'd inquired about several advertisements and one answer had come that morning. She'd be calling on her first prospective employer January 13th. This time with the responsibility of acting as a real governess. She hated to think about it.

"Really, I think Sam will take more than that. And you've gotten along so well here. We've had no mischief at all from—" Mrs. Penrith abruptly stopped.

"From Miss Pole?" Alexandra took a studied sip of her tea, unsure how to broach the subject of the woman on the stair. "I think I saw her, you know. At least, I saw a woman who could have been her twenty years ago. The woman I saw had no gray hair or lines on her face, so it seems unlikely it was truly the old governess. Still—"

"You—you—saw her?" Mrs. Penrith turned white.

"Yes. On the stair."

"Why didn't you say something about this before now?" The housekeeper's tone was sharp.

"It took me some time to conclude the woman was no servant. I thought about penning a note to Lord Newell, thinking I'd give him proof that she'd come back to the castle, but I could find none. Besides, I suspect he already knows what's going on around here. If Ursula in her madness has somehow made her way back here and has gotten into the castle, then she could be the one causing all the mischief, now couldn't she?"

"Oh, miss . . . oh, miss . . ." Mrs. Penrith keened.

"I'd have spoken of this before now but I saw no point in frightening everyone, especially since I'm convinced we'd never find her. With all the rooms to hide in, she's got plenty of choices. Why, she's probably coming and going at will, and if there's a nefarious servant helping her do it, then finding her will be virtually impossible. Of that, I'm certain."

"But she's dead, miss. She's dead. We all believe it. She *must* be dead," the housekeeper cried. "And wouldn't the woman have gotten her things if she'd come back? I don't know what's in the trunk, but I know it was all her worldly possessions. Wouldn't she take them back if she could?"

"The woman I saw was no ghost. I could have reached my hand out and touched her." Alexandra put down her teacup. It disturbed her, even frightened her, this focus on the otherworld. Evil penetrated Ursula Pole's soul, but the woman hadn't been a ghost twenty years ago when she was sadistically tutoring her charges, and she hadn't been a ghost when Alexandra had shrunk away from her on the stair. She would never be able to reconcile herself with this ghost business because her scientific mind rebelled every time.

"What do you know of ghosts, miss?" Mrs. Penrith's voice was but a scratchy sound emanating from her throat.

"I know what anyone knows," Alexandra said defensively.

"And you know for certain that you can't touch them? That you can't sit down to tea with one and hand them a buttered scone?"

"What is your point, Mrs. Penrith?"

"My point is that you don't know what you saw on the stair. If you believe it was Ursula Pole, then I say she could have been a ghost as easily as she could have been real and intrigued her way into the household."

"I almost believe you want her to be a ghost. It's easier to explain away her being in the castle, now isn't it? You can make excuses for the fact that no one has ever searched this place and looked for her. She possessed a cruel and twisted mind, Mrs. Penrith. I believe she's capable of sneaking around Cairncross and frightening people. Especially when that keeps her closer to him.''

"You mean John Damien?"

Alexandra didn't want to answer. It pained her that she might be encouraging servant's gossip, but there was no point in making up a fib now. "I understand she was in love with him, even though he was hardly a man while in her charge."

"She did love him, miss, but no one would desire such a love. It was wrought of possession and death. If he hadn't been away when she disappeared, I believe he might have killed her. She would have forced him to."

"No one has ever told me the exact story of his banishment so long ago." Alexandra waited, hoping the housekeeper would talk.

"It's an ugly story, Miss Benjamin," the woman answered stiffly, her mouth a serious taut line of ivory one shade darker than her skin. "It was scandal, pure and simple. They were in the stable, and they were doing things they should not have done. Oh, I'll believe until I'm dead and turned to dust that *she* made him do what he was caught doing. But a feeling is no defense when a woman has cried rape."

"Rape?" Alexandra was sickened. In a small voice, she said, "I had hoped it would be something less severe."

"I'm telling you facts, miss, facts any Yorkshireman would know. John Damien and Ursula Pole were sharing an intimacy when the stablemaster discovered them. The old Lord Newell had no choice but to banish his son. Miss Pole was his cousin, you know, and there was no one to defend John Damien. He was big for his age. He could have forced her."

The housekeeper heaved a sigh. "As with any story of right and wrong there are two sides to it. Some say he raped her, then killed her for crying rape. But I sided with his lordship. The woman forced *him* and not the other way around, and when she was caught, she cried rape to keep her respectability. I don't know why she disappeared, but I don't think Lord

Newell had anything to do with it. He was gone the night before she disappeared. You see, I still side with him now though he's grown to be a man who sometimes frightens me with the shadows that live inside him. Still, I fancy that I understand him a bit. Though just a bit.''

''If you will but tell me the facts, tell me this: why has he now returned to Cairncross? And why do they call him lord if he was banished as the older son?''

''There was only Sam left. The former Lord and Lady Newell were shallow creatures and filled with vice. They did what was convenient and what was expected and no more. Never any more. When there was trouble, they banished him, as they felt they must, given the scandal. When Lord Newell died in Paris only last year, it was stated in his will that his estate and title revert to his eldest son. A son he had not seen nor cared about for twenty years. But again, it was convenient and expected. The estate is entailed, so now John Damien owns all title and all, even as he despises it.''

Mrs. Penrith stared at Alexandra, as if she were gathering the words to explain the unexplainable. ''You must understand this, too, Miss Benjamin. There wasn't always so much tragedy here. Before Ursula Pole arrived, I believe the boys were almost happy. Yes, they yearned for their parents, John Damien in particular for he had the mind to understand they were much too absent, but with that aside, the boys got along here pretty well. They had their moorland in which to ride, the garden in which to play, and the servants took pity on them, being parentless and all, and they fed them downstairs in the kitchen with the rest of the families belowstairs. They got along right nicely, if I do say so, until that creature ruined their lives.''

''Do you think he still yearns for his boyhood?'' Alexandra looked at her, desperate to understand even one small facet of Newell's enigmatic character.

''I think the happy memories make him hold onto all this, but there's more to it than that. I believe he wants to change this castle from the sad place that it is. He thought he could do it with the new decorating, the drapery and carpet, but he'd found it hasn't changed. Oh, the veneer may be a different color and not so old, but the castle's the same, and it will always be the same as long as she is trapped here and will not leave." She leaned over and touched Alexandra's hand. "This castle stands for everything evil. He never seems to want to stay here and if not for Sam I believe he'd never come here. Now I believe he wants to win over this castle or lose to it. And that's what frightens me. Indeed, that's what terrifies me."

Slowly, as if the words came from nowhere and not her own mouth, Alexandra said, "The castle is winning."

"I fear it is," the housekeeper answered evenly.

"Because there's a part of him that wants the castle to win. I think I saw that the night of his accident."

"He's drunk too deeply of bad wine, miss. It taints his blood with its evil. If he were only more innocent, but that was taken away years ago."

"What will help him?" Alexandra waited for the answer.

"I don't know, miss. There's no one to understand him. There's no one who would dare try."

I would dare try, she said silently, suddenly overwhelmed with the need to bring him from London. She wanted him back at Cairncross. She wanted to see his face by the gaslight and take off his spectacles and touch his eyelids with the gentleness of her fingers. That much and more she had fantasized about. Now she burned to do it with all her soul.

The housekeeper watched her. Slowly, she said, "But even if someone could help him, Ursula would see him dead first. And you know that as well as I know it."

Alexandra couldn't deny it. She found her tongue anyway. "He's stronger than that lunatic and you know it. He's only tolerated this mischief because he's got better things to do with his time and most of it's spent in London. Besides, the mischief hasn't been that bad. Not yet."

"And what about his lordship's arm?" Mrs. Penrith asked.

Alexandra had no quick answer for it. Instead, she replied, "If he wants her gone, he will make her go. I know it. He's that strong."

''Then someone must make him want her gone. Don't you see the problem here? He's too accepting of the evil around him. He's too complacent.'' The housekeeper looked at her oddly, as if interpreting the sparkle in her eyes and the blush on her cheeks as something other than a result of her brisk walk on the moors before tea. ''Someone must make him want her gone. Someone.''

A pain settled in Alexandra's chest. ''The only person who can make him do that, Mrs. Penrith, is someone he loves. That is the prerequisite, and I fear that is something a governess cannot accomplish.''

''We'll see.'' Mrs. Penrith stared at Alexandra across the tea table as if wishing dreams could come true. ''We'll see,'' she murmured again, this time softly.

The lord of Cairncross took his brandy in the library of his London town house precisely at ten. There were nights when he was not at home; Lady Chester would be having a soiree, or a reception had been planned at Buckingham. It was well known that Victoria approved of the new baron, and also as well known that Albert did not.

But tonight Lord Cairncross was in; for some reason, Newell felt no impulse to venture to the docks. Abbey no longer seemed to pull at him. For some reason, one he didn't want to think about, he craved quiet tonight instead of violence. Silence instead of the snap of the lash. Abbey was right for him. He knew it. Like two species who recognize their kind in a mad wilderness, he understood her and she him. But there was no longer the need. And where there was no need, there was nothing to gain. The thrill would be flat and repetitive. No challenge.

Not like the challenge of that governess.

Little Miss Benjamin. He must stay away from her. He had to stay away, he thought, becoming lost in the swirling brandy in his glass. She was no toy. She was a woman of flesh and blood, one who nursed her aching heart right in front of everyone just by the expression in her eyes.

He wondered who the man was. There was a diabolical desire in him to go and look the chap up. He wanted to feast his eyes on the soul who had tossed aside Alexandra Benjamin in all her kind-hearted womanliness and cruelly cast her to the wind. *His* wind.

He hated that man, he decided. Hated him with the same force that he worshipped him. The thought that she had wept over some weak-kneed, impotent colleague made his tongue thick with disgust, and yet, his heart still soared. She might have married him. If the bloke had had the moral fabric that Alexandra had, he would have married her, and then the baron would never have set eyes on her.

Yes, he worshipped that man. He'd given him a girl who was just like the garden at Cairncross, pretty and walled-off. And because one couldn't see beyond the garden walls, it left one with the intense desire to climb the barriers and discover the garden within. The Eden that men dreamed about.

She was Eve, all womanhood. And as much as he wanted to take her hand and walk with her through paradise, he still found himself pulling back. He was right to leave her. She upset the balance. She made him have a conscience. So he must try not to think of her; he must leave her alone. Let her go to some weak soul who'd never known a moment of passion, but he must not touch her. He was not Adam. No indeed. He'd made his choices long ago, and it felt good to wield the power that a man with no conscience had.

He was the serpent.

Chapter
Fourteen

"There, Sam, now can you tell me what this is?" Alexandra scooped up a handful of pebbles that lined the walks around Cairncross. It was a temperate day, with just enough of the crisp air of autumn to make for an invigorating walk.

She had found Sam in the garden and now together they walked toward the moors while she thought of games to make him speak.

"Stones. Stones," he repeated, towering at her side while he watched her every move like a falcon on his perch.

"Very good." She rewarded him with a smile, struck by how much he yearned for her approval. It still could tie her heart in knots. "Now what is this?" She picked up her skirts and ran to a nearby oak, wrapping her arms around it.

He followed, much like a dog at her heels. Ever faithful. "A tree," he uttered, his tongue thick and unmanageable.

"Excellent, excellent." She looked around for more things, but the moorland past the castle was only heather and bracken and the occasional crag that rose up from the landscape like an altar to the gods. Too big and difficult to explain.

She looked down at her dress. Gingerly, she lowered herself and sat beneath the oak. "What am I wearing, Sam?"

"Preddy dress," he said, staring down at her like a giant.

"Thank you." She pointed to his boots. "What are you wearing on your feet?"

"Shoes," he offered.

"They are boots. Black boots. Much the same as Lord Newell has, I imagine." She paused. She hadn't meant to speak of Damien, but the words just came out. "Can you say black boots, Sam?"

"Blaaack boots," he repeated, heartbreakingly anxious to please.

She held out one of her black leather gloves. "And what is this?"

He looked down at the glove for a long moment. She thought to prompt him but suddenly she realized that he wasn't at a loss for words, he was frightened.

She looked down at her glove. It was innocuous enough, just a small, inexpensive black leather glove that any merchant might carry. But she had the feeling he wasn't even seeing her glove. He was seeing other gloves. The strange orange and green gloves Ursula Pole had.

"Sam?" Her voice sounded tiny and vulnerable. She stared up at him while still sitting nearly at his feet. With his back to the sun, she saw him only in silhouette, and his very blankness gave her a moment of unease. It never occurred to her before to find Sam threatening, but now as he towered over her, a very powerful emotion suddenly triggered like a pistol, and she was afraid.

A part of her wanted to get to the root of the trouble. She longed to rip away the curtains that hid Cairncross's devils and expose them once and for all.

But alone with Sam on the edges of lonely moorland, she wasn't sure if now was the time. Her cautious, "scientific mind," as Newell had called it, thought better of rousing dormant fears when there was no one near to help her should things go awry.

"We're finished for today, Sam. Let's return to the castle, shall we? I believe it's well past time for luncheon." She made a big play of taking off her gloves and putting them away inside her pockets as if the symbolism would make him overcome his fear. When at last the gloves were out of sight, she raised her bare hand and said, "Take it, Sam, and help me to my feet, will you please?"

She kept her hand up. He didn't seem to understand the gesture. She had the longest time wondering if she should just take his hand or lower hers. In the end, she grabbed his and held onto him in order to get to her feet.

"Sam, you've done so well today," she said lightly, beginning the walk home. "In fact much better than I've expected. What would you say to my asking Featherstone to write to your brother our progress and we could summon him home here for next week. Would that be agreeable to you?"

"Where's Dam'en?" the giant uttered, still standing beneath the oak tree.

"Damien?" she whispered, unnerved by the angry stare he gave her.

"Where's Dam'en?"

"Don't you remember? He left for London." She stopped along the path and waited for him to follow. He didn't. He simply stood beneath the oak and stared at her as if she were Beelzebub.

"Want Dam'en," he cried out, a child's wail of despair.

"Damien will be here soon, Sam, you must believe it." She stood motionless, trapped by the awful feeling that as he looked at her, he was seeing someone else. He was seeing *her*.

"You hurt Dam'en. Where is he?" he moaned.

"He's fine. He's in London. He'll be here to see you soon."

"Dam'en!" he cried out in inexpressible agony.

"Why do you think I've hurt Damien?" She wanted to comfort him, to throw her arms around him and hold him until he felt safe again. He seemed so alone and afraid standing there beneath the oak, but she was afraid herself. Sam was so big.

Twice her size. If he became uncontrollable, she wouldn't be able to do anything but helplessly let it happen.

"You take him away. I want him back!" He stepped toward her and for the first time she knew what it must feel like to be cornered by a lion.

"No, Sam, it's me, me, Alexandra, not her. I'm not Miss Pole." Her eyes must have said volumes, because he locked gazes with her, and suddenly he was pacified. Understanding somehow dawned in the ever-deep dimness of his mind and he was finally able to grasp the situation. He saw who stood before him.

"Do you see now? It's Miss Benjamin." She felt her limbs go weak with relief.

"I scared."

I scared too, she thought as she looked up at his great height. It almost surprised her how much better he spoke when he was angry. "There's nothing to be afraid of Sam. Nobody's going to hurt you again. You just make her go away. Tell her to go away."

"She's here," he said, shaking his head. "Always here."

Alexandra stared at him, her brow furrowed with concern. "What do you mean she's here?"

"Always here."

"You've seen her?" She turned around and searched the moor. But there was no one there. No one visible at the castle and no human figure marring the moors.

She turned her attention back to Sam. He stood next to her, shoulders hunched in the breeze, his eyes downcast as if he were fearful or contrite.

"Do you see her, Sam? Is she still here at the castle doing bad things?"

"Bad things. Very bad," he mumbled.

Alexandra stared so long she thought she might have drilled a hole into him. The dilemma she faced was like crossing a tightrope; one wrong move and she might tumble Sam into permanent muteness. But she would never have a better chance to get to the bottom of his troubles if she didn't take her chance now.

Without regard to herself, she put her arms around him and held herself to him. He didn't move, and yet he didn't quite accept it. He merely stood there on the path with her and allowed her to hug him perhaps because he'd rarely if ever had such a thing before.

"Sam," she whispered, taking hold of his big, frightfully strong hand, "you know I'm your friend. I would never ever hurt you, Sam, you know that. Is she at the castle now? Do you know where she stays?"

His eyes were afraid and mournful. "My room," he said.

"Everything is prepared, my lord. Her Grace, the duchess, has favorably replied and the soiree is all arranged. If I may say so, your lordship, I do believe this will be what is called a social triumph." The butler bowed and led Newell to the library, placing a stack of replies on the enormous mahogany partners' desk that fronted the bay of windows.

Newell watched Matthewsby leave, then he sauntered to the desk and thumbed through the numerous replies. It was indeed a social triumph. There wasn't a refusal among them. He supposed all and sundry wanted to meet the newest Lord Cairncross, perhaps to compare him to his father, but probably to assuage their curiosity. Even he knew he'd created a sensation. No one had ever discovered where the lord's eldest son had been all these years of his banishment. There was talk he'd traveled with Perry to Japan, there was also the ridiculous rumor that he'd spent years in Italy romancing a beautiful countess. Byron, it seemed, was still in these people's heads.

They didn't know that when an eldest son is banished, he goes to London. He finds himself in the poorest part of the city because being the next in line for a place in the House of Lords has not taught him a skill to keep his belly filled. He'd gone to Wapping and gained work as a stevedore on the docks. There he'd made his first ha'penny, and there he'd made several more as owner of the White Bear, the most notorious alehouse in London. More money passed under the table than over it. He never dealt in flesh but in everything else, the White Bear was the well from which all sin flowed. Extortion was not beneath him, nor was outright robbery, as long as the blunt came in. And it had until he could count himself among the rich.

Now he possessed more lands and money than he knew what to do with. The baron—as he had always called his father—had died only last year, leaving him, in a final ironic moment, all his estate. The baron had ruined his son's life at the age of fourteen, then he had salvaged it at thirty-four, all without ever knowing it had been ruined long ago by neglect, and salvaged long ago with the money of his own making.

Damien sat down at his desk and gazed out the window. The cherry trees were just beginning to yellow from an early September frost. He'd been gone from Cairncross for more than a month.

Restless, he rose and put his hands against the mantel while he stared at the lit hearth. Damien's *Inferno,* he thought sarcastically. The idea left him in a foul temper, and he then resumed pacing his library like a wounded bear, uncomfortable in the leather club chairs, too bored with the unread tomes stacked by his chair.

He had to quit thinking about going back. He had to quit thinking about her.

She was what he feared.

He'd gone as far as the train station in his desire to return to Cairncross, but even then, circumstances drove him back. A lone woman and child had waited on the platform, their faces slightly afraid as they watched all the strangers milling about, waiting for the train from Brighton. There was nothing remarkable about them. Their clothes were once fine, but now they were patched and mended as many working-class wardrobes were. The woman held her little girl's hand tight in the crowd so there wouldn't be a chance of losing sight of her. The child spied him watching them while the mother seemed engrossed in discovering sight of the train miles down the tracks and her blue, distrustful gaze lit upon him like St. Peter's.

He'd almost flinched. But then the train arrived, the one now headed to York, and the child was distracted. Mesmerized, he found he couldn't board the train until he made sure that whoever they were waiting for had arrived. Passenger after passenger passed them by without the slightest chord of recognition. A worry frown began to crease the woman's forehead and the little girl appeared almost ready to cry. But finally, a male voice called out from the crowd. A young man in mended trousers and a clerk's jacket shouted to them from the window of the train. The little girl's face cracked open wide with a smile, beaming just like sunshine. The man disembarked and she cried out in her little girl voice, "Father! Father!"

The man swooped her up in his arm, and saved the other arm for the woman who now looked fifteen years younger. He bussed them both on the cheeks and walked away with them, leaving Damien alone on the platform. The ticket in his hand unused.

Yes, they terrified him. These honorable women who loved their husbands and hugged their children. The ones that made life worth living.

He shut his eyes, not wanting to think of Alexandra Benjamin, and yet, he was compelled to do it, as he was compelled to think of Sam.

His brother, the intractable goodness. He'd agonized about Sam ever since his father had banished him. Twenty long years of suffering, wondering, imagining what had happened to the only person that had ever mattered to him. For twenty years, he'd been helpless to do anything about it but wait. Now he feared again for someone.

Alexandra Benjamin. The pretty little daughter of a Jew who was going to be in trouble if he ever went back to Cairncross. He could still see her quietly seated opposite him in the library, her face solemn, her eyes dark and expressive, too big for her face, filled with an exquisite mixture of fear and defiance.

He cursed the remaining dust of his conscience. He didn't

want to stay away, he wanted to be at Cairncross and force that governess to have a firsthand understanding of his cravings. Ursula was right in taking her haunts along the dark side. After all, what was evil but a force that he'd experienced every moment since he could remember. It was mired in his life like a muck that held him fast. Now he even wondered if salvation were extended to him like a hand, would he take it, or would he simply pull himself down further, comforted by the known, terrified of the unknown.

If he succumbed to these feelings and returned to Cairncross, Alexandra would be his downfall. She was his match in every way. He had no doubt about that, but he had begun to wonder if a life was measured in days and years, or in pinnacles. If it were years, he numbered thirty-four. If it were pinnacles, he was less than zero.

He had never before wanted joy. It was something ethereal to him, something more elusive than seraphim and angels. But now he suddenly had been given the urge to tally up the pinnacles. Sometimes he wondered if he didn't long to grab even the smallest measure of joy with both his fists, and it was all because of her. Alexandra. Her quiet self-assurance drew him like a raven to carrion.

But he had to leave her alone. She didn't deserve what he could give her. There was only evil in him. An evil she could not know.

My lordship,

I am at a loss as to how to begin. It is of great urgency that we find Miss Pole for I now have evidence that the woman has indeed come back to Cairncross and that she is here at the castle instead of the lunatic asylum she belongs in. In searching for the madwoman, I've recruited Mrs. Penrith, the footmen and the chambermaids. Of course, they found nothing—it was not unexpected—but I had hoped there might be some kind of proof that I

*could present to you of her very real physical being
residing here—*

Alexandra took the piece of paper she was writing upon,
wadded it up, and tossed it beneath the desk. It was no use.
She had to write his lordship and beg his return, but she couldn't
find the words. Every explanation sounded weak, especially
when her best evidence was only obscure references to her
intuition. Already, she'd written five letters that night. The
library candelabra now sputtered pools of clear wax, and she
had nothing to show for her labors. Five different forms of
pleading and still she couldn't find the words to implore him
to return.

Her frustration was mounting. She threw all the letters into
the coal grate. There was no way to explain intuition. It was
imperative; it was crucial that Ursula Pole be found because
then and only then would Sam find his peace. He was speaking
now, the words coming in slow fragmented sentences, but she
could see that he could do more if only he could trust. And he
would learn to trust only when his fears were finally put to
rest.

Yet she couldn't beg Newell to return on merely intuition.
She had to give him cold, factual evidence that Ursula Pole
was in the house, living in the house without detection.

Dejected, she lit a chamberstick and left the library. The
servants were all abed and the castle was tomb-silent, but she
wasn't frightened. Her inability to find the words to bring
Newell back to help them, left her feeling defeated. It made
her feel as if Ursula Pole had somehow won. And she wouldn't
win. Even if it meant that Alexandra must endure another
encounter with her on the staircase, she almost longed to see
the woman. Because then she might get the evidence she sorely
needed.

She found her darkened bedchamber and placed the chamberstick on her nightstand. Automatically, her hands went to
the buttons on her bodice to undress. It was then she found the
trunk wide open.

4 BESTSELLING HISTORICAL ROMANCES BY YOUR FAVORITE AUTHORS CAN BE YOURS, FREE!

Kensington Choice brings you historical romances by your favorite bestselling authors including Janelle Taylor, Shannon Drake, Bertrice Small, Jo Goodman, and Georgina Gentry, just to name a few! Each book is filled with passion, adventure and the excitement of bygone times!

To introduce you to this great club which is part of Zebra Home Subscription Service, we'd like to send you your first 4 bestselling historical romances, absolutely free! And once you get these 4 free books to savor at home, we'll rush you the next 4 brand-new books at the lowest prices available, as soon as they are published.

The way the club works is that after your initial FREE shipment, you will get our 4 newest bestselling historical romances delivered to your

doorstep each month at the preferred subscriber's rate of only $4.20 per book, a savings of up to $8.16 per month (since these titles sell in bookstores for $4.99-$6.99)! All books are sent on a 10-day free examination basis and there is no minimum number of books to buy. (A postage and handling charge of $1.50 is added to each shipment.) Plus as a regular subscriber, you'll receive our FREE monthly newsletter, *Zebra/Pinnacle Romance News*, which features author profiles, subscriber benefits, book previews and more!

So start today by returning the FREE BOOK CERTIFICATE provided. We'll send you 4 FREE BOOKS with no further obligation: A FREE gift offering you hours of reading pleasure with no obligation...how can you lose?

*We have 4 FREE BOOKS for you
as your introduction to
KENSINGTON CHOICE!
To get your FREE BOOKS, worth
up to $24.96, mail the card below.*

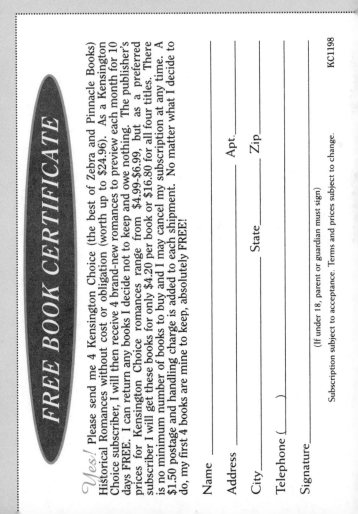

FREE BOOK CERTIFICATE

Yes! Please send me 4 Kensington Choice (the best of Zebra and Pinnacle Books) Historical Romances without cost or obligation (worth up to $24.96). As a Kensington Choice subscriber, I will then receive 4 brand-new romances to preview each month for 10 days FREE. I can return any books I decide not to keep and owe nothing. The publisher's prices for Kensington Choice romances range from $4.99-$6.99, but as a preferred subscriber I will get these books for only $4.20 per book or $16.80 for all four titles. There is no minimum number of books to buy and I may cancel my subscription at any time. A $1.50 postage and handling charge is added to each shipment. No matter what I decide to do, my first 4 books are mine to keep, absolutely FREE!

Name _____

Address _____ Apt. _____

City_____ State_____ Zip_____

Telephone (___) _____

Signature_____

(If under 18, parent or guardian must sign)

Subscription subject to acceptance. Terms and prices subject to change.

KC1198

AFFIX
STAMP
HERE

KENSINGTON CHOICE
Zebra Home Subscription Service, Inc.
120 Brighton Road
P.O.Box 5214
Clifton, NJ 07015-5214

Ice ran down her spine like the cold fingers of one of her father's cadavers. Pages from a diary, ones just like the page she'd found beneath the bureau lambrequin, were scattered across the gleaming wood floor of her bedroom. Mary had come to turn down the bed and laid across the plumped, crisp down pillows were a pair of odd green and orange gloves.

Alexandra spun around, her gaze searching every shadowy corner. She strode to the bureau and desperately wrenched open every drawer, then she sagged against it, her worst fears realized.

Her possessions were gone. Her presence in the room was wiped away like the dust on the shining beeswaxed bureau. And where every one of Alexandra's things had been placed: her brush, her tortoiseshell pins, her clothes; another's were now there instead.

The trunk's contents were neatly displayed as if Ursula Pole had never left.

There were a lot of things she had planned to do in her lifetime, but the last thing Alexandra Benjamin ever expected to do was to return to London with the express purpose of asking Lord Newell to come back to his castle.

Yet there was no choice. She couldn't handle Sam alone. They both needed Newell's help. There was more at Cairncross than even he knew about.

Her mind saw again and again her violated bedroom, but it was the atrocity within the diary pages left strewn about it that finally broke her. She'd picked them up and placed them in chronological order. Much was still missing, but one passage still drove horror through her very soul.

24 January 1838

   Seed and blood. That's what I want from him. I want both to spill for me now. He thinks he can escape me, but he's wrong. He's mine and shall be forever. For all

his manliness, he's still a child. I'll outwit him. I'll avenge
my broken heart with all that he cannot spare.
  Seed and blood.

The situation was out of control. Alexandra knew it the
moment she set eyes upon her room. She particularly knew it
when she'd read the passage from the diary over and over again
until she'd had every evil line memorized. The trip to London
had been fashioned in haste, and she hadn't even allowed Mary
to accompany her. Instead she'd diverted the maid with a story
about having to contend with her father's estate. It was partially
true: her father had left some loose ties and she could take care
of them through the family solicitor while she was in town.
But she was going for Damien. She wasn't going to stay in
Yorkshire without him. She was too frightened to do it. If he
wouldn't escort her back and take charge of what was going
on at the castle, she must leave.

And to leave, to abandon Sam just when he was beginning to
speak, to leave Cairncross and her chance to again see Damien
Newell . . . it seemed untenable.

Chapter
Fifteen

Fond wretch! and what canst thou relate,
But deeds of sorrow, shame, and sin?
Thy deeds are proved—thou know'st thy fate;
But come, thy tale! begin—begin.
— CRABBE'S HALL OF JUSTICE

"A young woman to see you, my lord," the butler whispered into Newell's ear while he and several guests, notably the duke and duchess of Underwood, were just beginning their first course. "Her name is Miss Benjamin," Matthewsby uttered behind a white-gloved hand. "She says she's come from Cairncross."

Damien looked down at the heavy vellum card the butler handed him. It read Alexandra's name along with the penned message, *I beg to tell you about the governess, your lordship.*

With absolute control, he nodded to his dinner guests, his expression a mask of blank eloquence. Murmuring an excuse to the lovely silver-haired duchess who sat to his right, he discreetly rose and left the dining room.

He saw her first. He entered the open door to his library and found her staring out the windows to the gaslit London street, her eyes held by the line of his guests' waiting carriages that formed all the way to Regent's Circus. She was exactly as he'd imagined a thousand times over in his mind.

Her hair was pinned to her nape in a thick, tight chignon. There was that primness about her that he found exquisitely challenging. The reward would be sweet, if the promise of her mouth could ever be fulfilled, but more than that, he was tempted by the soul. He knew it was pure, like pristine bedsheets were, before ruined by a spatter of blood.

He'd had two paths set before him. He could change, or he could change her. It was true that she might topple him; he could play with her goodness and in the effort shock himself to see if any goodness still remained within him. Or he could do the reverse. He could lure her goodness away. Seduce it into liking the dark.

Watching her, the challenge was sweet. He ached to see how corrupt he could make her.

"I thought your job was to see to my brother, and not to disturb me with the details of Cairncross."

She jumped at the sound of his voice. Those big eyes turned on him and he was glad he sounded angry. She shouldn't have come here. He had wanted to stay away from her.

"We've had a fright at Cairncross. It concerns Miss Pole." Her voice was exactly as he remembered, soft, well-schooled, but not cool.

Empathetic.

His insides burned with some unknown yet violent emotion. He didn't want someone to feel what he felt, to know what he knew. Especially her. It was too close. It made him feel as if he were skidding over to her side. But she was the one who'd come here unbidden; she was the one who'd taken a step into the dragon's lair. So it was she who would pay the consequences.

Without provocation, he walked to her and grabbed her wrist, hurling her into his chest. "I left to spare you."

He enjoyed the feel of her wrist in his grip. The bones were so fragile, so small; he could snap them without blinking an eye. Ah, but the expression on her face thrilled him even more. She was afraid. As well she should be. He wanted her afraid. Power and fear went hand in hand.

"Please, I beg of you ... return to Cairncross or I fear I cannot help Sam. He needs you." She looked deep into his eyes and whispered, "She's opened the trunk. She took away all my things. Where my corsets should lay, hers are now in the drawer. I don't think I can fight her—"

The fear on her face was not of him anymore. He released her. Irrationally, he became furious that Ursula had frightened her. It was his power to frighten, not some bloody shadow's that walked the halls at Cairncross.

She stared up at him, her eyes wide with need. Without wavering her gaze, she untied the heavy knot on her purse and removed a pair of orange and green gloves. She held them out to him like a sacrifice and whispered, "She stole my black gloves and put these in their place."

He took them in his hands. Her expression was one of revulsion and panic, but he didn't have the reaction he knew she expected. He was not afraid of the gloves or even repulsed by them. Feelings such as those were too long in his past to remember. The place where they should come from had long been callused over.

"Her favorite gloves," he uttered as if commenting on the color of a flower.

"These are *the* gloves, aren't they?" she whispered.

He looked down and took her small hand in his, and in her fear, she seemed to have no compunction to stop him. He stared at it for a long time, casting to memory the ivory color of her skin, the path of the blue veins that etched delicately across its back. He ran his thumb over it and marveled how fragile, how womanly her hand was. It was nothing more than delicately-boned fingers, a warm, soft palm, and a thin little wrist with all the strength of a child. He could shatter it so easily.

"I can't help you, Alexandra. I'm not returning. Leave Sam if you must, but I won't return." His gaze moved upward to her face. She stared at him with those large hazel eyes that he thought about every lonely night by the library fire.

"Why can't you help? I can't do this alone. If you force me back, I'll fail. So come with me. You're no coward and I know you love Sam—as I've grown to love Sam. We can't abandon him."

He looked at her and he could feel his expression fighting a snarl. "Sam's in no danger, nor are you. I've told you that. You may return to the castle without worry."

"She's there at the castle." Her voice took on an uncharacteristic edge of hysteria. "I've seen her myself on the stair and now she's gone into my room—"

"Her room. It was her room. You should have asked Mrs. Penrith to move you."

"But what about my belongings? Where have they gone?" She seemed unable to bite back her sarcasm. "Have they gone to some netherworld with her?"

"I'll have them replaced at once."

It was her turn to become angry. She snatched her hand away with a very quickness that surprised him. "You aren't listening to me, my lord. You heard the words but the meaning escapes you."

"I understand the meaning." He took a step toward her. It was with delicious satisfaction that he watched her move back from him until her back met the drapery. "But she doesn't concern me; you concern me. So don't plead for my return."

"What about Sam?" In her passion and anger, her cheeks seemed lit with fire. "He told me she stays in his room. His *room,* my lord."

Damien felt his heart lurch in his chest like an anchor twisting out of ice. The pain that suddenly came to life inside him was that much more acute for his never having felt it before. As if in a fit of paralytic revulsion, he lowered himself to the seat of a chair.

Quietly, she came to his side. "Now, my lord, do you know why I had to come?" she whispered, kneeling beside him.

"I'll send for him. I should have taken him from there long ago . . ."

"It isn't prudent now," she answered in a soft, feminine voice. "In his own small way, he's handling the horror of the situation. He's making progress. A change of environment could force us to go backward."

"She won't hurt him. She doesn't want him. She wants me." He glanced at her, then looked away, rubbing his jaw. He could have cursed himself for he had not meant to speak such things.

"I know."

He gazed down at her slim, kneeling figure. Her eyes were like a forest, dark and mysterious with flecks of sunlight amongst the leaves. They offered escape, peace, surrender. He could not look away.

"She's doing this to lure me back."

"Where is she? They say she's a ghost but I don't believe it. She's hiding in the castle somewhere. We've just got to find out where that is."

He watched her. Her face was a mask of need. She didn't understand the situation and she desperately wanted to. But the beauty of her was that she could never understand the things that haunted Cairncross, it wasn't within her soul to do it, and that was why he found himself suddenly aching to be beside her.

She continued, "I sent the servants out to look for her. We searched everywhere—"

"Not everywhere, love."

She reacted to his tenderness. Her face softened and he felt himself grow stronger. She wouldn't topple him. She couldn't begin to think as he did. If and when he desired it, he could make her into his kind without even an effort. "Cairncross was built over miles of Roman catacombs. A thousand men died in the battle of Eboracum in the fifth century and they were laid to rest in the caves beneath the castle. If Ursula is indeed manifesting the castle with her presence, she may come and go as she likes, for no man has yet to decipher the labyrinth beneath Cairncross Castle."

She appeared shaken by this news. Shaken but not defeated. With a thrust of her small, delicately pointed chin, she asked, "Is she there, Damien? I still feel you know where she is."

He said nothing. He merely stared at her and wondered what his life had come to. It seemed there had never been any salvation for him. Now even damnation was trying to elude his grasp because when he was with her, he didn't want to be damned.

"What did she do to you? I can see something in your eyes. What did she do?" he heard her whisper. He suddenly wanted to tell her, yet he found he could not speak. He closed his eyes to block out the honest concern in hers.

Slowly, there came the rustle of her skirts as she raised herself. He thought she was going to walk away, but she didn't. Instead, he felt her lean against the arm of the chair and pass her hand along one side of his face. He was numb inside while she placed his spectacles on the table. Then with excruciating slowness, she lowered her head and pressed her cheek against his as if she were comforting some kind of hurt child. "Pray, tell me about her. I need to understand. You must help me understand."

He didn't want to talk. It was against his nature to make confessions, especially those of his own doing. But the cheek, warm and soft, still pressed against his own. Of its own accord, his hand touched her hair and he swore he had never in his life felt something so soft. Somehow, in her brilliance, she had found the chink in his armor, and she was determined to get inside. He would have no choice but to destroy her.

His hand on her hair suddenly became rough. He tangled his fingers within her chignon and pulled her face to his. Words weren't necessary. He could see the pain on her face, the terrible expectation.

He kissed her brutally. Because he had to. Hard enough to make her bleed, he thought as his mouth moved over hers. She struggled to get away, but the attempt was laughable. She was no physical match for him, nor would she be a spiritual match. If softness would seduce her first, then he would be soft. He would be gentle first so he could be ruthless later. Slowly, he gentled. Deep inside her, he swore he heard her moan. Her lips seemed less reluctant as his turned more tender. Soon, he swore she was returning the kiss, and he wanted to shout in triumph. She was his.

Her hand went to his cheek. Before he even realized what she was up to, he felt her nails rake down his flesh, taking skin with them.

He released her. She looked like a cat that wanted to back away low on its stomach because it had just found a repugnant scent.

"Why did you do that? Why?" she demanded.

He said nothing. It almost hurt him to watch her. Abbey would have taken the kiss, enjoyed it even. Any other girl would run for her life. But not this one. This one was strong and curious. And perhaps bent on salvation. His insides were like raw, bleeding flesh to find her still in the room, still willing to give him a chance.

He violently stood up. His chest felt like an iron band had been wrapped and rewrapped around it until every breath was torture. The renewed self-hatred that churned up inside him felt good. It was like the relief of lightning in summer heat.

He forced himself to look at her. She stood by the chair, her hand on its back as if it held her up. The blood had left her face and she stared at him with shocked, sad eyes. For the first time in his life, he thought of going to a woman's arms for comfort and not just carnal amusement. It would be so easy to just let himself be drawn into this one's slim, pretty arms. He could rest his cheek on her soft breast and let the beating of her noble heart give him peace. It seemed such a simple thing to want, but he had never felt a woman's loving embrace. His own mother had forsaken him for Europe and a string of lovers the minute he'd been born. A soft, loving embrace was beyond his imagination, yet now, looking down at her, he wanted it with a hunger he'd never known.

"I'll go to Cairncross," he said.

"Thank God. We must find her. We must. She's a lunatic.

She's got to be locked up," she whispered, her face etched with disbelief and horror.

"I'll take care of her so that you may take care of Sam."

"Yes," she rasped.

"But remember who *I* am, Alexandra," he whispered harshly. "When you start with women the way I did, you develop very grand, very dark, appetites."

She began to tremble. Her hand shook as she reached for the back of the chair to steady herself. He couldn't tell what was going through her mind, but it involved terror.

"I've guests here tonight. I must return to them. We'll speak of this tomorrow," he said in a succinct tone, hoping they could return to a plane of cool normalcy.

"Of course." She nodded her head. "I should never have bothered you this evening, my lord, but I came straight here after I left the train station." She gathered up her long purse, nervously tying and untying the swollen knot that kept it closed.

"Did Matthewsby take the rest of your things?"

Her gaze shot up to his. "I'll be having a room at the inn, my lord."

"What inn?" It was all he could do not to laugh.

"The inn . . . well, the inn that I'll find accommodations in tonight."

"I can recommend one." He smiled darkly. "The White Bear in Wapping."

"I'll go to Wapping then." She clutched her long black purse, her fingers nervously playing with the tassel.

He couldn't stop himself from placing his hand on the wall behind her and leaning down to her, in essence capturing her. "You've never been to Wapping, have you, Alexandra?"

She tilted her face up to him. Her mouth was expressive, her eyes brilliant, yet shadowed; he couldn't read her thoughts and the challenge was exquisite. "I've heard it's a hellish place."

"They'll take your pound of flesh if you as much as blink."

"I take it you've been there?" She glanced up at him.

"It's there I learned what the world truly is."

"And did they take your pound of flesh, Damien? Is that why you enjoy frightening me?"

His stare locked with hers. No one on this earth had ever come closer to figuring him out than this woman. At times she came so near he was left almost breathless from the chance escape. But it angered him. He didn't want her to know about Wapping, about the dirty, sordid dealings he had at the White Bear. About the boys that came in peddling their wares. No, he wanted to protect her from such filth because she stood for everything that was good and blessedly out of his reach. Some unfamiliar part of him wanted her clean and safe. She did not deserve the abuse of an explanation of Wapping.

"You couldn't possibly understand such a place," he said, their heads just inches apart. "There, you quickly learn that they can only take what you value. So you don't value . . . *anything.*"

His words seemed to affect her. He swore he could see the gleam of tears in those beautiful eyes as she stared at him.

"My lord, then 'tis time you were given something to value."

"Give me that then."

There was wretched quiet while he stared at her. He didn't know why he even said it. The look in her eyes was sheer devastation.

He turned away from her. "My guests await," he said, his voice barely a growl. "I'll send for Matthewsby to help with your bag. We'll leave for Cairncross in the morning."

"I mustn't stay here."

"You *will* stay here and nowhere else."

"But tomorrow, before the next train to York, I have to visit my father."

"Where is he buried?"

"The Jews' burial ground in Brady Street, Whitechapel."

"Ah, yes, that one. The one with the thick vines that cover the tombs of doctors and lawyers and bankers. I've gone by it many a time. I'll take you there before we go to the train station."

She was so silent. He tasted her reluctance like an aphrodisiac. She was intelligent. Too intelligent. If ever in her life, she should be cautious, it was now.

"I don't think I should stay here, my lord."

"Whatever waits for you in Wapping is far worse than what waits for you here."

She began to yield, but only because she was afraid. He could tell she was not used to traveling without chaperonage. It must have taken all her courage to make this trip, and all to help Sam. His brother. Old slow Sam whom nobody ever loved save him. Now they had an angel of mercy.

"I accept your hospitality, my lord."

He needed to touch her and the feeling was so overpowering that it took all his strength not to act on it. She was right below him, trapped by the heavy velvet drapery and the arm he still held against the wall. They were parted by only a matter of inches and he could cross the distance and take her mouth. There were things he had done with Abbey that he longed to do with her. Wonderful, inglorious things . . .

His fists clenched; his chest tightened. They had miles to travel before she would be in his mercy. He would have to be patient. And he would have to be cautious too. She worked a kind of magic on him when she was around. There was an innocence about her that even he felt reluctant to defile. Sometimes the light grew too bright for him to resist. But he wouldn't surrender. He wouldn't give her the chance to make him mourn his mislaid soul.

Abruptly, he moved away. "Go find Matthewsby and have him settle you in your room. I must return to my guests."

She seemed hurt by his tone of voice. It had been calculated to be cold and rejecting, and he was glad. Glad when she stepped away, glad when the door closed behind her. The look in her eyes made him think she might have even fallen in love with him.

Alone, he could almost physically feel the pull of her lessening. The darkness seeped back inside with astonishing speed. He hadn't even noticed its absence until now.

His gaze turned to the chair where she had last stood. He

pictured her there again, appearing frightened and yet defiant. She would fight him. He knew it. But she wouldn't win. The essence of her soul was going to be crushed in his fist because she'd foolishly come to London to fetch him.

He could hardly wait to get to the castle with her and begin her reformation.

Alexandra stared in dismay at the little garret room Matthewsby showed her after the butler retrieved her from the library. She certainly couldn't say she merited the best room in the house for she was only a servant, if an elevated one, but the cramped, sparsely furnished attic room made Ursula Pole's room at Cairncross seem luxurious.

Yet, there were advantages to the place. This house held no madwoman.

She unpacked the few belongings she had left after Ursula had redecorated her bedchamber. Her entire body drooped with the bone-tired weariness she'd been fighting ever since she had taken the walk with Sam. But she fought the exertion, for if she succumbed to it, she might talk herself out of returning to the castle, and she could never do that. Yet as much as she hated to admit it, Ursula Pole was becoming too much for her. At first the woman was just a chilling curiosity. Now she had proved to be real, and the worst part was that Ursula knew about her. The woman had taken her things, she'd even perversely used *Ivanhoe* to flail her Jewishness. Her omnipotence terrified her. There weren't many perceptive enough to have chosen the novel; and it was diabolical that Ursula had exactly picked the right one. Now the lunatic had even taken her things—her undergarments, her lavender dress—things that she not only liked but needed. It left her blood flowing like ice.

And Sam. She couldn't get the image out of her mind of that red-haired woman she'd seen on the stair, hovering over Sam's bedstead like a specter. Always, the question of what Ursula might have done to Sam plagued her like a buzzard that was flying overhead. Damien had said that Ursula's abuse and attentions were only focused upon him and the diary pages she'd read gave evidence to that fact. But Ursula could have done things to Sam. The two men looked so much alike, even she herself had trouble sometimes remembering that Sam wasn't Damien.

She slowly sat on the edge of the lumpy mattress and thought of her encounter with Newell in the library. His kiss still caused her hands to shake. He'd tried to hurt her and she knew it. But the worst was when he'd been gentle. He'd seduced her then, and made her want the kiss.

She realized she didn't like John Damien Newell, but she also realized she was on the precipice of falling in love with him. He was damaged; even now she wondered if the damage could be repaired. Yet at times such as these, when she despaired, she thought of the garden at Cairncross. There was beauty within the grotesque. There was new life even within a crushed rose. It made her wonder if a gentle heart could seek out his and tame the ferocity he'd always needed to protect himself.

But he terrified her; he sent a chill through her very soul in some instances . . . yet, he'd at least touched her soul. More deeply and more completely that any man she had ever met. As much as she had convinced herself to stay away from him, she found out she couldn't. Even the lesson of Brian wasn't enough to warn her away. She wanted Damien. She wanted him because she sensed he needed her even more than Sam. It would be within all reason to take her valise and send for Mary and never think of Sam and Cairncross again. No one would blame her, least of all Newell. But she wouldn't leave. For every vile hint of Damien's darker side, she was only drawn in more, as a moth to a flame, convinced that there was a goodness inside him as well. One that would outshine any evil if she could only find it.

Downstairs, the bell-like sound of feminine laughter rang through the house. She rose and peeked out the attic window. The guests were slowly trickling out the door. Carriage after carriage arrived at the town house like phantoms rolling in from a deep London fog. Even the treetops from the park beyond the crescent where Newell's townhouse was built were shrouded in the thick gray fog, and at the end of the park, a woman stood motionless, covered in a hooded cloak as she stared at the departing guests that poured forth below.

Alexandra's heart froze. The figure was too still, too silent. It reminded her of the woman in the hall, a fabrication, perhaps, but no less hideous.

In mute silence, she watched the figure turn toward Damien as he stepped out of the town house to escort a regal, silverhaired woman down the marble steps to her carriage. There was a sudden intensity to the way the dark figure watched that trailed ice down Alexandra's spine. She expected any second for a bony hand to protrude from the cloak and beckon Damien away to a place so foul and dark, no one would ever find him again. Alexandra's very soul ached to cry out for him, because she knew she couldn't bear losing him to such a force.

"Miss? His lordship asked that I send up refreshment."

Alexandra spun around from the window and almost glared at the plain, young chambermaid who stood in her doorway with a silver tray. The interruption was another blow to the nerves.

"Thank you very much. You may set it on the bureau," she said perhaps a bit too tersely.

"Very well, miss. Enjoy it." The small maid put down the tea tray and scurried out the door.

Alexandra's gaze riveted once more to the park, her eyes scouring the mists for another glimpse of the dark figure. She was gone. Now a man and a woman were walking through the park, laughing arm in arm, as if they were newlyweds fresh from the wedding. The woman wore a long, black cloak, much like the one the figure had worn, but now the hood had fallen down revealing a wealth of blond hair.

She was not Ursula, and Alexandra made herself believe that the woman she had seen was this same one who now walked with the man. But she wasn't completely convinced. There was no telling where Ursula Pole was now. The woman could have followed her from the castle and now watched the town house hidden in the mist of the park. She would know Alexandra was there with Damien, her obsession, and she shuddered to think of the woman's reaction to such news. Ursula possessed a lethal combination of stark lunacy and sheer brilliance. Any woman who could remain hidden so long, even with the assistance of the miles of catacombs beneath the castle, had to be intelligent. She and Damien would have to be canny to find her and put her in the asylum where she belonged.

God save them. Ursula Pole was not to be underestimated.

Chapter
Sixteen

. . . and it is death who is my rival.
—Bois-Guilbert to Rebecca, in IVANHOE

The graves of the Jews were situated in Whitechapel at Mile End between such places of poverty as Goodman's Fields and Davids-In-Field. The Jews buried in this particular plot of earth weren't poor, but they and their ancestors had lived in Whitechapel for so many years, they could account for being there when it had been pastureland.

It was an honor that they had made room for Horace Benjamin, and Alexandra always felt proud to visit her father on such esteemed ground where even N. M. Rothschild had been buried when he'd died in 1836 as the leading stockbroker of all Europe. Her father, for all his impracticality, had been a man missed by his colleagues, and for that Alexandra would always be grateful.

Newell did not go with her into the graveyard. He stayed behind with the carriage, fighting the blustery wind while he waited against the graveyard's crumbling wall. Alexandra took her moment of peace to be with her father. Standing at his gravesite, she wondered what her life would be like had he not died. She would probably still be waiting for Brian and working with her father, still desperately trying to weave herself into the fabric of his life. Of both men's lives.

And then she thought of Newell, his collar up against the wind, his face, hard and drawn, as if fighting the unexpected cold, and something else, something deeper.

"What do I do, Father?" she whispered at the door of the granite tomb blazoned with the Star of David as if it were the Benjamin coat of arms. "Shall I run from him and be alone? Or do I take what little I'm offered in this life as I took and took from Brian?"

The questions were never answered. She reverently placed a laurel wreath at the tomb's threshold, noting that the roof was already covered with a fine green moss, turning brown in the impending autumn. It had been nine months since her father died. A life could be created in such time, but no grief could be expelled by then. With a heavy heart, she turned and found Damien at the gate, standing much as he had stood at the garden gate before he'd left for London. Only this time, he wasn't leaving her. In silence, he held out his hand. She took it and allowed him to help her into the carriage that would whisk them to the train station, and to York.

They arrived at the castle well after midnight the following day. Their train was delayed at Stirring and they were forced to take rooms at the inn. Newell politely acquired a room for her and stayed in another. There was no talk of sharing. In fact, Newell was the perfect gentleman. When Alexandra knew him better, she would know that when Newell was distant and polite was when he was most dangerous.

"I've thought about moving my room, my lord," she said to him when they had at last arrived at Cairncross and were taking a bit of refreshment in the library before retiring. "I don't think it wise for me to leave Ursula's room. It upsets her, my being there, I'm convinced of it. She'll be easier to catch, I think, if she's riled."

Damien sat opposite her, his palm wrapped around an amber liquid that he seemed to take no interest in. His gaze was fixed on her, and though it was her imagination, she swore it had not moved from her face since they had left London. "It's up to you," was all he said.

"I'll admit it doesn't seem judicious to stay there, but it might be a lure with which to catch her."

A wry smile tipped the corner of his mouth. He was so blessedly handsome in the gaslight, with his hair reflecting gold and his hard, desolate features softened by shadow. She ached to touch him, to kiss him. It was sheer agony stopping herself, but she knew she must bury the impulse. She'd melted once for Brian, and she was certainly wise enough to fear melting for this man who confessed to cruelties as easily as a child confesses a hand in the cookie jar.

"Why do you smile like that, my lord?"

The smile deepened. It was not altogether a nice one. "Sweet Alexandra, you're innocent and so good, and you understand so little. I'm not going to catch her, she's going to catch me. You can be sure of it."

"But you'll catch her. I know it." She lowered her gaze to his figure. He was such an impossibly strong man, so big and muscular, she couldn't imagine anyone taking him and winning.

He leaned forward and touched her cheek. It burned where he caressed her. His hand was rough with old calluses and she wondered where he had acquired them. Wapping? She really knew so little of his past.

"Alexandra," he said, "were I a more honorable man, I believe I would marry you and get you with my child so that I could leave this earth with less regret. If only I were an honorable man."

She clasped his hand to her cheek, the emotion suddenly running raw. "But you are an honorable man. You came back to save Sam. You came back to help me. Anything is possible for you, Damien."

"I'll have no sons like me."

"And daughters?"

He seemed to think on this a moment. "I would have daughters like you. But where is the guarantee they would be daughters? That's the risk I won't take."

"You're hard on yourself, my lord. I would be proud to have a son like you. You survived where many would perish. Isn't that an accomplishment?"

His stare met with hers.

She fought the impulse to go to him, to perhaps touch his cheek. But she knew it would accomplish nothing.

"I must retire so that I can begin once more in the morning with Sam. Shall I tell him you'll take tea with us?" She waited expectantly. The nod was almost imperceptible.

"Then I bid you good-night, my lord." She stood and turned to the door. It was almost a shock to feel his hand take hers.

"Don't bid me good-night." He stared down at her for a long moment, his face taut with intensity.

"Will you make me fall in love with you only to pass me by afterward?" She hated showing her feelings, but he left her no room for facades. "I'm beneath you on two counts, my lord: I'm not of the peerage and my father was a Jew." Her voice turned husky with emotion. "I've already learned which strike against me is the worst."

"Magdalene was a Jew. Jesus was a Jew."

"Yes," she whispered, "but once an infidel—"

"We're all infidels," he interrupted, his brow turned stormy. "Did you know that the worst infidel in this house is Featherstone? He was the one to first cast a stone upon me when Ursula cried rape. I believe he was in love with her. He was a sour old man even twenty years ago and when she worked her wiles on him, he fell like a cannonball, as all sour old men do when a pretty woman pays them mind. He fell in love with her and he betrayed me."

The news didn't really surprise her. She always wondered about Featherstone. Now she almost felt for him. "But he hates her now. What changed him? Why do you keep him on?"

The small wicked smile once more played at the corner of his mouth. "For years her seduction of him was all the talk of the servants' quarters. Apparently, she told him she needed money. The night she disappeared, she begged him for his life's savings because she feared a pregnancy. *My* pregnancy, can you fathom it? He gave her all his money and made an assignation with her in London. Naturally she never showed. He returned to Cairncross with his tail between his legs and he's grown ever more sour since." His gaze raked down her figure. It was a violent glance meant to intimidate. "That's why he doesn't trust you, Alexandra. He doesn't trust any pretty woman."

"So that's where she's gotten her keep from all these years. I wondered how she cared for herself without any money."

Damien made no reply. Instead, he thumbed the circles beneath her eyes. Something seemed to pull at him, as if he were trying to make a decision. He appeared jumpy, as if he were waiting to spring upon her. Finally, he turned away. "Go ahead up. I'll meet you on the landing with a candle."

She nodded. A flood of emotion spread through her. It seemed whenever Damien turned away from her was when he needed her most, but at those times there was no way for her to penetrate the armor that surrounded him.

She turned and left, with his caress still imprinted upon her mind. It had made it easy to pretend they were man and wife, heading upstairs after another uneventful evening by the library fire. She wondered if she could get used to such evenings, but she cautioned herself against such musings. Fantasy only led to disappointment.

Outside of the library in the hall, she shivered in a passing draft. It was near to jet blackness in the passage, and the only light seemed to come from the top of the stairs. She thought there was a lit gas lamp on one of the tables on the landing, but as she took each step upon the stair, she formed the cold realization that the light was emanating from a lit candle left on a tread far above her.

She paused on the landing. It was an instinctual reaction,

primeval even. Almost the way a bear scents danger. Yet she resisted the urge to run back down the stairs. Damien would be following, she told herself. He would be out from the library any moment and he would see what she saw.

She wanted to remain where she was, perched in the middle of the staircase, but all at once she was struck by a perverse curiosity. Someone had lit a candle and placed it on the stairs. It was there to light something, but what, she couldn't guess.

Behind her she heard the door to the library open. Gaining courage at the thought of Damien near, she lifted her skirts and climbed further upon the darkened staircase. Higher and higher she climbed, until below her the hall was nothing but a black maw, the landing succumbed to shadows.

Six steps down from the candle.

Five steps.

Four.

She saw what was displayed.

It was the book. Of course, it was the book. Slowly, as if she were a very old, very reluctant, woman, she climbed the final stairs. A cold draft rushed past her as she read the passage circled in an ominous crimson ink:

Farewell. I waste no more words on thee; the time that remains on earth to the daughter of Jacob must be otherwise spent.

From the darkness above, a hand reached out and touched her shoulder. She cried Damien's name like a wounded animal.

But it wasn't Damien who waited.

Chapter
Seventeen

"Lord Newell is here to see you, love. Is your head still a-hurtin'? Shall I send him away?" Mary looked down upon her, her familiar face hanging forward in dewlaps of pleasant wrinkles.

Stiffly, Alexandra sat up. Her head throbbed. From her place in the bed, she could see it was well past dawn. The morning light was blessedly clear and soft. Winter was soon in coming.

"I'll see him. I'm fine. Really, I am." She did her best to hide the grimace as she brushed back her hair.

Mary clucked with disapproval but handed her the black shawl and tucked the covers around her. "You gave us all a scare, you did, tumbling from those stairs. I never thought I'd see such a sight as Lord Newell bringing you to me in his arms, your head bashed from the terrible fall. 'Tis fortunate you're alive."

"I'm fine. A little headache, but no more." She stared helplessly at the maidservant. It was on the tip of her tongue to confess all that had happened the night before and to beg her to pack their things and leave. She didn't even remember being brought into her bedroom. All she remembered was the face, and then the terrible empty darkness.

Mary must somehow have read the expression on her face. Intuitively, the woman took her hand and Alexandra clasped it tightly, tears suddenly brimming in her eyes.

"Love, what is it?" the maidservant whispered.

Alexandra almost couldn't speak. "I don't know." It was the truth. She didn't know what was going on, all she knew is that she was frightened and yet she couldn't burden Mary with her fear. Even now she was pulling Mary along with her and she wanted Mary safe from what had happened on the stair. Above all, Mary must be spared. Alexandra loved her too much to entwine her in her problems. Besides, it was all Alexandra's fault that Mary was at Cairncross in the first place.

"Show Lord Newell in. I'm fine now. Really." Slowly Alexandra took her hand away. She raked her fingers through the hideously tangled mass of her hair and felt like some kind of wild creature. Without a comb and pins, controlling her hair was about as easy as parting the Red Sea.

"I'll see to tea. If you need anything, love, just ring." Mary draped the tapestried bell pull against the headboard. She gave Alexandra a worried, puzzled look, then she exited and allowed Lord Newell to enter in her stead.

Alexandra could find no words to say. She had to explain to this man what she saw, and what it meant. She had to change his mind; she despaired at the very thought.

"How is your head?" he asked, taking the seat where Mary had obviously vigiled at her bedside the night before.

"It hurts. I must have hit it." Her gaze wandered down his form. He looked more unkempt than usual. He had changed shirts, but there was a dark gold scruff of beard on his face and his eyes looked tired, especially when he rubbed them beneath his spectacles with his thumb and forefinger. She would have bet that he hadn't slept all night.

"How did you fall, Alex?"

She paused at the name. Her father only called her that in

times of deepest affection. A strange hurt crept into her. She didn't want to fall in love with Damien Newell.

"She was above me in the darkness." She began to tremble. "Such an awful face . . ."

He sat quietly on the chair, every muscle tensed. He was a lion before it pounced. "She pushed you?"

"I'm not sure. I saw a woman above me as clear as day, but then it seemed there were two figures. I swear if I was pushed, the push came from behind me."

The silence was like a wall of ice avalanching down upon them. She prayed he wouldn't speak, because she knew what he would say. He spoke anyway.

"I'll give you your year's wages and a recommendation. A train leaves from York this evening. This is your last chance. I suggest you take it."

"No, I don't want to leave. I want to help." She muffled the strange sob that seemed caught in her throat. She couldn't leave, she had no where to go.

"If you stay here you might jeopardize your life—"

"But Sam and I were making progress. He needs me." *And I need him,* she added silently, her heart wrenching at the thought of departing.

"The blow to your head must have rattled your brain, Alex." The lines framing his mouth grew deeper. "Don't you understand? She views you as an obstacle. She'll get rid of you to get to me."

"But how are you going to stop her? If she's living within the miles of catacombs, she's impossible to find. Besides, you won't even look for her."

His mouth turned hard. "I know how to stop her."

"How?" she pleaded.

"I've got to find out where she went when she disappeared. I've got to know what happened to her. Then I'll know how to get her."

"She's here in the castle now." She nodded toward the schoolroom door. "Perhaps she's standing even now on the other side of that door, listening to every word we speak."

"She may be. That's even more the reason why you must leave. Today."

"But I can't."

"Why can't you?" He suddenly turned ferociously angry. He grabbed her and shook her like a madman. "I'm giving you another chance. Another chance to be free. You're a fool if you don't take it!"

She stared at him, shocked at his outburst, unable to explain her tenacity in staying. There were no words to convey the basic need to be wanted, and deeper still, the yearnings within the heart of a lonely young woman. All she knew was that the thought of an empty flat in London with only Mary for her company was something she feared far worse than the wraithlike specter of Ursula Pole.

"I want to help. You hired me to help. Sam may know something about her that we can't even know until he has the words to speak. You must let me stay." She reached out to him in supplication and took his hand.

Slowly, coldly, he extracted it. "Remember, I gave you every chance. Every chance."

She looked down at her empty hand that had only seconds ago touched his. It was suddenly freezing. It seemed so absurd, all this tension for a madwoman who should have been caught and locked up months ago. His reluctance to find Ursula almost seemed like a ruse.

"Of course, I'm only a servant who doesn't know what's good for her, but I'm staying because of Sam. *Only* because of Sam." The defiant words tasted like acid and they were made worse by the strange feeling that Ursula was listening to them. The woman knew all her insecurities. Somehow she had realized how much *Ivanhoe* hurt. The words Rebecca spoke to Rowena at the end of *Ivanhoe* suddenly came to her through the mist of impending tears. Without wanting to, she whispered, "Let me not think you deem so wretchedly ill of my nation as your commons believe. Think ye that I prize . . . sparkling fragments of stone above my liberty? or that my father values them in comparison to the honor of his only child?"

He cast his gaze away. There was a heavy, oppressive silence, then he stood, as if at a loss where to go with it next.

"My lord," she said to him before he departed, "the face I saw, 'twas nothing like the woman I met on the stair. The woman I saw was red-headed and almost lovely if not for the cruelty of her mouth. Last night I saw another face altogether. It was ugly and distorted by wrinkles. She possessed a shock of white hair that seemed to stand straight up. Ursula would now be gray, would she not? The woman I saw earlier must have indeed been a servant."

He shook his head, his expression strangely relieved. "You should have told me this sooner. The face you describe from last night was Lady Bess. My grandmother is near a century in age. I've told you she lives separately from the rest of the household in the north tower. Sometimes she wanders and she's a fright to behold. No wonder you fell. You must have been surprised by her and slipped. She's a harmless creature, she wouldn't have pushed you."

"But who then set up the candle and the book?"

The disturbed lines reappeared on his brow. "What candle? What book?"

"The candle and book that were placed on the landing. The passage was circled and—" She stopped herself short. There was no way to explain *Ivanhoe* without stripping her emotional self naked. "Was there no candle and book when you heard me fall?"

"I didn't see any such things. I ran out of the library when I heard you fall. There was no one else there. Should I ask the servants if they found anything?"

She lay back against the pillows, inexplicably wearied. "They would have come to you if they'd found anything unusual."

"What book was it, Alex?"

She stared at the door to the schoolroom, her soul suddenly burning with a hatred she had never felt before. Ursula was torturing her and she wouldn't let her. She wouldn't.

"It was just a book, opened to a passage. I didn't really read it before I fell. I'm sure it meant nothing. Just another prank.'' She prayed Ursula had heard her. She wouldn't let that mad-woman get the best of her. She'd now go to her grave before she let that happen.

"Rest," he ordered, staring at her with an odd, perplexed expression. "I'll send Sam in later. Perhaps you can take luncheon with him. He'd like that. Mrs. Penrith said he missed you."

"I missed him too," she whispered.

Damien almost smiled. It fractured her emotions to see how difficult it was for him to do such a thing. "Good day then," he said before he left, and she knew he meant it.

Damien wandered into the small garden. The gate creaked on its hinges as he walled himself in. He breathed deeply of the air and sauntered through the dead, dried overgrowth. It was hard to imagine what the garden used to look like in the spring when his grandmother tended it. Pink floribunda roses dotted the top of the wall back then, their scent the smell of heaven. The hedges were clipped into topiary. He walked past one and remembered that once it had been carved into a fat, amiable rabbit.

He removed his spectacles and leaned his head against the cracked stucco wall. Clouds like cottonwool sailed with the breeze, playing peekaboo with the sun and casting shape and shadow across the garden. In the distance, a crag jutted over the garden walls, breathtaking in its empty magnificence.

His eyes burned. He'd been up all night. A tiredness seeped through his bones, but exhaustion was an old familiar friend. He'd been on intimate terms with it ever since he was a boy having to fend for himself on the streets of London.

Ursula had tried to kill her.

He couldn't escape the thought, even here in the garden where peace lived. Because there was no peace inside him.

He was beginning to care for her. It was a tightrope he never wanted to walk, but when he'd found her limp form at the bottom of the stairs, he felt a rage so raw and violent he could barely repress it.

He knew it had been Ursula even before he spoke to Alexandra. Ursula knew how he was beginning to feel. In the past, she'd known his vulnerabilities and his failures, and she'd taken advantage of them. She was doing the same thing now. If she couldn't get to him, then she would get to Alexandra.

Last night he'd dreamed of Alexandra. The garden was in full summer bloom and she wore a pretty muslin dress the same pale shade of pink as the roses. The color was beautiful against the dark of her hair. She took his breath away. He found himself at the garden gate just staring at her, unable to look away.

She went to him. Like a seductress, she took his hand and led him further into the garden. Licentiousness stole into his thoughts and he wanted to lay her down in the thick lavender, but she stopped him. He was confused, especially when she whispered, "Hold me," but then he understood. She snuggled into his chest and he found himself wrapping his arms around her. Behind them, the castle suddenly burst into flames. The gentle moorland became like a fiery Armageddon, flames bursting from every crag and cairn.

But there was peace in the garden.

He held her tight within his arms, so close it seemed to ward off the chaos around them. "I'm safe now," she whispered, and he wanted to deny it; he wanted to tell her she'd never been in more danger than when so near him. But he couldn't. The fragileness of her, the trust and need in her eyes gave him a feeling so sweet and pure he ached. He didn't want to let her go. He wanted to hold and protect her forever. And he wanted the spark of goodness that she had managed to ignite to never leave him. He wanted it to grow and devour like the flames from the castle all the evil inside him and leave only the goodness.

But then he woke up. And he was all alone. The same old Damien. The same old battles.

He slammed his fist into the garden wall. Chunks of green-stained stucco fell to the ground. His knuckles, when he bothered to look at them, bled.

The garden would renew itself in the spring, but not him. He was beyond rebirth. Whatever emotion inside him was fracturing. He'd stop Ursula, he had no doubt of it. He wouldn't let Alexandra be a casualty of the battle.

Oh, but he didn't want to feel for her. This feeling of wanting to protect her sickened him. It was so noble. So foreign. He felt it for Sam, but no one else. Not ever. Until now.

He reached out and grabbed a handful of dead rosebuds from a nearby bush. Their thorns imbedded in his bloody hand but he didn't care. He just wanted to crush them. To make them deader than dead. There was no rebirth in him and there would be none in these either.

It was no use. The flowers crumbled and flecks of seeds fell to the fertile earth. The roses would be back in the spring. Life had a will of its own. An awesome, undeniable power.

But so did evil.

He rubbed his jaw and thought of Alexandra. This morning, she'd looked so helpless lying in that huge bed, her pale face framed by wild, dark curls. Her vulnerability moved him. He could have done anything to her at that moment. With her maid gone, he could have trapped her beneath him in the bed and stilled her fight. He could have taken her roughly, then turned from her in the way he'd rid himself of dozens of women. He'd have been cold afterward. She'd have probably wept. The physical satisfaction would have been great, the power heady, the reaffirmation, assuring.

But he could have never looked into her eyes again. He would never want to see the emotion mirrored there.

Alexandra was going to make him lose this battle. If he fell for her, as he could see he was already doing, it would be his end. He couldn't endure life defenseless. He couldn't open himself ever again to that kind of pain. It was her or him. And if he lost, death was preferable.

With one shaking and bloody hand, he replaced his spectacles and began to walk to the garden gate.

Death was preferable.

"It's too cold for the garden today, Sam. Where would you
like to have our lesson?" Alexandra asked across the breakfast
table the next morning. A light frost dusted the yard beyond
the windows and the garden wall was just visible in the corner,
its mossed stones turned ochre from the early freeze.

"I want Damien." Sam watched her from the other side of
the table. His silver embossed spoon was stirring a steamy bowl
of porridge.

"Damien is busy, but I'll send him a note. Would you like
to spend the day in the library? Mrs. Penrith tells me there are
all sorts of volumes there. Shall I read to you today? Poetry?
We could repeat it together."

Sam just stirred his porridge like a spoilt child.

"What's wrong? Do you miss your brother even though
he's here with you at the castle?" Her lips tipped in a soft,
understanding smile. He finally looked at her.

"You're not Damien's friend." He scowled and returned
his stare to the porridge.

Alexandra was struck speechless. She couldn't quite understand what he was saying, nor why he had said it. "Why would

you say such a thing, Sam? Your brother and I have the utmost regard for one another.''

''But he doesn't like to be with you.''

A tiny frown appeared on the bridge of her nose. ''Why do you say such a thing?''

''He's never with you. He's only with her.''

She placed her trembling hands in her lap and gave him a cool, level stare. ''Who do you mean by *her*, Sam?''

''Her,'' was all Sam answered, before he shrugged and returned his attention to his porridge.

Alexandra was at a loss what to do next. Her first instinct was to shake him and force him to elaborate, but she knew such action would only serve to frighten him, and there was no point in it. Calmly, she sipped her coffee and analyzed the situation. But every avenue led her to Ursula. She just couldn't fathom what Sam had meant by Damien being with *her*. Yet she was determined in the course of their lessons, she was going to find out.

''Shall we go to the library?'' she asked lightly when he had finished his porridge.

Sam nodded and the underbutler helped her with her chair. Soon they were ensconced in the library with Sam perched on Damien's own chair while Alexandra scanned the volumes lining the walls for some suitable poetry.

''Here we are . . . how about this?'' She slipped out a volume by Thomson entitled *Liberty* and placed herself on the floor near the hearth. She'd found it was always better to assume an inferior position with Sam, for he became tense and quiet whenever she looked over his shoulder.

''Now, let's see if we can find something. . . . Oh, here we are.'' She raised the book up in front of her face and read a few lines, until she came to the passage:

> *Then from the bleak coast that hears*
> *The German Ocean roar, deep booming, strong*
> *And yellow-hair'd, the blue-eyed Saxon came.*

"Damien," Sam whispered, as if she were describing him.

"Can you repeat it, Sam?" she asked, hating the poem already. She wanted to get away from thoughts of Lord Newell and here she had found the one poem in the whole library that reminded Sam of him.

"Then from the bleak coast," she prompted.

"F'om the bleak coast," he mimicked.

"Then from the bleak coast," she corrected.

"From Cairncross, the red-haired Saxon came." Sam's mind seemed to slip into a world of his own. He whispered, "As I am now, so you must be. So take my hand and come with me."

"Sam?" She rose to her knees and touched his hand. She took both his arms and shook him finally to get him to look at her. "What are you saying, Sam? Who taught you those words?"

"As I am now, so you must be. So take my hand and come with me." He stared at her, with eyes so much like his brother's, but bereft of the intelligence that was Damien's.

"Who says that, Sam? Who taught you such a poem? Was it Miss Pole? Where does she talk to you? In your room?" She forced herself to keep her voice soft and her expression concerned but relaxed. It was near agony to manage it when she felt as if an army of skeletons were marching down her back.

"Not my room. She's not in my room. She's with Damien."

"But where does she talk to you? Can you show me?" She wanted to shake him and force him to take her there. Ursula was hiding in this castle and part of her cloak was this man's slowness. She had to get Sam to reveal her.

"Take my hand and come with me." He stood and held out his hand. With a snake of a shiver careening down her back, she took it.

They walked through what seemed to be miles of passages in the castle's east wing. Here the castle was built closest to the coast and there was many a breathtaking view of violent sea before they wound their way down the turret stairs to where the rock walls began to weep salt water.

"How far does this go, Samuel, all the way to the River Styx?" She looked below while he climbed lower and lower into the darkness. "Sam?" The chill air making her shiver, she held out the candelabrum she had taken with her and tried to spy him in the darkness.

Sam paused on the stair and looked up at her. "Down. We must go down."

She released a disconcerted sigh. Lifting her skirts, she continued the climb.

At last they reached solid ground, or rather, solid stone. From what little she could detect in the gloom they were in a large domed cave that must somehow lead out to the lower sea cliffs. There were casks of dry goods stored against one wall and upon further inspection, she determined they had been there for five centuries at least; they were the extra stores to ready the castle for war.

"You see her here, Sam?" she asked, dismayed that he would come to this dark, wretched place alone.

"Not here. Here." Sam wandered away into the shadows. Nervously she clutched the candelabrum and followed.

He led her to a fifteen-foot door carved into the face of the cave wall. Laurel swags and a ram's head adorned the top, and the sides were carved with numerous Roman trophies, armaments, and sacrifices. It was the entrance to the catacombs.

"There. She's in there. I see her in there," Sam said mournfully. Even in the near darkness, she could see his head bowed, his eyes cast downward in fear.

"Shall we have a look inside?" she asked, feeling more nervous than she wanted to. Damien had said the catacombs were almost endless, and staring at the maw of the entrance, she was suddenly hit by the instinctual panic of being buried alive, lost in the maze of tombs beneath the castle.

"Don't go in there!" Sam shouted abruptly, his normal cowering shoved aside.

Alexandra almost jumped to the ceiling.

Soothingly, she said, "I'll inform Lord Newell about this. He should have these catacombs explored as best he can." She touched his sleeve. "You understand, don't you, Sam? We can't have this madwoman running loose around here any longer."

"Don't go in there!"

Sam grabbed her. She cried out and the candelabrum slipped from her, clattering to the rock floor of the cave. The light extinguished and they were cast into an oily pitch blackness. The utter darkness of hell.

"God help us," she cried out with Sam's iron arm around her waist as he dragged her away from the entrance to the tombs. She struggled with him to let her free, but it was like fighting a Goliath, he was so big and muscular and strong she couldn't move an inch without his permitting it.

The stones along the cave floor ripped at her hem but she couldn't get her feet. With no light to tell her where things were, she was turned upside down and inside out. She had no bearings. She was being dragged through a universe of nothingness and it made her lose her sense of balance, indeed her very sense of self.

"Sam, I beg you—you're hurting me—what are you doing?" she whimpered, his fingers like iron spikes digging into her ribcage while he dragged her.

"Don't go in there," the giant mumbled like a chant. Then he tightened his grip most painfully to show his displeasure.

"Call for help. Call for help. We're lost in this darkness. Don't you understand—" Tears streamed down her face. Her heart beat frantically; it was difficult to catch her breath. The blackness was all hell. Her fear of Sam was surpassed only by her fear that he might let her go, and she would have to face the utter darkness alone.

Incredibly she felt a heavy thud and then another along her backside. It took her a moment to realize that Sam had found the stairs. The years of his journeys through the cave must have given him some sense of direction. Even in the thick and utter blackness of the cave, he'd found the stairs like a vampire bat finds blood.

She moaned and grabbed at the arm around her chest. She could find her way now and his hold was unutterably painful. Sam didn't know his own strength. He was near to choking her.

"Please—Sam—let me go. Let me go," she pleaded, the fingers still digging mercilessly into her ribs.

"Don't go in there. You can't go in there." He was weeping. His muffled sobs were the harsh, terrible gasps of a grown man.

"Oh, Sam. Oh, Sam, please let me go. You're hurting me. I know why you did it. I understand, but I beg you, let me go." She wept too. His grief and pain of his grip was too much for her.

Still, he didn't release her. It wasn't until they burst from the tower door into the belowstairs servants' passage did he even think to relinquish her. By then she was convinced he had broken one of her ribs. Her breathing was labored even after he let her tumble to the floor.

The passage was not well lit but compared to the nightmare below it, she felt as if she were basking in the sun, not beneath a smoky old oil lamp. Panting to catch her breath, she crawled to a space against the wall. Sam had placed his back against the door as if he feared she would take off down the stairs again the minute he wasn't looking.

She caught her breath and tried to tame her sobs. There was no one in the passage—or at least so she thought—when suddenly a figure appeared down the hall. It loomed closer and closer. Her breath caught in her throat.

"Damien!" Sam shouted out, his joy at seeing his brother erasing the terrible moment.

"Mrs. Penrith feared you'd come down here." Gently, he lowered himself to a kneeling position to look at Alexandra.

"My lord," she whimpered, her fears suddenly overwhelming her. She didn't want to do it; she knew he'd disapprove, but her needs got the better of her. Without the strength or will to do otherwise, she placed her head against his chest and began to weep.

"Alex," he said, his voice strangely constricted as if he were disturbed by her display of need. "Sam didn't understand not to bring you here."

"Our—light—went out," she sobbed. "There was just darkness everywhere. And Sam grabbed me. He was so angry."

"He wouldn't have hurt you. He loves you," Damien whispered.

"He just kept saying, 'Don't go in there. Don't go in there.'" She trembled all over. For some reason the implacable warmth of the chest she cried against seemed to coax out all her terrors and weakness.

"He was afraid you'd get lost. He's not good at expressing himself. You know that." As if he didn't even realize it, he reached out and stroked her temple, brushing away the loose curls.

The sudden awareness of their intimacy seemed to shock both of them in the same instant. She felt him stiffen. He tried to pull away, but she wouldn't let go. Her side ached abominably, and she was weak from fright, but she had never felt so . . . safe. So at peace. Where she was, was a place warm and secure. She never wanted to leave the wall of Damien's chest.

"Look at him," he whispered, his gaze flickering to his brother. "He's more upset than you are. You gave him a terrible fright, no doubt."

Alexandra wiped the tears from her cheeks and looked up at Sam. He hovered over them like a child witnessing a birth, all wide-eyed, wondrous and afraid.

"Oh, Sam, it was my fault," she choked. "I shouldn't have gone down there alone with you."

Sam said nothing, he just watched her, his face pale and intent.

"He's taken with you," Damien whispered, as if the words went against his will.

A tingle ran through her. Her gaze lifted and locked with his. Suddenly she had so much to say to him, but the words, the questions, the answers, wouldn't come.

She touched his cheek. "Damien . . . " she whispered.

"Don't." He lowered his gaze.

Tears fell on her face like acid. The expression on his face was that of one who was without hope.

"Perhaps it would be better to take Sam away." She stared at Damien. Now he was inscrutable. Not an emotion escaped the hard planes of his face.

"She doesn't want Sam gone. She wants you gone." The words were more harsh than she believed he meant them to be.

She leaned back against the corner. The floorboards felt hard and inhospitable against her bottom. "I don't want to leave." She was a fool to say such a thing. It was decidedly dangerous trying to live here. She couldn't physically control Sam, and she couldn't understand Damien. But instinct told her to stay. A feeling deep in her heart as she watched him beg her to stay until the feeling ended. Her fear was that the feeling was forever.

She slowly wiped the tears from her cheeks with the back of her hand. "I want to help. What should I do?"

"Tell me what Sam tells you. And stay away from the catacombs." His face was dead serious. "I would have them searched but they've fallen in places and they're not safe. The labyrinth is unexplored and extensive. You must understand." He stared at her. "Sam saved your life today. If you'd gone in there you might never have found your way out."

She nodded, cursing the tears that still welled in her eyes. "I'll stay away from it."

"There are passages all throughout Cairncross. If you come upon a passage, tell me."

"What kind of passages?"

"During a siege knights could escape the castle by exiting through the catacombs. There's a hidden passageway in most of the castle rooms. I know where some of them are, but not all of them. They enter the Roman tombs." His eyes darkened. "I've a ledger that accounts for the disappearance of fifty knights. They never reached the outside. Indeed," his darkly amused gaze skimmed the walls, "they may be lying but inches away from us now, on the other side."

She leaned away from the wall and shuddered. Thank God Sam had acted the way he had. Perhaps he had saved her life.

"How can you live here? This foul, wretched place," she whispered.

"There are times when it suits me." He tipped her chin up so she would look him in the eyes. " 'Tis a fair righteous place compared with Wapping."

His thumb brushed her tear-damp cheek. "Can you stand? I'll take you to your room and summon Mary." He rose from his knees and helped her up. She thought to walk alone, but he put his arm around her waist as if it belonged there. Together, with Sam bringing up the rear, finally calm, they took the steps to her room. They walked in silence, for now there was no more to be said.

Alexandra stared at her nude body in front of the walnut cheval mirror. Her hair was still wet from its washing, her limbs damp with droplets of water the linen towel had missed. A fire burned bright in the hearth and the room was jungle warm from the steam from her bath.

There were still bruises along her ribs where Sam had grabbed her. A week had gone by with no more incidents, but she continued to wear the traces of her misery in the black marks along her side. She had not seen Damien. The servants whispered to Mary that he'd been acting strangely since his return to Cairncross, but when Alexandra had questioned Mary about what they meant, the maidservant had merely shrugged it off with a comment stating that she'd always thought his lordship strange.

The clock on the mantel rang ten times. The evening meal had come and gone and Mrs. Penrith's cordial, always sent up at nine, still sat on the hearthside table, the chartreuse sparkling brilliant sulphur green in the firelight.

She walked over to it and placed the tiny footed goblet to

her lips. The flames it lit within her felt wonderful. Even necessary. They chased the chill that had seeped into her heart ever since her own return to Cairncross. She had not seen Damien for days. She had no claim on the master of the house, but she had thought there was at least a budding camaraderie in their quest to help Sam. Now she wondered if she had imagined it. A week was an eternity when one feared one was in love. That she believed she might have fallen in love with John Damien Newell, was becoming more and more true.

Her gaze drifted back to the nude form in the mirror. There was nothing to disparage in it; it was not the most lithesome, statuesque form, but it was pleasingly curved, full-breasted, round-hipped.

She leaned toward the curtain and swathed the hanging length around her figure. The lace undercurtain she demurely wrapped around her head, lifting a panel to place beneath her eyes in the manner of the Saracens.

Rebecca had looked like this. Her veiling had been of jewels and gold-spun cloth, not heavy Alençon lace, but she had peeked out from such a cover to capture the eyes of every man in the tourney, including Wilfred of Ivanhoe, including Brian de Bois-Guilbert.

She was a beautiful Jewess. Legendary.

Alexandra studied her image in the mirror. Her eyes were dark and pretty, but not quite exotic because there was too much mundane Irish in her blood for that. She was no exquisite Jewess, the kind that Sir Walter Scott had come upon in New York and written about in such a noble fashion. She was only Alexandra Benjamin, the bookish daughter of a Jewish scientist, a lonely woman, a woman who wanted . . . wanted . . .

What? What did she want? To become wife to the baron of Cairncross? The absurdity of it struck her like a slap to the face. She couldn't imagine such a thing, and yet there it was, torturing her in the back of her mind, terrorizing her with the idea that she might have fallen in love with him. That she might once more have tripped into such utter stupidity. Yet, day by day, it became harder to deny. She thought of Damien every waking moment of every day. Dreamt of him every slumbering midnight.

But he didn't deign to see her anymore. Perhaps he'd noticed her growing attachment to him and decided to do the gentlemanly thing by separating them before she had grown too fond of him. Before she had expectations. Before he had to do to her what Brian had done.

With a sigh, she dropped the curtain and lace veiling. Unhappily, she donned her dressing gown and took up her horn-backed brush. It would take hours to get her hair dry. She had to keep her mind on more ordinary matters, such as Sam's progress, and she had to forget Damien. He was not for her. She was attracted to him—most women would be—but his coldness was a blessing. He hid himself behind an implacable shield; she'd been allowed but the briefest glances behind it, and already she knew it wasn't going to be enough to just fall in love with him. His tortured soul had been calculated to touch her, so she must warn herself against such weakness. She had imagined Brian once with disturbing, deep emotions. His feelings, in truth, were as clear, temporary, and shallow as a seasonal moorland stream; she had only misread them. And she was misreading Newell as well. There was probably nothing more to the man than a deluded, self-absorbed lord who fancied himself in a pact with the devil. Why, there'd been thousands of those. Lord Byron had even made such dementia fashionable.

It was best they stayed away from each other.

She went to the curtain once more and held the lace beneath her eyes. *Rebecca. Rebecca.*

How she longed to be a dark foreign beauty who could seduce with a look.

Chapter
Nineteen

"You've an invitation, love, from a most mysterious source."
Mary left Alexandra's morning coffee on the tray and instead
brought her a wax-sealed vellum notecard. "Did you know
Lord Newell's grandmother lives here at the castle? I was struck
dumb, I was, to hear it. There are more secrets in this place
than there are legends about Ben Nevis."

Alexandra cracked open the seal. She read the note, then
absentmindedly returned to unplaiting her hair.

"Well?" Mary placed her hands on her hips.

Alexandra glanced at her, then laughed. "From now on, I'm
going to introduce you as my nosy Godmother instead of my
maid."

"I *am* your Godmother. There was no other at your birth."

Alexandra's lips tipped in a mischievous smile. "And I can't
be forgetting it with you here always to remind me—now can
I?"

"You still haven't told me what the note says." Mary was
so agitated that her silvery red curls were popping out from
under her cap.

"It's a note inviting me for a visit. It seems Lady Bess has of late discovered I'm here, and she's curious about me." She took the brush to her loosened hair. "I can't really refuse her."

"By all rights, she's the lady of the house. You can't refuse her . . . still—"

"Still, you don't like old women who roam the north tower like a haunt, do you?" Alexandra lowered the brush. The need to protect Mary once more rose up from inside her. "Please don't worry. I know you don't like anything about Cairncross, but it's only proper that I answer this missive."

"I wouldn't like the woman even if she were young and beautiful and his lordship's wife. She's part of this place and indeed, I don't like it."

"It'll only be for a short visit. You must understand, I'm just as obligated to his lordship's grandmother as I would be to his wife."

Mary paused. In the mirror, Alexandra watched the woman's features screw into a taut expression of ambivalence.

"You look as if you're bursting to tell me a secret, Mary." Alexandra stared at Mary's reflection.

"He'll be takin' a wife soon, I hear. There's talk belowstairs, you understand. Talk of an engagement."

The brush fell from Alexandra's hand. Slowly, she turned on the tufted seat and faced the maidservant. "What are you saying?"

"I've been hearin' talk, about a woman from London. She's the daughter of an old and infirm earl. Very beautiful, I'm told by the servants that come with him from London. He's been seen with her on many an occasion."

Alexandra felt as if the wooden floorboards had snapped beneath her feet. It hadn't happened twice in her lifetime, but it almost had. She had almost fallen for a man who was about to throw her over for another. It was only sheer fate that kept her from committing such suicide twice. At least Newell never knew where her heart had been leading her. She could pretend utter indifference and enthusiasm for his gossiped-about alliance. He would never see the humiliation that drove into her heart as if Brian were yesterday. She'd been spared that indignity at least.

"His lordship has probably a dozen young women in London who've set their cap for him," she said evenly, rigidly, oblivious to the damning evidence of the brush that lay at her feet. "Why shouldn't he be looking for a wife among them? He's handsome, he's titled and rich. . . . Why, any woman would want a peer for a husband."

"Yes, any woman," Mary answered, gently picking up the brush and handing it to her.

Alexandra brushed and brushed until she felt she must have pulled every hair from her head. Mary offered no words in the quiet, companionable, understanding silence. When Alexandra was finished with the last pin to her hair, she stood and her eyes met Mary's. They said nothing, as they had said nothing when Brian had left the town house almost a year ago Christmas Eve. The shared hurt was too deep.

"He's not for me. He's never been one for me and I knew it from the beginning. Don't think I was fooled, Mary, I knew it from the beginning." Alexandra finally said, yanking on her corset hooks as if violence would close them better than attention.

"You deserve a fine man. When we return to London he'll come along. I know it."

Alexandra bit back her reply. Her first notion was to tell Mary that they were headed for London this night; her work at Cairncross, though only begun, could be damned, for she could not stay in this house if Newell took a wife. But her more rational side took over before the offending words were out. They had shared little but a kiss and now Newell refused to see her. There was nothing to leave Cairncross for. If anything, a Lady Newell might make it a better place. She might get her husband's mind off of ghosts and the devil and place it on more holy thoughts. And a wife would keep him out of the governess's path.

"I'm off to see the good Lady Bess." She stood and nearly threw her gown over her head. When the pins were straight in her hair and her bodice was hooked to the throat, she flipped her shawl over her shoulder and left Mary to stew over her mistress, alone.

The north tower was easy to find. Not only was she getting used to the castle's layout, but the tower could be seen from nearly every window and battlement for it loomed twice as high as the keep. Alexandra found the winding staircase and ascended. At the top was a heavy oak door nearly turned to stone from age. She knocked softly, tentatively, then wondered at the haunt that might open the door. Below, the spiraling maw of the tower was dim; there was a draft that wafted up it, sending ice fingers to wander down her back.

She suddenly jumped at the cry of rusty iron. A latch was thrown on the other side of the door and with a shudder, the huge behemoth was shunted aside, and she stared at an unfamiliar wizened little woman who looked just like a witch from a child's fairy tale.

"And who do you be?" the woman asked, her voice curious but not unpleasant.

"Lady Bess summoned me. I'm Miss Benjamin. Samuel's instructor." She stared at the old woman. The elderly woman wore a cap with long heavy lappets, the kind not seen since the turn of the century. Her black gown was adorned with a clean but frayed linen apron. She was old, yet hers was not the face Alexandra remembered on the stair. This face was certainly wrinkled, almost prunelike, but the eyes that stared back were periwinkle blue and full of energy. She would have remembered this face, and Alexandra knew she had never seen it before.

"Ah, yes, of course, the new governess. Come in, Miss Benjamin, come in. Lady Bess has spoken of nothing but you for weeks. Come in." The old woman moved aside and bade her enter.

It was as if Alexandra had entered fairyland. The walls were draped with every colored silk imaginable and where the silk had run out, multicolored chintz in gaudy patterns of stripes, cabbage roses, and lilies was tacked to the ceiling giving the room the ethereal effect of a garden in the clouds. Sunlight

streamed through a mullioned window high in the tower, dap-
pling the room with spots of gold, only furthering the other-
worldly appearance. And there, below the window, as if upon
a throne, sat an ancient woman draped in black, the joyful
chintz the perfect foil for her morbidity. Her face had once
been beautiful, but age had satirized it, descending her features
into the grotesque. It was the face of the woman Alexandra
had seen on the stair.

"You're here." The woman announced, pointing to her as
if she were ordering her execution.

"Lady Bess." Alexandra made an awkward attempt to
curtsy. She was still not quite used to the peerage.

"Why haven't you come up to see me before now?"

The question was so pointed, Alexandra had a difficult time
answering it. "I—well, really—I didn't know you even existed
until but a few weeks ago in the garden—"

"He didn't tell you?" The old woman seemed quite affronted
now. Her white face almost matched the tufts of long silvered
hair that still persisted on her scalp. "The cheek of him to keep
me a secret from you."

"If you're speaking of Lord Newell, he didn't really keep
you a secret. I simply believed he didn't think I needed to
know." Her voice trailed. "I believe he didn't think I would
be here long enough to need to know."

"He thought *she*'d get you, did he?" Lady Bess tapped a
cane she held in the gnarled root of one fist. "Tea. Tea at once,
Millicent."

Lady Bess returned her attention to her guest. "Sit here with
me, Miss Benjamin. We'll have a chat, you and I. Then you
will understand me, and I will understand you."

Alexandra opened her mouth to say something, but she
wasn't sure what it was she wanted to communicate. That Lady
Bess was well into her ninetieth year was no surprise to her,
but the quickness of the woman's tongue was a shock; too was
the pointedness of her questions.

She sank into an aged, tapestried chair and waited while
Millicent appeared from behind some of the wall drapery with

a full tea tray. Lady Bess motioned for her to pour out and while Alexandra did so, Millicent disappeared between the parted cloth once more.

"Now tell me, what do you think of him?" Lady Bess took her cup and saucer in one shaky hand and stirred with a silver spoon in another. She stared at Alexandra from beneath lids as heavily draped as the walls. There wasn't the life within her eyes as within Millicent's. Hers were murky colored, a hazel much like Alexandra's, only faded and dimmed. Yet a keenness still burned within them and Alexandra was almost grateful for the veil of wrinkled lids.

"I think Samuel is going to talk like his old self again very soon and my task will be completed." She took a sip of her tea and glanced around her. She felt odd in the surroundings, as if she were taking refreshment in a Frenchman's campaign tent.

"You know I'm not asking about Samuel. He'll speak again if he bloody well feels like it and not a moment earlier. I'm asking you about Damien."

Alexandra gave the woman a look that she prayed was somehow quelling, haughty even. "I have the highest regard for my employer, Lady Bess, and to have further opinion would not be in my best interest at all."

The old woman began to laugh. It was a terrible choking sound that forced Millicent to pop her head from between the drapery to check on the ancient peeress.

When the laughter ceased, Millicent's head disappeared, and Lady Bess began to talk once more. "He told me you were unusually truthful and insightful. He was right, by God." The woman put down her tea. Her thinning white hair seemed to wave about her head like a halo beneath the glow of sunshine. "Now tell me, what do you think of her?"

Alexandra paused and studied the woman, assessing her fortitude. "If you mean Miss Pole, I despise her. Naturally. I thought you were her on the stairs. I hope I didn't give you a fright. No one told me you enjoyed wandering."

"I follow her sometimes. We weave through the passages

and taunt each other. It's quite a challenge, don't you see? I'm a ghost who's yet to be." The woman smiled. She had no teeth.

"I don't think you'll be haunting these halls for many a year yet. I understand your health is remarkable from what Dam— from what Lord Newell tells me." She could have kicked herself for revealing the familiarity, and she could have flogged herself when she read in Lady Bess's expression that the old woman had noticed it.

"Are you in love with him?"

Alexandra shook her head so hard she felt it might spin from her neck. "Of course not."

"Oh, you are, you are. All the women are in love with Damien. And in your face, I believe it's even genuine."

Alexandra had to force herself to keep her hands in her lap so they wouldn't fly up to her reddening cheeks and further betray her. "He's a handsome man, but he's my employer. It would be foolish of me to—"

"To what? Love him?" The woman leaned close to her, so close Alexandra could smell the rose water that covered the scent of shriveling flesh. "To love him is imperative. To love him is to save him."

"There's talk of an engagement—"

"He wants you."

"Don't be absurd. I'm only the governess here. Besides I'm—everyone thinks I'm . . ." She couldn't say it.

"A Jewess?"

"Yes." The word came out in a gasp. Like a dying man's last prayer.

"Why can't he be with a Jewess? There is no law forbidding it."

"There is moral law," she blurted out more acidly than she would have liked.

"Damien doesn't need morality. He needs to be saved. From *her*."

"He's a grown man. He'll catch her. You yourself admitted to finding her roaming these halls. It's just a matter of time before Ursula Pole is caught and placed into an asylum."

"You cling to that theory, do you?" Lady Bess clasped her hands in her lap. It was then that Alexandra noticed the jewels on her creased, blue-veined hands. There was a fortune in rubies, sapphires, and diamonds adorning her gnarled fingers. The dazzle was so brilliant, she could not look away.

"You like them?" Lady Bess whispered in her ear. "They'll go to Damien's bride when I'm gone."

Alexandra raised her eyes to meet the woman's gaze. "I cannot help but admire them, but I don't covet them. It's not my place."

"You're much too confined to your 'place,' Miss Benjamin. You're too demure and accepting. You should fight the constraints around you. Rebel, child. Do whatever it takes to capture Damien."

"I forgot my place once." Alexandra stared woodenly at her. "My father was not a religious man, so I learned everything I know about being Jewish from one painful lesson. I've no need to do it again."

Lady Bess seemed utterly bemused. She leaned back against the cushions of her armchair and studied Alexandra as if she were some kind of creature she'd never met before. "I can see why Damien speaks so highly of you. You're quite unexpected, my dear. Everything you say is difficult to dispute and how I want to dispute it."

Alexandra finished the last of her tea. She quietly placed her cup on the tray and began her departure. "It was most kind of you to invite me to your apartments, Lady Bess. Should you ever find you're in need of my services, please do not hesitate to request them. Your garden below is lovely and I feel privileged to have finally met you."

"Before you go, tell me one thing." Lady Bess touched her lightly on the wrist. "In your heart, do you believe Damien worth saving?"

She could hardly look at the woman. Alexandra felt as if her face had been frozen into a mask of studied uninterest. "Lord Newell, if he is in need of saving, can save himself."

"Yes, but he has to *want* to save himself." Lady Bess added in a harsh, urgent whisper, "I was blind to him and Sam years earlier when they needed me. Don't you understand? I've got to make up for it now. I've to see the damage repaired before I die. He needs you, my dear. He needs you."

"I really must go. The past is done, and I've a lesson with Sam this afternoon in the garden. It's such a lovely day today . . . so unusually temperate." Alexandra stood and bowed to the peeress. The need to leave pressed upon her shoulders like heavy ballast. The air in the tower room had grown thick and hot from so much suffocating drapery. "I'm so honored to have made your acquaintance, my lady. Please call on me should you need anything. Anything at all." Too hastily she went to the door and turned the latch. She was out the door and descending the tower stairs before she heard Lady Bess's final plea.

"I need you to save my grandson, that's what I need. Don't let him go the way of her. Save him. I beg you." The last was barely a ruffle of the wind. "Save him."

Chapter Twenty

Alexandra sought escape on the moors. Her conversation with Lady Bess had disturbed her more than any previous to it. Perhaps because it had no real bearing on Ursula Pole. Perhaps because it came too close to the slicing truth.

The day had started out fair and warm, but now she felt the ice in the wind. Clouds darkened the cairns on the glyphs to the north, creating an ominous, jagged horizon. Her walk should have settled her, instead it made her even more restless. She hugged the edges of her black cloak together, and wondered what Newell was doing at the moment. The stablemaster had had his horse readied for a ride before she'd left on her walk. Now she wondered whether he desired a gallop on the moors because he felt as agitated as she did. He'd kept to himself so much she was amazed that even in the castle's countless rooms two people could live their lives without ever setting eyes on one another. All the more evidence of Ursula Pole's manifestation.

The wind cut sharply now and she thought of returning. She'd gone farther than she thought. The walk home would be miserable in such a chill.

It was then she saw her.

She was very far away, a blur of black on the moorland. Still, Alexandra knew her. Fear glued her feet to the ground.

The figure didn't move. She stood in a patch of dying hare-bells, dressed in a black gown and veil, much as the dressmaker's dummy had been costumed, but now they were miles from Cairncross, not in some servants' passage. This was no mannequin, no trumped-up display. This was a woman, her form deathly still on a bleak landscape, her face directed toward Alexandra as if she'd expected her.

Anger suddenly lit within Alexandra. Here she was, finally face to face with her nemesis. She was going to catch the woman now, if it took all her strength.

"I know all about you," she cried out to the distant figure. "I know about your schemes and your plans!" She picked up her heavy skirts in two fists and began to run toward her, with no other thought on her mind but to grab her and see for herself that this Ursula Pole was of flesh and not imagination.

"I've read the diary!" she panted, running desperately to close the distance between them, but strangely, making no headway. "You remember it, surely! You left it for me!" Furious tears clouded her vision. She had never felt such indignant anger, not even for Brian. This creature before her had caused so much sorrow, Alexandra couldn't hold in her wrath. The woman must be caught and locked up so that she couldn't spread her misery any longer. And she was going to be the one to do it. And do it now.

But the woman drew no closer. It seemed no matter how far Alexandra ran, Ursula Pole's unnatural figure remained planted the same distance from her. Hysteria rose up as Alexandra ran and ran, all the while gasping for breath, and still, the figure loomed no larger, the details became no clearer.

Finally, with sobs cutting her breath even further, she stumbled on a patch of heather and fell to her knees. She sat there, tears streaming down her face as she looked at the black-draped woman, her anger suddenly being transplanted by utter perplexity.

It was not possible. She told herself this again and again until she had the energy to get to her feet. She ran some more, this time twice the distance as she had previously, but Ursula drew no nearer, and tears of frustration instead of anger ran down her cheeks.

"Come here and face me!" she screamed, giving in to the hysteria. Her side felt as if it might split open from the agony of the run, but still she kept on, determined to reach the woman and prove everything that she thought.

Alexandra didn't hear the rider gallop up behind; she didn't hear the man dismount, nor did she hear him harshly call her name. She was so fixated on the figure in the distance, that heaven and earth could have come to an end and all she would have seen was the black-garbed woman staring at her from the moors.

"Alexandra!"

With a guttural cry, she felt two strong hands pull her up short. She fought with her captor, unable to even register who he was, while she reached for the figure in the distance, convinced Ursula would disappear if Alexandra so much as paused.

"See her there, out on the moors? Get her! Get her!" She moaned in frustration as the hands held her tight. Slowly she looked up to see who it was. It was Damien. His gaze never even wavered from her face.

"Don't you see her?" she asked in a small, panting voice.

"You won't catch her."

"I ran and I ran and I still couldn't get near her. But she never moved. She never moved!" she wept hysterically.

Damien's spectacles had fogged in the sudden Yorkshire chill. She couldn't see even the outline of eyes. His was only a cold, handsome, anonymous face peering down at her. Offering no solace.

"You can run forever, but you'll never catch up with it," he said.

"Don't you see her? It's Ursula. *Ursula,*" she moaned, her eyes trained on the dark, veiled figure that now seemed to watch both of them.

"I see her." He looked up and gave the woman a cursory

glance, as if jaded to her appearance. "But no one can catch her. The figure on the moor isn't really there . . . and yet, it is there, but too distant for our pitiable mortality to reach."

"She's not a ghost. She's not," Alexandra sobbed, burying her head in his chest. The wind whipped at the numerous capes of his greatcoat making her feel as if she were enclosed within a flock of ravens. She couldn't bear to watch the figure any longer. It chilled her to the bone to think of her and Damien embraced on the moors, with that unnatural black-draped woman staring at them from a distance.

"Take me home, then, if you won't chase her. Take me home," she murmured, wondering when she would have the courage to peek out from the safety of his chest.

"You don't have to be afraid. I'm not afraid, Alexandra."

She wiped her cheeks and stared up at him. She could see everything but his eyes. His eyes were cloaked in the frosted glass of his spectacles.

Slowly, she reached out and took the wires from behind his ears. She wanted to throw the spectacles to the ground and crush them with her heel; instead, she put them in his hand and seized the opportunity to look into his eyes.

"Damien," she whispered, finally seeing the man he was. The emotions he hid behind the veneer of ice were now laid naked. She saw a flicker of his perished innocence, and she saw the stronger pull of the shadows. Fear was not anywhere there, and she knew it was because he understood, while she did not.

"What's happening?" she whispered, her voice fearful and raw.

The phantom of a wry smile played upon the corner of his lips, as if he were privy to a dark irony visible only to him. "My interest is in the fallen, not the mighty. Bear witness to it in the choice of swords I display in the Hall. Each of them, Cairncross's included, I bought in Persia, ancient discards from the Crusades, rendered worthless by the Arabic inscriptions of the men who took them from the dead. No one would want such relics but I. It fascinates me, as it fascinates *her,* this felling of angels."

Slowly, he uttered, "Don't you understand now, Alexandra? She wants me, and I—I want you."

Her insides froze as she absorbed his meaning. His words and his easy coexistence with the figure in the distance sickened her. She searched his face for even the smallest hint of human need, of human suffering, but his face was shorn of emotion. It was a slate, wiped clean of chalk. It was the Damien she first knew. A figure of ice, much as Ursula was now a figure of death.

His hand touched her cheek. The caress was gentle, but it didn't register within his eyes. There was no feeling there, only a void that she feared she might become lost in.

"Kiss me, Alexandra. Kiss me, and I'll make her go away."

Alexandra glanced at the figure of Ursula, her vision telling her what her mind could not accept. The woman hadn't moved, and though the wind whipped at their clothing like a tempest, the black-draped woman stood in utter stillness.

"I'm afraid," Alexandra cried out, tears streaming down her cheeks.

"Don't be. She's just a symptom. She's not the cause."

"Are you the cause?" she wept, her heart exploding as his mouth lowered to hers.

His lips crushed hers in a slow, hurtful kiss. She grew numb, and then melted with need. She loved him. Once, a small window had opened up within him and let her peek at the man he could be. And though that man wasn't here now, kissing her with tenderness, she believed he would return, and that alone kept her willing.

A sob escaped her as he moved more forcefully over her mouth. He drew her ever closer until she was locked against him, his desire much like a rod buried beneath layer upon layer of clothes. Marriage and all of society's polite little conventions didn't occur to her when he kissed her as he did now. His was no suitor's kiss, nor Brian's kiss, but one full of animal lust and doom. A sweet, beckoning doom that tempted surrender.

"Please," she moaned as his hand crept up her bodice. He cupped her breast, irreverently ignoring the confines of her corset. She was hot with shame, and hotter still with a sudden need. Her female desire, like wine, had had a long time to mature. She was more than physically ready for what he promised. If only her heart and her soul didn't scream warning.

"Don't," she begged. "She'll see us," she whispered, falling limp against his chest, her emotions torn apart with the war being fought inside her.

"She's gone. Gone. And yet we remain in hell."

Alexandra looked up. The moors were empty. The place where the figure had stood was now only an eternity of blowing, wavy heather.

"She's not a ghost," she whispered hysterically, then hid her gaze once more in his chest.

"Don't think about her," he said, tipping her head up with his knuckles. "Think about this. Only this." He kissed her again, this time dragging his tongue deep inside her mouth as if to taste her. A shock ran through her body as she weakened, and it coursed even stronger when his hand, still on her chest, squeezed and rubbed along the edge of her nipple.

"No," she said, tearing herself from him. She ran a few steps away, then turned to face him, her lips still burning with the memory of his mouth. "You kiss me and yet I hear even this day that you've a woman in London who begs to be your wife. What say you, my lord? Shall you take *her* to wife and *me* to mistress? 'Tis my particular honor to be able to turn down such a proposition twice in my lifetime."

"It's always honor with you, isn't it, Alexandra?" he said, clearly angry at her for placing between them the shield of her self-worth. Whatever he had intended now had been foiled.

"Yes, it's honor," she said acidly. "For I am my father's daughter."

"Ah, yes, the Jew. A descendant of people named Green

and Schoenburg. Those who had to take names like 'pretty mountain' because they lived in dark, squalid ghettos, banished as infidels.''

"My ancestors lived in poverty, my lord, but they lived in honor."

He walked to her and took her arms in a viselike grip. Behind him, the moors rumbled with charcoal-colored clouds and the threat of rain. "We'll see how well that honor stands by you."

"Is that what gives you glee, my lord? To test everyone?" She fairly spat the words at him.

"No," he said softly, a bare whisper. "Just you."

She stared at him, desperately trying to reach whatever goodness rested within his soul. When the effort failed, she broke away from him and ran toward Cairncross that was only a silhouette on the horizon. She didn't hear him remount his horse, nor did she hear him gallop away, as fast in the opposite direction as his steed and his daring would take him.

He was just a shadow man. Life and all its rich emotion remained forever out of reach, torturing him with its promise. He knew his soul was composed of nothing but a dark translucency; inside, he was merely a shade that searched desperately for a light that was not forthcoming. There seemed nothing left in him at times, and he'd never mourned the feeling.

Until now.

Damien urged his horse on towards the western hills. The thunder of the brewing storm was a balm for the hollowness inside. He savagely fought the urge to follow her. There were times, such as now, when he believed he could crush the very life from her body, but then there were times, such as when she'd removed his spectacles, that his emotions became like a fire within him, melting the protection of ice around him.

She knew fear all too well. He could see it in her eyes whenever she glanced at the figure. Now she was teaching him it. She was too disarming, especially when she laid her head against his chest as if, absurdly, she could be comforted by the beat of his ignoble heart.

He couldn't let this woman make him feel. Not when he'd spent his entire life dancing along the chasm that now had him almost swallowed up. He'd have to deal with her, but she'd left him unsure how to do it. There seemed no way to turn her around. She clung to her righteousness like a staff and there seemed no way to pry her fingers from it.

He'd have to follow her path for a while. He could see that now. Nothing overt was going to seduce her into changing. No, he'd have to go quietly to her, sneak up when she'd let her guard down. He had to win her trust. Then he could lure her to his side.

It was risky, going to that method. He knew it every time he pictured her in the garden with Sam, using gentleness instead of wrath to coax the slow man into speaking. She was difficult to hurt when he pictured her that way, her head bent softly to Sam's, his idiot brother staring at her with adoration, the way he wanted to stare sometimes if the feeling had not been like a stab through the heart. She was a merciful angel come to save Sam. And begging a salvation in return, he thought, now imagining her head pressed to his chest as she had done back there on the moor, the open, innocent trust on her face clearly proving that she believed he would help her.

But how could *he* help *her?* She was afraid of Ursula, yet Ursula was nothing compared to him. He couldn't make her see that the figure out on the moor was static and witless. A symbol. Nothing to contend with; an evil that simply laid upon the floor.

Unlike the one in him. The one that longed for a final release. That longed to find one victim to purge itself on. To let out the fires of all hell that lived within him.

He shut his eyes as if that would put up a shield to her terrifying goodness. As if that would fend off his uncontrollable wanting of her. Determination ran through his veins like poison. She didn't know it yet, but he was worse than Ursula. The pupil had eclipsed the teacher. Alexandra Benjamin had no reason to suspect it, but she was going to find it out soon. Not in the violence that she might run from, but in sweet, seductive whispers and solicitous caresses. The lonely daughter of a Jew would not be able to resist.

And it would prove to be her damnation.

Chapter
Twenty-one

*. . . for, if I am again repulsed, my vengeance shall equal
my love.*

—Bois-Guilbert to Rebecca, in IVANHOE

A lull occurred in the tension. It was as if a line pulled taut had
been slackened. The foreboding atmosphere now lay dormant,
waiting. Yet for what, Alexandra didn't know.

She tried not to think of the figure on the moor. Even days
afterward she had trouble reconciling herself to it. It had been
no ghost, but its very stillness disturbed her. Yet not as much
as Damien had disturbed her.

His talk was insanity; his behavior worse. Still, she could
not rip her thoughts from him. It was as if he were becoming
a part of her. She didn't like him, but as one doesn't always
like oneself, she could carry both her dislike and her love within
her heart.

She glanced at the tea tray she'd hardly touched. Her lessons
with Sam were over for the day and now the evening stretched
before her like an interminable, cavernous yawn. Mary kept
belowstairs more frequently now, not because the maid had a

sudden realization of her station, but she claimed the castle, especially the wing where Alexandra's room was, made her feel morbid.

She walked to the bedroom window. Ursula's trunk and its contents had been mercifully hauled away while she'd been in London. Still, the room held its malevolence. It was a comfortable, handsome room, but she was going to be glad to leave it when she must.

She turned her head and looked at the schoolroom door. It was locked and kept locked ever since that last visit there with Sam. She went to it. Her hands felt the warmth of the wood, a sharp contrast to the frigid draft that whistled around its edges.

She would never know what made her look down, but all at once, she spied a piece of paper stuck beneath the door with only a corner visible in her room. As she retrieved it, a chill wrapped around her like a wispy phantom. Already, she knew what it was. The paper was all too familiar. It was another part of the diary.

She straightened. Her eyes surveyed the familiar script. She only caught three words before her stomach tied into a knot and she found she could read no more.

Blood. Seed. Stable.

It was Ursula Pole's account of what had happened that last day with Damien in the stable.

Alexandra folded it and placed it in the top drawer of her bureau. She would read it, but she wasn't up to it now. Not after what had happened to her out on the moors. She needed strength and distance to read that last page. She wasn't sure when she would get them.

"Very good. Excellent. Sam, I do believe you've been the best pupil I've ever had." Alexandra took a sip of the coffee Featherstone had just poured her. It was a rainy morning, so she was giving lessons in the library. She replaced the Sèvres coffee cup in the saucer and returned her attention to Strathey's

Diagram of the Mouth. "Ohhh," she repeated while pointing at the appropriate picture.

"Ohhh," Sam mimicked, watching her carefully.

"Eeeee," she said.

"Eeee—" he began, stopping short when Mrs. Penrith burst into the room, with a perplexed frown on her face.

"Miss—I—Well—I just don't know how to explain it. You'll just have to come see for yourself." The housekeeper waved her forward. Alexandra glanced at Sam, murmured her apologies, and followed Mrs. Penrith, not realizing Sam was tagging behind her.

"What is it?" she asked.

"I was just upstairs with the chambermaid gathering all the stray oil lamps for the scullery maids to clean when I saw the most astounding thing. In your room, miss. Come along. Let me show you." Mrs. Penrith picked up her black silk skirt and surmounted the stairs. Alexandra looked over her shoulder and found Sam right behind her. With no real reason to make him stay behind, she took his arm and allowed him to escort her.

They followed Mrs. Penrith to Alexandra's room. The housekeeper stood in the doorway and pointed to the room's interior. "Do you see, miss?"

Alexandra poked her head through the door and surveyed her room. Nothing seemed out of the ordinary. There were no foreign belongings lying about and her own possessions were still neatly put away where she had left them. The chambermaid had made the bed . . .

"My God," she whispered, her gaze pinned to a spot below her window.

"That's right. It's back. We put it in the keep where his lordship stores all castle's old furniture. And now it's back where it always was, but I didn't request it be returned and it's heavy, miss. It took men just to take the thing out of here."

Alexandra walked into the room, Sam trailing behind her.

"I'm afraid to say it," the housekeeper murmured, "but I could never figure out why the thing remained in here all these years. Now I recall having it moved perhaps a year or two after

Miss Pole disappeared. It never registered that the thing came back. Until it returned this second time.''

Alexandra kneeled before it. It gleamed with new polish. The lock had been replaced also. She had no doubt Ursula Pole's belongings were folded neatly inside, just exactly as they were the day Ursula put them there.

"I can't explain it . . ." Mrs. Penrith said numbly.

"His lordship, I believe, could lift such a trunk. He could bring it here without the servants' help." Alexandra looked at the housekeeper.

Mrs. Penrith only frowned.

"Sam?" Alexandra looked at him. "Did you see Damien lift this trunk? Did he bring this trunk back here perhaps?"

Sam merely stared at her, then slowly shook his head.

"He hasn't the capacity to lie." Mrs. Penrith began to wring her hands.

Alexandra turned her attention back to the trunk. On one corner, there was a scraping of white paint, yet the trim in most of the castle that she'd seen was either varnished walnut or painted Prussian blue. "Now where on earth did that come from?"

Sam stood very still, his head hung low. All at once he went to her bureau. He shoved it aside and pressed on one panel of the walnut wainscoting. It sprang open, revealing a darkened maw painted white sometime in the last century.

"My heavens!" Mrs. Penrith exclaimed.

Alexandra scrambled to her feet. She retrieved the Argand lamp from the mantel and lit it. To her unspeakable relief, the passage was not part of the catacombs filled with dead Roman soldiers. Instead it was simply an old servants' entrance that connected with belowstairs.

"In all my years at Cairncross I never knew that was there." The housekeeper turned to Sam. "How did you know, my dear?"

Sam didn't answer, but whether he didn't understand or couldn't quite form the sentences was never to be known.

"Look, there's raw wood revealed on the trim here," Alexandra exclaimed, studying the passage with the lamp. "The trunk was brought through here and its corner bumped against the doorway." She looked at Sam, then at the housekeeper. "What powers of deduction, he has. I'd have thought he brought the trunk back here except that I can't bring myself to believe he would even touch Ursula Pole's trunk."

"She made Dam'en go 'way. She made Dam'en go 'way." Sam burst into tears. Alexandra's heart wrenched at the sight of this grown man blubbering like a toddler.

"But he came back, didn't he?" she soothed, taking him by the hand. The housekeeper replaced the lamp on the mantel and cleared a path for Alexandra to lead Sam to the crewelwork bench at the foot of the bed.

"Everything about that woman rattles him. I should have brought you here, alone, miss, to show you the trunk," Mrs. Penrith lamented.

"Sam," Alexandra said carefully, "don't be upset. I'm so impressed that you knew about the passage. And that you remembered it was painted white. You've helped us solve a bit of this little mystery. You mustn't cry. Damien came back for you, and he would be proud of you now, too."

Sam wiped his eyes on his jacket sleeves just like a young boy might who'd suffered a skinned knee. "I told you—don't go in there. Don't go in there," he sniffed.

"The catacombs? I didn't go in them because you saved me. You were a hero then, too, do you remember?" Alexandra placed her hand on his arm. When he nodded, embarrassed by her compliments, she could do nothing but wrap her arms around him and hold him to her breast, her emotions overcome with an overwhelming maternal love.

"Let's return to the library, shall we?" she whispered, finally loosening her hold.

A voice rang out from the doorway. "Yes, I think that would be best. Why don't you go first, Samuel, and I'll be down shortly."

Her gaze flew to the entrance. Damien stood there, a grave expression on his face.

Sam broke from her embrace and promptly did what his much-idolized older brother had told him. Mrs. Penrith murmured the excuse of being needed belowstairs, and suddenly Alexandra was alone with Newell.

She looked at him for a long moment and said nothing. Her emotions were still in turmoil from the last time they'd met. He was a dangerous enigma, so dangerous that he could even be wrapped up with that hideous creature out on the moor. Anything was possible.

"My lord?" she said, coolly lifting one eyebrow.

"Miss Benjamin," he countered, his voice as polite and distant as hers.

"Is there something you wish to speak with me about?"

He seemed on edge, as if he were somehow acting and speaking by memory and not impulse. "I came to ask you to dinner. I'd like to talk to you about Sam's progress." He paused and she saw a muscle bunch in his jaw. "After what I just heard, we really *must* talk."

"What did you just hear?" Her forehead furrowed.

"I believe Sam just gave us a clue about his last experience with Ursula. He said, 'She took Damien away.' I never knew his understanding of the situation went so far as that he blamed her for my banishment. This may lead us to the explanation of what she did to him in her final hours at Cairncross."

A tingle went down her neck. She hated thinking of what the woman might have done to Sam. Dear-hearted Sam.

"Did you know about the passage here to my room?" She was surprised by her candor, but her curiosity told her to shove aside the threatening memory of him on the moor and delve into the subject at hand.

"I did not." He glanced at her, then at the trunk. "So she brought it back, I see."

"She couldn't have. It weighs too much."

"Alas, our puny mortal strength." He seemed to bite back a smile. She now felt the chill waft down her spine.

"I don't want to dine with a man who only wants to speak of ghosts. There may be such things as ghosts, but I'll choose to keep my mind on Sam, not on the otherworld—that is beyond my reach."

Her talk seemed to sober him out of his libation of wickedness. He nodded and said, "Yes, tonight, let's speak of Sam. You must keep me informed of all he says, no matter its apparent lack of importance. As this incident proved, I'm a better judge of its significance than you."

"Yes, you can be assured, I'll report everything back to you."

He studied her for a moment, his gaze strangely worshipful and forlorn. He missed nothing; not the thick chignon pinned to her nape, not the fragile way she perched on the bench, nor the way she filled out her bodice. His stare gave her no small amount of discomfort, yet it gave her a strange pleasure too. It was exceedingly reluctant, and therefore, exceedingly complimentary.

"My lord, is there anything else you wish to speak to me about? If not, I really must see to my pupil. Sam and I weren't through with our lessons yet." It felt good to pull away. It felt powerful, but with that power came loneliness. When he tightened his mouth and nodded a curt farewell, she was loath to admit it, but she had never felt more alone.

"Have more pheasant, Miss Benjamin. I brought this brace from the Lake District myself." Newell had the footman refill her plate. She was satiated, but he obviously wanted indulgence. The repast was extraordinary, even though Cairncross's cook always concocted a good meal. It was almost as if Newell had asked for something out of the ordinary, as if he wanted to impress her.

She looked down at her newly filled plate. "Really, my lord, I don't think I can manage any more."

"Then you must have some more wine. The old baron bought this particular bottle in Paris. It was said to be purloined from Château de Malmaison after the Emperor was removed to St. Helena."

"No, really." She covered her wineglass with a sheepish smile. "It's wonderful but I've had enough."

"All right then," he said stiffly, dismissing the footman.

When they were finally alone, she studied him from across the table. He watched her too, his eyes barely detectible beneath the spectacles.

"My lord," she began, "you've hardly mentioned Sam all evening. I almost wonder if you wanted to discuss him at all."

"Ah, so you've caught me." The corner of his mouth tipped up in a wry, handsome grin.

"Caught you?" she asked, not understanding.

He put down his knife and fork, picking up his wine instead. "Is it so wrong to want company in this bleak place? Besides, a governess isn't really a servant. You can't take your meals belowstairs with the rabble. It's common for an employee such as yourself to dine with the family."

She was disconcerted. "After yesterday, I would have thought—"

"Forget yesterday," he interrupted. "I want things to change. In fact, I'd very much like it, Miss Benjamin, for me to be able to call you a friend."

If she was unsettled before, now she was reeling. "My lord, I—"

"Call me Damien."

She stared at him, unsure of what to say. *"Damien,"* she repeated, the name strange on her lips, "I just don't think I understand."

"We got off to a bad start, you and I. I want to make reparations. I want to begin again."

She felt as if someone she didn't know was talking to her. His cold, arcane mannerism that she'd thought she'd begun to understand was now replaced by a forced conviviality, and the reason for the change bothered her most of all. "We needn't begin again, Damien. Let's just go forward," she said simply.

"Yes, let's. And to start, I'm going to begin to pay you what I would have paid your father, Alexandra. You've already worked a miracle on Sam. I owe you that much at least."

She cautiously nodded and murmured a demure thank-you.

"Is there anything you would like here at Cairncross to make you feel more comfortable?"

"Yes," she said, her hands in a white-knuckled grip on the edge of the table. "I'd like you to discover who that wretched creature was out on the moor and make her leave this place. I think we'd all benefit from that. Perhaps Sam, most of all. Someone put that trunk back in my room. Someone. I'd like the wicked mischief to stop."

His face grew taut. The expression in his eyes was hidden. "It's done."

"How can you be so certain about that?" Her suspicions that he might be involved were only strengthened now. She sat across the table from him, suddenly aware of the game he played. He was trying to win her over. She suspected he would say anything that might sway her to his sympathies.

"I didn't do any of the things you think I did, Alex. All I want is a second chance to show you my innocence."

It was a nice, tense, dangerous dinner she was having with Newell, she realized. The battle between good and evil was still there, only now beneath the surface. "Very well," she answered. Her expression was cagey. "But you'll have to excuse me now, my lord—Damien. I suddenly feel the effects of the wine and I should like to retire."

"Of course."

He stood after she did, and he escorted her out into the baronial hall. They walked in silence through the shadowy cavern of limestone and armament. She averted her gaze when she came to the wall of captured swords.

"How mighty the fallen," he whispered, suddenly clasping her hand in his.

She thought to pull back, but his arm encircled her waist and pulled her to him.

He tilted her chin up. "Give me just one gentle kiss to ease the tortures of my soul."

Her stare was transfixed. She couldn't look away. The varnish of his manners had begun to wear thin and by the cruel slant to his mouth, the old Damien lurked behind it.

"This won't work. I see behind the mask, Damien," she whispered.

"What do you see?" he asked.

"I see a man I fear I might love." Her eyes grew dark.

Revulsion crossed his face. He looked as if he wanted to throw her against the wall and run away from her as fast as he could. "You flail with your honesty, do you know that?"

"Return it in kind then." She took the hand that was clasped in her own and held it beseechingly to her cheek. "Tell me what you want from me. I'm not your much-gossiped about London beauty who even now dangles after you. I'm not a woman such as you probably knew in Wapping who is easy with her body and with her love. So what do you want from me, Damien? I'm the daughter of a Jew come to teach your brother. By all accounts, I should have escaped your notice. I should be invisible to you, but time and again, I find you at my side, tugging at my very soul. And I want to know what it is—what it is that holds you in such fascination—"

He bent his head, as if in a gesture of defeat, and leaned against hers, forehead to forehead. Whispering, he said, "How are such things explained? Poets have failed."

"Our relationship is not poetry."

"I fear it could be."

"And *fear* is truly the word, isn't it? What did she do to you, Damien? What ruined you? Sam may one day speak of his agonies, but you'll be harder by half to open up."

"I don't want to think about her," he whispered.

She thought of the diary page still unread in her bureau. As much as she was loath to do it, she would have to read it, and tonight.

"I don't understand you," she confessed. "One minute you're backhanding a servant, and the next, moved to tears over your brother's little triumphs. You talk of evil as if you were bedfellows with it, and yet I truly believe it's the opposite of evil that you want. You want peace. Surrender . . ."

''Never surrender.''

The hand on her waist tightened, bruising her. She knew it was time to fight, or submit to his kiss. A hundred times, she told herself she mustn't want his cruelties, or his kiss. But she did want them; they were heaven and hell, but they kept her close to him.

''Alexandra, let me feel *your* want for once,'' he whispered against her hair.

She released a small moan. Loneliness was a toxin with no antidote for it but risk. She lifted her face, her mind believing she would protest, but all at once, she covered his lips with her own.

She kissed him. She pressed her lips to his and let her heart soar with the intimacy of it. She opened up to his searching tongue and she let him hold her so tightly, she could barely force out a breath. But she continued, her kiss saying things to him that words failed to communicate. Relentlessly, she drew his violence from him and coaxed him into gentleness.

In the back of her mind, she understood that kissing Damien was very much like flirting with the devil. Newell could hurt her. But suddenly she understood that she had to give to him, if even just this once, to see if there was ever hope that the malignancy within him could be excised.

''Don't go to your room tonight,'' he said, after she'd pulled away. ''Stay with me. I want you with me.''

Desire sang within her like a voice that could not be muffled, but still she shook her head. He wanted her, yet Brian had wanted her. Brian had lied and said he loved her, as Newell could easily lie. She didn't want to be told about love; she wanted to be shown love. And John Damien Newell wasn't near ready for such a step.

''No. I must say good-night.''

He grabbed her arm. The face that she knew as cruel, and that had tried tonight to appear affable, was now etched with a deep agony. ''Don't leave.''

Two forlorn words, yet they sent a lancing pain through her heart.

She met his gaze. Her own need pulled on her like a ballast, but she still declined. "This isn't the time. Not yet," she choked out. Then she broke away, gathered her skirts, and ran up the long flight of stairs to her room. His anger at her rejection seemed to bloom like a thick cloud of coal dust. Behind her, she heard the smash and clatter of swords as they fell to the stone floor, each ripped from the wall with his bare hands.

Newell sat in his darkened bedchamber, with a glass of brandy loosely held in his palm. He wasn't drunk. The bottle was half-empty, but still the raw feelings didn't numb. The confusion didn't lessen.

Somewhere out in the passage, the clock struck three times. It would be dawn in a few hours. Another agonizing day of holding back, and holding within.

A noise like the glide of silk over paper came from a faraway corner of the room. He squinted to see who was there; to make out the outline of a form, but his vision was obscured, partly from the brandy, partly from the shadows.

"At last, the foulness reaches my chambers too," he said.

The outline—or was it just hapless shadow?—of a woman was now visible through the dimness.

"Show your face to me, Ursula. Show *me* you haven't changed," he growled, leaning forward in his seat.

The shadow didn't move. The unearthly silence was not breached.

"You've come for me, have you?" He resumed his slouch in the chair. "Well, I'll come when I'm ready."

He stared at the form, his eyes malevolent slits. "And I'll take her with me."

All at once a breeze came up from the corner. A draft, perhaps, but he swore the figure's shadow-gown wafted toward him like black scarves in the wind.

He threw his head back and laughed. "You don't like her, do you? Good. I'm glad, you bitch." He took another deep sip of brandy. "And she doesn't like you, either. So which will win? I would have thought you, Ursula, but after she worked me over tonight, maybe she'll be the victor, after all.''

The breeze grew stronger, but the figure didn't speak, didn't move from the cover of the shadows.

''She looks at me sometimes as if she can see right through me,'' Damien whispered as if to no one. ''I want to hide my shame, skulk in the shadows like you do, Ursula, but then her honesty draws me out again into the light. She's no match for you and I. You might as well go back to your hell, creature of the night. I'm already in mine. I want her,'' he groaned, his hand clenched around the glass so tight it shattered in his palm.

Slowly the shadows melted back into the corner. With drunken, blurred vision, Damien glanced at his bloodied hand. Then he passed out.

Chapter
Twenty-two

The step between time and eternity is short but terrible . . .
—Rebecca, in IVANHOE

Alexandra paced her bedroom until well after midnight, unable to summon the stomach to look at the diary page. Finally, accepting the destiny that had led her to Cairncross and to this moment, she went to the bureau, drew out the piece of paper, and sat down to read it.

I got him to the stables because I told him his father had brought him a new horse. His lordship was never one to do such a thing for his son, but I smile even now just thinking of the trickery. One thing is constant: a lad always has his hopes about his father.

He is big for fourteen. His revulsion of me has caused a blackness to invade my heart. I gave him what he deserved. He hates me, but find I can live with that hatred as much as his love. He's grown tall this year, he looks much older than he is. I've tried to leave him alone, but always there is this need to touch him, to get him to touch me. I tell him time and time again that I have all the power and he has none. None . . .

Today I found him alone in the stable, looking for the new horse. He had stepped inside a fresh straw-bedded stall and I blocked the doorway. I could see on his face that he wanted to hit me. He could have easily pushed me down, kicked me out of his way. He was a giant of a youth, twice my size, but he was intelligent too. He could see I would have enjoyed the fight. And, I suppose, some faint streak of male chivalry kept his hands within his pockets.

I walked up to him and placed my hand at the very center of his manhood. I could see from the stunned innocence in his eyes that he was horrified I could make so bold a move, but he should have known better, the foolish youth. For I am bold. My hatred makes me so.

I unbuttoned him. He didn't move. He seemed as if his every limb was lifeless with shock except where I touched him. I put him in my mouth. He didn't move and I could see he'd never felt such a way before. The power was sweet, as sweet as his flesh was to my tongue.

He was overcome, just as I had hoped he would be. I worked on him as I'd done for no man, until his juice spilled into my mouth. Then I bit him. Oh, the ecstasy. I can still taste the blood and the seed seeping from the corner of my mouth, I can still see the agony and hatred on his face.

He hit me then. He shoved me off and ran out of the stables without even fastening his pants. The stablemaster saw him, and saw me fly out of the stall. I knew what I would do if he told and I was forced to do it. His lordship and Lady Newell were at the castle on one of their infrequent visits. I made sure the baron found me in the stall weeping. I'd torn my dress and smeared Damien's own blood on my linen. "He raped me!" I cried. He beat me into submission, I told him, and I had the red mark on my cheek to prove it.

There was nothing in his defense. There was gossip from the servants that he had shown his father his bloody cock but it only cemented my story that I was trying to defend myself. My acting was superb. I placed my tear-damp linen to my mouth and whispered, "I had to bite him, my lord, because I was forced into an unnatural act."

He'll be gone tomorrow. Sam has cried and cried about his brother leaving but I've ignored the idiot, as I always have. "His lordship was forced to banish him to keep the scandal to a minimum," I screamed at the sobbing cretin. "Your brother got what he deserved."

But I think, still, that banishment isn't enough. I shall follow him . . .

No one understands this need better than Damien.

Alexandra rose from her seat on the bench, slowly made her way to the basin, and retched. She dipped her handkerchief in the ewer and patted her face, trying to ward off another bout of nausea.

She knew Ursula Pole had been an evil woman, but she had never in worst nightmares figured she'd do something like this to a fourteen-year-old boy. Another wave of sickness assailed her. The woman clearly took pleasure writing every detail of her exploits in her diary. It was almost as if by penning each moment, she got to relive it again.

Damien, she thought, suddenly finding tears on her cheeks. She couldn't think about him without a knot of tears in her chest. His parents had all but abandoned him as a child, then when he needed them, they betrayed him by believing Ursula. It was no wonder his thinking was skewed. What kind of perversion could this have created in a young, formative mind when sex was equated with punishment, revenge and fear. He'd commented once on his appetites. She shuddered to think what this had done to them.

She fought the urge to go to his bedchamber, knock softly on the door, and when he answered it, put her arms around him and hold him. He needed someone more desperately than

Sam. Most of her life and her father's had been devoted to the deaf, to those persons who could not put voice to their needs. The deaf were trapped into muteness by their physical self. Newell was trapped by his spiritual self, the part that had been abused into silence. She must help him. That man that she glimpsed every now and then when the spectacles were off was worth saving. Worth loving.

She probably already did love him. Now, though it might even destroy her, she was going to save him. Her whole life had brought her to this moment, this destiny. She was terrified, but she would not run.

"Yes, my lord, it is a pretty day. Unusually warm," Alexandra commented the next day in the garden. She and Sam were ensconced beneath the lime tree while the sun beat upon the stone wall and reflected its warmth. Sam was quietly looking through some picture books she'd found for him in the library while she found solace in the silence. Her mind, her very soul, was still held captive to the diary and Newell. Both of these men, Sam and Newell, seemed to need someone, but she was beginning to understand that Newell's needs were much greater—and more difficult to assist—than Sam's.

She gazed around the garden, basking in the warmth of sunshine that reflected off the crumbling walls. The garden was a sanctuary. A place of peace. A place of hope. She touched a brown rosebud and watched it fall to the dry, weedy ground. There was no doubt that roses would burst from this bush in the spring. As there must be no doubt in her mind that somewhere, somehow, John Damien Newell had rebirth inside of him too. That one small seed of humanity still dwelt within him and could be cultivated.

Her gaze drifted upward. It was then she saw him. He stood tentatively at the garden gates as if reluctant to intrude upon them. His stare met hers and suddenly Ursula, the diary, all came back to her in one breathless shudder, but she was quick to hide it beneath a calm, inexpressive facade. When he strode toward her, one part of her longed to run away. And yet the other part found it hard not to fling her arms around his battered soul.

"I thought to take a trip into town tomorrow," he said tensely as he leaned against the tree. "Would you and Sam like to accompany me to York?"

Sam nodded eagerly. Alexandra trembled a smile, but still she found it difficult to meet his eyes. There was so much to see there now, so much that terrified her, she wondered how she missed it. "Perhaps that's just the medicine we all need: to get away from Cairncross, if but for a day."

He nodded. "Very well." He stared at her. His body tensed as if preparing for battle. He seemed to dislike the effect she had on him. She made a mental note of caution to herself. This dislike could turn dangerous before she might find a way to defang it.

The moment turned awkward. He suddenly appeared as if he wanted to say something but could not. She could only think of the diary page, and of the boy he used to be.

"What time, my lord?" she asked.

"We'll leave at first dawn." He glanced at her, then at the garden gate. Lady Bess and her strange nurse Millicent had just sauntered in, obviously on an outing to take the fresh air.

"Oh, what a glorious day, a glorious day!" Lady Bess exclaimed, leaning heavily upon a silver cane as she walked up to them. "Miss Benjamin, I apologize for my garden being in the undress of autumn. You must see her in the spring. Then she'll be as fine as a pink-cheeked debutante."

Alexandra laughed. "You have a way with words, Lady Bess. Won't you join us while Sam and I take our lesson?"

Lady Bess looked at Newell, the aged colorlessness of her eyes growing dim as she stared. "John Damien, 'tis not like you of late to visit my garden. What are you doing here?"

"Taking the air," he said woodenly, pushing away from the lime tree to assist her to the bench.

Lady Bess handed her nurse the cane and slowly eased herself down onto the marble. "Have you told Miss Benjamin about the garden? About how you and Sam used to play here as a boy?''

He nodded impatiently.

''Until, of course, you were forced out, and the old place became the home of ghosts.''

Alexandra gave Damien a glance. For the briefest of moments, their gazes met. Then he looked away.

''I'm taking Sam to York tomorrow,'' he said. ''Miss Benjamin is coming too. If you need anything from town, give Millicent a list and have her give it to Featherstone.''

Lady Bess leaned toward her, ignoring Newell's change of subject. ''Oh, Miss Benjamin, has Damien told you all the stories of Cairncross? Why, even the old governess has her stories.''

''I doubt very much if Miss Benjamin would like to hear such things, Bess,'' Newell snapped.

The wizened old woman continued to ignore him. ''After Ursula Pole disappeared—now what was it? Twenty years ago?—in any case, we could hear a woman screaming through the castle. Some say it was her going mad and just trying to frighten people because she could never frighten John Damien. But some say 'twas her ghost and that she's dead, and I believe the latter, for they still hear screams today when the wind off the sea is just right and there's a storm blowing in.''

Damien rubbed his chin in a weary gesture of impatience.

Alexandra decided it was time to cut in. ''What a creepy story. It almost sounds as if she were wandering through the catacombs.'' She flicked a glance at Newell. This only strengthened her theory about Ursula. She hoped what he'd said last night were true and that he was now motivated to take care of the woman before she hurt herself or anyone else.

''Miss Benjamin here believes that Ursula has returned, Bess,'' Newell said, a muscle jumping in his jaw. ''She wants me to find her.''

''And you should, you dear boy,'' the old woman said, her words low and ominous.

He turned to Alexandra. "After tea, Miss Benjamin, are you ready to explore the catacombs?"

Alexandra almost gasped. The last time she had even gone near them, she almost lost her life. Now he wanted to take her exploring and the glint in his eyes spoke of warning.

"Have you no answer? I thought you were anxious and determined to find her?"

She stiffened. "All right," she said, knowing she was being a fool to take his bait, but she was weak for him, especially now that she knew his past. "I'll go with you after tea. Together, we'll see what really happened to Miss Pole."

He smirked. "After tea then. I'll meet you in the servants' hall."

"Yes," she whispered, her eyes not flinching when they met his. "Hopefully we'll find some answers to the madness of Cairncross."

They met at four o'clock, just when the sun had slung low behind the cairns to the west. They said very little. It was on an unspoken dare that she'd come, and so not speaking, she took the proffered lantern and followed him down into the bowels of the castle.

It was all just as Alexandra remembered it. Seemingly miles of dank staircase, winding down into the earth, the air composed of ancient exhalations from the long since dead, and limestone's mineral smell of blood.

He took her hand in the darkness. She backed against the stair wall, suddenly afraid to go further, but then remembered the skeletons that he said lay in the catacombs, conceivably in every wall. Without wanting to, she whispered, "Please don't let go of me."

He didn't answer.

They arrived in the cavern and placed their lanterns by the old Roman door. Newell had brought a crowbar and he pried the doors open with amazingly little effort. It surprised her that even a man of his strength could do it alone.

"Come inside," he said, holding his hand out, beckoning her.

As I am now, so you shall be. So take my hand and come with me.

She paused. The lantern reflected in his spectacles, a sharp yellow light. He looked like Satan inviting her through the gates of hell.

Before she took her first step, she paused and looked at him. Questions burned inside her, demanding answers. "I go with you gladly, my lord," she said, "but before I do, I must tell you I fear this. And I can't help but wonder, and truly, I must know, does my fear excite you? Will you give me comfort for my fear, or only more fear?"

The light cast heavy shadows across his face. She couldn't completely see his expression, but it appeared as if in a struggle between two opposing forces.

"Will you come with me?" he finally said, not answering her question, "Or cower here alone and wait the eternity for my return?"

She took a deep, unsettling breath, then took his hand, and he pulled her into the catacombs.

They left her lantern to mark the entrance. Once inside the enclosure of the tomb, Damien's Argand was more intense, lighting all corners. She trailed behind him. The blood in her veins ran ice cold even while his hand wrapped around hers like an iron hot from the fire.

The walls were made of wet, crumbling stone with moldy polychrome paintings of the baths of Caracalla. The explicit nudes were not as unsettling as the darkness in front of them, still unexplored.

"How can she live down here?" she exclaimed.

"She doesn't want for mortal comforts," he said, turning to glance at her. He held the lamp out and studied the other side of the Roman door. She bent to it, noticing scratches along one side.

"What are they?" she asked.

"Perhaps the claw marks of the yet undead."

She shivered, but something else caught her eye. She motioned for the lamp, then gasped as she held it to the floor.

"Red hair. Clumps of long, red hair," she choked, repulsed by the sight.

"Her hair. Perhaps she pulled it out in a wild fit of rage." He paused, then said eerily, "But then perhaps, it fell from her skull as she lay here dead."

Alexandra felt a violent shudder run through her. Finding nothing more on the ground, she stood and returned the lamp to him.

"Shall we go further?" His voice carried a trace of wicked amusement.

"Yes." Her anger at his taunts battled with her desire for safety.

With his hand still clamped around hers, they went a hundred feet more, then turned a corner. There they found themselves at the intersection of six passages. Damien arbitrarily chose one and took her another two hundred feet forward. The utter blackness of the space set a panic inside her. Now it was dark behind them and in front.

"There's something ahead. Are you prepared for it?" he asked, a strange mixture of darkness and amusement in his voice.

She followed, too afraid to hold back and chance losing his hand.

Damien forged ahead. He paused at a shadowy break in the smooth wall. He looked at her, then raised the Argand lamp high.

Below Damien's lamp was a Roman skeleton, half-buried in the wall, its face almost all extracted from the mud casing, its bare mouth open in a gruesome smile. She quickly turned her head from the sight and felt her stomach lurch.

"Why does it reach like that?" she asked, not daring another look.

"He was probably buried alive. A slave to one of the warriors."

Fear caused her heart to hammer in her chest. Her stomach

heaved from one side to another as if she were being tossed about on a high sea. The idea of being buried alive was all too familiar after her last experience here. It left her feeling scared and tentative. The need to retreat was as powerful as a thunderstorm.

"I'm not sure I can do this," she said. "I thought I could, but now, after seeing that . . ."

He gave her a hard look. "Do you agree no human could live down here?"

"I—I suppose so. No sane human, at least."

He stared at her, then grasped her hand more tightly in his. Tracing their path back to the intersection, he led them through the right-most tunnel, and she was blessedly relieved to see her lantern light beaconing them.

Yet Damien took the left.

"Stop," she said, pulling back. "Our light is that way."

"This is the way we need to go. That isn't our light."

"Of course it is," she exclaimed, wondering what had gotten into him.

"We'll take this passage. This is the way we must go."

"But we left my lantern at the entrance, remember? If the light we see there isn't ours, what is it?" She studied him, her mind almost numb from disbelief. Ahead, his profile was hard and handsome against the steady light of the Argand. She could read nothing in it.

"This is the way we came, Alexandra. The light is a phantom light. It's not the passage we came from. You've got to either go with me, or go to the light alone."

"But we left a light burning. It must be the light we left."

"You asked, 'Will I give you comfort for your fear, or more fear?' Now I offer you comfort. Take it. This is the way out."

She stopped, unwilling to lose sight of the light burning in the distance behind them. "You tantalize with comfort, Damien, and yet your comfort comes with great fear. I tell you, we must return to the lantern. If we don't we might never find our way out."

He stepped closer to her and put his arm around her shoulders, pressing her to his chest. One hand held the Argand lamp, the other, he raised and caressed her cheek. "My love, what is life but pain and fear and agony? What will you do? Will you go to the light, perhaps to find a lonely freedom from these catacombs, or will you follow at my side, perhaps to die with me, lost forever in this maze?"

"Life is not always those things. If you think it is so, it's only because you've been taught by the wrong teachers. Life is renewal, it's hope, it's joy. You can find those things even in that which you fear most if only you will look for them."

She didn't know what the expression was on her face, but her heart held such honest emotion he seemed unable to look at her.

A strange, inexplicable expression crossed his face, wrought of pain, confusion, and the terror of loss of control. "If you say you will stay with me, if you care that much for my wretched soul, then I promise to take you out of here," he said harshly.

"Damien," she whispered, emotion choking her, "I fear these catacombs. But I know a greater fear, and it is not this place, or this darkness, or even you and your frightening moods. I know that I may chance to leave this place and the darkness must always turn to light; I understand full well that one day you may lose the thin control you sport when around me, and do violence towards me. But none of this, *none of this*," she repeated, knowing there was nothing left but honesty, "is as terrible a fear as that you may never love me as . . ." she forced herself to spit out the words, ". . . as Brian never loved me."

The hand on her cheek grew rough in its caress. He seemed torn again, until he summoned a deep groan, then took her hand and jerked her viciously to the intersection.

"But this is *still* the wrong passage," she wept as he strode forward through the darkness, her hand clamped to the breaking point in his iron fist.

"My comfort is death," he said, jerking her with him.

"What are you doing?" she sobbed. "Have you gone mad. This is the wrong passage."

"Do I look mad to you?" he rasped.

"No," she whispered. "Don't do this. I love you." She pulled back, if only to try to pull him with her. The light was gone from behind them. There was still a possibility of tracing their steps. "Damien, take my soul, take my love, but don't take my life . . ." she begged, searching for reason in his mad heart.

All at once, he stepped through an opening. He let go of her hand and she stood frozen in the light, unable to move. They were outside the catacombs, in the cavern. The Roman door stood ajar behind them.

"I—I don't understand," she said, staring at him.

He looked at her, a strange defeat on his face. He whispered again, "My comfort is death."

She ran to him and wrapped her arms around him. She cried against his chest, finally understanding. Their lantern had indeed blown out. The light they saw, be it phantom or reflection, was not in the correct passage. He had been taking them to his death. To their deaths. And yet, for her, he'd weakened and turned back.

"Your comfort will be my love. I swear it," she wept before tipping her tear-ravaged face to his for a kiss.

They stole through the shadows of the night, pausing on each landing for a kiss. And that Damien kissed like no other, Alexandra was certain, for his was hard, satisfying, demanding need in return. Not weak and gentlemanly as Brian's had been.

It was against good reason, she supposed, to follow him to his bedchamber. There were prices to pay for such folly, a heart to break, honor to be lost. But she didn't think of any of this as he kissed her before his bedchamber door, his one hand on her jaw, his other on the wrought-iron door latch. She only thought of him, of how he was inside her, part of her. And how she was meant to be here.

They didn't speak. There was nothing that needed saying. His loneliness and her loneliness were going to be executed at dawn.

He slowly removed the spectacles and tossed them on the seat of a leather chair. Staring at him, she found his eyes beautiful in the dim gaslight, darkened with desire, glittering with hope. And perhaps fear.

He led her to the bed.

She remembered his room well. Velvet and cobwebs. He kissed her, a deep, damp, needful kiss, before he sat on the edge of the mattress. He pulled her to him and intently began on the hooks to her bodice.

When all were undone, he eased the pins from her hair, letting her hair fall around in her Raphaelite splendor. She stared down at him, trapped between his legs. He met her stare, and he returned it in kind, deep agony engraved on his face, as he took her hand and held it tenderly to his cheek.

The hand left and in its place was a kiss. He toppled her on him as he lay back on the bed. They kissed again and his lips trailed a fiery length down her neck, bared by the open bodice.

"I've dreamed of you, of this," he whispered, rolling over her, capturing her beneath him. "It's always the same dream. I held you like this, then I looked down and you were gone."

She kissed him and felt her bodice give way beneath his practiced hands. He shrugged her out of the gown, then brushed aside the straps of her corset cover. With excruciating study, he unfastened all the buttons down the front of her frilled corset cover, finally reaching his goal: the tight linen corset beneath.

"Generous, so generous . . . as the woman is," he said, tonguing the burgeoning swell of her breasts as he unhooked her corset. "I'll dream of no other ever again," he murmured before his mouth caught her nipple and lit a fire deep inside her belly.

He pulled on the corset until it too lay in a pile by the bed. The strings of her pantalets were untied, and they too joined the growing pile, along with her shoes.

"Let me see you," she begged, suddenly aware of her nudity. All she wore now were her black silk stockings and her white satin garters.

His gaze raked over her body, then rested on her face. He

eased himself to his feet and pulled off his jacket and shirt. She remembered well his chest from that night that seemed a century before. It looked just as wide and rife with muscle as before.

She looked away when he began to remove his trousers. Her maidenly instincts sent a tremor of nerves through her body. She wanted this, but still, she wasn't very well-versed in being with a man. Before, she'd always believed she'd have the benefit and respectability of marriage when she gave herself to a man. Now such things seemed too far away, out of her reach. The physical need for such a union was strong, but none of it was stronger than her need to be close to him, to hold him and, just for a night, make the demons go away.

His weight came down next to her on the bed. Slowly, she turned her gaze. He gathered her in his arms and kissed her, his lips moving in hot, furious motion. The warmth of his hard chest was like a wall shielding her from the outside world.

His head bent and he kissed her breast. His handsome, shadowed face was taut with desire. She thought there would be more of this, the kissing, the caresses, but quickly, as if he needed the shelter of her, his hand parted her gartered thighs and, to her dismay, he drove inward.

Her moan was wrought from surprise and pain. Every muscle in her body tightened as if to ward him off.

He groaned and buried his face in the fan of her hair, his hips moving in primeval rhythm.

"Stop," she breathed, barely able to speak from the shock of his invasion.

"Alexandra, take me. Take me," he whispered in her ear.

She released a small sob and turned her lips toward his. They kissed until she finally felt herself give way to him. Inch by inch, her muscles relaxed and the heat increased. Like a flower that had blossomed in her lower regions, she felt a kind of wild pleasure never before experienced. Her loins no longer rejected him, instead they embraced him and demanded more.

Her head turned back and forth against the mattress as she

fought the sensation his thrusts sent her. But her womanhood had been held dormant too long. Her last vision before she threw her head back in a pagan ecstasy was Damien's face. He looked down at her with doom-filled eyes. And a terrible smile played at the corner of his mouth.

Chapter
Twenty-three

Thus, like the sad presaging raven, that tolls
The sick man's passport in her hollow beak,
And in the shadow of the silent night
Doth shake contagion from her sable wings;
Vex'd and tormented, runs poor Barrabas,
With fatal curses towards these Christians.
                              —THE JEW OF MALTA

Alexandra awoke. Her head pounded, every muscle ached, and there was a strange, alien soreness between her legs.

She turned over and found she was alone in the bed. In Damien's bed.

Disoriented, she sat up and looked around, all the details from last night wrathfully flooding back to her. The bedchamber was much as she remembered it, but now the gray leak of dawn filtered through the heavy burgundy drapery. And the chamber was empty. He was nowhere to be found.

She leaned back against the rumpled pillows, exhausted and confused. It was almost as if last night were a dream, but where she lay and the strange sensations still running through her body gave eloquent testimony that it was not a dream.

She tried to summon the energy to leave the bed. For some reason, the fact that Damien wasn't in the room, made everything seem worse. A cold aloneness settled in her soul. She was a ruined woman now, and she had needed his touch and reassurances.

Her clothing was scattered in the perimeter around the bed. She still wore one stocking and both garters; the other she had lost beneath the sheets. Slowly, as if she were very old, she left the bed and got to her feet. The sheets were damp, rumpled, and scented with lovemaking. She rummaged through them in a vain attempt to find her stocking, but the black stocking never materialized. She shook out the pillows, hoping it might fall from between them, but to no avail. She threw the last pillow to the mattress and sat on the edge, inexplicably tired. But then something on the sheets caught her eye. And her blood froze solid in her veins.

Unable to accept what she believed she saw, she turned up the gas lamp and threw more light on the bed. She reached out, her hand trembling, and she picked up the two long red hairs dangling off the end of the pillow.

She held them to the light, irrationally hoping they were hers. But she had no red in her hair at all, and these were brilliantly red. The flickering gaslight cast glints of fiery orange into each strand.

Her very soul felt weak and sick. She thought of the diary page and she wanted to scream in denial. "No, Damien! No!" her mind cried silently to her, hating to even think about the meaning of the hairs and why they'd been found in his bed, a bed they had just shared.

She stared at the hairs, repulsed to even touch them.

They were *hers*.

Her fingers let them go and the hairs drifted down to the white sheets. Even amongst the wrinkles in the bed, they were conspicuous.

With shaking hands, Alexandra gathered her clothes. The

room was like ice. Damien's dressing gown was tossed over a chair and she covered herself with it. She dressed by the hearth, her only thought being escape from this terrible room and her even worse thoughts.

The clock struck seven, and she realized she was going to have to steal back into her own bedchamber or risk giving Mary a seizure when her maid found her missing. She didn't know how she was going to manage seeing Damien again. There were so many questions and so many denials in her head, she didn't know how she would be able to look into his eyes and listen to his answers.

Once dressed, she left the bedchamber, gratefully encountering no one in the halls and passages. She entered her room, and, with a strange flutter of guilt, she mussed her untouched bed. Last night's dinner was stone cold by the dead hearth. Sickened by the sight of it, she then spied herself in the mantel mirror and was shocked by the image. Her bodice was unevenly hooked, and her face looked back at her, pale and nervous, beneath a wild, unbound mass of brown hair. She looked insane.

She turned away from the creature in the mirror. Perhaps she truly was going insane.

Feeling weak and nauseous, she undressed again and fumbled to run the brush to her hair. In her own dressing gown, with Damien's hid in the bureau, she sank into a chair and numbly recalled the night before.

Her cheeks heated just to think of it. She and everyone else had always considered her terminally logical and restrained. Last night had shattered that illusion. She had forsaken all that she was, and she had given everything to him. That he needed her, that she loved him, had seemed reason enough. Now in the harsh morning hour, with those two red hairs still stuck to the sheets, reality intruded as loudly as Mary did, bursting through the door with her tray.

"Good morning!" she said, bustling over to the hearth to lay out breakfast.

"Good morning," Alexandra said, wondering if her face betrayed her.

"It's another lovely day. A trip into York will be just the thing."

Alexandra closed her eyes in despair. She had forgotten the trip. Putting her throbbing head back against the wing chair, she wondered how she would get through it. It would be terrible seeing Damien in the carriage, trapped with him, yet unable to speak with him. All day, for the benefit of others, they would have to maintain their social distance. It would be torture. Especially since last night had made such a mockery of their social distance. Especially since there were two long red hairs in his bed, and she desperately needed a good reason for them being there.

And there was none.

Mary went to the wardrobe and laid out her clothes. Lastly, she took out Alexandra's black cloak and said, "I'll send this down to Featherstone for a good brushing. You'll need it, I imagine, at least for the ride home tonight."

"Yes. Thank you," Alexandra answered absentmindedly, her mind still reeling from shock.

With the black cloak slung over one arm, Mary picked up the abandoned dinner tray. If she was surprised to see it untouched, she didn't show it. Yet when the woman made it to the door, she paused and searched Alexandra's face. "His lordship never made it to the dining table either."

Alexandra felt the blood rush to her face. She didn't know what to say. Slowly, she fumbled for an explanation. "We— were—down in the catacombs. We got lost, but Damien found his way back." She glanced at Mary, unable to hide the uncertainty that ravaged her. She didn't know how to handle her lapse last night, and it only made it worse that anyone else might guess at it.

"It'll be all right, Alexandra. Just remember that, no matter what, you always have me." After that seemingly enigmatic confession, Mary nodded and left.

Alexandra had never been so grateful to her.

* * *

The carriage lurched and rattled along the pitted moorland road.

Damien sat facing her, his face wiped clean of expression save for a veneer of impersonal politeness. Sam was like a little child on his first outing. He glued his gaze to the passing landscape as if he dared not miss a foot of it. And Alexandra sat across from both men, her mind despairing with every mile.

There weren't many avenues left to a fallen woman except silence.

She gazed at Damien and wondered if his thoughts were as morose as hers. If circumstances were different, if they were alone in the carriage, she would take his hand, place it to her cheek, and ask him for the horrible explanation of the two red hairs. He might not know anything about them, but she didn't believe it, not when she looked into the emotional void of his expression and thought of Ursula's madness.

She despaired of the future. They had performed a consequential act last night, and at least in her case, there was no way to remain unchanged. The terrible thought occurred to her that even now she could be carrying his child.

Her emotions plunged into a whole new darkness. To demand that Damien marry her was laughable. He wouldn't bend to anyone's demands, least of all an employee's. And did she want marriage to this man? This man she loved, but couldn't really like?

If he could be released from the ghouls inside him, she knew she would like him, but in some ways, his damage was worse than Sam's. Mrs. Penrith had thought so and tried to warn her off of Newell.

But now there was no going back. She knew it every time his gaze met hers in the tiny confines of the carriage. She would never be a virgin again, and she would never be able to forget him, even if she did what she thought would be the best for her and left Cairncross. He would haunt her forever.

"You look tired, Miss Benjamin. Perhaps we were selfish

in bringing you along on this trip.'' Newell casually leaned back against the leather upholstery, but gave her a stare that robbed her of breath.

"I haven't slept well of late, my lord,'' she answered, proud that she could keep the tension from her voice. "And until the mystery of Miss Pole is ended, I fear I shan't sleep.''

"Ursula's influence diminishes as we speak, my love.''

He whispered the last two words like a prayer. She glanced at Sam to see if he'd heard them. He hadn't. He still gazed out the window in raptures over the new scenery.

She returned her gaze to Newell. His stare stopped her heart. And she knew unspeakable agony for not being able to talk to him, to touch him.

"I wish it were true,'' she said to him, her words nearly begging, "but I fear, as most sinners do, that evil's too strong a force to resist. It promises so much. It offers a seduction for which few are able to master their desire.'' She again wished they were alone. She wanted to throw herself into his arms and beg for an answer to what she found in his bed.

"Innocence offers a more tantalizing repast,'' he answered, his eyes not wavering.

"Do you mean instead 'goodness,' my lord?'' she asked.

He whispered, "Yes. Goodness. Everything that is you and *only* you, Miss Benjamin.''

She looked at him and felt a warmth seep into her soul that she had never felt before. The feeling was light, and beauty, and sweetness, all in one indescribable, never-before-experienced emotion. And as she stared at him and took her fleeting glimpse of the man she knew he could be, the two red hairs no longer seemed to matter. Whether Ursula was a ghost or a madwoman didn't seem to matter either. All that did, was that she was hopelessly, eternally, in love with this man, and she would wait for his salvation, if she must wait forever.

"Yoruk! Yoruk!'' Sam suddenly shouted, pointing to the distant heights of the minster rising up like a phoenix from the moors.

Alexandra leaned toward the window to watch for herself

their entrance into the walled city. Sam's excitement rubbed off on her and all at once she pressed her hands into Sam's and said, mostly for his brother's ears, "I do believe today is going to be the most wonderful day of our lives."

Alexandra remembered the minster like an old friend, only this time, she took in the view from the top of the central tower, with the wind blowing her hair from beneath her black silk bonnet as she and Sam held onto each other and drank in the sublime grandeur of the moors and the surrounding Pennines.

They took tea in a small tea house in the back of the Shambles, ducking their heads beneath the huge carcasses of meat hung in the open-air butcher shops as they ventured down the tiny medieval street. Above them, the half-timbered buildings were built so close together, it was said to be possible to reach out the window and shake hands with your neighbor across the street.

After their refreshment, Damien took her arm and escorted her to a museum tucked in the back of a crumbling seventeenth-century mansion along Marygate. The Hinchcliffe, as the locals called it, specialized in neolithic artifacts.

Alexandra had never found anything so fascinating. The museum guide, the old, eccentric Hinchcliffe himself, explained the difference between a henge and a howe in neolithic cultures, then he unveiled to his guests his lifetime prize. A bier made of huge blocks of chalk that he'd found in East Riding. Within it, he gruesomely detailed the three bodies he'd discovered. There was a man, coffined within the hollowed out trunk of a tree, with the bark still intact. A woman was entombed there too and around her neck she wore an amber pendant. Lastly, came the remains of a young boy, whose arms lay around the body of a gray fox speculated to be his pet. Most odd of all, the three of them were decapitated, but whether this had religious significance in neolithic culture, or whether they were all executed, old Hinchcliffe couldn't say.

The afternoon grew almost warm, and Alexandra found it

pleasant to sit in a small park situated beside the ruins of Clifford's Tower while Sam watched a roving Pierrot troupe perform for the children. Damien sat next to her on the bench, and without even being conscious of it, she'd discovered he'd put his arm across the back of the bench, and his fingers were caressing the small baby-fine hairs that were loose at her nape.

"It's been an extraordinary day, one I think we should repeat more often," she said, watching Sam's eyes light up when one of the Pierrots did a back flip.

"It was time to get away from Cairncross," he answered. A lazy smile gleamed in his eyes.

"Would that we could get away forever." She didn't look at him. There was too much she wanted. And it was all fantasy.

"I want you to stay with me again tonight," he said in a low voice.

She stared out the golden park, where all the hazels and oaks were wearing their autumn finery. "Last night was a chance occurrence. You must understand that I'm not the kind of woman—"

"I know what kind of woman you are. I had your virgin's blood on me. But we're not talking about morality now, we're talking about *us*."

"Then let's talk about us." She turned to him and saw the rising tension on his face. It probably matched hers. "When I awoke this morning, I found two long red hairs on the sheets. She's been in your bed, Damien, and I don't know which is worse, if she was in your bed with you, or without you."

Her heart sank to her knees. He appeared disturbed by the news, but not surprised. She stared at him, silently waiting for an excuse, a reason for his dearth of horror. His concerned acceptance. But there was none. He knew exactly what was going on with Ursula Pole and he wasn't going to tell her.

All at once, she snapped. She couldn't take it anymore. The speaking in riddles, the metaphors, the lack of forthrightness. Perhaps if she hadn't opened herself to him last night and given him so much closeness and intimacy, she could preserve a detachment to him. But she couldn't keep up the pretenses any more.

"I've got to know what's going on at Cairncross. I've got to know everything."

Grimly, he rubbed the bridge of his nose beneath his spectacles. "You know everything. Ursula Pole is dead. Sam was the last to see her alive. If you can get him to the point of talking about it, we might find out what happened to her."

"If she's dead, then what about the hairs in your bed?"

"Cairncross has other red-haired wenches other than the resident ghost."

Her gaze rested on him while sickening surprise gave way to anger. At first she wasn't sure what he meant, but all at once his meaning became clear, and it sullied both of them.

She stood and meant to walk away. Numb inside, she didn't want to speak to him, or even look at him. She took a step away, but quickly found his hand on her arm, holding her back.

"If you thought I'm as chaste as you, you thought wrong."

"But not with the servants," she hissed, her eyes filling with tears she refused to shed.

"This wasn't meant to ruin the day. Forget what you saw in the bed. It changes nothing."

She snapped her arm away and stared at him. "You ask me to join you tonight but I'm not a serving wench or a scullery maid. I'm a woman who has the money and means to take you to task for breach of promise."

He laughed. It was the old Damien. An awful sound. " 'Breach of promise.' At times you can be too quaint, Miss Benjamin."

She strode across the park toward the tower, unshed tears bright in her eyes. Whatever reasons drove her to commit so foolish an act as she had done last night now abandoned her. He didn't care for her; her love was wasted on him. He didn't have a heart, and he'd told her so a thousand times. She'd been a fool. Now twice in her life.

"What did you expect?"

She heard his voice behind her, following her. "Not this,"

she said, increasing her pace. She was only a few yards from the tower.

"Would you believe me if I told you that I know nothing about the hair in my bed? Would that make everything all right?"

"You'd be lying." The tears threatened to overflow. "I'd hear it in your voice."

"I thought to change you." He grabbed her arm, violently jerking her around to face him. "Last night I decided to be selfish and do it, but now . . ." His words trailed off as he looked at her.

She met his gaze defiantly, the tears not daring to spill from her eyes. "But now?" she prompted.

His anger returned. "But now if you're to stay at Cairncross, perhaps you'd best be like the rest of us."

She jerked free her arm and walked to the rubble that was once a tower built upon the ruins of the keep of York Castle. She thought he would go to Sam who still sat in rapt attention in the distance as the Pierrots performed their stunts and acrobatics. Instead, he came up behind her.

Without touching her, he said, "Did you know, Alexandra, that one hundred and fifty of your kinfolk died at this spot? Can't you feel the power of their souls screaming to you? They came here to the keep in 1190 to seek asylum from the anti-Semites. The Jews all perished in fire, all of them . . . infidels," he whispered.

She spun around. Without warning, she reached up and hit him across the face. Her hand left a red angry mark on his cheek. She choked back a sob and would have run if not for his own hand that took her by the wrist and forced her to walk with him.

"I think it's time we return to the castle," he said, making her practically gallop at his side as he walked back to Sam. He looked at her only once. Rubbing his face where she hit him, his eyes an emotional blank behind the reflecting glare of spectacles, he murmured, "Never fear, you may become my kind yet."

She wiped away her tears with her free hand. Damien took Sam from the Pierrots and the driver settled them all in the waiting carriage.

The ride back to Cairncross was made in complete silence, except for Sam who, upon sensing the tension, kept repeating the rhyme, "As I am now, so you must be. So take my hand and come with me."

Simple words that left a deadly frost over the day.

In years to come, Alexandra would remember her trip to York. She would marvel at the joy she felt taking Damien's arm to descend the two hundred and seventy-five steps from the minster's tower. She would always remember the lighthearted laughter as a female Pierrot gave Sam a paper flower and Sam innocently smelled it.

But she would never cease to marvel, either, at how the promise of the day could be so swiftly murdered.

Chapter
Twenty-four

*Let me not think you deem so wretchedly ill of my nation
as your commons believe. Think ye that I prize these
sparkling fragments of stone above my liberty? Or that my
father values them in comparison to the honour of his
only child?*
—*Rebecca, in* IVANHOE

Alexandra didn't dare fall asleep in the carriage ride home.
Damien's black stare was alone enough to keep her on guard,
but worse were the thoughts of nightmares, of ghosts and phantoms that lurked in shadowed hallways, taunting her with their
evil.

She kept her eyes wide open all through the tedious journey
back to Cairncross. The tension was like a rope pulled to the
snapping point. She wasn't sure she could bear much more of
it. Reveries of life in London intruded upon her thoughts as
she fantasized returning there, after Brian's hurt had finally
been wiped from her soul.

But she couldn't return to London and her old happiness, because there was no one to take Damien's hurt from her.

She wanted to weep every time she thought of the night before. It had been too close, too intimate, for her to ever forget. Damien had made Brian's wounds look like a mere scratch compared to the slashes now on her heart.

Once at the castle, she quietly bade both men good-night and left them in the baronial hall. In her room, Mary had left a pot of tea on the hearth and a plate of scones covered with a white linen next to the chair. Alexandra thought about eating but she wasn't hungry. She was weary, yet not tired. Restless, she undressed and slipped into her dressing gown, then remembered the other dressing gown in the bureau.

She opened the drawer and ran her hands along the silk velvet collar. Placing it to her nose, she inhaled deeply the scent she now knew too well. It was the scent of man and soul blended together into something undefinable but immediately recognizable. It was Damien's essence. A smell beyond description, like the smell of cobwebs and velvet.

She folded and refolded the dressing gown, unsure how to return it. Mary would find it eventually when she rummaged through the bureau for laundry. She had to return it, perhaps even taking the risk tonight.

She didn't want to do it though. It would make her too vulnerable to go knocking on his door after midnight.

Perhaps she should just rip it to shreds and burn it in the hearth, she thought ungraciously. He could certainly afford another.

While she ruminated on what to do with it, a knock sounded on her door. Rattled by a visitor at the late hour, she answered it and found Sam standing in the passage, a mournful expression on his face.

"Why, Sam, come inside. Why aren't you asleep?"

"Dam'en mad," he answered, a slight frown furrowing his handsome brow.

"Yes, but he's mad at me, not you. Come, have some tea and I'll try to tell you about it." She opened the door wide and let him enter. Settling him in the hearth chair, she poured them both tea, a strange feeling coming over her whenever she glanced at Sam's torn expression.

"Is there something else wrong, Sam? You—you look so strange." She handed him a steaming cup of tea.

"She was angry and made Dam'en go away." His gaze slid to the trunk. He seemed repulsed by it.

Alexandra perched on a little needlepoint footstool and gave him her total attention. "Are you talking about Miss Pole?" she asked softly.

"She was angry and now you're angry." His eyes turned to her.

"I see." Gently, she placed her hand on his own that rested near his knee. "Sam, are you afraid that if I get angry, *I'll* make Damien go away?"

A big crystal tear slipped from his eye. "Yes," he said, trying very hard to be brave.

"But I wouldn't, Sam. I couldn't. You must believe me," she rushed to say. "I would never do anything to take you from your brother. I love you. Do you know that, Sam?"

"She made Dam'en go 'way," he sniffed, glancing again at Ursula's hateful trunk. "So I made her go 'way."

Alexandra froze. She stared at Sam, unable to believe they had never guessed it. *"You* made her go away, Sam? Where did you make her go?" She cursed the nervous, high-pitch to her voice.

"I just made her go 'way." He shrugged, and by his dull-eyed expression, she couldn't tell whether he was hiding something or just couldn't grasp the particulars of the incident.

"Have you ever told Damien this, Sam?" she whispered, grasping his hand for her comfort and his own.

"No."

"If we told Damien, you and I, could we show him how you made Miss Pole go away?" She squeezed his hand further and tried her best to smile.

"I can't 'member everything. I scared."

"I know, Sam, I know," she almost wept, wondering if at

last they were going to get to the bottom of Ursula Pole's disappearance and the fright that had taken Sam's speech. It was almost amazing that no one had ever linked the two when it now seemed so obvious.

"Shall we go and show Damien tonight?" she asked, hoping to seize the moment while he seemed halfway lucid about the incident.

"I'm tired," he announced, suddenly standing.

She stood too and allowed her hand to drop from his. "All right then," she said in as light and pleasant a voice as she could manage. "We can always talk about this in the morning. Get some sleep now. We'll go and see Damien in the morning and then you can show us how you made Miss Pole disappear."

"You mad at Dam'en?"

Her heart pounded in her chest. This big, gentle giant just might have killed the last governess and it seemed prudent to mollify him the best way she could.

But lying wasn't the answer. Even one as slow as he was could pick up on emotions. Instead, she decided to tell him the truth.

"You know, Sam, sometimes you can be mad at someone and still love them. Remember when we were down in the catacombs and I went too close to the big Roman door? You were mad at me then, weren't you? You were afraid I was going to enter the tomb and get lost, and then you would never see me again. Do you remember this?"

He nodded.

"And do you remember how you felt? Were you angry at me just a little for scaring you like I did?"

He nodded again.

"But you still loved me, didn't you? Even though I made you angry."

He smiled. "You love Dam'en? Even if he makes you angry?"

"I believe so," she said, the admission making her feel exultant and terrible. "And so you see, you don't have to hurt someone when they make you angry."

"But I don't love her," he uttered, the frown returning to his brow. "I hate her. Dam'en hate her."

"She was a terrible person."

"Yes," he said as if there were a very old, very wise man inside of him.

She opened the door and bade him good-night, placing a kiss on his well-sculpted cheek. When she closed the door, she went into a panic to dress. She had to see Damien. Tonight.

It all made so much sense, she thought while she rehooked herself into her corset. She couldn't get the memory of the Roman door out of her mind. The red hair and claw marks that were left on the other side made her convinced Sam had somehow lured Ursula into the catacombs. To his simple mind, it was the perfect way to make her disappear.

A shiver of pure ice ran down her spine as she thought of Lady Bess's comments the other day in the garden. The screams. They were Ursula's screams as she tried to claw her way out of the oblivion Sam had put her into.

But he hadn't known he might kill her. In fact, she'd bet her own life on it that Sam didn't understand the tragedy he had caused. When Ursula never returned for her things, to his child's mind, he just figured she went away. He never figured on murder.

"Oh, Sam, dear Sam," she whispered, throwing her gown over her head and hastily hooking it. She wondered if he knew any kind of guilt or remorse for his actions. If they finally found Ursula's body, there would be no telling his reaction. It could be the stimulus for him to understand and be better. Or it could disturb him to the point where he could be dangerous.

She trembled as she slipped on her shoes and bound her hair with a piece of brown velvet. She must go to Damien and tell him what she knew. Sam's life, *her* life could be hanging in the balance.

The light shone under Damien's bedchamber door when Alexandra finally arrived. She knocked and waited, but no one answered. Again she knocked, but this time her pounding on the door made it creak open. It was unlatched.

She peered into the room. Damien sat by the fire, his blond head slung back against the chair upholstery in a gesture of weariness.

"My lord?" she whispered, creeping into the room.

He glanced over at her. His eyes lit upon her unbound hair and the tentative expression on her face. From her place at the door, she could see his shirt was unbuttoned, revealing a mass of glistening bronze-colored hair on his chest. He sat so near the fire, he was sweating.

She walked over to him. A slow drip of fear slid down her spine when she saw what he held in his lap. His hands were loosely wrapped around the pearl handle of a pistol.

"My lord," she said quietly. "Pray, what need you with a gun?"

He looked up at her. His spectacles were folded on the table next to him. She was trapped by the haunted beauty of his eyes.

"It serves no purpose," she said, keeping her words low and soft. "If she's a ghost, you cannot kill her. And if she's a madwoman, then it is too cruel."

She went before him and placed her hands on his. "And. . . . And if you were thinking of turning it toward yourself, you cannot do it, because . . ." She felt her eyes fill with tears. Pain choked her words. ". . . because I fear I love you and I cannot let you leave this earth right now."

He stared at her, saying nothing, not moving, simply taking in every detail of her appearance as if he needed to savor it.

"Damien," she whispered, leaning down to him. "What is it?"

Abruptly he pulled her down to him. He placed the pistol on the table next to his spectacles, then, cupping her face in his hands, he laid his mouth heavily upon hers. She was too shocked to stop him.

After a moment, she moaned and tried to pull away, but he still kept her head in the vise of his hands.

He kissed her behind her ear, then trailed his mouth down the curve of her neck. His tongue was lingering at her wildly beating pulse.

"What is this, Damien? What do you need of me?" she nearly whimpered as he buried his head in the long length of her hair.

"Remember yesterday," was all he offered.

She shivered. "But you turned back. You're not ready to die and you won't hurt me. You care for me. Say it, say it," she demanded, her wounds suddenly summoning tears.

"Yes, I care for you. Your better nature, how it intrigues me, beckons me. I want you with me." He stared down at her, his eyes on fire with lust and want. "I will have you with me."

"No, Damien," she whispered. "This is not love."

"But love is eternity."

In terror, she watched as his hand settled once more on the gun.

"My love, you don't have to do this." Her mouth went dry. Terror coursed through her body. But not hatred. Never hatred. She understood him too well to ever hate him. And she loved him too much. It was a love she'd never known about, never read about. It was heart and soul, it was all life and it exceeded death. She must not be afraid.

"Damien," she whispered, her shaking hand resting on his cheek. "We can find Ursula Pole, I know it now. And I can teach Sam to speak and get over his fears."

"But what will you give me?"

She took his hard-featured face in both her hands and said, "I'll love you. I do love you. That's all you need."

The hand slackened on the pistol. Slowly she pressed her lips to his. Her kiss said what words could not. It promised eternity, but also life. When his hand drew away from the gun, she took it and pressed it to her breast, right over her pounding heart.

"Teach me, then. Teach me," he said.

He stood and led her to the bed.

Chapter
Twenty-five

Nay, if the gentle spirit of moving words
Can no way change you to a milder form,
I'll woo you, like a soldier, at arms' end,
And love you 'gainst the nature of love, force you.
— *THE TWO GENTLEMEN OF VERONA*

Firelight gamboled up the shadowed walls like little devils, surging and retreating in perdition. Alexandra couldn't sleep. What they had just done weighed heavy upon her. And there were the needs of all those around her. The problems were so great and she felt weak and pitiable in her attempt to go against them.

A hand touched her hair. It stroked it lovingly. Her eyes turned to the man who lay next to her in the bed, his hand on her hair, the other resting intimately on her bare hip.

"What occupies your thoughts?" he whispered, his voice matching the rare tranquility in his eyes.

"So much," she said, nestling further into the barrier of his chest. "I came to see you tonight because of Sam. He paid me a visit to my room and told me the most extraordinary things."

"Such as?"

"I've reason to think Sam caused Ursula's disappearance. He blamed her for your banishment." She met his gaze and slowly raised her hand to caress his lean cheek. "In his eyes, she made you go away, and so he told me he made her go away."

He turned his head and kissed the palm of her hand that rested on his cheek. "I suspected as much."

"He implied that he closed her in the catacombs. The red hair and the marks on the wall could be hers. If she's dead, we must find her body and rule out the possibility that the figure we've seen isn't a madwoman coming back for revenge from such a terrible experience."

"She's dead, love. She's dead."

His words chilled her. She snuggled even closer to him. "But you haven't found a body. You don't know exactly what happened. And it's imperative we find out. I fear Sam sometimes mistakes me for her. He came to me tonight because he was confused about our argument. I fear he thought *I* might make you go away, and then he would have to do something to me. He doesn't mean to hurt me, I know that, but he's so muddled and frightened—"

"Stay away from him for a while."

"Do you think I'm in danger? I care about him so. I—I don't want to hurt him. I want to be prudent but I couldn't bear for him to think I'm rejecting him." The very thought hurt her. Sam needed her so desperately. She didn't like the idea of backing away now.

"I'm going to speak with him." His jaw hardened. Slowly he slipped on his spectacles and rose to find his trousers. "It's time we have out with it. He'll show me where he put her."

"We're assuming he killed her, but he might not have," she pleaded. "He might have only locked her in the catacombs. In some ways, it makes sense. The figure in the hall and out on the moor, all the gruesome tricks—they're devised by a woman

whose mind has shattered. If Ursula found her way out of the
catacombs, it is still possible to believe she might have come
back here to wreak some kind of terrible revenge.''

"But you forget one thing in your theory, Alexandra." He
leaned over the bed and gave her a sweet, heated kiss on the
mouth.

"What is it?" she whispered.

"Her experience in the catacombs couldn't have shattered
her mind. Her mind was shattered before she ever got to Cairncross.''

She watched as he pulled on his trousers. In her maidenly
embarrassment, she'd never really looked before, but now she
wondered if his manhood still bore the scars of his experience
in the stable.

Ursula Pole's mind *was* shattered before she ever got to
Cairncross.

Blood and seed.

Alexandra had to agree with him.

Alexandra crept into her room and disrobed. There was still
an hour or two before dawn, and she suddenly felt the exhaustion of the past two days. Without her usual orderliness, she
shrugged out of her dress and underclothes and tossed them
over the hearth chair. Once in her white cotton nightrail, she
slipped beneath the cold sheets and fell fast asleep, her dreams
filled with Damien and the devil.

"Wake up, miss! Wake up! Oh, come see it! Who did this?
This wretched, disgusting thing?"

Alexandra scrambled to a sitting position and blinked into
the morning sunlight. Mary stood beside her bed, her knuckles
jammed in her mouth. To stuff back the scream.

"What is it?" she asked, her dry tongue thick and unmanageable.

Mary simply pointed to the corner of the room that was on

the other side of the bed. With a chill racing down her spine, Alexandra looked behind her.

The dressmaker's mannequin was back. It now stood in the shadowed, forgotten corner to the left of her bed. But it was not draped in black. Not this time. This time it wore Alexandra's lavender silk gown. And the worst obscenity was that the skirt had been pulled all the way up like a harlot's and flipped over the figure's head, obscuring it.

Alexandra stumbled from the bed and released a deep, soul-wrenching moan. She would have run if the door had not been closed. Anything to get away from the lewd obscenity behind her.

"Don't touch it, don't," Mary whimpered next to her. "I don't want to see its face."

Alexandra grasped Mary's hand and pulled her toward the door. Anger mixed with horror as she glanced at the figure one last time. It had not been there last night, she was sure of it. So it had been set up while she slumbered. It was a message. A message.

But from whom?

"I removed it from your room. It was nothing but what you'd expect. I don't know how the dress got on it." Damien put both hands on the mantel and stared down at the hearty fire. The windows in front of him portrayed a blanket of frost. The fine weather had gone and winter had finally begun to dig its claws into the land.

Alexandra hugged her shawl to her shoulders. She couldn't seem to get warm this morning, and she thought it had more to do with the dressmaker's dummy in her room than the weather. "Would she call me a whore, Damien?" The question was high-pitched and brittle. "Or did you do it? You were the only one who knew I was with you last night. Did you do this prank to torture me with accusation?" Her eyes held no sparkle. She was becoming worn by the ordeal.

"I didn't do this. She did this and you know it." He studied her pale face. A muscle tightened in his jaw. "I'd call you no whore, but an angel for your mercy on Samuel." His gaze flickered over her, then he looked away. His words were less than a whisper. "And on me."

She sank into the settee. Weak and exhausted, she lowered her face into her hands and suddenly began to cry.

He didn't touch her. Not really. He stepped to her and his face grew hard. Slowly a hand went out to comfort her, but then he drew it back. As if there were no use.

"I'll have your things taken out of that room. You'll move into the room next to mine."

She sniffed and wiped her eyes on her handkerchief. "What would the servants think of that arrangement? Not much, I believe."

"I can keep an eye on you if you stay near me. And the servants won't talk. They won't know about it."

"But what about my servant Mary? She'll know."

"Then you'll send her away."

"I couldn't be all alone here. I just couldn't."

He gazed at her tear-streaked face. Whatever he wanted to say, the words didn't come.

"Perhaps it's time I move on," she said tremulously. "This . . . *weakness* you've found in me is not quite ladylike, now is it? Especially without the bonds of marriage. And I know all about the impossibilities of that."

"I asked you last night to teach me of love. How wide are the boundaries of your love, Alexandra? Are they beyond these silly human institutions that mean everything to society and nothing to the individual?"

"I would love without marriage. But . . . ." Her eyes darkened with unhappiness.

"Would you marry me then, if I asked? Would you bind your soul to mine and live in the agony that I live in? Are you that kind, that altruistic? Then I say you possess more mercy than a mere sinner should."

"I am only that. A sinner. But I love you and I could proclaim that love before God and man."

He stared at her for a long moment, his face battling some indefinable emotion. "Then I *shall* marry you. And may God have mercy on your soul."

She looked up. If she meant to hide her shock at his proposal, she did a poor job of it. Even now she could feel her heart skip a beat in her chest. "Did I hear you correctly, my lord, or did you just consent to marriage?"

He didn't meet her gaze. "I do not ask you to marry me. I beg you."

A silence settled in the room after he spoke. Each seemed to grapple with their destiny. Alexandra watched Damien as he went again to the fireplace and stared into it, as if the flames could speak prophecy to him. She herself wondered what had happened to her life. Everything had once been mapped out and catalogued and analyzed, just like her father's research. Now everything was spinning out of control. Her feelings, her future, her logic.

"Yes."

His head snapped around to look at her. "What did you say?"

"This sinner says yes, I will marry you. I must marry you."

He plucked her off the settee. His massive strength made her nothing but a rag doll to him. "We'll marry in a fortnight. In Cairncross's chapel. It hasn't been used for a century."

"And shall Miss Pole be maid of honor?"

His face turned grim. "She'll be gone by then. I swear it."

"What can I do to help, my husband?"

He looked down at her. She ached to take off his spectacles and place kisses all over his fine lips and eyes.

"Tonight, I'll explore the catacombs once more. But first, I must speak to Sam. We both have to. He knows more than he's yet been able to tell us. That will be a start."

"Yes," she said, her heart suddenly, inexplicably light. "That will be a start and so will our marriage."

"I'm still moving you from your room. I'll tell the servants we're to be married. That should keep them quiet about any sleeping arrangements."

She wanted to hold onto propriety, but still she wanted the safety of being by his side. Of sleeping by his side. The fright she'd had this morning was something she never wanted to repeat again.

And she wouldn't, she thought defiantly. She gazed into his eyes and her heart filled with an apprehensive happiness. He would protect her from all the horror.

Unless she were to find out that he was the one behind it.

Chapter
Twenty-six

Damien rubbed his jaw; it was the only indication of the tension in the room. Sam sat happily next to Alexandra on the settee, scarfing down cook's famous currant scones. As she and Damien had discussed earlier, the mood was kept as light as possible. There was a tabby in the stable that had just had kittens, and Alexandra brought one to Sam before tea. The black piece of fluff had already gotten into the creamer, then tried to climb up Damien's leg. Even Damien had laughed once he'd extracted the prickly, wide-eyed kitten from his trousers.

"Sam," Damien began when they'd quieted again, "Miss Benjamin and I would like to ask you some questions, is that all right?"

Sam stared dumbly at his brother, then at Alexandra. The kitten settled down in his lap and began to purr.

"Ursula is frightening me, Sam, do you understand?" Alexandra laid her hand on his. "You don't want her frightening me, do you?"

He looked slightly confused. "But I put her away."

"That's what we want to speak to you about," Damien said.

"Where did you put her, Sam, when I went away so long ago?"

Sam glanced at Alexandra. She swore she saw guilt. "I put her down in the ground."

"In the catacombs?" Damien asked.

Sam didn't seem to want to answer. All at once, he blurted out, "She made you go 'way. Why she made you go 'way?"

Alexandra kept hold of his now clenched hand. But he was so strong. She remembered his strength with trepidation. "Sam," she said gently, "she was a wicked person and she caused a lot of trouble."

"Can you show us where you put her?" Damien asked.

Sam gave his brother a vacant stare. "She screamed, Damien. She hit me. I hated her and I scared. So I put her away."

"Where, Sam? Where?" Alexandra begged.

He stared at her and she was convinced he was overcome by guilt. All of a sudden, tears began to stream from his eyes. He rocked back and forth on the settee, knocking off the kitten. "As I am now, so you must be. So take my hand and come with me," he repeated over and over again.

"Hush," Alexandra whispered, putting her arms around him. She looked at Damien and shook her head. For now, the situation was hopeless.

Damien stood. Softly, she asked where he was off to.

"The catacombs," he said grimly, his eyes filled with some unnamed emotion as he watched his brother sob upon Alexandra's breast.

"He won't talk," Alexandra whispered to Damien as she closed Sam's bedchamber door behind her. "I sent for the physician and he gave him some laudanum. That should make him sleep." She heaved a sigh of despair. "I don't know how to approach things now. Perhaps in a day or two he'll come out of this and be back to what he was. Or perhaps . . ." She didn't want to think of that possibility.

"I found nothing else besides the hair and scratch marks we

saw the other day. If he put her in there, she died somewhere else besides near the door.''

"Or she escaped. And now she's returned.''

Damien drew near until she backed flush against the walnut door and was trapped between his two arms.

"She was down there with me as I searched,'' he whispered, his voice cold and dispassionate. "I could feel her there, bumping against the walls like a wraith. Are you going to tell me a mortal woman knows all the passages in this castle while I know but a handful?''

"She's had years to study them. We don't know how long she's been here—''

All at once, he bent his head and kissed her. His mouth was hard and his kiss was thorough. She put her hand on his chest in a lame attempt to ward off his fury, but it was no use. She wanted his kiss. Always.

"What was that for?'' she asked breathlessly, her lips feeling bruised and tender.

"We have a strange truce right now, Alexandra.'' His head bent to hers and his knuckles caressed the soft plane of her cheek. "But the war isn't over yet. I want to marry you and clasp your hand in mine, never to let it go. But then I see her, and I feel my own monster inside me. I don't know how it's going to end.''

"You'd never harm me. I know it.'' She said almost too boldly, as if the more she believed it, the more it would come true.

"I don't want to hurt you. I need you. You know it.'' His eyes darkened. "But she's still here, still a symbol of the evil that lives inside me.''

"Damien.'' She ran her hand along the arm that had carried the wound from the falling chandelier. "We all have evil inside. That's why we need love. Love reconciles us to it.'' She met his gaze and held it. "I don't fear you, and I'll not fear you. I love you.''

He leaned against her. His powerful frame seemed held up by her puny one. "Sometimes, as when I was down in the catacombs, I feel the lure too strongly. But times such as now, it's as if it never existed—out there or in me. But,'' he said grimly, ''it's not over.''

''No, Damien,'' she begged. ''It's not so. Besides, she's after me now. The mannequin, she was calling me a harlot. I know it. She's jealous.''

''She wouldn't dare hurt you.''

''Why?'' she asked, surprised by his conviction.

''Because she doesn't want you with her in all hell and damnation. She wants me.'' He thought a moment. ''And perhaps that's what we should do. Set a trap for her.''

''But if you're right, my lord, how does one set a trap for a ghost?'' She raised one eyebrow and stared at him.

Damien looked down at her. He kissed her again, long and full and moist. ''With bait,'' he said, before taking her to his room.

Sam rose in the dark from his bed. The laudanum made his steps slow and uneven. He pulled on a jacket and trousers and felt along the wainscoting for the servants' jib door. When he found the panel, he pressed it and peered into the dim recessed stair that led to the kitchens.

He took a candle and descended the staircase. Once belowstairs, he found the door leading to the catacombs and lost himself in the darkness.

The cave was no different at midnight than at noon. A permanent black inked the recesses. Sam's lone candle shone like a pinpoint in the maw. The light stopped at the Roman door. He stared for a very long time, not opening it, not touching it. A distraught, guilt-ridden expression marked his face.

He turned around. Carefully retracing his steps, he left the cave. Once in the servants' passage, however, he took a different door. This staircase was old and musty, and obscured with spiderwebs.

He went to the top of the stair. A jib framed the landing and he pushed it.

It was *her* room.

He placed the candle on top of the bureau. To his right was the door to the schoolroom, still closed. But that was not his destination.

He stepped to the trunk, his face a sickly, pale hue. Closing his eyes tight, he seemed to suspend the moment and hold inside all his fear and dread. Then, as if he had to be sure, as if he had to see, he snatched the candle that now trembled in his hand, and he removed an old iron key from his jacket.

He undid the padlock.

With a gasp of terror, he threw open the trunk lid, his eyes wide with mute horror as he fed his gaze upon the contents. Whatever meaning they held for him was conveyed by the helpless animal groan that reverberated from his throat. As quickly as he opened the lid, he closed it and fell upon his knees as if he were fighting some unseen force that now deigned to keep it open.

He held the trunk for a very long time. And all the while he cried like a terrified child, his moans and tears echoing through the abandoned rooms to be heard only by ghosts.

Chapter
Twenty-seven

The rose, wherein the world divine makes itself flesh.
—Dante

The next morning Damien asked Alexandra to meet him in the garden. It was a bitterly cold day, but the sky was a dome of unmarred azure and the horizon was endless except for the menacing crags that jutted up from the west.

Bundled in her cloak, braced against the frigid wind, she entered the garden. At first, she thought the garden was empty and that he had forgotten the meeting. But soon she felt his strong arms around her waist.

"Where were you, my love?" she said to him. "I daresay, sometimes I fear you are more ghost than she, the way you can sneak up on a body." She turned her head to him and smiled. He looked down at her, his eyes so blue, cold, and want-filled.

She let him kiss her mouth. It took them a long time to part.

"I've been waiting here, behind the garden gate. I wanted to surprise you," he said.

"I never knew you to be so mischievous." Her mouth tipped in another smile.

He kissed her again and whispered, "Not even after last night?"

She blushed. It was wrong what she was allowing to happen. It was all wrong, but so infinitely powerful and sweet, she couldn't find the moral strength to stop it. The constraints of society seemed to flee when she was with him and her brown, mousey self fled with them. For one small moment, in his arms, she bloomed. And her love for him became like a rose, the petals, her body; the fragrance, her soul. She gave herself to him with unprecedented candor and she refused to hold back any emotion, even fear and darkness. And her honesty wrought a bond that had become stronger with every day. She found that even after Brian, she had the capacity to take her happiness with both hands and hold onto it with a passion and a greed she'd never known she'd possessed.

"I've made more mischief," he whispered playfully. "Give me your hand."

She poked her hand through the part in her cloak and stood shivering in the wind that scoured over the garden wall.

He dug something out from inside his greatcoat. Then he placed it on her trembling finger.

It was a ring of diamonds as blue as the sky above, as fiery as their union. The weight was foreign to her hand.

"No matter what happens, you are to be my wife." He stared down at her, his face taut with emotion and cursed by the unholy emptiness that she feared might never be filled.

"I'll be your wife. I swear it," she whispered.

He kissed her against the garden wall and, for one aching moment, they found refuge within the sublime goodness of the garden, of each other.

It wouldn't last. She knew nothing would while evil still walked the halls and passages of Cairncross. But the climax was near. Her instincts roared with the signals of impending danger. The peace would fracture soon, and whether they would both be strong enough to withstand the onslaught remained to be seen. All she knew was, that with every kiss, with every soft word, and every night in Damien's bed, they angered the evil within Cairncross. The black-draped figure, human or not, didn't like a soul set free from its grasp.

They had set a trap; their love was the bait. And a sweeter lure, she never knew. Not even in dreams.

Damien entered the tower room. He shot one censorious glance to Millicent and sent her scurrying behind the wall of chintz. Lady Bess was in her "throne," her head lolled against a pillow as her mouth admitted a loud even snore.

He sat in the chair next to her and took in his hand the gnarled claw that had once been soft and feminine. His grandmother sputtered awake with the touch, and she stared at Damien with sleep-clouded eyes.

"Why have you come to see me? What a rare occasion this is." There was no missing the note of reproach in her voice.

"I have some news." He paused as if not sure how to begin. "This may come as a shock, but I'm going to be married."

Lady Bess sat up straight in the chair. Her eyes pinned him to his seat. "Not to that viscountess you left back in London? The servants have bandied her name around so much I can't remember it now—what is it? Lady—Lady—"

"I'm not marrying Lady Compton."

Lady Bess made a grimace. "It's not that creature down in Wapping I hear you go to—"

"No, it's not her either." He leaned back in his chair and studied his grandmother, as if he wanted to note every nuance of her expression when she got the news. "I'm going to marry the new governess, Alexandra Benjamin."

She clasped her crooked hands together almost in a gesture of thanksgiving. In a delighted, high-pitched voice, she said, "Just what I would have wanted for you. I like her. She's . . . why, she's real, now isn't she?"

"Yes," he said softly.

"She'll be good for you, Damien."

"She's already been good for me, but I," he paused, his face grew hard, "I just can't say how good I'll be for her."

"She loves you. I could see it in her eyes when she came to visit me. She softened every time I mentioned your name."

"She's a spinster. She was probably prone to falling in love with the master of the house." He stood and paced the room, his face a mask of marble. "I worry that I've been hasty in this. Greedy even. I want her but still . . .."

"But still there is the past."

"The servants might tell my fiancée things they would not tell a governess."

"But I was the only one to hear you and Ursula in the tower that last day."

"I've never been sure about that. The only blessing is that she was so hated by then, no one ever came forward." His eyes clouded. "But they might come forward now. For Alexandra."

"For her, you must take the risk. Perhaps she'll understand. *I* don't blame you for whatever you had to do. What else but death was going to stop her?"

"I said we were never to discuss that."

"Fine. We'll say no more. The past is gone. Marry your Jewess, Damien. She loves you so."

"Pray for me, grandmother," he said, his face ravaged by doubt. "I can't risk losing her. If she ever turned away from me . . ."

"Don't test her love. Just take it and hold it close."

"I wish it were that simple. But still, there's Ursula."

Lady Bess leaned forward and whispered harshly. "Why haven't you put her in consecrated ground? She would walk no more if—"

"I want you to be at the wedding," he said, cutting her off. He was clearly jaded to Bess's suggestion. "We're marrying in two weeks, down in the chapel."

"If there's still life in this body, I'll be there."

He knelt before the old woman and kissed her hand. "In two weeks then. I'll either see you dance at my wedding, milady or you'll dance on my grave. I don't know which."

"Get her in hallowed ground," the old woman chanted as Damien exited her apartments.

Sam drifted further and further into his silence. Alexandra refused to give up on him, but this time his muteness grew tough and unyielding, stronger than before. He seemed caught in a strange kind of spell. Damien said it was fear, but Alexandra began to guess that this time it was something else. She had the inexplicable notion that what captured his tongue now was of his own making.

It was the very next evening that Alexandra came closer to solving the mystery. Damien had asked the servants to gather in the baronial hall at eight in order for him to announce their engagement. Alexandra had thus far even refrained from telling Mary the news for fear she would have it spread belowstairs before it was official. Damien, too, had been very particular about appearances. He'd said it was only proper to make an announcement to everyone all at once because to tell people piecemeal would only add fuel to gossip and speculation. He wanted to announce it to all, he'd said, then, almost under his breath, he'd said that anyone opposed to such a match could speak to him.

Alexandra didn't think to question him. She was the daughter of a Jew and Damien was a member of the Church of England. There were bound to be objections voiced among Cairncross's throng of the Christian servants. Because of Brian, she just assumed the objections would be about her. She was only a governess and he was a peer. There were a thousand reasons to object to such a union.

And not once did she ever think that the objections would lay upon Damien's head and not hers.

The servants were lined up in the hall four deep as the clock struck eight. Damien searched the crowd as if wanting to make sure everyone was there. Alexandra couldn't believe the number. She stood between Featherstone and Mrs. Penrith and scanned the faces around her. There were servants she had never laid eyes upon and couldn't even guess their function in the household. The sheer numbers of the crowd only hardened her to the belief that Ursula could be living amongst them at Cairncross, undetected.

"I've an announcement to make that will affect everyone in this household," Damien said in a strong commanding tone, instantly quieting the masses.

All eyes turned to him, while Alexandra's heart pounded nervously.

"I'm to be married," he said, his gaze roving the anonymous crowd. "I've finally found the woman who is to be my baroness and my wife. The woman who is to become your mistress."

A current of hushed voices ran through the crowd. Alexandra knew that speculation already was running amuk. She glanced at Mrs. Penrith. The woman stared at her master, her face placid and accepting. Alexandra fought the strange sensation that bloomed inside her as she wondered what the housekeeper's expression would be like once she found out that the new baroness was to be none other than herself.

"Miss Benjamin?" Damien said, holding out his hand to her. Alexandra clasped his with the hand that now bore his diamond ring.

"I want everyone to meet the future Right Honorable Lady Cairncross."

If the murmurs had run through the throng like a current, the gasps ran through it like a shudder. Alexandra tried to smile and there were some, such as a few of the scullery maids whom she'd come to know, that even looked upon her with envy.

But not Mary. Her maidservant merely stared at her as if she were in a walking dream. Mrs. Penrith frowned in amazement as if she were watching a murder, but Featherstone's expression was the worst of all. He opened his mouth in utter shock and stared at them both, viewing their clasped hands like a dese-crated altar. Then all at once, he seemed to remember himself. Alexandra watched in horror while the other servants stepped to them to offer their congratulations. Featherstone did not. He merely removed his thunderstruck expression, and departed the hall. His actions were more than sufficient for dismissal.

Afterward, while she and Damien took cordials in the library, Alexandra broached the subject of Featherstone. She was nervous about it, instinctively knowing she would be delving into places she preferred not to go.

"It must have been a shock to him after what Ursula did. I think we must find it within ourself to understand him just this once," she said calmly, sipping her chartreuse.

"What he did to you, to me, was unforgivable. By tomorrow, he'll be on the next pony cart out of here. I'll have my man from London sent up until we find a replacement." Damien's gaze kept shifting to the door as if he wanted to be elsewhere. She would have put money on the guess that he was anxious to go to the servants' quarters and fire the butler.

"How old is he, my love? He looks sixty if he's a day. What are his chances of finding another position, and without references?"

"Then he should have thought of that before he walked out of the hall!" Damien almost shouted. His anger was palpable.

Slowly, she rose and perched on the arm of his chair. She touched his cheek and turned his head to face her. "Let me talk to him. I'll find out why he did it and perhaps we can work something out. There's no need to put an old man out on the streets for one mistake—"

"Two mistakes. Two, Alexandra," Damien bit out. "You forget about the past. My father forgave him his indiscretion with Ursula. I find no need to forgive him twice in this lifetime."

"And perhaps it was reverberations from the past that made him act the way he did just now. We need to find out what he was thinking. I've never been overly fond of him, but he's served you quite well as long as I've been at Cairncross. He's been with the family most of his life. It just seems wrong not to go speak with him—"

She found her words devoured in a kiss. When they parted, he said, "I'll take care of this, Alexandra."

Alexandra stared down at him. She was not yet Lady Cairn-cross. The servants were still his domain. "I think I must retire for the night. It's been another upsetting day."

He took her hand and laid a kiss within the sensitive palm. She felt the heat of his mouth like the flames from the hearth.

"I'll come to your room later."

She slowly removed her hand. For some reason, his obstinance over Featherstone rankled her. The butler had clearly needed a reprimand, but the idea of him being let go was overburdening. She was the cause, no matter how innocent she was. She burned with the questions of why he'd done it. Featherstone belonged at Cairncross. She couldn't understand what could be so objectionable about her that he could not work in a household where she was its mistress.

"I think I need to be alone tonight," she said, her words, her body stiffening. "I'll see you in the morning, love. Sam and I will take our lesson in the conservatory."

Damien didn't look at her. "Good night then," he said coldly.

"Good night," she whispered, wishing once and for all that his mysteries were solved.

Alexandra left the library and climbed the stairs to her new room adjoining the master's. There was a dark figure at the end of the landing and her heart skipped a beat. But all at once, the figure moved, and Alexandra released a gasp of relief.

"Mrs. Penrith, you should know better than to lurk in the shadows," she exclaimed.

"I've got to speak with you, miss. It's about Featherstone."

"That really is his lordship's domain. I don't think I can change his mind."

"I'm not here so that he may keep his position, miss." The housekeeper stepped further into the circle of gaslight from the wall sconce. "I'm here for your sake. We must talk. Featherstone's behavior this evening is but a symptom of what may be yet to come. He reacted to what you don't know, miss. And now that you want to marry his lordship . . ." The housekeeper's nervous, birdlike gaze darted to Damien's bedchamber door, exactly opposite Alexandra's own, ". . . now that you might marry him, miss. I think there's more to the past than you know. And you *must* know."

Alexandra slid her hand from the doorknob and faced the housekeeper. "What is it that I need to know other than I love him?"

The housekeeper nodded. "Please, shall we go to my apartments and discuss this?"

"All right," Alexandra said hesitantly, her eyes dark with reluctance. "If you insist."

"Thank you, miss. Thank you," Mrs. Penrith murmured as she touched the baize-covered jib door. The passage door sprung open, leading to a maw of cold, oily blackness. She handed a candle to Alexandra and allowed her to go first, then she, too, disappeared into the labyrinth of servants' passages.

Chapter
Twenty-eight

"He seemed quite out-of-sorts by the announcement, but I had supposed it was because of his being duped by Miss Pole." Alexandra lowered herself to Mrs. Penrith's worn horsehair settee. "Still, I can't understand how he could object so much as to risk a dismissal."

"It was my fault," the housekeeper moaned. "Oh, why didn't I just keep quiet?"

Alexandra looked at the woman's white face. "How could this possibly be your fault?"

Mrs. Penrith lowered her eyes, and Alexandra swore they were filled with tears. "I should never have done it. I should have kept the secrets to myself. I told Featherstone about that last day in the tower. It was a mistake, I know it now. To keep such a thing buried all these years, then to go and spill it like I did, I'll never forgive myself." The housekeeper grabbed her hand and held it tight. "It's just that we were talking about his lordship, you understand. For some reason, he seemed almost desperate to know more about the day Ursula left the castle, and so I told him. I don't know why, it's just that I suppose it felt good to unburden myself after all these years. But his reaction . . .'' She squeezed Alexandra's hand. "Don't you see? You can't marry his lordship, miss. You can't.''

"Why can't I?'' Alexandra asked, as a sick feeling invaded her soul.

"Because he's a murderer. I know he murdered her. Most only speculate that he did, but I know he did. Before he left all those years ago, I came upon him and Miss Pole in the tower. He doesn't deny—''

"He denied it to me,'' Alexandra interrupted hotly. "I asked him if he murdered her and he denied it.''

"And what do you make of that, miss?'' the housekeeper asked quietly, her stare giving Alexandra the shivers.

"I believe him. He would tell me if he had.''

A small, dark smile lifted the corner of Mrs. Penrith's mouth. "Yes, he wouldn't lie. He'd have no reason to. There's no reason at all for a man to want to gain the confidence of a pretty woman like yourself.''

Alexandra knew her cheeks betrayed her. "I still don't believe you. He had no reason to want to seduce me. I'm just the governess here. No conquest at all. None at all.''

"You're different than what he's had before. There have been other women, even some of the servants, but you—I could tell from the beginning there was something about you that he just couldn't stay away from. Now he wants to marry you and I tell you, you can't do it—his mind is gone. He's dangerous.''

Alexandra turned away. She didn't want to believe it. She loved Damien, and if his need for her was great, she suddenly realized her need was greater. The loneliness of her future without him was untenable.

"I'll admit at times he's frightening,'' she said calmly, "but Damien has had such a wicked beginning—the neglect, and then Ursula—I've always found it in my heart to understand him. And I've read her diary. I know the horror of what she did to him that last day . . .'' She stood and said passionately, "Perhaps he had to kill her. Perhaps what we've seen walking about here *is* a ghost, but I'll always believe she drove him to it.''

"And yet he won't admit it to you. And then there's Featherstone. What can be done about him?"

Alexandra allowed the housekeeper to pull her back to the settee. "I don't understand why he reacted the way he did. Why should he care if Damien and I are wed?"

"He was in love with her." Mrs. Penrith clutched a linen handkerchief she'd removed from her sleeve. "All this time, he'd thought she'd duped him. Then last night he told me she came to him. She said Damien and I knew the truth of what happened to her and only we could tell." The pitch of her voice grew higher and higher until it was near hysterical. "This morning Featherstone demanded to know what it all meant. I broke down. I shouldn't have, but he seemed in agony. He was in love with her, he told me, and he'd grieved for her though he was convinced he'd been duped. He said this morning that he feared it was a ghost that had visited him last night. And he wanted to know if Damien killed Ursula Pole." Her voice suddenly dropped. "And I had to tell him yes."

"How do you know this? How do you know he killed her?" Alexandra demanded, hysteria in her own voice.

"When the old baron banished his son, Ursula took one last moment with him. Damien met her in the tower stair. I was just going up to give Lady Bess the news when I heard the voices. They were terrible, miss. Unholy. He was shouting at her, and she was weeping. He described how he wanted to kill her. He wanted to 'place his hands around her throat and squeeze the life out of her,' were his words. And then all I heard was silence. No more weeping, no more confessions of a sick love. All I heard was silence. And a heavy groan of relief. Nothing more."

Alexandra numbly realized that she was crying. She touched her cheeks and found them wet. Her tongue tasted salt.

"Miss Benjamin. You cannot marry him. I know he killed her. And if I ever told him that I heard the conversation on the tower stair I'd live in fear of my life. But I've spent my life with the Cairncrosses and I know no other existence. He is my master, and I love him in the strange, ridiculously tolerant way of old servants who've served their master from nappies to the grave. But I couldn't stand silently by and watch you marry such a dangerous unpredictable man. Nor could I keep my silence and leave Featherstone in his agony, though we might all be better off for my silence.''

"So why did Featherstone walk out now? Why didn't he submit his resignation?''

The housekeeper wearily shook her head. ''I think he probably was as shocked as I was over the announcement of your engagement. We had no warning of it. Perhaps his behavior this evening was out of a regard for you. He may have a perennial vulnerability for the governess, or perhaps he couldn't bear to see the master take a bride when he now imagined John Damien had destroyed his chances for marriage so long ago.''

Alexandra extracted her hand from the housekeeper's. As if in a dream, she stood and paced the room, her thoughts going in a thousand morbid directions all at once. ''We must warn Damien of Featherstone.''

"He's already packed and gone, miss. I can't know there'll be any kind of revenge. Besides, it's not Featherstone that has me concerned. It's yourself. Sam has moments where he cannot understand reality. Sometimes I think he speaks of you as if you were Ursula Pole. This could be his slowness, or it could be the anguish she put both lads through. Remember, of the two brothers, Damien's been through the worst. I'm terrified that one day he'll turn on you.''

"He wouldn't hurt me.''

"Have you proof of that?''

Alexandra became perfectly still. She wanted to shout her affirmation for the whole castle to hear, but she couldn't. She loved him and he needed her. But did he love her? Was love something only a sane man could feel?

She again lowered herself to the settee, this time moving as an old woman. Her mind shoved away all the terrible possibilities, and now when she needed her logic above all, it was irretrievably lost in the quagmire of her emotions.

"There, there, miss. I know you love him,'' Mrs. Penrith

said. Her face was shadowed with concern. "But what could I do? See you wed to a murderer? I've too much regard for you not to tell you the truth."

"We don't know the truth. Not the entire truth. I think no one does but Miss Pole." Alexandra put a trembling hand to her lips. She felt disconnected and numb. Deep inside she wept, but her physical tears no longer fell. The ache was too great. She loved him. Now she wondered which was worse: to love a murderer and one day find him turned on you, or to live forever in the dark, oblivious to the treachery around the corner.

"I'm going to find her," Alexandra said. "Whatever it takes. I'm going to search her out if I must dig up her grave to do it."

"Her truth may be no different than mine."

"I've got to warn Damien about Featherstone."

The housekeeper stopped her. Mrs. Penrith's face was drained of blood and her hands shook as she rung them. "You—you can't tell him about what I've just said, miss. He never knew I overheard him in the tower. I've worked here most of my life. I'm not like Featherstone, I've nothing and no one. Please, miss, you can't tell him. I can't sacrifice myself for you and Ursula Pole as Featherstone has."

Alexandra stared at the housekeeper, her heart torn. She understood Mrs. Penrith's plight, but she was frightened for Damien. Featherstone had never struck her as being a kind, levelheaded old gentleman. Upon this information, she wondered if indeed he wouldn't come back for revenge for his imagined love affair with Ursula.

"I'll tell him nothing of our conversation," she said finally to Mrs. Penrith, "but I've got to tell him something of Featherstone. Surely you understand that. It's for his own safety."

"Yes, yes, but you must leave what I know out of it. I can't risk losing my position here. It's all I've got." The housekeeper forlornly took a glance around her small parlor and Alexandra felt a tug on her heart. The housekeeper in all her years of work possessed nothing more than two tiny, rather shabby rooms and a position in an old creepy castle. The woman had never married and whatever respectability she possessed wasn't through a husband but through her work. It was all too easy for Alexandra to picture herself thus, aging and alone, still a spinster.

Her hatred of Ursula Pole came like a thunderbolt. She thought she despised the woman before but it was never like this. This was hatred, an emotion so black and so pure, Alexandra was left breathless with the violence of it.

Damien probably had murdered her. He was probably unbalanced and not the best prospect for a husband. But it was all because of Ursula. Ursula had done it to him. She had lured him into the darkness, the darkness that was inside everybody. And if he'd killed her, she had driven him to it.

And now Ursula Pole had ruined Alexandra Benjamin's life too. She'd made Alexandra understand a whole new facet of the darkness inside of her. A darkness Alexandra had never wanted to admit existed.

"I must retire for the night, Mrs. Penrith. Of course, you understand what a trying day I've had. There's a lot to think about, a lot to discuss. Please, excuse me." Alexandra rose to her feet and walked to the door. She reached out her hand and placed it upon the knob, then said, "Good night. I'll keep your name from Damien. I suppose I owe you thanks for what you've told me tonight."

"Don't thank me, miss. I know as kind as your heart is that you don't mean it. Believe me, it wounded me to have to tell you. I had no idea you were falling in love with him." Mrs. Penrith dabbed her eyes.

The picture burned into Alexandra's mind: the tiny, black-clad housekeeper, perched like a bird on her settee in her small, shabby parlor, dabbing eyes that always beheld so little. Alexandra said good-night and left for her room, but still the picture haunted her.

She feared it was her future.

* * *

He was waiting for her when she returned.

Alexandra closed the door to her shadowed bedroom and leaned tiredly against the doorjamb. Damien sat in a needlework chair by the bedside, cloaked in the darkness of dim gaslight.

She went to the gasolier and reached for the key to turn it up. She wanted light to flood the room, to make it bright and alive. The shadows were becoming too much for her. They were filling up her very soul.

"Don't," he whispered, taking her outstretched hand in his.

"It's too dark in here," she said, suddenly nervous.

"I like the darkness. It softens the edges." He pulled her down onto his lap, but he didn't try to kiss her. He merely stared at her for a very long time, as if he were trying to read the shadows inside of her. "Where were you? I've been waiting here a long time."

"Featherstone has left the castle and spared you the trouble of dismissing him."

"Who told you?"

"I met Mrs. Penrith in the passage. She told me," she said, offering only the bare bones of information.

"What else did she tell you?"

She shivered. His tone was ominous. She ached to remove his spectacles and throw them in the fire. They distanced him from the rest of humanity.

"She asked me to her parlor for tea. She wanted to—" Alexandra was forced to swallow the tears that suddenly threatened. "She wanted to wish me happiness at our engagement."

"I wish us happiness too," he said, his voice filled with doom.

"We will be happy," she said, suddenly burying her head in his shoulder. The tears she'd tried to hold back came without warning. She held him to her and wept. Numbly, she felt his hand stroke her hair.

"What is this?" he asked, placing a kiss at her temple.

"Nothing," she lied, not daring to tell him.

"But it is something. You're very upset. I see the dismal emotion in your eyes. They're . . . without hope."

She fingered the tortoiseshell buttons on his jacket. Somehow she had to come up with a story, but she was terrible at such things. "It was just so awful of Featherstone to do what he did this evening. It still has me rattled."

"The last time I saw you, you defended him and asked me to forgive him. What changed?" His jaw tightened. She could see he didn't believe her.

She wiped her eyes. It seemed she'd spent the last weeks doing nothing but shedding tears. "I fear Mrs. Penrith did tell me of his departure. He fancied himself in love with Miss Pole, but you know that. He somehow has recently gotten the notion in his head that she didn't dupe him as he believed. He feels you took her from him." Her voice lowered to a frightened, confused whisper. "I fear he may want retribution. You must be careful, Damien."

Damien stared into her eyes as if searching for her very essence, as if searching for truth. "For years, the servants have bandied about the idea that I murdered her. Featherstone never believed them. He was too angry. So why does he believe them now, Alexandra?"

His tone of voice froze her. The anger he held back was like a taut piece of rubber, just waiting to be released. Trembling, she left the circle of his arms. "I asked you before if you murdered her. I got my answer, and I'll keep it still."

"You'll keep it, but obviously as Featherstone doesn't believe it anymore, you don't believe it anymore, do you?" The words were like ice.

She couldn't look at him. She didn't dare. If she saw a different reality in his eyes, she would go mad.

So she looked away, like the coward she now knew she really was. "I—I've found pieces of her diary, my love. She was beyond evil in what she did to you. The past is gone. Why dredge it up again and again?"

"You think I'm a murderer." He grabbed her arms and forced her to finally meet his gaze. "And you wonder if you can marry a man who murdered a woman, a man who might have taken her in his hands and broken the very life from her body.''

''Yes,'' she choked, unable to hide any longer. Her emotions were like glass, shattered in all directions from the boulder Mrs. Penrith had thrown at it.

Slowly, he removed his hands. He held her stare for a long, interminable moment while she groped to see the mortal behind the spectacles. But she found nothing, but cold, terrible darkness.

''I bid you good-night, Miss Benjamin. And I suggest you lock your door tonight, for I might take it within this head to— to—'' He stared at her, but didn't finish. He didn't seem able to. She watched in horrid fascination as the muscle in his jaw bunched and tightened in an angry knot. He gave her one last forsaken glance, then he left, slamming the bedroom door behind him as she slowly sank to her knees.

Percival Featherstone had probably never been a sane man. Over the years, he'd butled well, as his father did, and his father before him. But if the truth be known, his mind had always been weak and prone to suggestion. Particularly by young, pretty women.

And now his mind was gone.

It was probably most apparent by the fact that he conducted an entire conversation—all the while speaking clearly and articulately—even though he was the only one in the room.

''She is so beautiful, so beautiful,'' he whispered, mindlessly stroking the pistol he held before him like a phallus. ''She hasn't aged a day. She is still so beautiful and come back for me at last.

''But why didn't you come to see me before now? 'Tis been so lonely here without you. I've needed you as no other. No one else ever touched me like you did.'' He rose from the little child's desk where he had sat. He threw open the shutters and shed moonlight into the old abandoned Cairncross schoolroom.

''I'm waiting, my true love,'' he whispered into the night.

''Tell me what you want to avenge this tragedy. He won't take his happiness when he tried to destroy ours.''

He turned around. The pierced skirt of Ursula Pole's mahogany desk threw fascinating patterns of moonlight on the far wall, mesmerizing him. One silhouette appeared as a man's profile and he walked up to it. ''Is this what you want?'' he whispered. Sweat broke out onto his lined forehead. He lifted the pistol and positioned it to the silhouette's temple. He pulled back the hammer, then fired.

The hammer came down with a leadened thunk. The gun wasn't loaded. Yet.

He tipped his head back and laughed. He pulled down the hammer, again and again, and kept firing into the shadow's temple.

But then he heard a noise. One of the panels had been released along the wainscoting and a figure stood there, obscured in shadow.

''Is that you, my love?'' he whispered, going toward the musty-smelling figure. Beyond, where the tunnel turned into a stone staircase, he saw Roman paintings of laurels and rams' heads flickering in the light of a lone, distant candle. It was a secret entrance to the catacombs.

''Tell me what to do. After twenty long years, my will is yours to command,'' he rasped.

The figure pulled him into the catacombs. She put her lips to his for a long, terrible moment.

Then the panel was replaced and they were gone.

Chapter
Twenty-nine

Alexandra lay abed the next morning, her heart heavy, her soul weary. Mary had come with tea and toast, and now bustled around the little room, opening drapery and laying out clothes. Alexandra just watched her. Mary had never even given her good wishes on her engagement. She was conspicuously silent. She did not approve.

But Alexandra wondered if there would ever be a marriage of which Mary needed to approve. Damien had become so cold last night. He seemed to break. Everything was shattering like a piece of crystal fallen to the floor. There seemed nothing Alexandra could do about it.

"Shall I send for some hot water and see to your bath?" The maidservant stood at the bedside and held out a dressing gown.

It wasn't her dressing gown, it was Damien's left from so long ago. She'd never gotten the chance to return it. Now it damned her.

All at once, Mary, too, noticed that the garment wasn't hers. Then her face dawned with the recognition that it was a man's dressing gown.

Alexandra met Mary's gaze. By the horrified expression in Mary's eyes, Alexandra figured she'd drawn all the correct conclusions. She suddenly felt ill. Even now she could feel the blood drain from her cheeks.

"There, there, love. We'll put this one back. I can't imagine how this got here," Mary said, obviously trying to spare her.

"It belongs to Damien. You should have it taken to him." Alexandra saw no point in lying. The truth will out. Besides, she needed to be honest with Mary. Her maidservant's friendship was all she had in this world. She couldn't tolerate deceiving Mary and begging for her support at the same time.

"I know you love him now," Mary said quietly, folding the dressing gown and placing it on the hearth chair.

"I do love him," Alexandra whispered, her eyes dark and worried. "But I'm so afraid . . ." All at once the tears returned. She laid her head against the pillow and gave in to their wrath.

Mary came to the edge of the bed and put her arms around her. Alexandra sobbed against her shoulder, finding release for all the torments within her.

At last, when the wave of tears subsided, Alexandra took the proffered handkerchief and said, "What should I do? He frightens me, but I want him. I've given myself to him. I love him. Yet I don't even know if he *can* love. Mrs. Penrith thinks I should leave, and the sooner the better, but something keeps me here. A tiny flicker of hope. The light in his eyes when he sees his brother Samuel. If I love Damien, will that be enough for all these problems? Will it tame the darkness in him? Or will it make him turn on me?" She wiped the silent tears that still streamed down her cheeks. Nothing was any good anymore. She couldn't imagine returning to London now, because Damien had forever changed her. She might even be carrying his child. There was no way to begin again as if she'd never been here, never known him.

"In my heart, I feel I must fight," she choked out. "There's goodness inside him. He loves his brother. He'd surrender his life for Sam without a moment's thought. But I just can't get a grip on what it is I am fighting here." She looked at Mary who simply held her and let her vent her emotions. "I—I don't even know *what* I'm fighting. Am I fighting a ghost or a madwoman, or worse, am I fighting the madness inside Damien?"

" 'Tis perhaps too soon to know. I just fear for you, child. I just fear for you," Mary whispered.

As usual, Mary's graying red curls were peeking out from her cap and it suddenly struck Alexandra how Mary was so perfectly the opposite of Ursula. They both had red hair, but Mary's showed her age and proved her blessed mortality. Ursula's, chillingly, did not.

"I'm going to stay, Mary," she said. Her thoughts of Ursula turned her tears to stone. "But I think perhaps I should make you return to London. Just for a little while. You see, I've decided I'm going to fight her. Simply because I despise her so much."

"That's not a good reason, love. Better it should be because you love him so much."

Alexandra wondered if this was how Damien felt inside. She wondered if the expression in her eyes hinted at the devastation inside her, or if she had finally learned to hide her vulnerable feelings behind a frigid, distant veneer, the way he did. She whispered, "I do love him so much. God save me, I do."

It was bitterly cold the next day. A light rainfall turned to snow by noon and covered the distant hills in white. The moors and crags were now ghosts looming on the horizon, beneath a churning wintry sky.

Alexandra began arrangements for Mary's trip to London. The woman protested, but Alexandra was afraid. She didn't want Mary caught in the evil of Cairncross out of devotion and love for her charge. She loved Mary. Above all, it was imperative that Mary be kept safe.

She had her lesson with Sam though he still would not speak. At four-thirty, when Mrs. Penrith arrived with tea, Alexandra watched from the music-room window as Damien braved the snowfall, mounted his horse, and galloped out to the moors.

"Where is he going?" she had asked Mrs. Penrith.

"Out to meet his pact with the devil, I suppose," the woman had said before shaking her head and departing the room.

Alexandra tried to drink a cup of tea, but she couldn't even concentrate on that mindless task. Sam sat in his chair, quietly rocking back and forth as if taking succor from the motion. The panes of glass in the west-facing windows were frozen with a pattern of blowing snow. Her worries for Damien were eclipsed only by her need for the truth.

"That will be all, for today, Sam." She reached out and touched his cheek. Briefly their gazes met, then he lumbered to his feet and left, not saying a word.

She gathered her skirts and prepared for the long climb to the tower room. Her visit would be unannounced, but she had to see her. Damien's grandmother knew more about what went on at Cairncross than she had ever revealed. And now was the time to make her have out with it.

"If she's napping, then I'll wait," she told Millicent upon her arrival.

"Miss, she's not been feeling well of late. We don't let her have visitors who just spring upon her," the servant said, emphatically wringing her hands.

"Who's there?" rang out a voice from behind the chintz panels. Lady Bess then appeared, her thin, scraggly hair unpinned, her face still heavy with sleep. She looked just as she had done on the stair that night she had frightened Alexandra.

"Damien has announced our engagement. He and I are to wed." Alexandra paused and waited for Lady Bess's reaction to the news. She was taken aback by the happiness she saw cross the old woman's face.

"So it's finally official now. My dreams have come true. Thank God. He needs you so much," Lady Bess said, clapping her hands.

Alexandra helped her to her chair.

"Oh, this is wonderful news, lovely news," the aged peeress

exclaimed. She tapped her cane on the floor. "Millicent, bring us a sherry. We must celebrate!"

Alexandra took her palsied, wizened hand in her own and kneeled in front of her. She stared at the old woman. A dark expression shadowed her eyes. "I think that would be premature."

"What?" Lady Bess gasped. "What could go wrong?"

"I've grave doubts about Damien's character. I need to know everything you know. I feel I've got to make my decision soon."

Lady Bess stared down at her, her expression filled with a strange mixture of guilt, dismay, and dread. "You must marry him. You'd make him a good wife, Alexandra Benjamin. He needs someone level-headed like you."

"He needs me, and in my own way, I need him as badly." Alexandra paused. The words were difficult. "But this is about more than need. I have to know whom I'm to wed. I need to know about Damien. I need to know if he murdered Ursula."

Lady Bess's hand seemed to go ice cold within her grasp. The old woman looked away, a frown carved deep into her lined face.

"Did he?" Alexandra urged in a whisper.

Lady Bess nodded a dismissal to Millicent. The old servant promptly disappeared behind the loose panels of chintz. When they were alone, Lady Bess said, "I don't know what you want from me. Did I see him murder her? No, I did not. Should you love him and cherish him in spite of everything? Yes you should, because he can be loved. And because he needs someone to teach him about love since his family . . ." her words grew gravelly and thick with tears, ". . . since his family failed him in that matter so abysmally."

"You were an old woman even twenty years ago. There wasn't much you could have done to help Damien even if you were able to." Alexandra bent her head and stared pensively at the floor. "You mustn't blame yourself anymore for the past. 'Tis done and I'm only here for the future. If he murdered Ursula, perhaps in time I could forgive him such a sin. Nonetheless, I need to know. I've a right to know if I'm to be his wife.''

Lady Bess put a gnarled hand to her hair and lovingly stroked it. ''I didn't see him kill her, but there was a conversation in these tower stairs before Damien was banished. He had every cause to murder her, and by his words to her, he explicitly proved the desire to do it. I wish I could say otherwise, for I fear you might leave us, and we'll have nothing then. I don't know if he murdered Ursula. All I know is that he's certainly never denied it.''

Alexandra felt as if a great weight had just been thrown upon her already overburdened shoulders. There seemed no way to deny Damien's guilt now. He had murdered Ursula Pole, and the question was, could she, Alexandra Benjamin, live with it. She feared the answer was no.

''I know it's a shock. The very idea is repulsive,'' the old woman explained hastily, an edge of desperation in her voice as she stared at Alexandra's white face, ''but he had cause to do it. Remember, he had cause.''

''He may have had cause. I believe he had every right to hate her. But whether she deserved killing, 'tis not for me to judge.'' Slowly Alexandra rose to her feet. She felt no urge to cry. Inside there was only an emptiness, a howling darkness where before had been her heart.

''Marry him. Don't lose him to her. Fight for him. Please.''

Alexandra walked numbly to the tower door. ''It's not her I must fight.'' Her voice cracked but not enough for tears. ''But at least I know that now.'' Without a glance of farewell, Alexandra departed. She didn't see the old woman reach out to her in mute supplication. Nor did she see Lady Bess finally lay her head in her gnarled hands only to release a terrible, forsaken sob.

She waited for him in the baronial hall. Tomorrow Jaymes was going to take Mary, and perhaps even herself, to the train station in York. They could conceivably be settled in a flat by week's end, Mary picking up her normal routine of servant, Alexandra unable to picture anything being normal again.

Damien came in well after ten o'clock. Outside, the drifts were almost a foot deep, and his shoulders and head were wet with melted snow. Without Featherstone to meet him, there was only a lone footman to take his ice-covered greatcoat.

She observed him from her seat in the shadows. He slicked back his damp gold hair, and wiped his spectacles on his shirt-sleeves. His face was handsome, yet severe, and she ached, remembering how a caress across the cheek could soften it.

" 'Twas a long ride you took, my lord,'' she said.

He turned and squinted into the shadows. Warily, he replaced the spectacles, looping each gold arm around his ears. "Alexandra,'' he acknowledged, his expression scrupulously cleared of feeling.

"I waited up to speak with you.'' She stepped from the shadows.

He watched the footman disappear through the baize-covered door. When they were alone, he said, "Come. Speak with me upstairs.''

"No. I can't be with you anymore. I mean to tell you I'm leaving.''

He rubbed his jaw and she swore she saw a flash of anger in his eyes before he shuttered the expression. "You won't go.''

"Tell me the truth about what you did to Ursula Pole and I might stay. But I need the truth.''

"I didn't murder her. I could have. I even wish at times that I had, but I didn't.''

"Bess and others say you did. I need to know.''

"Why?'' The anger within him seemed to seep out the edges. "What difference does it make? Perhaps you're right and she's not even dead, and we will have wasted time disputing the identity of her murderer.''

"You never told me you threatened to kill her in the tower.''

"Would your regard for me increase if I told you such a story?'' He met her gaze and his mouth twisted in a dark, cynical smile. "I can see from your face what you think of me now that you believe I'm a murderer. So I ask you, what is the incentive to confess to killing Ursula? Will it better the situation? Will you love me even more?"

His logic was irrefutable. Her insides bled for him, but it didn't change the conclusion. "I can't stay with a murderer, I just can't," she said quietly. "I find I can't believe your denials. So it doesn't matter what you say, I'm leaving with Mary in the morning."

His jaw hardened. There was a dangerous glint to his eyes. "I asked you to be my wife, Alexandra. *My wife.* You gave yourself to me. That binds us together forever. You will stay with me."

"No," she said, her voice beginning to shake. "That's why I must leave now, before it's too late."

He took a menacing step toward her. "I'll keep you here against your will if I must."

She edged away, but slowly, not allowing him to see the fear in her. "This is not your kingdom, my lord, to do what you will with your lieges."

"This may not be my kingdom, but if I keep you here, who would come for you? If I sent your timid little maidservant Mary to London, would she come back with a force to retrieve you? Would your beloved Brian realize his love too late, and storm Cairncross as if he were stepping from the pages of old Watty's novels?"

His sarcasm stung. She began to tremble with anger. "So you know about *Ivanhoe* then? Was it you who set about tormenting me with that copy of it? Was it just a fortunate guess that this jilted daughter of a Jew might find that novel particularly raw on her nerves?"

"Is that what you think? That I'm a lunatic, sneaking around here, playing these sick pranks on you?" He released an unpleasant laugh and took another step toward her.

She backed away.

He began to stalk her. "You must think I'm a madman, Alexandra," he said, shoving aside a blackened oak armchair, "and you know what? I am. Because I'm not going to let you leave, not tomorrow, not ever. You will stay by my side, and if it takes a madman to keep you here, then a madman I'll be." He reached for her.

She slipped from his grasp and bolted, but he blocked her way.

"You'll stay with me, Alexandra."

"Not like this," she panted and turned, pushing chairs in his way. "I pledged my love to you, but not by force. Never by force. That was her kind of love, not mine."

He stopped. Their eyes met and he looked at her for a long moment as if studying every plane of her face, every glitter of emotion in her eyes. "No other man will worship you as I worship you. No other man will need you as I need you," he said, his voice hoarse with emotion.

"If you revere me so, why haven't you told me the truth? Why haven't you told me about the conversation you had with Ursula in the tower that last day? Lady Bess told me. You murdered her, didn't you? Didn't you?" The last question dissolved into a moan of hopeless agony.

He took a step toward her, his body tight with implied violence.

She stepped backward, but her skirt caught on a sword point from the display. She stumbled, and he caught her dead center into his arms.

"Don't," she gasped as she stared up into his unforgiving gaze.

His arms tightened like the steel jaws of a trap.

"Please, don't do this. Please," she begged.

He ran his teeth along the tender skin of her earlobe, pulling and tugging in erotic invitation.

"Tell me there'll be no pleasure here for you and I'll make you a bigger liar than me." He bent and captured her mouth with his. She tried to turn her head, but he locked it in place with his two hands.

She let out a moan of despair. Her lips accepted him, but her mind screamed rebellion. And all the while, she cursed the betraying warmth that had begun to spread from her lower belly.

"Pleasure is not the greatest seduction, Damien," she pleaded as he pulled her to the staircase.

"And what moves men to destruction faster than the lure of pleasure?" he rasped, taking the treads two at a time.

"You can find it with any woman," she cried and tugged on her arm. "So take one of the serving wenches and leave me be."

"But I choose pleasure *and* love." He strode to his bedchamber door, her arm locked in the shackle of his grasp. He backed her against the closed door and trapped her within his arms. "Tell me you hate me, Alexandra, and I'll let you go. It's your love that draws me near, that tantalizes me with its rareness. Tell me you loathe me and the pleasure will die like coals left untended in the hearth."

"I do hate you," she cried, gouging his cheeks so that he might free her from the iron lock of his embrace.

"Look at me and tell me the truth." He grabbed her arms and shook her.

She quieted, letting her breath come in great gasps as she leaned against the door frame. Finally, she looked up at him and found herself caught in the net of his unholy gaze. "I do hate you . . ." The words were as difficult to think as they were to say, ". . . and yet I love you as well. And *that,* my lord, is why I'm leaving in the morning."

He lowered his head and bent so near, she could feel his breath like a warm caress to her cheek. "No, Alexandra, *that* is why I'm going to keep you until I'm dead in the grave and my dust has blown across the moorland."

Her gaze violently met with his.

He whispered, "Deny that I mean it. I dare you."

She lowered her gaze. A mistake. It signaled surrender.

Her instincts told her to keep her dignity and distance from him. He probably was insane. All the tricks had probably been executed by him, and even now he was probably maniacally amused by all her frights.

But she loved him. And through that love, his struggles had become like her struggles, his passions, her own. And now in every way, he'd proved he was the opposite of Brian. Brian would have let her die by neglect and disloyalty. Damien was going to kill with obsession.

He jerked her to him.

She tilted her head to him. Perhaps, deep in her mind, she was forming an eloquent protest, one that was but at the tip of her tongue. Yet when his mouth crushed over hers, no protest came. And as the kiss deepened, she discovered no protest ever would.

She felt as if she were in a dream, one from which she could not awaken. She realized she had let him take her by the hand and that he had pulled her into his room. When he lowered her to the mattress of his looming bed, all her sanity begged her to flee, but still, she didn't. And she realized with his every heated kiss—to her throat, to her hands, to her tightly corseted bosom—that love was not sane. In a truly sane existence, such as she had had before, it was not even necessary.

But once the dam broke into madness, there was no bucket large enough to put the water back.

The river simply ran free.

Chapter
Thirty

Alexandra opened her bleary eyes. Every muscle in her body cried out, stretched and pulled to the limit. Her nude body was tangled in a knot of bedclothes. Her mind burned with memories of the night before.

She knew, by some sixth sense, even without turning over and looking, that he was gone from the bed. Her surprise was that he was even still in the room. Lying on her side, she faced the windows, and she found him by the windows, clad in only a pair of hastily pulled-on, unbuttoned trousers. He stared out at an unfamiliar white landscape that had only yesterday been the dun-colored moorlands. His figure was still and silent, and when he glanced back at her, his face held only nothingness. It was as purified of feeling as the snow-draped hills were of color.

She closed her eyes. A darkness settled in her chest like a lead weight. It was too much to expect him to blithely await at her bedside, perchance pouring her morning coffee like a doting husband. It had been too raw last night for such a performance; too raw, too wicked, too cryptic and sexual for them to kiss and pet each other this morning. But deep in her woman's heart, she still yearned for the sweetness. In her daydreams, she pictured herself as the pretty, young wife of a worthy man. She wanted healthy, bright children, and she wanted simple, pure moments when she might sit on her husband's lap, and perhaps stuff bonbons into his mouth until they fell against each other, weak with laughter.

Now last night seemed to wipe away the possibilities of that, as cleanly as Damien's eyes were wiped clean of feeling.

She couldn't even remember how many times he'd taken her, but each successive coupling eloquently accounted for her sore, aching muscles. And how, with each joining, he'd grown a little rougher, as if he were driven to possess her.

The last, he'd pulled her on top of him and drove her to do the work. She moaned she couldn't do it, but his large, powerful hands guided her, almost forced her hips into motion. The final shame had been the speed of her pleasure. She fell upon him, weak with terrible satiation, and then, to her humiliation, he made her take it again, as he greedily cupped her breasts in his hands and coaxed her with whisperings that no other man would ever have her, need her, want her as he would.

There was a time when just thinking of such things would have turned her face flame red, but now as she lay tangled in the sheets, want and desire had taken her beyond embarrassment. His method of seduction was diabolical, and it was working. He wanted her to understand the darkness; last night, she had begun the journey. With every brutal, selfish kiss he'd taken on her reluctant mouth, with every carnal embrace he'd held her down with, he'd created a need inside her she didn't want to know, let alone acknowledge. He'd begun the descent into ferociousness; and while it was a facet of her character she'd always known was there—for it was undoubtedly inside everyone—it was something that was best flirted with on the precipice; otherwise one might find oneself falling into the abyss.

She stared at his broad, unapproachable, naked back, and she thought of last night.

She was indeed falling into the abyss.

She had to save herself. If only because she wanted sweetness, gentleness, along with the ferocity. She had to pull away, because if she couldn't spare him, she must at least spare herself.

Disentangling herself from the twisted covers, she covered her chest with her hands and crept to a nearby chair where she found a dressing gown. She clutched it to her bare breasts, all the while keeping her eyes on Newell, hoping he would still be looking out at the snow.

He was not. He was staring right at her. His gaze went flickering down her nude body as she groped to cover herself with the cut-velvet robe.

They said nothing. The silence bonded them as captive and captor, pupil and student. Quickly she slipped her arms through the silk brocaded sleeves and covered herself, but not before his gaze traveled the length of her body, lingering on the heavy plumpness of her breasts as she raised her arms, struggling to get into the garment.

"You rush to hide yourself from me. Where do you think you're going?" His mouth quirked.

She glanced at him, then accidentally caught the vision of herself in the mantel mirror. She looked like a haunt. Her hair was knotted and twisted, wantonly thrown forward over one shoulder like a country trollop's. Beneath the frazzled mass of dark hair peered a face, white from fear, with dark lavender circles beneath eyes that looked unspeakably tired.

Desperately, her gaze searched the room for her clothes. They were gone. There was nothing scattered in the room but Damien's shirt that lay on the bedside table where he had discarded it last night, and the dressing gown that she now wore.

"If you're looking for your clothes, I've sent them belowstairs to be cleaned and pressed. The minister is coming at six this evening to marry us."

She backed away into the corner between a wall and his mahogany bureau. His words made perfect sense but she still couldn't understand him. They weren't going to be married today. The wedding wasn't for weeks. To be legally and morally bound to the man she'd met last night would destroy her.

"You look like a bird trapped in a snare, Alex."

He went to her.

She put out her hands as if to ward him off. Her palms met the warm wall of muscle on his belly and she pushed, but it was like trying to move a cairn. In a panic, she felt his knuckles slip inside the dressing gown. He brushed aside the garment from one shoulder and kissed her there, moving his mouth lower and lower from her collar, until he managed to bare her breast.

She entwined her fingers in his hair and pulled his head back before his mouth covered her nipple. He glared at her, his eyes almost demanding she pull harder, then he jerked his head forward and clamped his mouth around the tip of her breast.

"I won't . . ." she gasped, feeling his teeth dig into her flesh.

He pulled only harder. He was a master at skirting pain, but with every encounter, the pain came nearer, looming ahead as a matter of course. Now his lip-covered teeth ground hard upon her nipple, and when she cried out, it was as much from ecstasy as from the fear that he was soon to cross the threshold into damage, pain, and destruction.

Her hand groped helplessly across the surface of the bureau and met with the silver handle of a hairbrush. She grasped the brush and whacked it across the side of his face. He violently pulled back.

He grabbed the brush from her, nearly breaking her wrist in the effort. She covered her face with her hands and waited for the onslaught. But there was only quiet. The only noise in the room was from her struggle to take each terror-stricken breath.

Painfully, she lowered her hands and looked at him. He stared at her, his eyes opaque beneath the spectacles. In contempt, he knocked the brush back onto the bureau. It skidded across the smooth surface, then thunked to the plush wool rug on the floor.

"I won't marry you," she whispered.

"You will marry me, or I'll spread the shame of your wantonness all over London." His words were succinct, heartless.

She ached to hit him again. "I'll not continue this. You won't win, Damien. I'll make sure of it. I want gentleness. I want someone who cares for me. Or there'll be no marriage. I'll die first."

His face hardened. "Either way."

She leaned against the bureau top and turned away. He terrified her. "You *can* love in that way, I know it. I've seen it. But I can't fight the dark side of you forever. I can't out-think you at every turn, so I must leave."

He casually lowered himself to the large needlepoint armchair by the hearth. Without responding, he let his gaze go to the fire and there it stayed while she stared at him.

He was between her and the door.

She nervously clutched the lapels of the dressing gown.

She took a step, then another and another, toward the door. He grabbed her hand and twisted her down to her knees until she knelt before him in the chair.

"I want you so bad that I'm losing my mind over it." He stared down at her. His face strained with hidden agony. An ugly bruise was already forming over his cheek where she'd bashed him. "I knew you'd do this to me."

"Let me go," she gasped. A part of her ached to reach out to him and caress his face where she'd hurt him, but she couldn't risk weakening, so she stared back at him, her eyes filling with tears. "This isn't how a man loves a woman."

"And how does a woman love a man? I'll tell you how. She seduces by the bliss of her orifices, then kills just when her lover can't live without her, she *destroys*." He viciously grabbed her hair and yanked her head forward between his knees.

"Damien." She released a sob and buried her head in his thigh just as he put his hand through the unbuttoned top of his trousers. She released a sob. "No."

In horror, she watched as he pulled himself out.

She tried to jerk away.

He held her head down and savagely whispered, "Take a

look at it, Alexandra. You've been so busy using it of late, you probably never paused to examine it, to put it to the harsh glare of light and appreciate it thoroughly." He pulled her head up further.

"See the marks? They're still there. All the little scars where I in my youth trusted when I shouldn't have."

She looked up at him, frightened and shocked. But what she saw in his face was worse than the scars he was trying to force her to see. He was bereft of any knowledge of love, a man completely alone. A man who hated the world because he believed he had no place in it.

"I'm not Ursula, Damien."

"No, you're not." He paused. "You're worse."

"No, you're wrong." Her words were breathless as she fought the pull of his grip.

He ran his free hand through her hair, watching her with an odd kind of detachment. Then he took a long angry breath. "But you are worse, Alexandra. She kept her distance. She never made me feel for her the way I feel for you. I didn't need her." His voice grew thick. "And she never did all of this, then try to leave me."

"I love you, Damien. But not this side of you," she sobbed, turning her head to his knee. "Love is kind, love is tender and good. It tames, Damien. It tames." With a heartwrenching sob, she ripped his hand from her hair and scrambled to her feet. "I won't let you do this . . ." She ran to the door and flung it open.

It was then she felt the liquid on her bare feet. She looked down and found herself standing in a pool of cheap carmine made to look like blood. The spatter began behind Damien's door, passed across the hall and disappeared into the chamber that was now her room.

Without the will not to look, she slowly dragged herself across the hall and threw her door wide open. The sight sucked the air right from her lungs.

The windows were all shattered, and a frigid wind filled the room. A ruffling sound came from the bed. Her gaze fell upon the object. It was *Ivanhoe,* laid open, its pages turning back and forth at the caprice of the violent breeze. The mannequin was back, this time also in the far corner by the bed, its skirt once more obscenely flipped over its anonymous face. And the trail of carmine was everywhere, splattered on the white coverlet, pooled in the shards of broken window panes, finally ending at her bureau mirror, where the pot was dipped and dipped again with a finger, to draw a huge Star of David across the bureau mirror.

The horror of it robbed her of all that was life; of breath, of thought, of emotion. She turned by pure animal instinct, looking back at the beginning of the trail. Damien stood in his bedchamber doorway, just as she feared he would, staring at her with his thoughts unreadable, obscured by the implacability of the spectacles.

There was no surprise in his expression.

It must have been him all along.

Her vision dimmed, and she crumpled to the floor in a dead faint.

Chapter
Thirty-one

Alexandra opened her eyes. Panic still gripped her heart. Her gaze darted wildly about as she tried to discern her surroundings. She was back in Damien's bedchamber and at the other end of the room, Damien stood in the doorway. His stare was scoured clean of feeling, but fixed on her.

Mary's voice shattered the silence. "There, there, love, lie back and take some time to get your bearings."

Alexandra snapped her head around. The maidservant had just wrung out a cloth in a basin and was holding it out to her.

"His lordship told me you fainted," she said stiffly as she laid the cloth to Alexandra's forehead. Mary's expression was of worry mixed with fear.

Alexandra's gaze once more found Damien. He stared at her as if taking in every plane of her face, every fleeting anxiety in her eyes. He nodded, a curt, dismissive gesture, then without saying a word, he left the room.

"Where is he going?" she burst out, paralyzed with a sudden, inexplicable doom.

" 'Tis all right, miss. 'Tis all right. He said we're to leave today. Jaymes has already been instructed to ready the carriage.

We'll spend the night in York and take the train first thing in the morning.'' Mary seemed to whisper a silent prayer. ''Thank God,'' she murmured.

Alexandra looked down at her apparel. She still wore Damien's dressing gown. Her eyes turned to Mary. The woman's face held no accusation, only concern.

She tried to get to her feet but her head still felt light; her limbs unwieldy. ''He told me I could never leave.'' She couldn't hide the hysteria and confusion in her voice.

''When he summoned me, he explained that you had fainted.'' Mary's eyes darkened. ''He was terribly concerned. He said you were frightened here, and unhappy, and he couldn't bear to make you so. Then he said when you awoke, you and I were to be taken to York.''

Alexandra looked around the room, then again at her dishabille. ''I—I don't know how to explain my attire,'' she said, color creeping into her cheeks.

''You thought you were to be married, miss.''

Mary suddenly hugged her. The maidservant's trembling arms seemed to offer solace and absolution, but Alexandra couldn't allow herself such forgiveness yet.

''Have you seen my room?'' she whispered, her soul filled with grief.

''It's a mess,'' was all Mary offered.

''He did it. It must be him. He's been tormenting me.'' A tear slipped down her cheek.

Mary said nothing.

''All this time, I thought it might be Miss Pole. I thought she was playing the tricks on me because she didn't like me having Damien's attention. Now I know it's true. His mind is gone.'' She began weeping in earnest. ''I thought I could help him. He sat one night with a pistol in his hand and I feared he might do harm to himself. But what can I do now to save him? I can't marry a murderer. And these—these—gruesome pranks, they're diabolical in their very intimacy. How can I save him from such dementia without sacrificing myself to it?''

Mary took her hand in her own. ''I can't explain what's

happened here. Your room is certainly torn up, but did he do it? I don't know; he may have. I didn't see him. But we don't have to think of him anymore, miss. We're leaving. As soon as you can gather yourself, we're leaving. And I thank God for the escape. It's come none too soon."

"I don't think I can help him anymore." Alexandra wiped her cheeks and then let the tears flow free. She never felt so close to hopelessness. Her life seemed expunged of all meaning. The future was something now to endure, not to look forward to.

"Come, I've brought you some clothes from your room. Let me help you dress, then I can gather your things and see you off in the carriage."

Alexandra nodded, but her sight was blurred with tears, her heart filled with agony.

"I must say goodbye to Sam," Alexandra said when Jaymes had all their trunks lashed to the top of the carriage and Mary was down in the kitchen instructing cook as to what to pack for luncheon. "Where is he? I haven't seen him."

Mrs. Penrith wrung her hands and swept her gaze around the baronial hall. "Now that you mention it, miss, I haven't seen him of late either. Let me go summon the footmen to see if they can fetch him."

The housekeeper left and Alexandra was alone in the hall. The vast emptiness of it depressed her. She walked over to the Cairncross sword. Her finger trailed along the ancient, pitted edge and her mouth whispered the words of the motto. *Sunt hic etiam sui praemia laudi.* "Here too virtue has its reward." The motto had proved false. There was no virtue at Cairncross. And the unbearable pain of the discovery was hers to endure for the rest of her life.

She looked up at the enormous oaken staircase at the end of the hall. There was no sane reason to want to see the old schoolroom again, but she wanted to, nonetheless. Perhaps in the back of her mind, she hoped to see Ursula. Perhaps, she hoped for one last stab at an explanation of the madness that was ripping her in two. Whatever the motivation, she found herself lifting her skirts and walking up the treads to the third floor.

The schoolroom was empty. A strange kind of quiet had settled in the room once more. The shutters were closed and locked again. Dust was again accumulating on the desks and woodwork. Alexandra Benjamin's presence in it was being erased, day by day, dust mote by dust mote.

She went to the bookcase. Leather-bound novels were sentineled perfectly within the shelves with no gaps. All the Waverley novels were intact. *Ivanhoe* had been returned to its proper place.

There was nothing here for her. The story was over. The heartache begun.

She walked to the passage door and turned the handle. But a noise stopped her.

It was a small scratching sound on the other side of the door that led into her former bedroom. Ursula Pole's bedroom.

She crossed the schoolroom and tested the knob. As in the first time she had encountered this door, it was open when it should have been locked.

She turned the knob and as she opened the door, the hinges shrieked. Her old bedroom was dim also, the shutters latched firmly against any leakage of sunlight. Her eyes took a moment to adjust, then she saw what was making the noise.

"My God, Sam, here you are. We've been looking all over for you." She stepped into the room and bent down to his languid form. He held onto the old trunk as if it were his ship in a churning sea. His fingers were scratching repeatedly at the sides as if he were losing his grip on it.

"Come along, Sam. You mustn't be in here. What is it?" she said gently, kneeling down to him.

He started, and looked at her. It was as if he had not known until now she was there.

"What is it?" she whispered, a frown of concern wrinkling her brow. She took his hand from one side of the trunk and realized only afterward that it was warm and sticky with blood. He'd been scratching at the trunk until his nails were pulped.

"Sam, you're terrified. Why? Why?" she pleaded, suddenly understanding that if she could just get him to talk this once, a huge fragment of Cairncross's mystery might be solved.

He stared at her, his face handsome in the shadows. As achingly handsome as his brother's was.

"You can tell me. I won't hurt you. Please, please," she begged, "let me help you."

"I made her go away!" he burst out, a dry sob choking his words. "I made her go away but I put her back. See? I put her back. I'm a good boy."

A tingle of dread filtered down her spine. She felt the hairs on her nape rise in warning. "Where did you put her back, Sam? In the trunk?"

Sam took a long moment while he stared at her. His simple mind seemed to weigh her character. He wanted to trust her. She could almost taste his want.

"May I see that you put her back?"

Hesitantly, he nodded.

Alexandra rose to her feet.

Her hands were ice cold as she grasped the latch. She opened it. The heavy wooden and iron piece groaned with the effort. The lid dropped back with a rusty clank. The sound muffled the silent scream inside Alexandra's throat.

Chapter
Thirty-two

"Well, then, turn the tapestry," said the Jewess, *"and let me see the other side."*

—*IVANHOE*

Alexandra's entire body shook as Mrs. Penrith handed her a bracing cup of tea. The women had taken refuge in the housekeeper's parlor while the house remained in an uproar. Mary was white as a sheet as she sat by her mistress's side, trying to tend to her.

"I suppose when I found him in Ursula's room, somewhere in his child's mind Sam believed he was finally caught." Alexandra shuddered. "That's why he let me see inside the trunk. He kept telling me, 'I put her back. But I put her back.' Now I understand what he meant."

"The physician says she'd been dead a long time," Mrs. Penrith said. "Ursula's in a remarkable state of preservation though. The good doctor told me she had to have been somewhere else other than that trunk all these years. I told him I suspect it was the air inside the catacombs that kept her looking as she did.''

"It makes sense. So much of this now makes sense," Alexandra held the cup to her quavering lips. "Sam kept saying the other day that he made her disappear. After he saw Damien forced from the house that day, he must have confronted Ursula. She became enraged and terrified him, so he locked her in the catacombs." Another violent shudder went through her. "That accounts for the scratches inside the Roman door, and the red hairs scattered about. The hair must have fallen in patches from her skull as she decayed."

"Oh, our poor dear boy. He'll never get over this," Mrs. Penrith clucked as she poured herself some tea.

"I don't know. In some ways I think having the secret out has been good for him. She was so cruel, and he was obviously so terrified of her. Knowing it's over seems to be cathartic." Alexandra could feel herself begin to calm. Mary had gotten her a handkerchief with smelling salts. She was beginning to feel more invigorated, but every time she closed her eyes, she pictured the trunk and the macabre red-haired corpse of Ursula Pole inside it.

"But if Sam put that woman in the catacombs, why on earth did he retrieve that trunk from storage and put her in it?" Mary finally asked, holding tight to Alexandra's hand.

"I believe, in his simple mind, he'd always known he'd done something wrong." Alexandra tried to give Mary a reassuring pat. "I think that's why he refused to talk all these years. When I almost walked through the Roman door that day with him in the catacombs, he was terrified I would disappear through it as he'd made her disappear. I suppose without even realizing it, the memory of what he'd done so long ago returned to him then. He checked up on her after our experience down in the catacombs and when he discovered her body and the state of her decay, guilt made him want to make reparations. To his mind, since he made her go away, he thought he could put her back in her room, in her old trunk, and everything would be all right."

"Ghastly stuff," Mary exclaimed.

"Yes, it is," Alexandra said quietly. "But at least now we know Damien is no murderer."

"No," Mrs. Penrith answered pensively. "And yet there's still no explanation of what's been going on around this castle for years. Was Ursula a ghost then, after all?"

Alexandra didn't answer. She couldn't. The hideously dried corpse of Ursula Pole bore no real resemblance to the woman she'd seen on the staircase, nor the obscured figure on the moor. But in life, Ursula wouldn't have resembled the thing they'd discovered in the trunk. No one could say whether her ghost was really haunting the castle, or if it was all coincidence and the result of Damien's twisted mind.

"I can't go, without seeing him," Alexandra said, putting down her teacup. "If I've misjudged him as a murderer, then perhaps I've misjudged him entirely." She turned to Mary. "I want you to leave now with Jaymes."

"You can't be serious, miss! And leave you here?" Mary looked as if she were about to go into a fit of apoplexy.

"It's just that I must find out the truth." Alexandra's voice lowered to a whisper. "At last, I must know the truth, no matter what it is."

"But I'll stay here, miss, for as long as you want me to. You know I will—"

Alexandra shook her head. She looked into Mary's eyes. "I don't know what's going to happen. I only know that I must see him one last time. The carriage is ready. I want you to go to York and wait for me. I want you out of here and safe."

"Oh, love, don't ask this of me. I can't go, thinking you're here alone." Mary's face was filled with horror.

"I don't know how this is going to end. I may join you in the morning, or I may send for you this evening. I just know that I want you out of here." Alexandra's eyes glistened with unshed tears. "This is difficult to understand, but I love you, Mary. You're the only family I have in this world. I can't go fighting these dragons here at Cairncross thinking you're in danger too."

"And I can't let you fight them alone. Please, miss, just come with me. Let's leave while we have the chance." Mary looked at Alexandra, then at Mrs. Penrith, as if she could talk some sense into her.

"Miss." Mrs. Penrith took Alexandra's wrist and bade her stay. "You might as well go with Mary. He won't see you. He's been in a state ever since you decided to leave this morning. He's locked himself in his chambers and he won't see anyone. Not even when we told him we'd found Ursula."

"He'll see me. Surely he will."

"I don't know, miss." The housekeeper shook her head. "He's not himself. I've never quite seen him like this. When he spoke to me on the other side of the door when I told him we'd found her, he didn't seem all there. It was as if he was drifting away."

Alexandra's heart quickened. She couldn't escape the remembrance of the night she'd found him with the pistol. A sick feeling churned inside her gut. "I've got to go to him." She turned to Mary, her face pale and drawn. "You've got to promise me you'll leave now with Jaymes."

"Don't make me, miss."

"I care about you so much, Mary. Ursula, if she is some kind of lingering entity, knows that. Damien knows it too. If everything goes awry, I want you gone. *Promise me.*"

Perhaps it was the urgent, near-hysterical tone of Alexandra's voice that finally did it. At last, Mary put her head in her hand and wept, "I'll go, miss, but I'll pray for you. Please God, let me see you on the morrow."

Alexandra kissed her, then wiped her cheeks clean of tears. Trembling, she walked to the door.

"Why are you doing this?" Mrs. Penrith asked.

Alexandra paused. "If I've wronged him, I've got to see that he forgives me."

The housekeeper looked at Alexandra's white face and appeared to sense the urgency. "Go then, miss. Go quickly."

Alexandra rushed out the door, forced to ignore the foreboding in her heart and Mary's grievous weeping. She couldn't make any more judgments or decisions. She only knew she had to see Damien. Immediately.

The terror of her imaginings made her bunch her skirts in her fists and run.

Damien's rooms were empty.

Alexandra went through every corner in a frantic attempt to make sure, but he was not there. In the end, she lowered herself to a tapestried inglenook bench and simply stared at the abandoned bedchamber, as if by reading the evidence of his departure, she might guess at his whereabouts.

"Ah, the bride has come for her handsome groom."

She twisted around in the bench to see where the voice had come from. To her shock, a panel of the wainscoting moved back and Featherstone's cruel face loomed over her.

"*His* new bride, and yet he took mine away for all eternity." He reached for her.

She leapt from the bench and backed away. Her heart quickened as she saw the gleam of insanity lighting Featherstone's eyes. "Where is Damien?" she demanded.

"With her, with her." Featherstone released a laugh.

"He didn't kill her," she said, as her gaze covertly went flickering around the room looking for an escape. "We've found Miss Pole's body in the trunk in her old bedroom. It was a terrible accident, really. Sam didn't know the fate he'd sentenced her to when he shut her up inside the catacombs."

"And that's just what they'll say of me, Miss Benjamin." Featherstone was quick for his age. Before she could scramble out of the way, he leapt out from the panel and toppled her to the ground.

They struggled. She dug her nails into the side of his wrinkled face and drew blood, but to no avail. He was aged, but wiry, and in his delirium, he possessed the strength of two men. Quickly, she lay beneath him, panting from her futile efforts, staring up at him with an expression of loathing.

"She's dead, Mr. Featherstone," Alexandra whispered to

him, urgently making a plea for sanity. "I saw her myself. She was in the trunk, decaying, a hideous smile where her lips used to be, and long red hair sprinkled throughout the trunk where it fell from her putrefied skull. She's dead and Sam mistakenly caused her death. It was not my fault. It was not Damien's fault."

"She says otherwise." He peered down into her face. She nearly swooned from the rotting smell of his breath. "And she doesn't look that way. It was some other woman you saw in the trunk. Ursula is still young and beautiful. She hasn't changed—"

"And why hasn't she changed?" Alexandra demanded. "Because she's dead, Mr. Featherstone. And what you've been seeing is a ghost."

He laughed. "I've touched her. I've held her." He leaned closer and the odor forced Alexandra to turn away. "I've kissed her. She is of real flesh, and Damien deprived me of her all these years. So I'll deprive him now." He pulled her violently to her feet and dragged her into the inglenook. A mineral, earthy smell wafted from the panel where he first appeared. It was no servant's passage, but another twist of the catacomb's maze.

"Would you join your lover?" Brutally, he shoved her inside the panel, then followed her, replacing the wainscot so that no one would ever know they'd been there.

The tunnel was pitch black. Groping for her bearings, she felt along the wall until her hand shoved through an opening in the stonework and she grasped the hollow pelvis of some long dead warrior. Sickened and terrified, she sank to the floor, unwilling to move. The further she crawled into the passage, the further she'd lose her sense of direction. Featherstone could do his worst now, she wasn't going to take another step.

The flare of a phosphor-tipped match lit the interior of the cavern. She looked around and realized Featherstone had found an oil lamp. But the entrance from where they'd just come eluded her even in the light. The doorway was obviously sealed somewhere into the stone wall and without Featherstone's knowledge of where it was, there was no discerning it.

"Come along," the old butler ordered, with a strange, mad smile tacked on his face.

"Where's Damien?" she demanded, moaning as he shoved her ahead of him.

"I'll take you to him. *As he is now, so you must be, so take my hand and come with me.*" He tipped his head back and howled with laughter.

The sound sent gooseflesh climbing up her arms. "She's dead, Featherstone. I saw her. She's dead."

"You're lying." He grabbed a fallen hank of her hair and brutally pulled her to him. "I know your kind. I always have. You're just a lying little Jew and I won't hear you speak of her no more."

"She's dead. You're making love to a ghost. One day you'll turn to kiss her and watch the necrotic flesh fall from her cheekbones." She was unbalancing him further, but she knew she could no longer appeal to the sane man inside him. That man was as dead as Ursula Pole.

"You've never seen her. She's beautiful. That woman in the trunk wasn't her."

"It was her. And I *have* seen her. Her ghost, at least. She passed me on the stair one day, and she watched Damien and me from the moors. It makes sense now what I refused to believe then. Unless there is another just like her who has the need to play such trickery, I'll believe to my dying day what I saw on the moor was a ghost. *Her* ghost."

"Your dying day is near," he said in an angry, disturbed voice. "So get along with you. Keep walking. We'll see how Newell cherishes his bride."

She was shoved to the front and he held up the oil lamp. The passage was nothing more than a horizontal pit of darkness. She began to walk, but each step was slow and hesitant, afraid of the next turn and bend. She wanted to run to Damien, but Damien was somewhere in the shadows ahead and without

Featherstone's malicious guidance, she knew she'd never find him.

Damien stood at the Roman door. He pulled it open. His massive strength was just barely enough to work it. On the other side stood a dark figure. The one he'd come to see.

"The decision is made," he said to it, his voice harsh and raspy. "Show me the darkness you know so well."

The figure didn't move. It stood in the far passage, a crino-lined silhouette in the flickering lamplight.

"My purgatory is come. Show me the future. Prove to me the hell on this earth is worse than the one you live in." Slowly, he drew a pistol from the waist of his trousers. He held it in his hands, his eyes trained on the figure before him.

"Show me what you really are." He raised the pistol. In his eyes was a glint of willful, determined self-destruction.

The shadowed figure didn't move. It was still and expectant. The embodiment of a held breath.

"Show me, Ursula," he whispered just as a light passed in the tunnel to the right of him.

"Who goes there?" he commanded, the pistol lowered to his side.

The light grew more brilliant. The dark figure seemed to melt away into the shadows.

"Your lordship, 'tis I, your former butler," a voice rang out. From behind the lantern's glare, two forms appeared, locked in a macabre embrace.

"Damien," Alexandra whispered, shoved forward with the cold metal shaft of a gun pressed to her temple.

Damien looked at them, his eyes noting his former butler's pistol and the harsh grip of Featherstone's arm around her neck. For an infinitesimal moment, his gaze met with Alexandra's; hers was pleading, his, unreadable. Then he tore his gaze away.

"What do you think you're doing?" he impatiently asked Featherstone.

"I loved her, Newell, and you took her away from me."

"She didn't love you," Damien growled. "She was a whore who used you for the blunt you'd stashed away all the years of working for me. She never loved you. She never loved anyone."

"She did love me. She did!" Featherstone squealed. He shoved Alexandra forward, viciously allowing the gun to knock her head. "And now, your lordship, you're going to pay. Watch your bride-to-be while I—"

"While you what?" Damien interrupted. "Kill her? Go ahead. She can join me then."

"Damien," Alexandra gasped, her eyes filling with tears and disbelief.

"You don't want to die, Alexandra?" Damien mocked. "You think this life and the agony with it goes on forever?"

"Sometimes it takes courage to live, my love." She stared at him and her expression was one of terror and confusion mixed with staunch, implacable love. "Sometimes good and evil aren't predetermined paths laid out before us but choices that are made blind, and in darkness. I know you didn't murder Ursula. We discovered Sam trying to hide the mischief he'd wrought twenty years ago. I should have believed in you, but even when I thought you were guilty, I loved you," she whispered, her words barely audible.

He gazed at her but didn't comment, his face showed no emotion; the expression in his eyes was blurred by the spectacles. Perhaps mercifully.

"I'm going to kill her now, your lordship," Featherstone hissed. "And then I'm going to kill you. My own true love awaits."

"I'd rather see her die by my hands than those of a stranger." Damien raised the pistol he'd held casually at his side until now. Featherstone started, clearly surprised by the sight of another's gun in the lantern light.

"So you think to do the honors?" Featherstone asked, while Alexandra struggled within his neckhold.

"Why not? She was to be my wife."

"No, Damien, no," Alexandra pleaded, tears falling down her face like a waterfall.

"I see now that I made the choice before you even got here, Alex." Damien looked at her, his face like chiseled stone. "You can't change things."

"She'll win if you do this, Damien. I know she's only a representative of evil, but nonetheless, if you give up, she'll have won, and then you should have submitted to her long ago." She released a small, mournful cry. "I love you, Damien."

"But will you love me in death and in evil, Alexandra?" he said, cocking the gun.

"In death and in evil then," she whispered, her agony-filled gaze not wavering, "just return my love. Give to me what I've given to you and all life will be possible."

"I didn't put that carmine in your room. It wasn't me," he said. A fleeting emotion across his face said he wanted her to believe him.

"I know it wasn't. It was her all along. She knew about *Ivanhoe* because of what she was, not who she was. Don't do this, Damien," she begged, still struggling with Featherstone's maniacal hold. "I'd rather we both die at the hands of a madman than perish by the evil in ourselves."

"But there's so much inside me," he said in a tight voice.

"I know," she wept, "but that's why you must choose to live. I'm here now. That's why I was brought here. You must fight this thing. That's the sole purpose and meaning of love. Love reconciles us to the evil inside all of us. I love you. And what's more, I don't believe you really must die ... because I think you love me," she whispered, her face, her tears, her voice begging for an answer.

He stared at her for a long terrible moment, the gun pointed straight at her head. The silence was like a thunderclap.

No one would ever know if it was just the uneven flicker of the lantern light, or if a tear really did materialize behind the spectacles and slip down Damien's cheek. It was dim in the catacombs, and if his expression changed, there was no tangible indication of it.

"As I am now so *you* must be, so take *my* hand and come with me." She held out a trembling, supplicating hand.

He stared at it for a long moment, not speaking, not moving. Behind her, Featherstone had begun to laugh.

"You were wrong about Ursula," the butler cackled. "She's not dead at all. She's standing behind you, Newell, so pull the trigger on your lover, and then pull it on yourself, and make my own true love happy."

"I love you," Damien said to Alexandra as she began to sob at the picture of whatever stood behind him. "I do love you."

Then he pulled the trigger.

Epilogue

. . . thou hast in me found thy match.
    —*Bois-Guilbert to Rebecca in* IVANHOE

Alexandra watched as the two brothers walked ahead of her in the garden. It was a cold winter's day but no new snow had fallen, and the afternoon sun shone cheerfully from behind the crags. Sam forged ahead, making snowprints in the patchy crusts of snow that still lingered between the rose bushes. Damien walked right behind him, looking every bit like the contented lord overseeing his estate.

But he wasn't all content. There seemed something missing. All at once, he turned around and held out his hand. Alexandra picked up her pace and took it. She had an open, loving smile on her lips.

"How long has it been today?" he asked, holding her close to his side so they could walk in tandem.

"You ask this every day, my love. Are you going to do it forever?" Like the happy wife she'd become, she picked a bit of lint off his black greatcoat and brushed up the woolen nap with her gloved hands.

"I'll ask it forever, if I must just to make sure it isn't all a dream from which I fear I'll awaken."

She touched his cheek. "We were married on Christmas Eve. Let me see, that makes us married fifty-five days."

"I won't rest until it's fifty-five years." He looked ahead to his brother. The clouds danced in the reflection of his spectacles. He still wore them, but they'd ceased to be ominous to her. Ever since that last day in the catacombs, he never frightened her anymore. The truth had come out, the path had been chosen. Every day he grew more gentle, more tender. He said she was an excellent teacher, but it was inside him all along, she told him. She'd always seen it in his treatment of Sam.

"Does Sam want to visit the graveyard again today?" she asked, trying with a laugh to keep up with her husband's long stride.

"We'll ask him. He seems to enjoy putting flowers on her grave."

Alexandra looked up at him and nodded. "I don't believe he would be speaking again without the reparation of tending to her gravesite." She looked out at Sam, who gravely scrutinized the garden wall as if he were searching for the figure she and Damien had once seen on the moor. "It's been good for him to visit her. I'll never believe he understood that his putting her into the catacombs would kill her."

"I just want him happy and talking again. I don't care who killed her." Damien's thoughts seemed very far away at that moment.

Slowly, she squeezed his hand and pressed it to her burgeoning stomach. "She's gone, my love. We've not seen her since she was buried in consecrated ground the day of our wedding. And I don't think we'll ever see her again. She lost, remember?"

A muscle tightened in his jaw. "You've never told me how she looked when she stood behind me before I shot Featherstone."

"Does that matter?" Alexandra said softly, grimly. "We've got new life to look forward to. Besides, I told you, she appeared much as she did when we found her in the trunk only . . . only . . . she was animated with hatred." Alexandra didn't realize how her face drained of color whenever she thought of it. There weren't words to describe the evil that Ursula Pole represented, that last moment in the catacombs. It was an evil felt more than seen. And for a few seconds, though she would never admit it to Damien, she knew the evil had claimed her very soul.

"I need your strength, Alexandra."

She looked up at her husband and saw the worry in his eyes. These days the spectacles hid nothing. "You have strength of your own, Damien. You could have killed both of us when you had the chance. It was the escape I think you always wanted, but you chose to live. And so, dear husband, I'll chose to live by your side all the years of my life."

"Pray we have a daughter just like you, my love," he whispered.

"Pray we have a son who will learn the meaning of love as eloquently as his father has learned it," she answered, letting him crush a kiss to her lips.

When they parted at last, they clasped hands and continued their stroll along the wintry garden path. The rosebushes were only skeletons, pushing their bare, thorny claws to the warming sun. But in a few months they would be green again, and rosebuds would be bursting out from the thorns. Life would begin anew.

Alexandra watched her husband gaze warmly at Sam. She couldn't help thinking how brotherly ties grew deep especially when they'd shared the same horror. In the years to come, the fear wouldn't be as acute as it was now. Trust and gentleness were things to be learned over time. She knew Damien would learn them. He was already learning them. And with the child growing inside her belly, they looked to a future that was bright and warm with shared love. Sam seemed to understand the changes, too, for his speech came rapidly, and he seemed happier than he'd ever been.

Back at Cairncross, the servants had boarded up the unused schoolroom. The new nursery and schoolroom would be built in another wing altogether. The old governess's room was still abandoned and the chambermaids continued consciously to overlook it when time came for cleaning. It was a bad place, they whispered to one another, anxious to fob off the responsibility to an underling, until the room remained in neglect, just like the old schoolroom, a chill-swept, uneven place that still held the residues of the evil that had lived inside it.

No matter how Alexandra ached to change things, she knew the past at Cairncross would remain. Transcending that past was a continuing battle, but one she was ready to fight every day, with the man she loved at her side. She touched his cheek. He gave her a tilted smile. Together they walked through the garden.

Though it seemed that something—a darkness—lingered in the castle passages like shadows, restless, permeable, yet ever-present, and worst of all, forever present, Ursula was gone. Still, Alexandra knew she could not conquer all the evil that had manifested at Cairncross.

But she was determined. Her baby moved strongly under her corset, and joy rushed through her. Perhaps, just perhaps, with the ever gentle touch of her lover's hand, the memory could become, at last, only a series of quiet, cumulative shudders.

Set me as a seal upon thine heart, as a seal upon thine arm: for love is as strong as death.

                                                                    Isaiah 8:6

ROMANCE FROM ROSANNE BITTNER

CARESS   (0-8217-3791-0, $5.99)

FULL CIRCLE   (0-8217-4711-8, $5.99)

SHAMELESS   (0-8217-4056-3, $5.99)

SIOUX SPLENDOR   (0-8217-5157-3, $4.99)

UNFORGETTABLE   (0-8217-4423-2, $5.50)

TEXAS EMBRACE   (0-8217-5625-7, $5.99)

UNTIL TOMORROW   (0-8217-5064-X, $5.99)